The
Goddess
Village

The
Goddess
Village

Nuala Woulfe

POOLBEG

Published 2011
by Poolbeg Press Ltd.
123 Grange Hill, Baldoyle,
Dublin 13, Ireland
Email: poolbeg@poolbeg.com

A catalogue record for this book is available from the British Library.

ISBN 978-1-84223-460-0

Typeset by Patricia Hope in Sabon 11/14.5

Printed and bound by CPI Group (UK) Ltd, Croydon, CR0 4YY'

www.poolbeg.com

About the Author

Nuala Woulfe writes books and, now she is 40, has taken to trying out all kinds of dance (I was a child of the 80's and didn't get my *Fame* or *Flashdance* moment so I'm having it now!). She also harbours pretensions of being a painter of sorts and has a recurrent waking dream of trying out for the *X Factor* – much to her children's horror. When she is very old she intends to become an actress – there will be few grannies with snow-white hair and bad teeth on the acting circuit so she expects she will have her pick of great movie and TV roles. A million years ago she used to write the odd newspaper article. Then she wrote *Chasing Rainbows* (2009) and *Two to Tango* (2010).

Acknowledgements

I'm not usually one for gushing acknowledgements but I thought oh, what the hell, I'd go and thank a whole bunch of people for this book.

Firstly, thanks for everyone who allowed me to ask endless banal, annoying or even frustrating questions in the name of research. The great thing about being a writer is that you can get into other people's worlds and get an idea of what their lives and careers are like. So thanks to all the archaeologists, dancers, bog-snorkellers, women farmers, sex-and-relationship therapists and lesbians for your frank and informative discussions. Thanks to everyone who told me about lifeguards and gyms and a very special thanks to the separated wives to whom I spoke who told me of their past pain, their daily realities and their future hopes and dreams.

Thank you, Paula in Poolbeg for never holding me back in my writing – I feel I've grown a lot since my first book, *Chasing Rainbows*. Thanks, Gaye, for your meticulous editing – the copy for *Goddess* came back unbelievably clean first time round – either you went above and beyond the call of duty on this one or I'm turning into a cracking writer – only you know the answer!

Thanks to the Munster Goddess Bellydance Troupe, Abby, Val and Mary – who provided a great distraction from the writing when I needed it this year. I'll never forget that haffla in Limerick – thank you, Karen, for making it all happen both in Tipperary and in Limerick! It really was a wonderful year of dance. What a pity I had to break my toe at the start of the summer!

A very special thank you to the guy who fixes my computer when it occasionally throws a wobbly – you're the one who has been there through all three books, paragraph by paragraph. Won't say anything even remotely gushy but I appreciate everything you've done – thanks.

That's it, I'm not going to go so far as thanking the goldfish or every one of my family as much as I love them. Hope you all enjoy the book!

For my dad – I love you.
This one's for you. Nuala

1

India Jennings looked over her sleeping-beauty boyfriend and knew she was the luckiest girl in the world. "Gorgeous, you're bloody gorgeous," she whispered under her breath to her sun-kissed Australian lifeguard with his golden hair as she traced a finger lovingly over his six-pack. Nathan O'Driscoll, all six foot four inches of him, was India's man-fantasy come true when she met him in Sydney on a break from her event-management business. Still, it had taken a full year of Skyping, emailing and Facebooking to get Nate to her state-of-the-art two-bed eco-apartment in Little Cloonsheeda – the exciting, 'green' eco-village being built in the heart of Ireland.

Turning on some music in her just about eco-acceptable diesel jeep, India headed off to a festival-committee meeting thirty miles away. As she exited her driveway, her dark-brown eyes skimmed over the development that promised so much to its 21st-century residents. Little Cloonsheeda, with its nut and fruit-tree lined walks and communal living areas promised to be a mouth-watering slice of paradise when it was finished and India felt lucky to have

1

found a Sex God to grow old with in this heaven – it only troubled her slightly that, despite their red-hot affair in Sydney, she hadn't actually had sex of any kind, mortal or otherwise, with said Sex God in weeks.

"We're a gorgeous, fun-loving couple and there is nothing to worry about," she told her overhead mirror before she tossed her sleek black bob, clicked on the wipers to ward off the January rain and turned her stereo up high to rid herself of any doubts of worldly imperfection.

Anna Gavin looked at the assorted cardboard boxes at her feet and felt the panic rising as she took in the virgin walls and floors of her amazing but frightening high-tech eco-home. Reality hit hard as the day's light drew to a close.

"Jesus Christ, what have I let myself in for?" Anna whimpered as she steadied herself against the doorframe of her new sitting room which was completely bereft of furniture. This was the start of her new life in Little Cloonsheeda now that her split from Big Paddy Gavin, one of Ireland's most famous politicians from one of Ireland's oldest political dynasties, was officially public, but the change in her life circumstances was anything but joyous.

Gone now was the old life of certainty in the big house in the west of Ireland, of always nodding to someone on the street in case they were a supporter of Big Paddy, long-standing member of parliament, publican, father, husband and complete bloody bastard. Gone was the life of always having to have the face brightly painted and having a few good coats on standby for the obligatory photo where she would pretend to be the loyal wife standing beside the worthy husband and decent 'party man'.

"A new life, nothing to fear," she gasped as a pathetic mantra, but Anna Gavin was lost without a man, even a useless man like Paddy Gavin.

In her forty-three years Anna had never had a panic attack but as she stood flattened against the door of her lovely eco-home, heart racing, her breath shallow, her mousey brown hair flattened with sweat to her forehead, she thought now might be as good a time as any to give into a nice little bout of hysteria.

In a modern country mansion with every kind of mod con, useful and useless, two-year-old twin boys were throwing cereal around until their strikingly exotic, flame-haired, sallow-skinned mother flung her biro and archaeology notes aside on the Danish-designed table, narrowed her sumptuous chocolate-brown eyes, and gave in to the legendary hot temper of all natural-born redheads.

"Jack . . . Sam . . . Christ Almighty, but you two are a bloody handful! Whoever said two were as easy to raise as one never set foot in my household!" Rebecca Gleeson ranted as she parted the boys from their supper and, realising the time, chased them upstairs for their bath, all the while fuming, plotting and despairing. At this rate she'd never get through her assignments for her outreach archaeology course, it would take two years just to get a diploma and what she really needed was a degree if she ever wanted to be taken seriously by anyone with a brain.

Under the bubbles the boys were as raucous as ever, fighting over an orange duck, but before the mirrors steamed over Rebecca stopped to consider her full-length figure.

"Did you know your mum used to be the best-looking woman in the whole county before you two messers arrived to ruin my looks?" Rebecca sighed as she pivoted on one heel.

The boys splashed water over the sides of the bath, oblivious to their mother's frustrated dreams. Before she fell pregnant Rebecca had completed an instructor course in pole-dance fitness but, now she was thirty-three and a Size 12, Rebecca considered herself too old and fat to twirl around a sexy dance spire. Yes, far better to park the dancing and concentrate on doing some respectable studying instead. Besides, the fashionable new eco-village in nearby Cloonsheeda, which her husband Mark was developing, would give her a bit of kudos on her archaeology course with big-brained intelligent types whose acceptance she craved more than sugar.

"Yes, I remember Daddy said 'You have them, honey, and I'll help', but where is he tonight, boys?" she asked the expensive ceramic tiles. Then from the corner of her eye she saw Jack belt Sam with the end of a plastic boat he'd found near the oversized, chrome-plated taps and a full-throttle screaming match began – and she hadn't even tried to wash their hair yet. Definitely, she definitely needed one of those things that everybody raved about – what were they called again? Oh, yes, an au pair – and soon.

Young Willie Cleary pulled back the lace curtains, rimmed with black mould, of his rundown village cottage and peered out into the Main Street of Old Cloonsheeda village, checking for any signs of annoying callers coming to the house with a goat, horse or dog, or perhaps even a small child that needed mending. Being the son of a legendary bonesetter was nothing but hassle for the handsome, slightly built, dark-haired young man, what with the constant flow of people coming, often un-announced, to see his father Dan. Everyone said the father's talent was a 'gift from God', but as far as Willie could see this running of fingers down the flank of human or beast was a worthless gift in the modern world, especially as Dan's tight-fisted customers were often reluctant to part with much cash once the healing had actually been bestowed.

"God does the healing, boy, money's not important," Dan would hush him and Willie would bite back the resentment he felt at his father's stupidity.

Seeing no donkeys or babies waiting outside to delay him, Willie, who happened to be the double of famous Irish actor, David Ron Dwyer, escaped through the front door as he set out for some groceries. Passing by the wacky new eco-housing development Little Cloonsheeda that was bringing strangeness of all sorts to his home parish, Willie loitered at the cross and daydreamed as he lit a hand-rolled cigarette, his beautiful countenance serene, his naturally sexy pout the only hint of a possible bad-boy tendency in the making.

"Well, what are you waiting for, a personal fucking invitation, get in the car!" snarled his friend, Tom Skeehan, a pony-tailed black-haired youth, still young enough to have toned arms and the remnants of a six-pack torso despite his own fondness for liquid six-packs since his early teens. With nothing more than a sharp nod of acknowledgement, Willie jumped into the passenger seat of the clapped-out, rusting vehicle and stared out the window.

"Got a smoke?" Tom asked, raising one thick black eyebrow, and Willie lit another rollie before man and machine spluttered off to the city for the weekly grocery shop.

Despite a little self-loathing, Willie's tongue watered at the thought of the culinary delights he'd soon sample; for the city was the best place in the world for cheap eating if dumpster-diving was your trade and late-night 'just out of date' edible waste your luxury choice of food.

Tanned, toned and sun-bleached, Freeda Petersen shut the door of her bike shop on the Main Street of Old Cloonsheeda village and threw her leg over the fastest, flashiest, lightest, most expensive bicycle the townland had ever seen this side of the new millennium for the two-minute cycle back to her home in Little Cloonsheeda. The shop was doing well. Tandems, trailers and kiddy-seats were particularly popular as were bells, bicycle-clips, helmets and all manner of cycling clothes. Today the thirty-seven-year-old San Franciscan had sold a kid's cycle, some bells, assorted clothing and a trailer. Not a bad day's work for a new business in a small village, although keeping afloat was going to be a constant challenge, especially since the Irish weather was so bad the natural inclination of the natives was to seek the inside of a pub rather than sit on the saddle of a push-bike.

Still, moving from the West Coast of America to the centre of Ireland had felt like the right thing to do from the moment she'd read on the internet about Little Cloonsheeda and the type of innovative people who were signing up to a new environmental way of living for the 21st century. Of course there were days when she still got a yearning for big-city delights, like sushi and skateboard parks, or missed the intense white sunshine of home, but Freeda had heard so much about this land of mist and mythology, of porter and poetry from her Irish lover that she felt she needed something of its essence to heal her badly broken heart.

As she turned the key on her two-bed apartment, Freeda let slip the smile she had on her lips all day for the customers. "Oh why, my Irish love rat – why did you have to steal a bit of my soul?" she whispered weak and low.

Dinner times were always stressful for Sinéad Winterbottom, who at twenty-seven and with three young children, Jane four and a half, Peter three and a half and Andrew fourteen months, was permanently bypassing the present so she could zoom into the future and somehow make everything right for everybody – except, of course, herself. On the upside, despite permanent domestic madness, she was a woman who had the consolation of knowing she had a sensible life mapped out for the next few years – thanks mostly to the perseverance of her logically-minded, no-nonsense husband, Henry.

At only twenty-one Sinéad was already on the road to ruin when she fell out of a Newcastle nightclub, drunk to her eyeballs, wearing less clothes than you would find on an autopsy victim, and nearly flattened the sensible archaeologist Henry – a reluctant clubber steeling himself for a night of loud music on a colleague's going-away do. Heartbroken, after a rollercoaster fling with a dark-eyed, rugged Geordie lout with an accent ten times more seductive than any Irish lilt, Sinéad was ripe for some logical, controlled support and was impressed when a calm Henry, eight years her senior, understood her drunken gibberish, stuck her in a cab and called her the next morning and many mornings after with tips to get her life on track. Eventually, realising she was a hopeless case, Henry decided the best thing to do was to marry this Irish girl with a child's pale-blonde hair and lock her into a sensible marriage for life.

Back in the present and staring at tonight's dinner, which consisted of the mildest of chicken kormas, Sinéad smiled as she remembered all the fiery, spicy meals of her past before she had children, before she began dating Henry whose guts abhorred any trace of the exotic.

"Mummy, I *hate* this dinner," Jane pouted as she wiggled her nose in disgust.

"*Yeuch!*" snapped Peter as he crossed his arms in defiance.

Andrew, bless him, was too young to put up a fight and was digging his fingers into his bowl, exploring all the possibilities of korma and rice and spreading them all over his happy little face.

"For God's sake, Mr Winterbottom, do you think you could please help our baby just a little?" Sinéad asked in a flustered voice as Peter pushed his bowl away in defiance.

Sighing, Mr Winterbottom, his greying fringe and glasses just about visible as he pored over some academic notes, stood up and stroked the creases out of his sensible navy trousers. "Sinéad, as we have already decided that we are atheists, or at the very least humanists, do you think you could possibly eradicate the use of 'god' from your conversation at some stage in the future?"

"So sorry, Henry," Sinéad apologised as she played

with her engagement ring, Henry's grandmother's hand-me-down green emerald. "You forget I grew up in Ireland, a country steeped in 'godness'. Now, Mr Winterbottom, before everything goes cold, could you please come to the table!" As with every time Sinéad said her husband's name out loud she winced inwardly; she'd never really got used to Henry's surname. Henry, of course, had insisted that Sinéad hatchet her maiden identity and take his bottomy name. In fact Henry wanted their betrothal, their marriage, their entire life to be perfect and proper and, now that they lived in the most eco-gadgeted house in the whole of Little Cloonsheeda, it would be – once Sinéad knocked out baby number four (Henry hated uneven numbers – it upset his mathematical brain, although he did have a certain fondness for the stubborn beauty of a lone prime number).

"All's well, Mummy Winterbottom, I'm ready to be served now," Henry said calmly as he got the baby started on more food and sat authoritatively at the head of the table with yellow, industrial earmuffs glued to his head. Sinéad didn't bother registering her distaste at her husband calling her 'Mummy' or that she found his wearing earmuffs at every meal objectionable, although he never ceased to make the case that the only way he could get his sensitive academic brain through mealtimes with noisy, untrained children was by wearing heavy-duty ear-protection.

"More rice, please, Mummy Winterbottom," an artificially deaf Henry roared over the din and Sinéad wondered if, in the entire history of domestic disharmony, a husband had ever been clubbed to death successfully with nothing more than a plastic serving spoon.

As she finished lighting her tenth beeswax candle Demelza

Spargo settled down in the circle of low flickering light and began her meditation to the beautiful Áine, the Irish goddess of love and fertility. It had been a difficult year, moving to Cloonsheeda to write her first book in time for her fiftieth birthday in May, and she'd been treated with suspicion by the locals, who thought everything about her peculiar, from her vibrant dress, her musical accent and of course her fantastically ornate Cornish name. Currently dressed in a long, flowing white robe and ropes of coloured wooden beads, Demelza cared not for the culture of youth, still her breasts were high and her hair a mass of black corkscrew curls, her skin as clear as moonlight on water and her sexuality as obvious and natural as the shadows of firelight in a darkened room.

Incense swirled around her as she began her meditation for tonight. Things would work out somehow, even if her adopted 'nears and dears' persisted in some-times calling her 'that English witch' behind her back and mocking her name as fabrication – which of course it was not. Demelza Spargo was as Celtic as any Irish name. It wasn't her fault that her new neighbours knew not that the Cornish had a long and rich mythology of fairies and giants and their own mysterious Celtic tongue.

A plaintive mewing alerted her to her Cornish Rex Cat, Bast, wanting to get her mistress's attention but afraid of the candles. Laughing, Demelza picked up the animal with its long and pointy ears and rubbed the strange black curly hair which was peculiar to the breed. Mischievous by nature, Bast began to paw the wooden beads around her mistress's neck before Demelza lifted the scrawny animal and settled her into her basket for the night.

Another day was over but tomorrow morning as always Demelza would run up the black and white Cornish flag outside Mermaid Cottage as a symbol of her identity and other symbols would follow – symbols that she suspected might bring trouble.

"What will they say, my handsome, when they find out mummy be not a horrible 'English intruder' after all but a gifted sex therapist instead? Ah well, it be as I always say, 'An it harm none, do what thou wilt'."

Bast replied with a lick and a strange little miaow of understanding as her mistress gave her head one last rub and returned to her meditation inside the beckoning ring of golden light.

Sixty-two-year-old Mossy 'the Giant' Skeehan, six foot five and built like a slurry tank, seethed with silent indignation as he headed up the fields for his dinner. Things were bothering him by the day and he didn't seem to have the words to express all his worries and frustrations. Cloonsheeda, his home village, had once been a sleepy little place where everybody knew everybody else, their business and their ancestry. Now, with the arrival of these peculiar people from all over the globe at this Little Cloonsheeda, this village within a village, the proper order of things had been lost and at his age he shouldn't be expected to have to deal with such irritating changes and upheavals.

Worst of all was the antics of that mad bra-less English eccentric who insisted on flying her peculiar flag every morning from her cottage on the main street, making statements about things that Mossy couldn't fathom. Mossy's own wife, Rita, was a woman beyond all reproach. Tending to the animals with him on the farm, being in the Countrywomen's Association, baking pies for the local charity fests – and she'd given him four children as well, Lord bless her – it wasn't her fault they were all girls. The hour was late, but Rita would have his dinner already made and later on he might get to see a programme on the telly before rounding off the night with the rosary. The problems of Cloonsheeda were too big for even a big man like Mossy Skeehan to fix. They were problems for the Lord himself or perhaps for a man with a more direct approach and sexier hardware than Mossy's farmyard shotgun – Robert de Niro in *Taxi Driver* with his Smith and Wesson Model 29.

"You talkin' to me?" Mossy drawled in an American accent as his arthritic sheepdog Jangle greeted him at the door with a weak nuzzle and a slow lick to the hand. "You poor bastard, sure no one talks to you! No one talks to me either, boy!" he said as he opened the door and allowed the old soldier to creep slowly inside to his bed.

As the sun died and hid its head in the grey-black blankets of the sky, the moon rose surely and shone bright as a cat's eye, watching over everything; the cycles of the season, the land and the animals on the dark earth, everyone and everything in the pretty parish of Cloonsheeda where everyone used to know everyone else's name and, if it was worth knowing, all of their neighbours' most private business too.

2

Mark Gleeson sat back on the leather chair in the auctioneer's office founded by his mother and scowled, first at the moon and then at the expensive, glossy brochures on Cloonsheeda's Eco-Village. A well-built dark-haired man in his early forties, the auctioneer-developer had a natural animal magnetism about him, an irresistible sexiness in a rough-around-the-corners kind of way, especially when he scowled moodily as he was doing to great effect now.

Interlocking his fingers, he brought his hands to his chin and brooded over his current problem a little more. Little Cloonsheeda was meant to be his flagship 'green' development; every home whether apartment or house had the same façade with multiple extra features available to those willing to part with the cash, but things were not turning out quite as well as he'd hoped. Interest in the first phase of houses had been strong but then some buyers failed to commit and deposits were pulled so that Mark needed to shift the remaining units fast.

"A penny for your thoughts, son?" Mark's mother, herself a formidable businesswoman, leaned against the desk, the backs of her hands gripping the top tightly.

"Oh, just thinking about Cloonsheeda and how we can capitalise on promoting it over the next while . . . with less than half of the houses built . . . well, you know yourself . . ." Mark sighed as he tapped his pen rhythmically on his desk.

"It'll come, you'll see. These things always plateau then gain momentum again. It'll work out. That Eddie Ferris will help persuade a few more buyers and then we'll be snowed under with deposits." Dee leaned forward and patted his hand tenderly. He was her favourite son after all and probably her favourite person in all the world if she was completely honest.

Mark drummed his fingers off his desk as he considered what impact eco-celeb and trendy broadcaster, Eddie Ferris, Ireland's foremost celebrity campaigner for Green living, sustainable development and all things organic and natural, would have on sales when he came to film a documentary programme on site.

Tomorrow the *Independent News* would be sending a journalist and a photographer to cover Eddie's meet-and-greet, and such publicity would surely stimulate more interest in the days to follow. Not that Mark cared too much for Ferris or the good, clean life himself but for now he'd espouse the clean, Green way and work all the hours needed to get Little Cloonsheeda into profit. Besides, anything that kept him in the office and away from his perpetually discontented wife Rebecca would in itself be a blessing.

"Then there's that old bat on the Main Street . . ."

Mark looked up at his mother with smiling eyes as if he was almost embarrassed to talk about such things. "You know that mad English one with the zany clothes and the heaving bosoms . . . giving me grief about that young oak on the site, which, as you know yourself, accidentally on purpose got bulldozed last week. Daft cow attacked me on the street, ranting about oaks being sacred and I'd be cursed for not showing proper respect to ancient sites. God, I knew when we started this project we'd attract some oddballs as well as the upmarket environmental types, but still, sometimes I think it's more than my job's worth." Mark rolled his eyes and Dee threw her head back and laughed loudly.

"Lord God above, but I didn't take you for being the superstitious type! I'll tell you now, Mark Gleeson, I didn't raise any son of mine to be bested by trees or by oddballs either. Maybe this interfering oddball could do with getting an accidental belt with a bulldozer herself?" Dee's voice lilted playfully and Mark smirked like a brazen schoolboy.

"Well, hopefully tomorrow will be the end of it. Jerome's coming at the crack of dawn to cut the oak to a stump before Ferris arrives with the TV crew. And of course I'm not superstitious, it's just sometimes I wonder if someone 'up there' has it in for me on this damn eco-project and then Rebecca doesn't do much to ease the stress since she took up her archaeological studies . . . well, to be honest, I think I preferred her the way she was when all she cared for was shoes, fast cars and playing the odd game of women's rugby!" And having loads of sex – he kept that thought to himself.

Dee smiled to show she sympathised with Mark's

troubles but still she stiffened at the mention of her daughter-in-law's name. The simmering animosity between herself and Rebecca had remained constant over the years, and even the arrival of children hadn't endeared either to the other.

"Go on home, you work too hard," Dee soothed. "Tomorrow will look after itself."

Like a small boy Mark heeded her advice and drove the short distance home, sitting in the car for a full ten minutes before he headed for the front door of the house, bracing himself for all the screaming and whining – his wife's as much as the twins'.

Demelza Spargo came out from her hour-long reverie in honour of the goddess and looked again at the carved, painted sign in her hands. Tomorrow she would arise at first light and hang the beautifully crafted wooden feature over the front door of her cottage. It was better than she had hoped, this carving of the goddess, naked except for a snake around her thighs, all of the image radiating female energy and strength. More than two hundred business cards were also printed ready to advertise her new 'Goddess Sex Therapy Clinic'. Demelza would lose no time in handing the cards out tomorrow. With the arrival of that eco-guy from the telly, publicity was a given. A mischievous Bast, who'd escaped from her basket, rubbed against Demelza's shins and Demelza scratched the top of her lovely head and whispered into her soft velvet ears. "Mummy be planning to shake up this sleepy little Irish village, m'lover – I only hope we can all withstand the earthquake!" She laughed as she carried the pet to her basket for a second time and tucked her up with a faded blue blanket for the night.

The plan to spend the first night in her new house on a blow-up bed was not exactly going to plan for Anna Gavin. The foot pump seemed to be faulty, either that or the mattress had a tear. All of the contents from her previous home, especially her doomed marital bed, had been sold with the house. Bar two chairs, a table, two giant beanbags, a pair of barstools, a chest of drawers for her bedroom and an uncomfortable old rocking-chair, Anna had started her new life bereft of all furniture but with plenty of emotional baggage.

When Paddy's three-year affair with his bit of fluff, the bleached-blonde beautician who did his media make-up, became front page news, Anna couldn't bear the look of pity and embarrassment on the faces of other women she passed on the street, and in the days immediately after the formal separation there were many so-called 'friends' who deliberately dashed to the other side of the road and pretended they hadn't seen her at all. In some ways, she supposed, she couldn't blame them. Paddy was the charmer, Paddy had the magnetism that made people want to be around him; she was just the boring workhorse keeping things going in the background for her popular politician husband and her two energetic boys, both now at college.

Frustrated with her lack of progress with the mattress, which was only half-inflated, Anna rooted in her suitcase for the bottle of whiskey that she'd packed away for emergency rehabilitation purposes.

"Well, Anna, here's to you – congratulations on

getting that new life you wanted – let's hope it doesn't kill you," she toasted as she took the first swig of burning liquid, then by the silver light of the moon gulped back more from the neck of the bottle and prayed that the tomorrow of difficult life decisions might stay away for a week or two at least.

In the car park of Ireland's premier supermarket chain, young Willie Cleary kept a quiet watch while his friend Tom stamped about in a giant, smelly metal dumpster looking for 'good enough to eat' food by the light of the miner's torch on his cap.

"Found anything good yet?" Willie asked, pulling the collar of his coat up to his chin – it was beginning to drizzle and the air had turned cold and damp.

"Lots of vegetables, a bag of about thirty heads of broccoli and I hope you like carrots, Cleary, because there's a million of the bastards in here . . . hang on till I move them . . . oh Christ, whatever that is smells worse than your farts after a night on the beer . . . my feet are getting wet . . . I think I've only gone and stood on a hundred bleedin' rotten eggs."

"We should get some wet gear if we're going to continue on in this line of business," Willie answered back, not a trace of sympathy in his voice.

"What? Hang on, I'm gonna throw some stuff your way . . . not sure what's in it, so keep your wits about you."

Warily, Willie looked round the car park to see if anybody was watching. Dumpster diving wasn't illegal, but the stores didn't exactly like divers or Freegans as they were sometimes called, competing with the vermin and feeding their bellies for free.

"Got it!" Willie called as he caught Tom's plastic bag fired from the belly of the metal bin: an assortment of pre-packaged processed meats tied at the top with heavy black duct tape.

"Hang on, man, got a huge bag of bread here as well . . ."

Tom was deep inside the dumpster now – from the strength of his voice Willie guessed he was foraging close to the bottom.

"Could you hurry it up? I think we've got as much as will fit in your pile of shite car anyway!"

Without warning a flashlight popped up beside him and Tom was grinning in his friend's face.

"Everything good comes to he who waits, brother. There's steak in this one, I'd swear – you'll be feasting like a king tonight!" Tom laughed as he swung a white carrier bag under Willie's cold and reddened nose.

I am no better than a rat, Willie thought, knowing that if Tom's bags were really full of prime cuts of meat he'd swallow his disgust as easily as his steak, back in the hovel of his youth where cheap, knock-off or second-hand were nothing but second nature.

The drive back was unpleasant. Willie was dying for a fag but the smell of rotten vegetable juice from Tom's clothes was making him feel nauseous. It was a relief when they pulled up outside Willie's cottage and began to unload their hard-earned booty.

"Your old man about tonight?" Tom asked as they hauled their dumpster cargo into the back kitchen and left it in piles on the grubby work surfaces.

"He's staying with the widow in Carrigmore town, some sort of vigil or retreat – stays in her place half the time now when there's something religious on," Willie answered brusquely.

"Well, I suppose he's been a widower long enough – a man has to get his leg over sometime," Tom said a bit too bluntly and Willie scowled his disapproval.

"Sorry man, I didn't mean anything by it, was only having a laugh; I mean everyone knows your dad is one of nature's gentlemen what with all the healing he does and all."

Another black look from Willie and Tom silently began to sort through their haul of plastic bags, wiping down the outside of packages with a cloth if there was any trace of rotten vegetable juice on the plastic wrappers. Most of the stuff they'd salvaged was only recently out of date, or out of date that day: potatoes, vegetables, fifty packs or so of meat slices, cheese, yoghurts and the find of the night, just as Tom predicted, four just out-of-date steaks.

"Want yours fried with mushrooms and onions?" Tom asked excitedly as he went searching for the blackened iron pan in Willie's cupboard.

Half an hour later the two mates sat down to a late-night plateful of pot-luck dumpster food and Willie immediately felt sick – not from the food itself, in the six months that he'd been dumpster-diving he'd never been poisoned – it's just he never thought he'd be living the life of a rat in his mid-twenties. Living like a rat shouldn't have been an option for a man so young, a man who happened to be the spitting image of Irish movie star, David Ron Dwyer.

"You alright?" Tom asked as he ripped into his bloodied meat like a rabid dog.

Silently Willie nodded as he skated his spuds along some thick packet gravy.

"Well, you don't look so good. Dinner's the finest – get some steak into you and you'll be a new man," Tom encouraged through mouthfuls of stolen food.

Somehow Willie picked up his fork and began the process of eating, finding it hard to swallow from the lump in his throat, a lump which had been bothering him on and off since he'd left school, thrown his books in a corner and just stopped, stopped doing, stopped dreaming but never really stopped caring. I am a rat, but this steak's good, he told himself as he dreamed he was in a fine establishment, somewhere flash, somewhere where his doppelganger David Ron Dwyer would undoubtedly hang out: London, Paris, LA, so much of the world to see and all of it still a mystery to his eager but unworldly, small-town, boyish eyes.

Standing in her heat-efficient bathroom, Mrs Henry Winterbottom gazed into her mirror and took a number of long, deep breaths. Inside their sustainably harvested bedroom where the bamboo bed would be swaddled with organic cotton sheets, she knew Henry would be stark naked on the handstitched craft duvet, reading some stuffy book by the soft orange glow of a salt-rock crystal lamp. Tonight Sinéad was ovulating and tonight it had been decided the Winterbottoms were going to make baby number four. The fact that Sinéad was still breastfeeding her youngest was a moot point – it was after all still possible to breastfeed and be pregnant, Henry had pointed out; although possibly it might be just a trifle inconvenient and more than bloody exhausting, she thought.

Unsure of her destiny, Sinéad bit her lip and, feeling like a sacrificial lamb, walked towards the bedroom where she heard the first strains of mood-enhancing Bach, or was it Handel, escaping from the sustainably-managed eco-door? She hoped Henry wouldn't quiz her; not being able to distinguish one classical great from another infuriated him terribly after all his years of patient tutorage and she would always apologise for her lack of sophistication. Growing up a country girl on her father's nearby farm, Sinéad sometimes longed for a draughty big farmhouse, some kind of domestic imperfection that felt homely and right, and a little raucous Irish music that would sound unbearably painful to Henry's sophisticated classically trained ears.

For a moment she was struck by the memory of being six. One leg of her parents' big bed had broken and her father had propped it up with cement bricks until he bought a new bed when she was twelve. Her father, Mossy, never had time to fix things around the house, not when he was so busy around the farm. Thinking of being little Sinéad Skeehan again, with farmyard chores but no real responsibilities, made Sinéad sad as she remembered that despite their new proximity she didn't talk to Mossy any more. As she opened the door, Henry looked up with an air of a man who knows what is expected of him and can literally rise to the occasion. As the rising began, Henry folded away his book and put away his glasses in preparation for the momentous event to follow.

"All set?" he asked as he patted the bed beside him presumptuously.

"Uhm, actually Henry, I'm feeling a bit off tonight,

my head is pounding and my tummy feels just a tiny bit icky – must have overdone it on the korma – it was spicier than I thought!"

"But you're *ovulating* and I've been saving up my sperm and wearing loose underwear for days now for this precise moment of release, Sinéad!" he fumed.

"I know, I know, and you've been very considerate, Henry, but tomorrow will probably be okay too – and if it's not, well, there's always next month," Sinéad smiled, outwardly playing it ditzy but inwardly feeling the budding strength of something unfamiliar, something that might vaguely be approaching iron-willed determination. "So maybe tonight you could find some other form of release – you know, maybe you could find a suitable magazine or something on the internet to do the job instead?"

Scowling, Henry jumped out of the big bamboo bed, shot his wife a scathing look and thumped huffily into their spare bedroom. He wasn't happy, no. Underneath his enforced reserve Sinéad could tell he was furious as hell. Feeling very much a 'bad wife' but distinctly relieved, Sinéad hopped into bed and was just about to switch off the light when she remembered she hadn't fed her virtual fish all day. God, if you didn't feel the little blighters, or clean out their tanks with virtual brushes, they got sick and the entire population could be wiped out in an instant. Maternal fish guilt kicking in, she sneaked downstairs and turned on the kitchen computer. Having virtual fish was not something that Henry would approve of, it was most definitely a brain-dead and time-wasting activity, but Sinéad had been raised with animals and since her husband abhorred smelly pets and was allergic to shedding hair and dander, virtual pet ownership was the only route open to his wife – and besides, they really were the cutest little things – they even did tricks. Most rewarding of all, however, was that she had a vital maternal role to play in their fish world: keeping their tank clean, feeding them regularly and buying them toys so they would be healthy and stimulated enough to mate and have lots of lovely little fishlings! God, when it came down to it, these were the only new babies she needed right now. God, she really had to stop saying 'god' or Henry would divorce her for being such a scatterbrain.

Checking her appearance in the mirror one more time, India Jennings winked at herself seductively. That morning in a village fifty miles away she'd met a graphic designer to sign off on brochures for a new summer festival, then it was into a two-hour committee meeting for an oyster festival on the Atlantic coast, followed by typing up press releases on her laptop, answering email on her phone, sending a comedian's home phone number on to a media contact, troubleshooting and checking everything twice before driving to a marathon meeting of a vintage tractor festival where she had to listen to infighting over every small, petty detail before finally driving forty miles back home.

Festival event-management work in Ireland, the land of festivals, was chaotic and mostly India loved having her own business, deciding who to work with and keeping her own hours, but the downside was that work could become the only thing in your life. Nathan, who'd already started a new job as a lifeguard and gym instructor in the hotel in nearby Carrigmore town, had been really understanding about her commitments and tonight she wanted to thank him for his patience, by surprising him with an extra special present – herself!

Already she'd spent a precious half hour brushing her hair, touching up her make-up, doing her nails and spraying some of her sexiest perfume on her cleavage and pulse points and Nate wouldn't be able to keep his hands off her when he saw her in her new saucy black-lace rigout with a frilly 'almost there' skirt. Her feet were already beginning to pinch in her five-inch heels as she click-clacked into the bedroom to make love to the sex-god import of her dreams, but from the doorway she heard his snores crescendo. Sulkily she kicked off her heels and got into bed, making sure she gave him a dig in the ribs before stealing the duvet.

"Sex Gods are *not* supposed to fall asleep," she yelled loudly in his ear and, startled, Nathan twitched like a dreaming hound dog and whimpered ever so softly.

Drinking a cup of skinny hot chocolate but feeling fat and useless, Rebecca Gleeson ripped through the internet like a madwoman. Dinner with Mark had been an ad-hoc tense affair and half way through they'd had a stand-up row about parenting where Mark just about came short of calling her a bad mother and layabout wife.

"I just need help and I've had enough of your putdowns about my mothering skills so I've decided – we're getting an au pair and, I promise you, she won't be one bit good-looking either, Mark!" she'd screamed at high decibels. "All you need to know is she's going to be German. All the yummy mummies on line say German is the only way to go. Now, if you don't mind, I'm off to do some studying." Rebecca had slammed the door and headed for her computer.

Watching her storm away, Mark decided to pour himself a whiskey and mull. When Rebecca was angry she was as sexy as hell. If only she'd give up the books and concentrate all that energy on him instead. Sighing, he decided to make his drink a double, but he knew the fire of the amber liquid was no substitute for the fire of his wife who once liked nothing better than burning up his bed.

Under the duvet, snuggled up for the night, Freeda Petersen allowed herself to cry for the first time since she'd touched down on Irish soil six months before, grieving for the Irish lover who was responsible for luring her to the Emerald Isle. Every other day there was enough distraction with the shop to keep her stable, but today was the anniversary of meeting her Irish lover in a coffee shop in downtown San Francisco five years ago.

"Why, why, am I always, always attracted to the worst kind of shits and heartbreakers?" she berated herself as she gripped her pillow tight. Quickly the sobs built to a scream but Freeda didn't care. After all, what was the point in having energy-efficient insulated sound-proofed walls if you couldn't throw a nice big fat wobbly now and then without having to worry about the neighbours overhearing and reporting you to the authorities as a screaming nut-job who caused an unacceptable level of noise disturbance?

3

After days of drizzle and rain, the sun had decided to favour the inhabitants of Cloonsheeda with its warming rays and Demelza, who looked to nature for meteorological and astronomical signs on almost an hourly basis, thought the sunshine a most fortuitous omen. Picking her way through her garden of stone mermaids and heather, she ran the Cornish flag up the metal pole, smiling at her naturally scraggy cat who was mewing frantically for breakfast.

"Time to get out Mummy's pink drill and trusty old tool box – Mummy's got work to do," she told the restless animal.

Half an hour later Demelza smiled at her handiwork – her three-foot-high Goddess sign battened to the wall of Mermaid Cottage. The reign of the Goddess Sex Therapy Clinic had well and truly begun.

"Come now, my lovely, time for tea and toast."

Bast nipped at Demelza's fingertips and licked her hungrily with her hot and coarse tongue and together they slipped into the cottage from which a curl of sweet blue turf-smoke was already meandering towards the soft morning sky.

Mossy Skeehan was in terrible form as he bumped across the main street of Cloonsheeda in Glenda, his tractor, with feed for his dry stock at the other end of the village. The wife had a wicked tongue on her the night before, ranting on about how she was sick of making dinners day in day out for thirty years and how he never lifted a finger and her just as much a farmer as a housewife. What did the bloody woman expect? Certainly, she was a farmer's wife and had driven Glenda and her predecessors when needed, milked the cows when they still had a small dairy herd, with the children milling around her ankles, but he was still just a man, not trained in making dinners and baking bread and surely there was no point in Herself wishing any different at this stage of their lives?

Still, Rita's outburst made Mossy fret. Rita was always steady, not one of these New Age Feminist women who was always demanding more of this and less of that and wanting it now and not yesterday and the like – but since they'd reared their family of girls and had converted their dairy herd to dry stock, Rita had had a peculiar notion to photograph and paint cows. Cows with their calves, calves in their stalls, calves down laneways, cows being milked – she'd been painting every breed, every colour in every situation for more than a year and Mossy had paid little heed but now the woman was talking about approaching their neighbours to see if they wanted their beasts photographed and then immortalised in pastel, oil or acrylic. It was too much and Mossy had told her so over last night's dinner and now the blasted woman wouldn't speak to him. Mossy was still mulling over his domestic problems when he nearly fell from the tractor cabin in shock as he took in Demelza's topless goddess sign, complete with snake, swinging from the front wall of Mermaid Cottage.

"Well, now, that's nothing short of offensive. By God, that one has gone too far this time!" Mossy muttered to Glenda, as he pulled up outside the front door of the parish priest to talk about the immoral ways of the village witch and the confusing ways of women in general.

Polish immigrant Jeronim Sawicki had been meant to start on the final butchering of the oak tree on Little Cloonsheeda an hour ago but his Irish wife Sylvia, who was heavily pregnant with a new daughter, had felt strange in the belly and, worried that he'd have to rush her to hospital, he stayed with her until her funny spell was over. A well-built guy, Jeronim or Jerome as he was known locally, had deliberately damaged the oak, on what some said was a fairy fort, a few days before so his boss Mr Gleeson could get on with the business of developing his site without delay. The heavy work had been done already but Mr Gleeson wanted him to make the tree as inconspicuous as possible and cut the broken tree to a small stump and tidy away the smaller branches before some eco-celeb and a reporter arrived on site. Mr Gleeson would not be pleased that he'd arrived late. But cutting through a tree was a potentially dangerous job so, slowly and methodically, Jerome began the business of powering up the saw, taking away a few light branches before tackling the main stump itself, slicing through it at an angle, and as he did so he froze, then fell to his knees shouting hysterically in his native Polish tongue.

Mossy was just about to jump down from Glenda and seek out the advice of his priest when he saw the big Pole fallen to his knees, screaming frantically with the chainsaw in his hands. Fearing the worst, Mossy raced like a young fella of twenty across the field but the Polish labourer didn't need rescuing at all. In fact, up close he was wildly ecstatic as his eyes never once left the butchered oak.

"It is her . . . do you see . . . in the wood? It is her! The face of the Virgin," Sawicki gasped excitedly as he switched off the saw, pointed to the tree stump and blessed himself hastily.

"Mother of God, Queen of the Heavens, I do!" said Mossy excitedly. "It's the very shape of the Virgin's face and cloak all together, all immortalised in the blessed wood! She's come to show us the error of our ways and chastise us for all this village wickedness and blasted snakes!" Mossy fished for his grey rosary beads which he kept at all times in his pocket.

Then two grown men prayed to a tree stump, one in an almost inaudible mumble of English and Gaelic and the other in loud and excitable Polish.

Mark was straightening his tie at half past nine when the phone rang with a message from Maura Simmons, Dublin PR guru and manager of the sustainable village at Little Cloonsheeda, to tell him that celebrity architect, eco-warrior, author and TV presenter Eddie Ferris, was definitely on the way with some trendy media types on his heels. Maura and Eddie were officially in a relationship for the last twenty years but not actually bound together in marriage – that would be expecting too much of two creative, deliberately child-free, highly individual people. Both of them also had apartments in Dublin – the necessary centre for their work if they were to sustain their sustainable living project in rural Cloonsheeda.

"Oh and Mark, I think we have a bit of an unusual situation developing here in Cloonsheeda – perhaps you could get down as soon as you could and take a look," she added sharply.

Jesus Christ, what was it now? As he got up from his desk and hauled on an overcoat, a call also came through from his wife on his mobile and without a moment's hesitation he let it go straight to voicemail. After all, what did Rebecca have to worry about in life? Probably she had broken a nail on the dishwasher and was having a little nervous breakdown for herself or maybe the twins had refused to eat their breakfast. Either way, Rebecca could wait.

"Bastard!" Rebecca snarled as she heard Mark's answering message kick in. Believing, quite correctly, that her husband was avoiding her, she left a scathing message of her own then began doodling on the spiral notebook in front of her nose. All she'd wanted was a short chat and some encouragement for her au pair quest. Quickly the doodling turned more savage as Rebecca gouged out holes in the blue-lined paper with the tip of her ball-point pen. The two agencies she'd rung already had instantly shot down the German nanny dreams, telling her German au pairs were in high demand because their English was so fluent and her chances of getting a nanny were slim anyhow as most young people liked to be placed within striking distance of a city.

In desperation Rebecca made one more call.

"Hi, I'm based rurally, Carrigmore is the nearest town, and I'm looking for an au pair, a German, someone eighteen, nineteen, twenty, definitely no older than twenty-five," she began brusquely. As this was her third phone call that morning Rebecca knew exactly what she wanted and didn't waste any time in communicating her requirements to the slightly stunned woman at the other end of the phone.

"Oh good morning, Madam – well, as you can imagine, Germans are usually very proficient in English so they are very much in demand –"

"Yes, yes, I know all that, when can I get one?" Rebecca interrupted rudely. The twins had been watching TV for nearly two hours now and could erupt in violence at any minute.

"Well, unfortunately, at this moment we have no one who fits your exact requirements but we could put you on the waiting list."

"What! But I need one now! You have no idea how *crazy* my life is!" Rebecca wailed.

"I'm sorry, but just before you rang I had a woman on insisting she needed a German too – she thought it would be good for the discipline of their home, for herself and her husband as much as the children."

"I'll pay you extra. How much money do you want

to let me go straight to the top of the list?" Rebecca interrupted.

"Madam, please, we operate a completely professional business here and try and suit everyone's needs on a first-come first-served basis. However, we do have a Spanish girl we're looking to settle at the moment if that would be any use to you? Things didn't work out so well with her previous host family. They thought she was too clingy and she thought them too cold and they also went a little mad because she wasn't used to using a grill and kept burning the children's sausages. Match-wise things weren't the best – the Spanish really like to be part of the family, need a lot of TLC. She's mature too – twenty-nine."

Stuff that, Rebecca wasn't holding the hand of any 29-year-old incompetent already rejected by one family and needing constant TLC when TLC was what she herself needed in bucket-loads since having the boys. Besides, her kids lived on sausages – working knowledge of a grill was an essential requirement in the Gleeson household.

"Oh wait now, it's in the notes that she won't go rural, she wants to be based in a city, but if you're prepared to broaden your requirements we have Italians coming over in the next while for work. They do like their coffee though – most of them bring over their own coffee-making machines . . ."

And spend their time drinking coffee and not looking after the kids, Rebecca suspected. Italians were probably gorgeous as well; there was no point in dangling a luscious young Latin in front of Mark's eyes day in, day out.

"Now I won't lie to you – it could take months to find a girl who meets your exact age and nationality requirements. The only good thing about your situation is that Germans often prefer the country experience. Often they like taking Irish dancing classes and even Irish language classes. Do you want me to keep your details on file?" the woman asked politely.

Without answering Rebecca hung up. There was nothing left but to go on-line. At least she'd then get a chance to see what these au pairs looked like. Something told her that while she might be able to request the nationality of her au pair, specifying that she wanted an ugly one wouldn't go down too well. Searching in the cupboard, she found a giant packet of popcorn and poured two bowls out for Jack and Sam. The she put on a full-length Disney feature. Of course she knew some mothers didn't give popcorn to children under the age of four in case they choked, but Rebecca thought that that was over-mothering – there was something to be said for the survival of the fittest, and she didn't want her boys to be the kind who constantly whinged when they caught a cold or fell down and banged their knees.

"Okay, boys, I know you've watched a lot of TV already today, but trust me, you'll thank me when you both turn into the next Neil Jordan or Quentin Tarrantino," she said as she turned the DVD on and spent the next two hours drinking coffee, having the odd nibble on filling but calorie-insignificant popcorn and surfing for the Teutonic teenager of her dreams who would maybe, maybe help make her life worth living again.

When Mark pulled up in his luxury saloon in

Cloonsheeda, he parked on the street a short walk from the eco-development as he didn't want to draw attention to his petrol-guzzling car, especially as super-fit Eddie Ferris cycled everywhere he could and was arriving down from Dublin that morning by train. It looked like interest in Ferris was considerable – a large crowd was forming around the village development and for a moment Mark was pleased until he realised the crowd was mostly at the other end of the site, near the oak tree, and although Mark hadn't been to Mass since he was a teenager there was no mistaking the sounds of the 'Hail Mary' as that bullish farmer, Mossy Skeehan, led the crowd in a decade of the rosary. Worse still, beside Skeehan taking notes was that sexy young blonde reporter from *Independent News* who was meant to be covering the Ferris man's visit and who'd the sense to team a pair of funky, flowery welly boots with her black, to-the-knee, trendy office suit.

"And why exactly do you think the Virgin is appearing in Cloonsheeda at this time, Mr Skeehan?" Mark heard the young hack ask as Skeehan and the stump were photographed from every possible angle between excited 'Hail Mary's' and the odd 'Glory Be to the Father'.

"Well, to me it's a no-brainer," Mossy ranted. "It's obvious Herself Above disapproves of all the shenanigans going on with these outsiders, these green self-sustaining people we've had to put up with over the last while. We were always a moral people here in the parish before this development started and we're moral still, but these people with their strange ways . . . did you know there's a woman taken up residence in these parts, a sex therapist she is too, I only found out that bit myself this morning, and she's put up a female sign with – well, I hate to say this in front of a lovely young woman like yourself – but with female parts displayed and a snake entwined around her lady bits too," Mossy ranted.

"And where does this eh, sex therapist live then, Mr Skeehan?"

"Well, now, come here and walk with me a bit to the entrance of the eco-village till I point out her cottage on the main street . . ."

Mark, with a seasoned nose for trouble that might cause him to lose any business, knew he had to do something fast before the whole day turned into farce. He quickly moved in beside the young reporter and took a hold of her elbow.

"I'm sorry – Isobel, isn't it? Mark Gleeson from Gleeson Auctioneers. Sorry I wasn't here to meet you but I've just got a call to say Eddie is on the way for the official presentation to the fiftieth occupant of Cloonsheeda. I think *that's* the piece we've run past your editor for today so if you'll come this way I'll show you where the presentation is taking place. He has probably arrived by now."

The reporter scowled at Mark's intrusion. Young in years, she already knew that bringing her editor into the conversation was a not-so-subtle reminder as to where her priorities should lie; still, she didn't like being told her business by this presumptuous albeit very sexy older guy. Besides, her nose could smell where the real story lay in this dump of a village, miles away from a wine bar or a decent beautician's.

"Take more pictures, make sure you get a few good

shots of the Polish bloke and his massive forearms holding the saw, then follow me up to the Ferris thing," she hissed at the photographer, showing a savviness well beyond her years and Mark cringed knowing that she was going to be like a dog with a bone with the Virgin in the Tree Stump story.

In the central courtyard, his hands plunged into the pockets of his jeans, Eddie Ferris rocked back and forth on his high-heeled boots (he was five six in his stocking feet) and pushed a long red-brown curl back from his high forehead. Well liked amongst the public as well as the media, Eddie's opinions on sustainable living and eco-developments were considered to be both rational and cutting edge and today the fifty-something presenter's famous one-green one-blue eyes shone as he shook hands all round. Maura Simmons kissed him affectionately on both cheeks and, without displaying a trace of their personal history, thanked him for taking time out to publicise Little Cloonsheeda, a development he'd been supportive of from its initial conception.

"Eddie, as always great to see you," Mark subtly interrupted as Maura moved to mingle. "Let me introduce you to Isobel White – she's doing a piece on the eco-village for the *Independent News*," he announced warmly but authoritatively.

Isobel White nodded curtly at Eddie but Mark could see her saucer eyes were being drawn back to the tree stump where the 'Hail Mary's' were still in full voice, although Mossy had left, probably to feed his cattle. Down at the stump now, Father Fintan, his hands in the air, was pleading for a bit of quiet from the chanting madness so he could speak – hopefully a few words of sense – to the crowd.

"And who is the fiftieth occupant we're making the presentation of wild boughs and berries to today as a good-luck gesture?" Eddie asked, his mismatched eyes crinkling as he smiled.

"Anna Maguire. I have it written down right here," Maura beamed back.

"Right, let's do this so," said Eddie, straightening up his shoulders, shaking out his famous goldilocks curls and broadcasting the famous friendly cool-dude smile that could light up a nation.

The doorbell rang once – then again, this time more urgently. Anna had got a woeful night's sleep on the now-defunct blow-up mattress. During the night the damn thing had collapsed so completely that in the end she might as well have slept on the floor. Not that she really felt the discomfort as the whiskey had numbed her against all pain. Again the doorbell rang and then someone rapped on the window. Damn – it must be important. Fearing that something might have happened to one of her boys, Anna wrapped a dowdy dressing-gown around her T-shirt and leggings and opened the door, to be shocked at the sight of a cheering crowd and a big bouquet of evergreen and wild berries being held aloft by Eddie Ferris.

Disbelief and horror must have been written on her face because Maura Simmons immediately stepped up and whispered urgently in her ear.

"Anna – Maura Simmons from the Development – talked to you on the phone and sent you a card two weeks ago reminding you we were planning this little celebration of your being the fiftieth occupant of the Village. You *do* remember, don't you?"

"I - I remember now – but I just thought it was something simple – not – not this." Flash photography began to blind her eyes. "I just got in last night, you see," she faltered.

Maura smiled and nodded in pretend sympathy. *Jesus, the woman reeked of whiskey.*

From amongst the crowd Isobel White pushed forward, an eager look on her face. "You're Anna Gavin, aren't you, Paddy Gavin's wife, I mean newly separated wife? Our paper ran a piece on Paddy's new life and love in the weekend supplement last week and we were trying to find you for a comment. How are you coping without Paddy, Anna? What do you think of his setting up home with Lana Phillips, a woman fifteen years his junior? Are you going to go ahead with a divorce, Anna?"

The young woman pushed a recording device close to Anna's face and Anna visibly shrank away.

"I . . ."

"What did you think of his new girlfriend posing on Paddy's lap in a variety of designer dresses in our weekend special? Everyone says she has knockout legs."

"I . . . well . . . I . . ."

"Have you reverted back to your maiden name then, Anna – Maguire, is it? Do you think you'll ever find love again?" Isobel White's questions were rattled off as fast as an automatic tennis-machine and the reporter never took her eyes off her victim as she ruthlessly tore, probed and dissected with endless personal questions.

"I . . ."

39

Anna looked at Maura Simmons for support and Maura shrewdly decided to wrap things up.

"I think we'd all just like to welcome Anna Gavin . . . I mean, Maguire, to Cloonsheeda today and hope she'll be very, very happy."

With her eyes Maura motioned to Eddie to hand over the bouquet of leaf and berries and a shellshocked Anna smiled brightly until her cheeks ached although smiling through disaster was second nature for an ex-politician's wife. 'Smile,' Paddy would say to her, 'smile, smile, smile no matter what you feel or what the occasion' and she had obediently done so through scandal, controversy, disastrous election results, the affair and now through her own personal mortification, acute embarrassment and a bruised and battered heart.

4

Mark Gleeson went through the morning newspaper on-line and groaned. The coverage in the following day's paper was nothing short of horrendous. The *Independent News* reporter hadn't just landed one scoop at the eco-village but several scoops in one go, between the tree stump and the oak-worshippers and finding Anna Gavin looking dishevelled and reeking of drink a week after her husband's kiss-and-tell in the papers. Isobel White had even interviewed the Cornish oddball about her Goddess sex-therapy practice and sought her opinion on the view that the miraculous tree stump was Our Lady's warning against debauchery and immorality in the village, particularly for those who were setting up sex-therapy clinics.

"It be not so much the Virgin Mary who'd have an interest in this place as the fairies or in Cornwall what we call the pishkies," Demelza was reported as saying as she was photographed outside Mermaid Cottage, her dark-black curls blowing in the wind, a scarf of purple, orange and yellow blowing at her throat. *"Why, even the name Cloonsheeda is a corruption of the Gaelic,*

meaning 'fairy meadow', and up until last week there be an oak tree on the mound until it was mysteriously knocked by a digger. Terrible bad luck will befall he who orchestrated that little accident!" The oddball was also photographed inside her cosy cottage with an animal she referred to as her Goddess Cat.

Abruptly the phone rang and Mark heard his mother pant down the phone.

"Jesus Christ, Mark, did you see today's paper?"

"Could anybody possibly miss it?"

"Mark, this is bad. Five people rang already today requesting their deposits back and there were no callers from any new buyers, only call after call from reporters and nut-jobs – and a band of bloody witches or maybe they were Satanists, I can't remember, are thinking of coming to Cloonsheeda to get, what was it their coven leader said, oh yes, a 'feel for the fairy place', and a band of religious zealots are also threatening to lynch that Cornish wagon for, what was it they said again, oh yes, 'debasing the virginal nature of the tree stump with her brazen sex-therapy lark and pagan talk of the fairies'."

"I know, Mother, it's truly awful – you couldn't make this stuff up if you tried."

"Oh and it gets worse. That Maura person from the development is furious her friend/lover whatever he is, Eddie Ferris was eclipsed totally in the news piece. There was no mention of the ecological advancements being made at the village or the new permaculture course or was it a seed-saving course they're running for outsiders – and she went on and on about the state of that poor fucking eejit Anna Gavin answering the door with the smell of drink oozing out of her bloody pores . . ."

Yes, his mother was very distressed indeed. Throughout her life, Dee only ever cursed under extreme pressure.

"And I'm getting it in the neck from your father as well – he's furious that you knocked an oak tree, you know how superstitious he is about those things despite him usually having no morals when it comes to anything involving money . . ."

Mark couldn't take any more of his mother's ranting into his ear so he put her on speaker and read a bit more of the Cloonsheeda horror on his computer.

"So, to cut a long story short, I'm washing my hands of the entire spectacle and anyone ringing from now on will be getting your number instead, and I'll warn you now the English media have already got whiff of this tree stump thing. Good luck, son."

Abruptly Dee hung up and immediately Mark's mobile began to hop with one unfamiliar number after another. Then he noticed Rebecca's mobile coming through and considered ignoring it, but from experience he knew it was sometimes better to just answer and take whatever tongue-lashing she was planning for his punishment.

"Just to let you know I've found her! On the net."

"Found who?"

"Our new au pair, you idiot! She's German just as I wanted – very organised, smart, young and *definitely* not attractive. We don't want you being distracted by any eye candy about the place." She laughed joyously with just the slightest trace of venom in her merriment.

"Jesus, you've only started looking, don't you think you're being a bit casual handing over our kids to – how old is this au pair anyway?"

"Nineteen – nearly twenty."

"Christ, a schoolgirl and from a place we don't even know . . . a girl you found over the *internet*! Rebecca, have you lost your mind?"

"The internet is as good as place as any to find an employee and she might only be nineteen, Mark, but she's got great maturity. I could tell that the moment I talked to her on the phone this morning – we'd already been back and forward on e-mail. It's perfect, she's the homely domestic type, *big* into experiencing Irish culture, doesn't care about the bright lights of the city, which is just as well seeing as we live in Bogsville. I think she'll do just fine but, out of courtesy to you, seeing as you are technically the other parent of our boys whom you never see, I've sent you an email of her details, just as a formality, because as I've said I've decided – she's the one!" Rebecca finished in a triumphant rush.

Her incessant talking was enough to make Mark's head explode and he wanted to get her off the phone so he could ring the *Independent News* and eat the face off Isobel White's news-features editor instead.

"Yeah, okay, Rebecca, I'll have a look at the e-mail and get back to you?"

"Mark, there's no need to be so bloody formal – I *am* your wife you know, not one of your bloody business associates," she yelled in annoyance, hanging up the phone.

Sighing, Mark checked his email and clicked on the file for the au pair. Attached was a document about the girl's small achievements to date. Nineteen-year-old Liesel Hoffman seemed to have led a quiet studious life, was the eldest of three children, had done the usual baby-sitting stints and a first-aid course and was fluent in English and French, loved horses and thought she might want to be a homeopath someday. Mark breezed through her résumé in about thirty seconds, somewhat anxious that Rebecca hadn't gone to a proper agency. Still, he knew Rebecca; if she wanted this Liesel Hoffman there would be no peace until Mark gave in to her wishes.

Quickly he moved away from the girl's CV and snapped the mouse onto the accompanying digital photo and felt himself hold his breath as he took in a full-length photo of their new au pair. Immediately he could see why Rebecca would think the young girl unattractive: she was five foot seven at most and he guessed was a plump Size 16 or more, but the girl had an earthy sexiness that perhaps only a man could spot. Sure, her hips were wide and her backside more than likely generous, but her waist was nipped in and her breasts were miniature planets, and at nineteen Mark knew those orbs would be full, firm and perfectly ripe. The girl's gentle face was round and possibly could be described as plain, but her complexion was peaches and cream and around her cheekbones and on her throat she had a soft pink flush as if she was fresh from the farm. Her nose was perhaps a little too long and her big cow's eyes a little too far apart, but her mouth was soft and full and her honey-blonde hair was heavy and worn in one loose plait to her shoulders.

Jesus Christ, Rebecca wasn't serious about moving this curvaceous young beauty in to live with them for the next year or so, was she? Mark was straining in his underpants at the mere thought. Maybe it would be better to voice some objection straight away, that this Liesel Hoffman was too homely or that her countenance was a trifle stern and the boys mightn't find her much fun. Then again, he thought about the pain in the ass Rebecca had turned into since she'd become a mother, always whining about her study and lost business opportunities, almost making him grovel for monthly sex. Screw it, if this Liesel Hoffman was what his wife wanted, let her go ahead and hire her – nothing would happen anyway; he was far too old to stand a chance of corrupting this girl's mouth-watering innocence.

He left a message on her phone. "Hire her if you want, just check her references and, Rebecca, make it on a trial basis for a few months so we can get rid of her if needs be," he told her curtly. Bloody hell, he'd have to coax Rebecca into having sex with him soon or else she wouldn't be able to blame him for developing a roving eye. That creamy complexion, those heavy bosoms and those big, hypnotic cow's eyes could drive any man wild with lust given enough time and just a little opportunity.

Freeda Petersen was cycling back home from work – the bike shop was already paying for itself so she felt justified in working half-days occasionally, like today. Her personal enthusiasm was drawing in the customers, especially when they realised she had lived the great outdoors dream and cycled many interesting places. All around her shop she had pictures of her past cycling adventures: the Americas, the Alps, China and Europe, places she'd seen alone or sometimes with someone special. The thought of that 'someone special' was like a thorn in her brain but as always exercise helped Freeda clear her head – she always got her best ideas for business out cycling.

As she turned the corner of the village, she nearly fell off her saddle at the sight of possibly several hundred people tramping around the corner field, all praying loudly and looking towards the heavens, while at least two TV crews filmed their every move. Yesterday's fuss had turned into a full-blown furore.

"Now don't get me wrong. It's great that people seem to be returning to prayer but praying to a tree stump that may or may not look like the Virgin Mary isn't necessarily the kind of thing I'd approve of," the elderly Father Fintan, who had the decency to look a bit embarrassed, was telling a reporter from *Sky News*. Amazed at these developments, Freeda locked her bike into the bike frame outside her house and smiled a crooked smile. "This place is just as wacky as San Francisco," she muttered to herself, then shook her head and laughed out loud.

Anna Gavin née Maguire had spent the entire day in her new home ignoring the knocks on the front door and bangs on the window from nosey reporters intent on analysing the exact reasons for and the aftermath of the break-up of her marriage. Unfortunately she was severely deficient in groceries and ravenous with the hunger. Distraught and panicky from the onslaught of the media scrum, she tried to phone both her sons, Liam and Niall, for a little bit of moral support. Neither of them answered her calls but let her messages go straight to voicemail and the lack of connection made her feel lonely, so utterly friendless in the world. Reality was crushing as she realised if she couldn't count on her boys in her hour of need, she couldn't count on them ever. What would she do with the spare room she'd set aside for her sons for weekend visits home from college, family weekends that she suspected might never actually happen now?

In her small childhood bedroom Liesel Hoffman began emptying her drawers of clothes for her trip to Ireland while her mother leaned against the doorjamb and tried to talk her out of the madcap adventure she was so abruptly embarking upon. Liesel knew her mother was shocked at her sudden departure but she had to grab this job, this opportunity to escape, before it escaped her!

"When will you just apply for university, Liesel? You're far too intelligent to go to Ireland and look after some other woman's brat children!" Maria Hoffman berated her only daughter.

"This is an opportunity to see a part of the world that interests me. The relaxed way of life in Ireland appeals to me, the culture, the music . . ." Liesel sighed as she rolled a big pair of knickers up tightly and stuffed them into the side pocket of her rucksack.

"You call that whining noise the Irish make in pubs music? You're deluded, Liesel! Mozart, Beethoven, Wagner, Bach, now *that's* music. And what's so important about their culture? Anyway, what use is any of this going to be to you in the modern world?"

"Why does everything have to have a use, Mother? I want to do these things because I want to do these things, because they interest me and I need no better reason for doing them than that!" Liesel snapped.

"Have it your way, but you're only running away from your future, Liesel. When was any music ever that important to you?" Her mother shrugged and turned to go and have her habitual afternoon coffee and cake in the kitchen.

On her own in her bedroom surrounded by posters of Hollywood heartthrobs, Liesel fumed at her mother's musical taunt. Maria Hoffman had sent her eldest child to piano lessons every week for years to instil some 'proper culture' into her but Liesel had quietly rebelled, never playing for pleasure any of the hated music she learned, just putting in the bare amount of practice at home.

All Liesel wanted was to be free of the expectations of her mother and the responsibility of being the oldest sibling and the appointment in Ireland with the two little boys seemed the perfect excuse to escape. Her new Hausfrau promised she would be working no more than twenty-five hours a week, the wages were adequate, the Irish language course she wanted was promised, a car would be provided and the family seemed rich with a big house and lived in beautiful surroundings near an innovative ecological village which would no doubt be full of lots of interesting people. No, Liesel would trust her instincts; she needed a big life experience. College could wait, she thought as she stuffed more socks into her backpack to cosy up to her selection of big, sensible and decidedly ugly cotton knickers.

In Ireland Rebecca Gleeson was ecstatic. The new au pair would be with her almost immediately and then Project Overhaul Rebecca could begin in earnest. Naturally an impatient woman, Rebecca hadn't bothered checking the German girl's references – she didn't fancy spending hours on the phone talking to Germans. Besides, there was so much to do – after all, her personal grooming was in a sorry state and she'd work to do on her archaeology course, some of which was being taught by a new Professor Winterbottom. Slowly but surely Rebecca would gain some free time from her children and become, not only a well-respected academic, but the sex object of her past with the perfect Size 8 to 10 figure. From now on she would eat only soup and salad *and* study religiously. Impetuously she emptied most of the contents of the fridge into the bin, while reading from a textbook. The fact that most of the binned food items were Mark's favourites didn't bother her in the slightest.

5

The doorbell-ringing and window-banging of the previous day had continued on to the next morning but for the last hour or two there had been silence and Anna felt she could just about breathe again. Thankfully, the praying at the Holy Tree Stump had completely eclipsed her marriage break-up as around the village enterprising individuals set up stalls selling rosary beads, religious icons and statues of the Blessed Virgin – and for the media, hot dogs, coffee and giant chocolate muffins. Yes, fortunately, the lunacy was distracting from Anna's unfortunate situation – but, still, she had the sense not to venture out of doors without a hat, a scarf and the obligatory oversized sunglasses covering half her face.

Today was the start of February and Anna wondered if a new month would bring better luck. Keeping her head down low and her hand on her oversized shopping bag, she headed for the village's mini-supermarket to stock up on essentials. All she'd had to eat for the last day were her fingernails, half a pan of stale white bread, some wafer slices of processed ham, a packet of wine gums she'd found in her handbag, a tiny tin of beans, some breakfast cereal and bottled water. Passing by the new sex-therapy clinic Anna paused and bit her lip, then pulled her hat over her eyebrows, readjusted her sunglasses and ploughed on towards the store to face into the drudgery of shopping when all she really wanted was a gallon of fizzy orange, a six-pack of crisps and a crate or two of paracetamol to set her right again.

A happy glow enveloped Demelza like a giant bubble as she walked outside her front door and touched her favourite mermaid, sitting on a dolphin, just for luck. Yes, Demelza's auras were definitely very much aligned this morning – her whole body radiated warmth from her fingertips to her toes and she was feeling supremely optimistic as she passed the mermaids, who were combing their hair on her front pillars, and walked down the main street of Cloonsheeda wearing dramatic elephant flares in denim with red velvet patches around the knees and crotch.

A meeting on the education needs of the new eco-villagers was being held that very morning in the local church hall and Demelza thought she'd pop her dark, curly head in and meet some of the new arrivals from around the world, many of whom would certainly need her attention as they all moved from the dark of winter into the joys of spring.

In the church hall which smelt of sickly perfumed must, Sinéad Winterbottom with three children stuck to her legs gave the impression of listening attentively to the speakers while all the time her focus was on her bored, slightly whiney acrobatic brood.

"There's so much mention of religion in the schools and no mention at all of any of the world's enlightened scientists," Tilda, a very determined Swedish pharmacist who had lost the faith in 'real drugs' and who worked in the local café and health food shop, let rip. Nodding heads of assent encouraged her to continue with her worldly observations. "My daughter, Sameera, is coming home from school very confused, telling me that when it rains it is because God is crying because the world is so naughty. As a non-believer coming from Sweden this is very shocking so, yes, if you need to put together a committee to look into an alternative school system for Cloonsheeda I would be happy to do what I can."

Sinéad smiled a smile of support and nodded sympathetically, although inwardly she was a bit torn. Like Tilda, Henry was a fully signed up atheist although Sinéad preferred to tell people she was a humanist – it made her sound more 'nice' and less 'intimidating'. Then again, she had gone to the little country school in Cloonsheeda where first class and second were merged, giving her the dubious satisfaction of almost making her First Communion twice. Still, the religion hadn't done her much harm – she actually liked the hymns and the making of the May Day altar to Mary – and so she found it easier to say she was a humanist or 'somewhat spiritual' than going the whole hog and labelling herself an atheist.

Even her own mother Rita, whom Sinéad had always thought of as being fairly broad-minded, had initially been stunned when she'd brought up the 'atheist' conversation a few years ago. She could still remember every word even now. "Oh God, Sinéad," her mother had fretted, "if you don't have a religion, well, that's one thing – but an atheist is another thing entirely. How will I explain to Auntie Maureen, especially since she does the angel readings and has seen granny's ghost in the bathroom?" Ever since then Sinéad had become a 'humanist' – there was no point in upsetting everyone. Her mother had come around to her beliefs or lack of them, but not her father – humanist, atheist, or spiritual, if his grandchildren weren't baptised it wasn't good enough for Mossy Skeehan. For most of the row Sinéad had been in England with her children and an agri-business qualification that meant nothing to her father, but now newly back in Ireland she had yet to set foot in her childhood home and her parents had yet to call.

As the debate in the church hall intensified, Sinéad watched as her two eldest were lured away by 'child friendly' activities at the end of the hall. Shaking of maracas and banging of tambourines began as some children followed a ponytailed flautist called Enda, husband of Tilda the Swede, around the room. A preschooler or two hung out of Enda's purple-cord trouser legs as a multi-coloured children's play parachute was produced and billowed up and down in the air for the children's delight.

"Well, does anyone have an opinion on setting up one of those schools that concentrate on practical skills where reading and writing aren't the focus of early education? As I don't have children myself, I appreciate all opinions," Maura asked in her usual brisk, no-nonsense manner.

"Oh, I know the ones you mean," Tilda said, combing her long white-blonde hair with her long slender fingers and crossing and uncrossing her even longer legs in irritation. "Those schools wouldn't suit my value system at all – full of woolly-headed types. I want education, just no religion."

"Anyone interested in a Montessori primary?" Maura continued to probe.

"It's still largely based on the national curriculum though, isn't it?" asked Sylvia Sawicki, a heavily pregnant homeopath in her early forties who looked like a bush in an enormous green turtle-necked, vegetable-dyed wool sweater.

Sinéad was sick of looking at that turtle-neck sweater. Sylvia seemed to be wearing it the entire time, including when the media were interviewing her about her husband Jeronim's discovery of the Virgin Mary in the Holy Tree Stump.

"What about getting a multilingual school off the ground?" Maura suggested.

"Well, since my husband Jeronim is Polish and also speaks German and I have some French, I find that a very interesting suggestion," Sylvia trilled. "My husband, as everyone probably knows by now, is quite religious, although I myself don't really care too much whether or not there is religion in a new multilingual school."

For a moment there was silence as the other people in the room tried to work out their own position on education for their children. Nobody would admit it but basically they all would support any system that would turn their prodigy into the kind of wunderkinder who might one day inherit the world.

Spotting the first gap in the conversation, Sinéad self-consciously cleared her throat. "I . . . I was just wondering . . . well, my kids are still young, I know, but I had thought of homeschooling and wondered if anyone here had tried it," she asked, blushing crimson at her own audacity.

"My sister tried it in the States for a while with her two eldest but the kids were just too high-energy for her and in the end she was just dying to get them into real school." Freeda Petersen, who had just dropped by to hand out discount leaflets on kids' cycle seats and helmets, answered briskly.

"We have a friend who just *loves* homeschooling, but I agree with Freeda here it might not suit everyone," Maura added – again very diplomatically.

It was then that Sinéad's nose began to wrinkle from the smell – there was an overwhelming stench escaping the nether regions of her toddler and her body tensed with anxiety. "I'm sorry, could I just get by you there, I have to pop off, the baby needs changing," she apologised in a loud whisper to an earthy woman feeding a young baby with a purple-veined boob resembling a giant oozing turnip. The sight made Sinéad glad that she was weaning her baby off his night feed and could soon claim full ownership of her body.

"Oh, if you need a changing mat I've one here you can borrow," the breastfeeding woman kindly offered. "I'm sure nobody would mind if you laid him in the middle of the floor. I'm the home-birth midwife for the area. Believe me, when it comes to babies I've seen everything!"

"Ehm, no thanks, but . . . well, he's a bit temperamental at the moment . . . you see, he doesn't like anyone *seeing* him get his nappy changed, bit sensitive about it in fact," Sinéad stammered, aware that she sounded completely ridiculous. Frantically she tried to catch the eye of her older children, still entranced by the Pied Piper in purple trousers.

"Are you using cloth nappies or the compostable nappies as well for out and about?" Maura asked in a sharp but friendly manner. "From the padding around his bottom I suspect the latter."

Sinéad blushed crimson – how the hell was the woman so perceptive when she didn't have any children?

"I have lots of nieces and nephews," Maura added, as if reading Sinéad's mind.

"Cloth is definitely best. Never did the eco-disposable nappies for long myself – they're meant to be compostable but we had some in our bio-degrader for a year and *nada*, nothing, not even a morsel broken down after twelve months," Sylvia snorted from deep inside her green-bush jumper.

Sinéad smiled painfully – the pressure was mounting. From experience she knew if she didn't escape soon the leg-guards of the nappy were in danger of being breached. In a situation like that she would be forced to accept the loan of a changing mat and then her horrendous secret would be discovered. For despite the fact that she lived in an eco-village, Sinéad was still a cloth-nappy virgin, preferring to use cheap brand-name non-biodegradable, disposable nappies. Not only did she find them more convenient but the truth was, the Winterbottoms had spent so much money on their eco-house, they had no choice but to buy household items from the cheapest supermarkets – certainly costly biodegradable nappies were not on her list.

At the back of the hall her two older children were

now having great fun kicking the shins of Enda the Pied Piper who was laughing off the extreme pain like a really, really good sport.

"Well, sorry to have to rush off, next time perhaps we could investigate setting up a multi-ethnic but non-denominational, child-centred, unstructured school which embraces all the major European languages and maybe a few minor ones too," Sinéad joked as she was leaving.

Everybody blanked her, except for the smiling woman in the orange poncho and velvet-patched flared denims. Inside Sinéad withered. God, if there was one thing she hated, it was any sort of confrontation or being disliked. God, she really must erase God from all her thoughts as Henry found her constant lapsing into God this and Jesus that very, very disappointing.

Dragging herself and her crying children out the door (they wanted her to adopt the pain-proof silver-flautist), Sinéad was consumed with maternal responsibilities both real and vaguely ridiculous.

Back home, the feeding of her starving computer fish and cleaning of their fish tank had resulted in their having four babies. Running a domestic human home was a non-stop battle but taking care of a school of fish was almost twice as stressful. Sometimes she lay awake at night wondering about her fish family, how they were doing alone in cyberspace behind the blackness of the computer screen. Was the algae overgrowth at critical levels? Would there be any new fish babies when she switched on the home computer in the morning? There was nothing nicer than babies and, God, fish babies were just the cutest little things, but the stress of looking after them, God knows where it all might lead!

In drizzle and under overcast skies, Liesel Hoffman arrived at Dublin Airport and waited and waited and waited for her new Hausfrau Rebecca Gleeson to collect her and her few belongings. After an hour and more of pacing up and down in her scuffed Doc Marten boots, she figured out the payphone system and got through to Rebecca's mobile phone.

"Oh great, you're here," Rebecca answered brusquely. "I'm not coming to Dublin today after all, so just grab a taxi and ask for the train station and then get a train to Carrigmore town. Ring me when you get to Carrigmore and I'll see if I can pick you up."

"But you *promised* to pick me up!" Liesel spluttered in disbelief.

"Look, what's the big deal? You're an adult, aren't you?" Rebecca's irritation grew. Her PMT had reached near-violent levels since she got up for the smallest of yummy-mummy breakfasts this morning.

"But . . ." Liesel's money was running out at an alarming rate. All of a sudden the last of her supply of coins was eaten and everything went dead. Shocked, she left the airport building and found herself at the taxi rank, staring blankly.

A businesswoman in a green suit caught her eye. "Everything okay?"

"I don't really know. How much would it cost to get a taxi to the train station?" Liesel asked in her very polite, very precise German accent.

When the businesswoman told her the approximate price she went visibly pale.

"You could get the bus into the city centre and then get a bus or the Luas, that's a tram, to the station," the woman said a little briskly. She was glancing at her watch. "Do you know how much a train to the town of Carrigmore would cost?" Liesel asked anxiously.

"No idea but the trains in Ireland are quite expensive."

Liesel bit her lip and drew in a breath. This was a setback. The travel costs to reach her host family would rob her of her emergency money but she was sure her Hausfrau would reimburse her in full – she had seemed so nice when they had chatted by email and once or twice on the phone, before today of course.

"There's no train to Carrigmore until this evening and it's a commuter train so it'll be packed," a railway worker told her when she finally entered the train station. "It's a pity you didn't look up the timetable before you got here so you wouldn't be waiting." he added.

It was then that Liesel's eyes filled with tears and the whole sorry story of the inconsiderate Hausfrau came tumbling out and how all her money was being eaten up in travel expenses.

"Jaysus, that's bad form alright, leaving a lovely young girl like yourself to travel halfway across a foreign country. Make no mistake, some people are complete bastards," the man sympathised, rolling his eyes. "Here, take this, at least it might cover the price of a cup of coffee." He handed her four euros in coins.

"No, you are very kind but I couldn't possibly," Liesel protested.

"Go on now, take it and get a coffee into you. I know it's what all you continentals live on."

Despite the fear, Lisa smiled tightly and accepted the coins, grateful that someone was treating her with concern. For several hours she listened to her iPod, read discarded magazines or papers from the newsagent's and bought two cups of coffee and a chocolate bar. Come evening, as predicted by the railway staff, the train – an awful carthorse of a train, such a contrast from sleek German engineering – was packed but luckily she got a seat. Two and a half hours later she reached Carrigmore and, cold and hungry, she tried to phone her Hausfrau several times over the course of half an hour but again there was no answer. Reluctantly she traipsed back into the station and got the number for a taxi.

"You're going to the castle, are you?" the taxi driver asked.

After a twenty-minute drive over windy blackened roads Liesel eventually came to her new home – a mansion in the countryside with an avenue of gravel up to the door and big electronic gates.

"Bloody hell, you're late!" Rebecca greeted her. "Come on and I'll show you to your room. Make sure you get a good night's sleep, the twins get up early and are always ready for action."

Inside her bedroom, Liesel fought to keep her thoughts steady. Was this really the start of her grand adventure? As no answer was forthcoming; she fell into bed and instantly collapsed into the equivalent of a medically-induced coma.

6

It was seven o'clock in the morning and India Jennings was already up answering emails, a cup of tea at hand, a blanket draped over her shoulders. There was one from the graphic designer asking her to sign off on brochures, a request from an arts official of the tractor festival to set up some interviews with local and national media, a reminder to update their festivals web page and a rather cheeky request from a journalist hoping for a contact.

After forty minutes or so of reading and typing, India picked up the phone and dialled the number of a hotel in Galway to sort out accommodation for a stressed-out friend's hen night. It was a favour really and, although India could organise any event in her sleep, hysterical brides didn't make for the easiest of clients and she didn't want to ever make the mistake of finding that out for certain by organising a wedding from start to finish for a friend.

Having checked hotel prices and availability India took a break and scooted off to make some warm, buttery toast then watched her lover sleep – that amazing six-pack and his muscley thighs made her mouth water with desire. It was no wonder she'd forgiven him his recent crime of being as dead as a rock the night she'd come home to seduce him. A woman could forgive a man as beautiful as Nate anything – even sex deprivation.

Watching him as he lay there motionless, breathing deeply, India was struck by the fact that Nate still slept like a single person whenever he got the chance, hogging all the bed, his feet and arms sprawled wide. Immediately she felt an overwhelming desire to dump the toast and nibble his ear with her buttery lips and tongue but the movement triggered him like a bomb and suddenly he sat straight as a plank in the bed, his face white as limed water, his eyes blank and wide.

"Crikey, what time is it?" he panicked.

"Not yet eight."

"Eight! Why didn't you wake me? I'm going to be late for work!" he ranted.

"Hey, don't blame me. I don't know what hours you're working!" India defended herself.

"I'm meant to be there at six forty-five this morning."

"Well, you'll have to get your act together. It's not my fault you're late, Nathan – try using an alarm clock!"

"Shit, I was working till ten thirty last night and then I went for a few pints with one of the blokes down the boozer, well, maybe it was more than a few, course he's not in till two thirty this afternoon, the bastard, so it doesn't matter if he's wasted or not. Fuck, fuck, fuck, fuck, fuck!"

Kicking back the duvet and scrambling out of bed, he went on a mad tear looking for his cycling gear.

"What are you doing? Wait, I'll drop you in the jeep," she said.

"I'm late anyhow. I might as well get the exercise and work out a believable excuse. Crap, all I need is a verbal warning my first week. The bloody Sheila who runs the place is a right ballbreaker too," he moaned as he hopped round the room dragging a sock onto his foot.

From her upstairs window India watched Nathan's rock-hard buttocks disappear round the corner in his tight cycling gear. He was so fit and so good-looking it was enough to make any red-blooded woman scream but, if the last few weeks of sex famine was a future indicator of their relationship, India might very well be hooking up again with an old friend from her pre-Nathan days, ignored but not quite forgotten – her vibrator.

The Gleeson twins had just had breakfast in their pyjamas, smeared half of it on their faces and on their hair, and new au pair Liesel Hoffman was in a definite state of shock at her new role and responsibilities.

"Come on, Jack, hurry and finish those chocolate crispies, there'll be nothing else until Liesel gets your lunch," Rebecca harried.

Instantly, companion-in-crime Sam tipped a packet of cornflakes from the table onto the floor and jumped on the crunchy mess with his fat little piggies, laughing and screaming with joy. Liesel couldn't believe it, such outrageous behaviour from a child *and* in front of a parent.

"That's very bold, Sam! If you don't behave, Liesel will put you on the Naughty Step," Rebecca warned crossly.

"Is that part of your discipline system?" Liesel asked, encouraged that *some* rules might be part of the Gleeson family set-up.

"No, but you could try it. I never got them to sit still anywhere for more than two seconds – it was always easier to turn on the TV." She shrugged, grabbing her handbag. "Okay, I'm off so, Liesel. I'll be gone a few hours. I need to go to the gym and then I have a few things to get in town. Taking care of the boys should be lots of fun but put the TV on if things get too wild. And if you really need me, in an emergency you can call my mobile." Her eyes narrowed uninvitingly.

Liesel wasn't impressed; she already knew from experience that Rebecca was a call-dodger on the mobile when it suited. "Please, my Hausfrau, I must talk to you about my train fare and taxi expenses and when will I be insured to drive the car you promised me?"

"Hmm . . . oh yes, we'll discuss that later, gotta go, must get to the gym before lunch or there'll be no point in going at all!" Air-kissing her boys, Rebecca charged out the door like a greyhound just out of the traps.

Abandoned to the homestead, Liesel clapped her hands loudly and, with as much authority as she could command, spoke to her energetic new charges. "Come, boys, time to get out of your pajamas and tidy your beds."

Immediately both pointed at the TV sulkily.

"Noddy!" screamed Jack.

"Tractor Tom!" insisted Sam.

"No, boys, TV later, clothes first, come along."

"Noddy! Tractor Tom!" they both screamed at the top of their voices and then a joint attack was launched

as Sam went to bite Liesel's shins and Jack opted for a good kick to the ankles.

Completely taken by surprise, Liesel screamed but then her nerve steadied. A certain amount of defiance in a two-year-old was to be expected – Liesel knew that from her baby-sitting experiences in Germany and toddlers were of course like live bombs at the best of times – but she could not, would not tolerate violence from a small child without there being consequences.

"Come, boys, you will sit on the step of the stairs until you realise hitting people is very, very wrong," Liesel said sternly.

An hour later, with their pyjamas still on, the boys were still refusing to comply for any longer than three seconds on the Naughty Step and Liesel's arms began to ache from constantly putting them back in the sitting position, but giving in was not an option. Liesel Hoffman was made of sterner stuff than the will of two little boys whose collective age was only five. Still, close to eleven Liesel was definitely in need of some decent coffee and a biscuit at the very least. Hunger made her weak of will – so she finally turned on the television and let the defiant toddlers watch some drivel. Famished, she began a shakedown of the house for some kind of adult nourishment but there was nothing nice to be found – not a biscuit, piece of bread or even a yoghurt. Inside the fridge was mouldy cheese, out-of-date processed wafer-thin ham, two kiddie cheesy yoghurts and a tray of sausages. The sausages were a no-no – Liesel was a vegetarian. The yoghurts, awful-looking though they were, were still somewhat tempting but Liesel wondered if they were for the boys' lunch. Continuing on her desperate journey she tore open another cupboard and found about a dozen packets of dried soup and half a pack of soft, stale crackers. Feeling downhearted, Liesel's eyes scoured the room and landed on the fruit bowl which contained two half-rotten apples and several blackened bananas. *Gott im Himmel*, what in heaven's name did these people actually live on?

Willie Cleary was feeling moody and out of sorts as he stood in a damp field on the outskirts of Cloonsheeda, puffing on a roll-up and looking into the distance at a copse of trees. Beside him, Tom was squinting down the barrel of his pump-action shotgun ready to fire on a few boisterous crows just for fun. Desperately wanting to be anywhere else, Willie replayed the moment in the newsagent's that morning when he saw cover after cover full of the news that his doppelganger, bad boy David Ron Dwyer was snapped coming out of a top model's apartment in London days after the lady announced her engagement to a rock star, and once again Willie couldn't help wondering why Lady Luck should favour David Ron Dwyer over himself when if anything he was even better looking than the Irish Hollywood heartthrob.

"What's eating you, Willie?" Tom asked abruptly, taking a swig from a can of beer as the crows exploded away from the trees in terror from his gunshot.

"Nothin' but you'd better go easy on the drink or you might end up shooting more than crows and shoot your fucking toes off as well and since your da died from the drink and you're the eldest son you'd think you'd pay some heed," Willie snapped tetchily just as Tom suddenly took the notion to annihilate one big, black raven.

"Don't be such a fucking dry shite, Cleary, you and your sympathy for shagging crows – and leave my old man out of it! Sure, what's wrong with shooting bleedin' crows anyway? You need to lose your misery, man – isn't it a great life we have here in Cloonsheeda? Aren't we a million times better off than some sad bastard who goes to work every day in a suit, the taxman taking all his money? Shooting crows and a few tinnies – it's a fucking deadly life!"

"You think?" Angrily Willie stubbed out the fag on the ground. He wasn't into killing defenceless animals, even if they were as Tom called them 'flying rats'. In particular he hated it when Tom shot ducks and the birds would run around with no heads before the life fully went from their small bodies. Years of seeing his father helping distressed animals had worn off on him, he supposed.

"Here, Willie, hold my drink, would ya? I see a bunny straight ahead that's going to end up in my pot for dinner."

A blast of fire and it was all over and Tom ran over to claim his kill.

"Great eating in a rabbit, there is. We'll do a stew back at your house tomorrow once we've hacked, gutted, skinned and salted the fecker in a bucket overnight. Aren't we in luck there's a load of veg left over from the dumpster-diving too. Man, I just love this life of mine, not answerable to no one, living off the fat of the land! You just couldn't ask for more, could you, Willie?"

Barely raising his eyebrow in acknowledgement, Willie took the can off Tom and drank deeply, hoping to anaesthetise his brain against this wonderful indolent life Tom loved so much and made Willie sick to the pit of his small-town stomach.

If Rebecca wanted to be really harsh in her assessment of her body, she'd describe herself as plump and fleshy, but the gym mirrors told her that as a mum of two, and in her early thirties, she was still very much a hottie, even if she had a few stubborn, undesirable post-baby curves. When she checked into the leisure centre this morning she *knew* the cute Australian man-babe at reception was definitely giving her 'the eye'. Just a minute ago he'd flashed a grin in her direction as he scrubbed down a rowing-machine with a sponge and disinfectant while she was puffing and blowing on the nearby cross-trainer.

"G'day!" the golden Sex God greeted, looking up from his bucket of suds as she disembarked from the machine and wiped down the non-existent traces of moisture from the chunky, black, plastic handles.

"Oh hi again, you've really caught me out, puffing and blowing like this, I'm a bit out of practice," she answered in a voice so sweet and low she was almost doing a Marilyn Monroe impression.

The handsome man-boy in front of her just smiled and she felt the illogical need to keep chatting just to fill the silence. "I have twin boys at home, you see, just gone two and a half and I'm studying archaeology at college as well – distance learning mostly – but still it's hard to fit everything in," she gushed, aware that she was trying to impress this guy who was several years her junior.

"Got brains as well as beauty," he teased, then

immediately apologised. "Christ, I'm sorry, you must think I'm a right sexist pig. We're not always so careful with our words where I come from."

"No, that's okay, don't worry." Rebecca waved her hand then tucked in a wayward red lock behind her right ear. "We're all way too PC these days anyway, don't you think?" She smiled up through her dark-brown mascara'd eyelashes.

"Well, you need any help with the equipment give me a shout," he said as he wrung the sponge dry and moved on to wiping down another machine.

"With all that scrubbing ability you'd be a fine catch for any woman," she flirted outrageously as she casually arranged her hand towel around her neck.

He began to laugh. "Yeah, they don't tell you in college when you sign up for any of these fitness courses but there's always lots of cleaning when you get a real job – scrubbing down machines, mopping floors, lots of not-so-glamorous stuff . . . the boss was as mad as a cut snake with me this morning too . . . between you and me, I think she's laying on the cleaning as extra punishment because I was way late. I'm Nathan, by the way." He looked like he was going to extend his hand for her to shake but then he remembered he was wearing gloves. "I've only been in the country a few weeks but I think I'm still jetlagged," he laughed, pushing golden curls away with the back of one gloved hand and showing dazzling white teeth as he beamed.

God, he was gorgeous, super fit *and* friendly. What Rebecca wouldn't give for one look at that torso under his tight gym top! She always had an eye for a man in top physical condition. It wasn't that Mark wasn't

70

handsome – her husband had a devilish black look about him that often made her want to eat him up with a spoon – but Mark was in his forties now and bar the few months several years ago where she'd walked out on their marriage and he'd started pumping iron again, he was apt to develop a bit of a paunch. Of course he blamed the demands of work, but if he didn't work out regularly he couldn't blame her if she sometimes had a roving eye.

"You know, if you want you could come in for a physical assessment in the next few days. I could design a personal programme for you based upon your fitness level, flexibility and personal goals," Nathan continued, sponge in hand, scrubbing temporarily suspended.

"Sure . . . sounds good if you think it would be for the best," Rebecca simpered as she took a very slow and very deliberate mouthful of mineral water from her small plastic bottle.

"Well, if you're a busy mum and student I can show you how to get the best results for your time – that is, if you want to of course. In my opinion you're fine just the way you are too."

"Hey, no need to flatter me, Nate, I know I've got a few curves," she giggled like a schoolgirl, "but it's curves of steel I'm after now, so sure book me in for a personal programme."

"Ace, I'll check the appointments book for you on the way out then."

Rebecca nodded, already mesmerised by the sing-song happy Australian inflexions in his voice. With stupendous willpower she checked herself from licking her lips right there in front of him. What was it about younger guys that always made her pupils dilate and her heart beat faster? And what was it about Australia and men that always came back to haunt her? Two previous boyfriends had disappeared to Oz, including a very hot toy boy she'd almost had a full-blown affair with that time she'd split with Mark and he'd given her carte blanche to get 'everything' out of her system because she'd married young and maybe needed a few more experiences. Trouble is 'everything' could be like a dormant virus, capable of reactivating at the slightest hint of temptation.

Letting her imagination run away with her, Rebecca left the gym fantasising about next Tuesday's appointment with Nathan. Plonking her newly aching bum in her car she headed off to check out Carrigmore town's best shops and boutiques. High on her list was some skyscraper heels, plenty of low-fat nibbles and some sexy new gym gear. "Sexy hot Momma, here I come!" she told herself in her overhead mirror, imagining her new, fabulous life unfolding just as she'd planned.

7

Sitting at her computer screen, Demelza drank a brew of mint tea and felt the fog clear from her brain. For most of the previous night she'd been up writing her sex-therapy goddess manual for the modern woman, but now morning was here she was still possessed with wild creative passion. This book would set the publishing world on fire because it was timely, deeply spiritual and mindful of the stresses women faced in the modern world. And of course it was full of sex – and Demelza was astute enough to know sex always sells.

In fact Demelza's amazing insight, that every woman should have an assigned goddess to help unleash the power of divine sexuality and femininity in her, combined with her own practical sex-therapy experience and her unique meditation practices, would result in a book so ground-breaking that women everywhere would find release from the constraints of the one-sided, modern, patriarchal world. Once she could convince someone to buy it.

"It be all coming together," she told Bast as she

brushed her with affection and so it appeared when the phone rang and a tight English accent announced itself at the other end of the phone.

"Hello, I'm looking to speak with Demelza Spargo," a lady in a clipped voice demanded in a manner that suggested she wouldn't wait more than a minute for someone of that name to make themselves known.

"That be me," Demelza answered softly as she pushed a disgruntled Bast onto the floor.

"Antonia Marshall here. You sent your manuscript to me for consideration. I have to say that I find your manuscript somewhat intriguing – a bit rough, of course, but I think you might be onto something with your goddess theme all the same."

Demelza felt a warm glow of heat rise to her chest. So far, out of a total of thirty agents she'd sent her work to, this was the only one with the decency to contact her with anything more than a polite but firm written refusal.

"Goddess identification be universal, it's just that we've forgotten so much of it," Demelza quickly said. "The Hindus have a goddess for every village, although when it comes to this book I be concentrating on Celtic culture, like Áine, goddess of love and fertility, not forgetting one of my favourites, Medb who led men into a war so she could steal a bull. My writing be all about the resurgence of the feminine in this male-dominated world." For five more minutes Demelza rattled off her goddess knowledge and certain book publishing potential and could almost feel the quiet thought processes at work down the phone as instant decisions were being made.

"Hmm . . . well, if you write the entire manuscript I might consider it, although I am very busy. Hey, great pen name though, Demelza Spargo – how did you come up with it?" Antonia jocularly inquired as a sort of sweetener before finishing the conversation.

"Pen name! Demelza Spargo be not a pen name! It be my given name and it be proper Cornish through and through!" Demelza sizzled.

Antonia coughed nervously and then the line went dead.

"Well, that be the end of her," Demelza told Bast.

Still, if she wasn't quite setting the literary world alight at the moment at least things weren't going too badly with the sex-therapy practice. The phone hadn't stopped hopping since she'd advertised her services, even if some of the messages were abusive and potential clients sometimes hung up before they left a message. Clients would ring back; they always did when they managed to strengthen their nerve. Tomorrow two definite ladies were booked in for sessions and somehow Demelza felt it would all happen for her eventually – the book, the practice, the goodwill of the local people – and closing her eyes momentarily she imagined how wonderful it would feel when such things came to pass. Playfully, Bast broke her reverie by jumping on her desk and poking her paw into a jar of pencils on the windowsill.

"Alright, m'lover, I know I be ignoring your requests for titbits but Mummy has a job to do, a job that not even a very special little goddess cat like you could possibly understand," Demelza laughed as she buried her rosy cheeks into the cat's curly pelt and accepted wholly and without question the little animal's warm and honest love.

A woman in the mini-market was stalking her, yes, definitely stalking her, thought Anna as she placed a tub of luxury ice-cream into her trolley to join the other three two-litre tubs, jostling with a giant bottle of fizzy orange and some chocolate biscuits. In fact, she thought she'd seen her the last time she went shopping too.

"Anna, Carol Delaney here from the *Evening Mail*, Irish edition," the stalker suddenly burst out as a photographer stepped into Anna's personal space and began to take shots – they'd been to the Holy Tree Stump to take pictures of the rosary-praying.

"I couldn't help but notice how you're buying so much ice-cream. Just wondering, are you bulimic since the separation, Anna?"

Anna was speechless.

"You used to be a ballet dancer didn't you, Anna? Dancers always have eating disorders, don't they? Some of them even use appetite suppressants and cocaine to stay thin – did you ever use cocaine, Anna, maybe with Paddy, are you using cocaine now?" The woman rapid-fired the questions as she stuck her recording machine in front of Anna's nose.

Refusing to answer a single question, Anna steered her trolley to the till. Damn that bloody tree stump for causing a media frenzy in what was meant to be her idyllic, anonymous new world.

Anna slid down the inside of her front door and tried to forget. What a cow that woman reporter was! True she'd lost two stone in the last six months with the stress of separation, but what woman breaking up from her marriage didn't fall to pieces physically as well as mentally? Right now Anna could do with a proper drink, but she'd thrown the remainder of her whiskey down the sink after the Eddie Ferris debacle. Still, there was no ignoring her body's hunger for something raw and powerful in her veins – anti-depressants, sleeping tablets, nicotine, something, anything to kill the pain – but she'd come off all the lovely happy tablets that had first helped her deal with Paddy's affair and then with the actual separation proceedings and feelings of shame, mortification and absolute primal fear.

For the want of human comfort and kindness, Anna tried her eldest son's mobile again, desperate to talk to anyone and be heard. To her surprise a voice answered at the other end on the third ring.

"Mum?" Liam asked wearily and with that one word she wondered when that had happened, when had her beautiful baby, her lovely little boy started to sound like the irritated parent and her the awful needy child?

"Oh, so good to hear your voice, Liam, really it's so good to hear your voice!" she babbled over-excitedly. "How's college?"

"Same old same old," he said, every word dripping boredom and then she heard a female voice mutter something low and giggle stupidly in the background.

"Just wondering when you might come and see me for a visit, Liam? Just because we sold the old house doesn't mean you and your brother don't still have a home here with me. I was hoping we could have a little housewarming party, just the three of us – maybe next weekend?"

"Sorry, I'm spending a lot of weekends in my digs studying, going to parties, going off to friends, you know the way it is."

Anna frowned, the socialising part sounded right but not really the books. "But you *will* find the time, won't you, to come and see me, Liam?" she asked, increasingly anxious.

The giggling and the background noise seemed to intensify tenfold – more girls had arrived.

"Look, Mum, gotta go!" The phone went dead and, after looking at it trancelike for a few seconds, Anna fired it across the floor in anger.

"I'm strong, I'm stronger than this," she raged at the mirror in the hall. "I used to be more than just a mother and wife. I used to be somebody, a woman who danced in London, a woman who danced flamenco and the cancan on cruise ships in the Med, a woman who set up her own dance schools until it all became about the boys and Paddy, Paddy fucking Gavin and his political life at the cost of mine!"

With a weariness in her bones, Anna picked up her shopping bags and caught her reflection in the mirror as she passed to the kitchen. Small lines fanned from the corners of her eyes and her mouth. Was she still pretty, would anyone ever again find her attractive now she was single, did she actually care? Unloading the nearly melted ice cream onto her kitchen worktop, she fired the newly bought cartons into her freezer to join the two other untouched cartons inside. Bulimic indeed! What a stupid question! Anna bought ice-cream for her boys, her boys loved ice-cream, her boys could eat a whole tub each at one sitting and she wanted to be ready for her boys when they came to visit. And they would come to visit, she hoped, she prayed – someday soon.

On the way home from visiting the boutiques of Carrigmore, Rebecca decided to swing by Cloonsheeda to see how things were shaping up with the devotions to the Blessed Tree Stump. In some ways Rebecca felt partly responsible for the whole media frenzy. Mark had wanted to demolish the whole mound, both tree and earth, until she'd told him that earth mounds of so-called 'fairy forts' were archaeological features protected by law but that there was nothing stopping him knocking the actual tree – except that it might attract the attention of the Looney Brigade. At the time even she had no idea just how looney. Hopefully things would have died down by now, the crowds not having witnessed any actual miracles melted away and gone about their business. Even though Rebecca wasn't always the most supportive wife, she understood Mark was anxious to sell the remainder of the development and when it came down to it, his money was her money, a fact she hadn't forgotten while spending plenty of *their* money out shopping.

Discreetly she parked her gas-guzzling car on the main street and began to amble towards the Cloonsheeda development where she noticed some old biddies in heavy anoraks and welly boots were still battling the elements to stare at the stump, but at least the media had scarpered – there was only so much mileage you could get out of a tree stump once it had been photographed and filmed from every possible angle.

As Rebecca sighed, thinking how the shifting of more

units would result in more cash for herself, she didn't even notice Maura Simmons swiftly walk by to accost the leggy young woman getting out of a jeep.

"India, India, wait up! Just wanted to ask how you're settling in?"

India felt her chest tighten as Maura Simmons roared a greeting into her jeep, knowing from experience that such friendliness usually meant the inquirer wanted something and probably for free. "Maura, oh hi, meant to pop into the community hall a few times over the last few weeks for some of the information sessions, but things have been really hectic," she blustered. "My boyfriend Nate and I are still choosing furnishings and buying pieces of furniture for the apartment. Nate's the one on the eco-friendly bike, by the way, while I'm the baddie who, as I'm sure you noticed, has a tank of a jeep, but hey, at least it's diesel!"

"Oh, well, sure with you at least the jeep's justified, you must be travelling all around the country with your job, battling floods and burst rivers and going to places up the mountains!"

Maura beamed and this time India was certain a request of sorts was coming her way.

"Yes, well, it seems every small village in Ireland wants to run a festival and it's my job to help get committees off the ground," India said, smiling so much her jaws were aching. Maybe she could make a mad dash to her apartment by citing a weak bladder and a long drive home.

"Actually it's your work I wanted to ask you about, your work with festivals, that is. It's just with all the –

well, I won't say 'bad' but shall we say unwarranted publicity over the, ehm, tree stump and the politician's wife," Maura dropped her voice to a whisper, "I was thinking we should do something fun and sophisticated to put Cloonsheeda on the map. Actually it was that Spargo person who gave me the idea after she said in the papers Cloonsheeda meant 'fairy meadow' in Gaelic. I thought we could organise something for Bealtaine, the beginning of the Celtic summer. *Be-ahl-tin-ah*, you don't think it's too awkward as a festival name, do you?"

"No, not at all, it's fine, and ordinarily I'd *love* to help, Maura, but I'm just so busy at the moment and there's so much planning around a festival you wouldn't believe," India hinted hard before this Bealtaine Festival became another task on her never-ending 'to-do' list.

"Just a few meetings in the parish hall, you and a few others – just to gauge interest? I admit I am trying to appeal to your community spirit here, India. I mean, this festival is for the community, the community that *you* have chosen to live in."

Damn, but the woman was a prize manipulator with lots of friendly charm. "Okay, look, I'll see what I can do, maybe print out a few leaflets, help with a few contacts, that kind of thing." India smiled weakly.

"You're a real trouper, India, this will be great. I'm sure lots of other people will lend a hand with the planning of the festival too," Maura trilled.

Somehow India wasn't so optimistic, if life had taught her one thing it was that 'lots of other people' much preferred to sit on their bums and watch TV.

Feeling physically wrecked and craving the protectiveness of strong male arms, India opened the door

81

to her apartment and immediately sensed the place was empty although the signs of male life were all around assaulting her senses: underwear, deodorant, smelly trainers, dumbbells and lad mags strewn on the couch. Sighing, India switched on her TV and then wondered what the hell she was doing – she had a business to run, a hen's night to finalise and now an unwanted festival to organise as well and something told her that for this festival she wouldn't be getting paid too much if anything at all. Community spirit indeed.

The tension was getting to Mark Gleeson as he drove home in silence but he was trying hard not to show it. The Holy Joe Brigade would make it impossible for him to shift any more eco-units at Cloonsheeda, but he knew his mother's advice to sit tight and wait for things to blow over was all he could do. At a deeper level, though, he knew the tension he was feeling wasn't just about business, it was about Rebecca. When he'd first met her in her early twenties on a trip to London, she was a brassy air stewardess with a sexual charisma to match his own and had made him chase her hard, but after a few years the things he loved about her became things that bothered him and he began to see her as spoilt, arrogant and selfish.

Then for a while he'd glimpsed her softer side – when they took time out from their marriage and she'd come back a new Rebecca – more settled, ready to start their marriage over. That Rebecca was warm, slightly vulnerable, a woman he'd wanted to come home to every day, a woman he didn't want to leave every morning. But things changed again when Rebecca had the kids. After the justifiable shock of the first eighteen months, she'd hardened again and was acting as if she was a woman with only a few months to live, wanting to do everything at once – study, lose weight, set up a pole-dancing business – and Mark was worried about the effect on the boys. It's not that he was so old-fashioned that he wanted her to stay at home and just look after the kids; after all, his own mother had been a career woman and he'd been virtually raised by his grandparents. Yet on an unspoken level maybe that's exactly what he wanted, a mother at home for his boys.

Pushing all thoughts aside, including his mother's, who wondered why a carefree Rebecca needed an au pair at all, Mark breezed through the door, pretending to be looking for a briefcase that he'd deliberately left behind so he could check up on the new au pair. The kid had seemed sensible enough but you never knew what she'd be like once Rebecca was out of the house and he didn't think Rebecca would have the time or inclination to come back and check her competency for herself.

"Daddy, Daddy!"

The boys ran into his arms as soon as they saw him enter the kitchen and he swung them both around until they were screaming with excitement. Putting the boys down on the floor he fed his briefcase excuse to Liesel while the boys hung out of his trouser-legs and tried to climb him like a tree.

"Just popped back . . . forgot some papers . . . see you're feeding the boys lunch." The smell of sausages was delicious but Mark noticed Liesel seemed to be wrinkling her nose in distaste.

"Your wife left strict instructions on cooking sausages: two minutes on high, then turn, then two minutes and turn again to complete turning four times until they are browned all over. I have each two minutes on the timer," Liesel announced with a tight smile. As the beeper went off she turned the sausages clockwise once more.

"Yes, right, it all sounds very efficient. Well, you seem to have everything all under control here," Mark said, smiling awkwardly. He knew she knew he was checking up on her.

The toaster popping in the background was a welcome distraction and Mark buttered slices of white pan fast to help Liesel out, cutting off the edges so the toast would be acceptable to fussy toddlers. As he licked a large lump of melted butter off one of the leftover crusts with his tongue he saw Liesel look at him with something approaching desire, her moistened lips parted longingly, her pupils dilating hugely and, Jesus Christ, was that a quick flick of her tongue?

"Right, I'd better head so. You two terrors will be in bed by the time Daddy gets home so here's your night-night kiss," he said, hugging the boys close before tearing down the hall and out the front door. Flattening himself against the outside of the door for a minute or two, he allowed himself to dream wildly. Did the little German housemaid entertain wild notions about him, perhaps only showing her true desires when Rebecca was out of the house? You're losing it, old son, this eco-village problem is screwing with your head completely! He laughed at himself as he scrambled into the front seat of his car and headed back to town.

Hunger. Wild, bottomless, animal-like hunger was taking over Liesel body and soul. The little German au pair was so ravenous that when she saw the boys' father lick the leftover pieces of toast that she'd planned to have for lunch along with three tiny packets of raisins she'd found in the back of the cupboard, she was completely overcome. Now, with not a scrap of bread left in the house Liesel was fighting the lure of leftover sausages, for Liesel sometimes still craved the taste of meat even though she was a strict vegetarian on moral grounds. Hopefully, her Hausfrau would remember her vegetarian status when she came home from the gym, presumably laden with groceries to restock the fridge. Perhaps she should have broached the lack-of-food issue with Herr Gleeson, but he had disappeared out the door so quickly once he'd found his briefcase. Oh for just a lick of full-fat cheese or some smoked tofu sausages! Liesel could feel the tears build behind her eyes; her mother would be delighted at all the trouble she was encountering in her new adoptive country.

Hours later when Rebecca arrived home and threw her keys on the hall table, Liesel blocked her path in the hall like a dog pining for a bone, but to the teenager's dismay there was no sign of any bags that looked like they held groceries but plenty that contained shoes, trinkets and assorted garments.

"My Hausfrau, the children will need dinner soon and there are no groceries," Liesel almost whined.

"What, we haven't run out of milk, have we? I'm sure there's cereal around somewhere for a bedtime snack, have you tried the store cupboard?" Rebecca retaliated, clearly annoyed.

"But the children need *real* food – rice, pasta, vegetables, meat!" Liesel protested.

"Oh that, well, I mostly buy those ready-made frozen kids' meals, low fat, low salt, everything organic, they cost a fortune so I know they're packed with vitamins and stuff, you'll find them in the freezer," Rebecca said as she breezed by.

"And what time will I eat – with you and Herr Gleeson?" Liesel continued desperately.

Rebecca couldn't contain her laughter as she swung around. "Herr Gleeson, dear Liesel, eats mostly in the pub, has been doing it for years since his wife was never much of a domestic goddess and I'm watching my figure at the moment – a light chicken salad from the deli in town is all I need and I'm afraid I never eat more than packet Japanese seaweed soup after six and if I feel really peckish after that I might munch an apple – no bread obviously – carbs as we know are the food of the devil!"

"But please, Frau Gleeson, what will *I* eat then?"

For a moment Rebecca seemed puzzled, as if trying to decipher a foreign language. "You?"

"Yes, what will I eat? You must remember I told you I am also a vegetarian?"

Again, Rebecca's face registered blank. Perhaps she was thinking Liesel had enough fat reserves to keep her going for several weeks at least.

"Also, I was thinking while you were out, if I was insured to drive the car you promised me then I could go shopping for food *with* the boys," Liesel tried to reason.

Rebecca frowned. There was no way she was putting this au pair in the 4x4, she needed that for getting to her archaeology digs at the weekend and she definitely wasn't putting her in her Saab convertible. In fact, she had no idea how she could persuade the insurance company to insure this teenager at all at an affordable price – and there was the risk her no-claims bonus could be wiped out.

"Oh yes, the car," Rebecca mused as if it was the first she'd heard of the idea.

"*And* my travel expenses," Liesel chimed in.

"Uhm, yes, of course, we'll sort all that out tomorrow. I'm just going upstairs to work on my archaeology report now – it has to be finished today."

"Work! But I've had the boys all day! I thought you would be taking over now!" a tired, hungry and emotional Liesel began.

"Oh sorry, not today, Liesel, this is my study night. I have to drive an hour to the city and spend three whole hours at lectures and then drive home again. After that I'll be wrecked. No, Liesel, you're definitely holding the fort tonight."

"But, my Hausfrau!"

"Oh and try the packet Japanese Miso soup if you're peckish later on – it's in the cupboard nearest the fridge – I'm pretty sure it's vegetarian!" Rebecca shouted as she flew up the stairs and locked the door of her upstairs office behind her.

Two hours later, after Liesel had changed nappies, cleaned up spills and settled illogical toddler disputes, Rebecca scrambled down the stairs, air-kissed the boys goodbye for the second time that day and headed for the city for her outreach archaeology programme.

Over seventy students were signed up for the two-year diploma course and when Rebecca arrived they were waiting patiently for the new specialist guest professor to begin his lecture on the Bronze Age.

"Good evening, class, my name is Professor Henry Winterbottom," the bespectacled academic informed the group in a clipped English accent and immediately Rebecca's pupils began to blacken with interest.

Everything about him was attractive – his stance, his well-fitted sports jacket, casual chinos and brown suede shoes; his whole demeanour oozed authority and self-confidence.

Silently, he took off his glasses and cleaned the lenses before returning them to the bridge of his nose.

"Welcome to my course, but I must tell you from the start I fail more than 50% of pupils in exams so pay attention if you want to pass!"

On hearing his sexy, no-nonsense English voice, once more Rebecca felt a shock of electric energy jump across the room into her entire body. Somewhat flustered by the effects of this electricity, she crossed her legs and let her shoe dangle from the end of one foot while literally gnawing at her pen. She was, she realised, ever so slightly hungry and feeling her body burn through fat always super-charged her libido; it was as if the hunger for food had to be satisfied by something else. Bloody hell, the world was full of sexy men, she thought. First there was that Australian Sex God at the gym and now she had stumbled across this wonderfully seductive academic whose classes were mandatory for the rest of the term. Determined to be the best student in this man's class, Rebecca took down pages of notes, nodded appreciatively, smiled sporadically and stuck out her marvellously ample chest almost, but not quite, unconsciously for Professor Winterbottom to quietly consider and to grade where appropriate.

8

The following morning Rebecca woke up from very pleasant dreams where a multitude of men in a Turkish harem were kissing her breasts and licking her abdomen appreciatively while others (probably eunuchs) brushed her hair and painted her fingernails and toenails a vibrant pink ready for her meeting with the Sultan Winterbottom.

Meanwhile Liesel awoke from a nightmare where to the strains of Bach her mother, dressed as a burnt sausage, chased her around screaming: "I told you so, they're going to eat you alive!" Then, having escaped from the Mad Mutti Sausage, Liesel looked upwards to see a baby grand piano hurtling at speed towards her surprisingly naked body.

"Mein Gott!" Liesel gasped as she awoke fully and sat upright in bed. After hours and hours of juvenile drama the previous day, she thought she could still hear the twins screaming but there were no sounds coming from the bedroom next door and relieved, but still traumatised, she collapsed onto her pillows and heard her heart pound inside her chest.

The night before, when she'd been alone with the children without either of the parents around to help, she'd thought about calling her mother for reassurance but she couldn't bear the smug condemnations down the phone. No, she'd have to sort her au pair problems on her own.

Deliberately she ignored the first stirrings of the boys and let them go and wake their mother instead.

With relief she heard: "My boys, my sweeties, give Mum a big kiss!"

Hearing the boys laughing happily, and hoping that Rebecca might be in a good mood, Liesel got up, pulled on her dressing-gown and knocked on the door which the boys had left open.

"Good morning, my Hausfrau, I hope you slept well."

"Liesel! Good morning! Is everything alright?"

"Yes, yes – however, I feel I must tell you that –"

"Liesel, Liesel, come in, won't you, and sit with us!" Rebecca insisted.

The au pair, thrown by the spontaneity of Rebecca's affection, did exactly that – relieved to see there was no sign of Herr Gleeson.

"Thank you *so* much for baby-sitting last night. I know we agreed you'd only baby-sit two nights a week – we can work out later what other night suits us both. So then, have you thought what you'd like to do with your time off while you're in Ireland?"

"Ehm . . . well, I wanted to hear Irish music and learn some set dancing, my Hausfrau," Liesel spluttered, somewhat baffled at Rebecca's sudden softness.

Rebecca winced. "Sweetheart, I'd been meaning to ask you, would you mind dropping the Hausfrau bit? It's just it makes me feel, I don't know, like somebody's granny. Call me Rebecca, for heaven's sake! I had really hoped you might come to see me as a kind of big sister while you were here. Now, Liesel, I want *you* to relax this morning and I'll make you breakfast. Do you like porridge? I picked up some from the 24-hour supermarket on the way home along with some berries and natural yoghurt."

"Oh, yes, I *love* porridge," Liesel almost sobbed and Rebecca patted her hand and smiled, glad that her offer was being accepted as making porridge was one of her few domestic-goddess abilities. Besides, there was nothing as slimming as porridge, berries and low-fat natural yoghurt.

As Rebecca worked busily in the kitchen Liesel good-naturedly helped the boys to get their bowls and waited while Rebecca put a generous portion of hot porridge in front of her with berries and yoghurt in adjacent bowls ready to be spooned and poured. The porridge was flavoured with cinnamon instead of sugar and, to Liesel's starving body, tasted absolutely gorgeous. How stupid she now felt about last night where she'd almost phoned her mother for support. Suddenly she realised Rebecca was a nice person after all; she just had a lot of pressures on her at the moment what with college and being a mum and trying to get fit. Truly satiated for the first time since she'd arrived in Ireland, Liesel smiled as Rebecca cleared the bowls away and poured some aromatic freshly brewed coffee.

"Now, Liesel, when you're finished your coffee, if you could just stack the dishwasher and switch it on that would be brill."

91

Immediately Liesel's back stiffened in response; instinct told her Rebecca was going to abandon her – again.

Sensing resistance, Rebecca began the big sell. "I'm just running into town to get my fitness assessment done at the gym and afterwards I'll be popping into my usual restaurant for lunch but when I come home I *promise* you, the rest of the day will be yours to do what you want with. Perhaps we can even go on-line and find out about those set-dancing classes you want to do, you know, for the 'Irish experience' you're looking for?" Rebecca smiled, catlike.

"But I will have no money to pay for them, my Hau . . . Rebecca. Will you be bringing my money back today from your trip to town?"

"Er . . . yes, of course, not a problem," Rebecca waved her hand in a conciliatory manner.

"Will you bring lunch for me too?" Liesel asked fearfully.

"Absolutely! Vegetarian – right? Boys, give Mum a big kiss goodbye now!" Rebecca corralled the twins. "Back three o'clock, three thirty tops!" She said this while making strong and hopefully reassuring eye contact with her au pair. It was a trick she learnt from her air-stewardess days when trying to reassure passengers that the plane wouldn't crash – as if she could possibly know that stuff anyway when even the pilot couldn't always be sure he'd land safely. After holding eye contact for at least five reassuring seconds, Rebecca disappeared like a tempest. In suede heel boots, sexy skinny denims and a tight-cut leather jacket, clothes hardly appropriate for any gym, Liesel thought.

She was hardly out the door when both toddlers presented their stinky daily nappies simultaneously. Couldn't they wait till their mother was home and why weren't they toilet-trained by now? Liesel sighed as she hauled out the changing mats and began the task of wrestling the twins around the kitchen floor.

"Oh, I'm *so* sorry I'm late this morning and I'm not even in my gym gear yet. God, this morning was such a hassle, I didn't think I'd escape from the house at all!" Rebecca lied as she greeted Nathan the Sex God at the front office of the gym.

"No worries, Mrs G! I have to check the pH levels of the pool anyway. You go ahead and change," Nathan smiled in his friendly manner as she sauntered off to the ladies' locker room.

Banging her bag into the locker, Rebecca dreamed of the next half an hour where she would get to be up close and personal to that toned and tanned midriff and those rock-hard biceps.

"You ready?" Nathan chirped cheerfully five minutes later when she returned to reception.

"You betcha, no pain, no gain."

"Great, let's see what you can do then."

Baby, you don't want to know what I can do, Rebecca thought as she fixed a smile on her face and dreamed of being a Happy Cougar with a very yummy toy boy to play with just for fun.

Opening the downstairs window of her house, Demelza ensured the smell of sandalwood in her newly designated therapy room would not be overpowering. Sandalwood

93

was one of the sensual oils for both men and women and also calmed those of a nervous disposition, allowing the opening up of innermost thoughts and desires. Quickly Demelza swept a broom over the floor to clear the space of negative energy. Leaving the door slightly ajar she went to get dressed, hesitating over her choice of outfit. Turquoise tunic dress or flared green bellbottoms? Eventually she settled on turquoise, the colour of communication, sensitivity and creativity. Over her shoulder she wore a scarf of gold, the colour of the heart and protection and individuality. Finally, Demelza pulled on a crazy pair of short tan leather cowboy boots. It was an outfit that spoke words, but not too many, she thought, as the doorbell rang and she went to welcome her first troubled soul in need of goddess therapy.

Willie and Tom were walking the back roads of Cloonsheeda, not doing much, kicking the odd stone with their boots, Tom occasionally stopping to moo at the cows in the fields. It was a pretty useless talent to have, but Tom did a great moo all the same, a really long plaintive one and a second one which sounded like a startled cow or perhaps a cow in premature labour. He could moo undetected from a distance as well. Earlier that morning they'd hid a bit away from the Holy Tree Stump, as it was now known locally, and Tom had let out a few deep sorrowful moos which had startled a large gathering of the faithful. Numbers had been on the increase again since Tom's Uncle Mossy had spent an hour in the driving rain two days previously, staring at the stump, and swore he saw it move – slightly. The 'moving' 'holy' tree stump had brought back the media for another good laugh at the ways of Cloonsheeda, despite Father Fintan's continual pleas for communal sanity.

"Stop mooing at the cows, would ya? You're wrecking my head, Skeehan!" Willie snapped as he took a deep drag of his cigarette.

"Jesus, what is it with you these days, Cleary? You moan if I shoot a few crows and now my mooing is getting on your wick too? I've been mooing since we were both in Primary!"

"That's the whole fucking point, asshole! Maybe it's time you grew out of the mooing!"

"Ah, you thought it was funny this morning when that fella from Sky TV nearly jumped out of his skin before we legged it over the back fields!" Tom joked.

"Thank Christ we had our hoods up. The last thing I want is for the Social to catch sight of my mug on TV doing cow impressions and asking me if that's how I'm spending my time looking for work." Willie shook his head.

"Who cares about the Social anyway? They've got more to worry about than us two layabouts. Got any more fags on you, Cleary?"

Willie shook his head and pulled his fleecy grey hat around his ears.

"Give us a drag of yours then, will you?"

Silently Willie handed over his cigarette and, after taking a few puffs, Tom handed it back and started playing with the flame on his lighter. Picking up a discarded crisp packet from the ground he lit it around the edges and held on to it as it melted towards the centre.

"What?" Tom asked, knitting his brows together when he saw Willie's black looks.

"You've been pulling that stunt since we were in the Primary too," Willie accused.

"You know what, Cleary, you can shag off! If it's nagging I want I'll go home to the mother!"

"Fair enough." Willie flicked the end of his fag between his forefinger and thumb and walked away in a huff.

"Ah Jaysus, wait up, will you, and stop being so thick!" Tom roared after him, insisting on inflicting his company on his friend as they walked shoulder to shoulder down the lanes.

"You're worse than fleas, Skeehan, do you know that?"

Tom ignored the abuse and continued on with the conversation.

"So tell us, are you coming to Keogh's tonight? There's a bit of a session on – free pints for the musicians of course – and sure you haven't given those pipes of yours a good clean-out in years!" Tom kept his face straight but his eyes were wrinkling into a laugh.

Willie deliberately ignored his friend's smutty double entendre. "Well, I know why you're so interested in me being there. I'll be so busy playing that you'll be the one scabbing my free pints."

"And sure what's wrong with that? Haven't we always been brothers in arms, you and me, brothers in pints and best fucking mates since Junior Infants?"

"Are we?" Willie asked.

Tom gave him a playful punch to the shoulder. "Course we are and brothers in bins too, and it's time for another spin to the big smoke to load up on takeaway grub, because unlike you, you spoilt only child, my two younger brothers would eat a small child through the back of a chair if they got half the chance, so I'm all out of food. What do you say, fancy a spin into the city's dumpsters tonight and a few pints in Keogh's afterwards?"

"Get a life, would you, preferably one without me in it," Willie scowled.

"I'll take that as a yes. I'll pick you up around seven so and don't forget to wear your boots – you're the one going into the bin juice this time, baby. Aah, bin juice, I can smell the lovely rotten smell of it now!" Tom gave his friend another friendly 'brotherly' punch, this time to his upper arm.

Back at his front porch Willie, who was in no mood for nonsense, was met by a wiry little man wearing a patched overcoat, green wellington boots, a torn checked flat hat and leading a sheep.

"It's your father I want. I've been ringing and knocking on the window the last ten minutes," the little man blurted out by way of introduction.

"He's probably out so," Willie replied brusquely, hoping the stranger would take off.

"Well, when will he be back? I've travelled an awful long way to be here and my sheep is in terrible pain," the man panted.

"Don't know, he never takes off too far, he'll probably be back within the half hour." Willie had the front door unlocked now and was hovering over the threshold.

"Ah sure, my creature here couldn't stick the pain for that long. Look at her, look at her face, it's not a normal sheep's face at all, it's fairly contorted with the pain," the distressed owner fretted.

Willie looked but, not surprisingly, saw nothing more than an ordinary sheep's face. Not for the first time he wondered why these people didn't take their animals to the vet for a proper diagnosis. It probably had something if not everything to do with money. Sighing, he took out his mobile. He knew this chancer wasn't for turning away easily but would be 'bleating on' about his and his sheep's problems until the father returned to the cottage.

"Da, there's a man here, problem with a sheep . . . face contorted in pain . . . no, not the man, the sheep . . . yeah, okay . . . I'll tell him so." He hung up and turned to the man. "The father says he'll be back in ten."

"Grand."

"Suppose you'll be wanting some tea?" Willie offered half-grudgingly.

"That would be the finest but what about the sheep?"

"Sure bring her in, we've no women here," Willie said, nodding curtly.

Ushering both man and sheep into the house, Willie closed the door firmly behind him and shook his head in wonderment. Why was it that he should be stuck in such a hole of a place as Cloonsheeda living such an obscure bloody life? What Willie wouldn't have given for just a taste of normality! Being the son of a doctor, now that would be the finest. Having a lovely ma baking pies and sultana scones every other day, now that, that would be just heaven. Being David Ron Dwyer holed up in London with a young one with legs up to her armpits, now that would be the stuff of young Willie Cleary's wildest fucking dreams.

"Okay, is there anything you want to tell me?" Nathan asked Rebecca as she lay on the floor, in the fitness centre off the main gym, hardly a bead of sweat on her brow after a good run on the treadmill and a few stretching exercises.

"What do you mean?" she smiled back.

"Well, you're super-flexible, your pulse rate is low and your weight is well within your BMI range. So, why exactly am I giving you a fitness-assessment? Because you must be doing something else as well as just recently hitting the gym, Mrs G."

"Okay, I confess, I'm actually a qualified fitness instructor, did the course just before I got pregnant with the twins. But I only did the fitness side of things so I could do a follow-on pole fitness course and I've been brushing up on the dancing lately with my DVD and my pole."

"You're a pole-dancer?" Nathan said, grinning gleefully.

"A *fitness* pole-dancer," Rebecca emphasised. "Although I did a bit of the strutting-around-in-heels stuff too but that's before I did the courses. I don't think the high-heel stuff belongs in a gym although a lot of people start off that way and then get a qualification."

"Yeah? Hey, maybe you could teach pole-dancing here?"

She got up and brushed her hands down the side of her lycra pants. "'Fraid it would never work, Nathan. I used to work here a few years back – on the beauty side of things – but I was a bit of a naughty girl and kind of took an extended sabbatical without telling the management. It was a time in my life when I needed to get my head together. So I doubt I'll ever work here again."

"Pity, I'd say you'd be bonzer at it!"

"Well, thanks for the vote of confidence. I am hoping to open up somewhere with the pole-dancing in the future, although I'm very busy studying for my exams in archaeology as well."

"You're a real survival woman, aren't you? Exactly the kind of Sheila who'd give it a burl Down Under!" Then his brow creased slightly as he realised he'd overstepped the mark again.

"It's okay," Rebecca laughed, cooling his embarrassment. "Look, I'm kind of just hoping to do a bit of cardio to burn fat, so I'd mostly like a programme to focus on that."

"No worries. I'll show you the best machines to use to get the quickest results. Maybe you should come along to my Pilates class too. Pilates is great for core strength, you know."

"You teach Pilates?" Rebecca couldn't stop a smile curling at the corner of her lips.

"Hey, don't be so sexist! Lots of blokes do Pilates, it's great for the gut," he defended himself.

"Okay, point made. Who knows, maybe I'll come. I'll just have to check my schedule first. You wouldn't think it, but I'm actually a very, very busy woman, Mr Crocodile Dundee!"

Despite all the thought that had gone into her immediate environment – the plants, nice paintings, the nice smell of something or other – Sinéad Winterbottom shifted uncomfortably in her seat as she waited for Demelza to return to the room with some paper and a pen. It had been difficult enough to get Henry to mind their three children while she took off on a voyage of self-discovery – she'd told him she had a doctor's appointment. Henry and small children were not exactly an easy fit. But, as he was self-employed and had a home-based archaeological business as well as a part-time lecturing post, Sinéad found herself insisting that he commit to his parenting responsibilities today so she could get away from their brood.

In fact, considering the amount of time she'd spent at home with the children over the years while Henry was travelling all over the place working on development excavation projects in Ireland at a time when the Irish were building motorways like lunatics, she'd definitely earned a break, although she never actually took one, from the parenting madness.

"You know, I really don't know why I'm here at all." Sinéad smiled nervously at Demelza who was now seated in a soft armchair opposite her, legs casually crossed at the ankle, concentrated stillness oozing out of every pore. "Anyway, it won't be long till I'm pregnant again and then I won't have any time for thinking about my relationship or my sex life."

Demelza listened and nodded encouragingly but she was more interested in the young woman's uncomfortable body language than her words.

"Is pregnancy a means by which you try to forget about your relationship and sex life then?" Demelza asked briskly, her biro poised over her notebook, waiting for a response. Sinéad's blank expression told Demelza more than any words.

"Oh God, shit, sorry, I shouldn't have said that, the 'god' bit I mean, I'm an atheist you see, more of a humanist actually," Sinéad blurted out, squirming. "It's just, well, Henry and I always said we'd have four and I might as well get them over with while I'm young."

"So, you see children as a chore to be gotten over?" Demelza probed.

Again, the silence implied secrets and, realising there was a lot of work to be done, Demelza changed tack. "Let's start at the beginning, shall we? Tell me how you first met Henry."

All of a sudden the words poured out as Sinéad told her about how Henry had saved her from her wild self and set her on a sensible path with clearly defined goals and a lot of self-discipline.

"And what was the sex like, when you first met Henry?" Demelza asked abruptly, stunning Sinéad into silence. When no response was forthcoming, Demelza decided to introduce a few lightweight questions to lure Sinéad into some degree of free expression. "Okay, let's try something different for a moment. Tell me, Sinéad, who be your favourite male film star or personality and what qualities about him do you most admire?"

Names of desirable men began to tumble out of Sinéad's mouth but the qualities of her ideal mate sounded most unlike those of her husband. Then, most surprising of all, the young woman started to talk about fish. She had a whole tankful of them apparently and, although they were a source of great excitement, they were also a constant drain on her mental resources. Demelza sighed inwardly. Fish babies! Hopefully, the client who'd booked for later that day would be a much more straightforward case.

It was four o'clock and the effects of Liesel's porridge had worn off about two hours before. Now starving for lunch and awaiting the return of her Hausfrau, the German teenager was living off handfuls of dry cornflakes from the kitchen cupboard. In desperation she'd even brought a bit of leftover toddler sausage to her nostrils, inhaled deeply and briefly considered running her vegetarian tongue down its brown and greasy shrivelled flank.

"I'm home!" Rebecca shouted excitedly as she suddenly swept through the front door, full of optimism and rejuvenation. One look at Liesel's angry, near-tearful face and Rebecca knew she'd better crank the sweetness in her voice up to near-nauseating levels. "How have you been – how have the boys been?" She touched Liesel lightly on the arm.

Liesel didn't trust herself to answer in case she sobbed hysterically or ripped her Hausfrau's head clean off her shoulders.

"You promised lunch!" Liesel at last whimpered, half in reproach, half in hope.

"You're right, I did, and I have it right here," Rebecca answered, very pleased with herself. "There you go! Everything vegetarian, just as you asked."

Inside the cardboard takeaway carton were a few scraps of limp lettuce, three cherry tomatoes, some broken-up bits of celery, one tiny scoop of rice and a piece of potato salad that looked like a lump of rock surrounded by mayonnaise mush. Liesel's face almost collapsed in agony. There was no sign of any protein – chickpeas, beans, a lick of egg salad or any bona-fide complex carbohydrate to keep her feeling full. In shock she forgot to complain as Rebecca flew up the stairs, mumbling something about checking her email.

Sitting down at the table with a large glass of water, Liesel was so famished she ate every morsel daintily and chewed repeatedly before she swallowed a single bite and then actually licked the inside of the empty box.

"Enjoy the salad?" Rebecca self-congratulated as she reappeared in the kitchen doorway.

"My Hau . . . I mean Rebecca, thank you for bringing me lunch but I must tell you I need more food than this!" Liesel blazed, her eyes shining with a brightness that hid a well of tears. "Looking after your boys makes me very, very hungry!"

"I don't understand? Is there a problem? You said you were vegetarian – did I make some mistakes?" Rebecca asked, a blank expression on her face.

"As I said before, perhaps if I had the car you promised me I might be able to go shopping for everyone and then you wouldn't need to worry about me," Liesel insisted.

"Yes, I've been thinking about transport. I'll run a few ideas past you tomorrow, okay?"

"What about the set dancing? You said I could look it up on the computer when you came home. And did you get my money when you were down town?" Liesel continued, leechlike, hunger fuelling her bravery.

"Oh Liesel, your money! You should have rung to remind me, I completely forgot! And don't worry about set dancing – there's a musical session going on in Keogh's tonight in Cloonsheeda and that's almost as good. I think I even have ten euros in my bag for drinks – oh yes, there it is. So I'll write you an IOU for your expenses and you can write me an IOU for lunch – it was seven euros by the way. Back in a minute! I just have to pop upstairs and ring a friend from my archaeology course – I have a sticky question to run by him."

"*My Hausfrau!*" Liesel near-screamed as her employer attempted to escape once again.

"Rebecca, it's Rebecca, remember?" Rebecca shouted into thin air as she bolted for the stairs.

Unbelievable, the woman was unbelievable, Liesel thought as she heard Rebecca charge into her office and lock the domestic world out once more.

9

Turning out her bedside light Freeda mused over the session she'd had with the unorthodox sex therapist, Demelza Spargo, that day. It wasn't the first time Freeda had tried counselling or therapy. In particular she remembered being a paranoid sixteen year-old who felt pressured to conform to the button-nosed female stereotypes of her cosmetic-therapy-obsessed American peers. Later, thankfully, she'd found a wonderful therapist who helped her understand something of who she was, but it had never ever entered Freeda's head to go to counselling to find out why exactly her relationships always crumbled – until now.

Demelza had been quite incisive at that day's session when Freeda blurted out that her last lover had been a great conversationalist. She'd asked was that maybe not the problem, that as a couple they were maybe doing too much talking and not having enough lovemaking?

Closing her eyes, Freeda began her guided meditation with the Celtic spiritual guide Demelza had selected for her: Abnoba, goddess of forests, rivers and the hunt, the protector of all women. Bit by bit Freeda submitted to her trance as she felt her breathing deepen and her knotted brow unfurl. There were just two weeks to complete this phase of her homework before seeing Demelza again and progressing on to the next level of her spiritual awareness and Freeda was committed to doing a thoroughly good job.

Back home after another fruitful night of dumpster-diving, Willie wiped down his share of plastic-wrapped groceries and, having shown Tom the door, showered for more than ten minutes to get the smell off his hair and skin, then dressed anew before returning to the kitchen to cook for his father. Technically clean, he still couldn't shift the smell of vegetable decay from his nostrils and his brain.

"Here, get that down you, old man," Willie commanded as he handed his father a light meal of just-out-of-date sausage, brown sauce and buttered wholegrain bread. Dan took the meal graciously. He wasn't at all disapproving of the bin-foraging – in fact, a deeply spiritual man, he felt it was a sin that supermarkets threw out perfectly good edibles so casually. Besides, here in Cloonsheeda they lived in a 'green' zone and rescuing waste food was about as 'eco-friendly' as you could get.

"Dirty night – off to the pub?" Dan asked between slurps of milky tea and bites of bread.

"The rain won't put me off my pint tonight and at least it's scared off the crowds devoted to the Holy Tree Stump. Not even that eejit Mossy Skeehan would stand for hours in this wet," Willie smirked condescendingly.

"Ah well, each to their own, not that I need the

Mother of God to appear in a tree stump to know that she's real," Dan answered gently, licking brown sauce off the end of one finger.

Willie shrugged his shoulders dismissively, not wanting to get caught up in a conversation anyway about beliefs, disbeliefs or religion in general.

"You're taking the pipes?" his father asked cautiously, a hint of excitement in his voice as Willie laid his hands on his instrument and announced he was heading for Keogh's for the last pint.

Willie just nodded curtly and his father smiled warily.

"I'm pleased, son, greatly pleased. You have the gift in your hands – you shouldn't fight it or ignore it, it's not natural!"

"Ah, Da, don't start all that old talk again! I'm just taking them out for the night, don't read so much into it!" Willie snapped.

"Seven generations of Clearys played the pipes and mended beasts as well. Is it any harm that I see the same talent in my only son? Those fingers would heal God's creatures too if only you'd try, boy – if only you'd believe in yourself the way your mother always believed in you, son."

Looking at his father, Willie saw the longing in the old man's face, the longing for his only son to embrace tradition, to give away his talents freely but Willie didn't believe he had the same altruistic nature as his father. It was an accident that saw his father limping for life and on disability, just barely surviving on social welfare, but it was stupidity that saw him turn away payments for his 'beast-mending' as he called it, it was stupidity to not want to grab everything that came your way with two hands whether you were entitled to it or not.

"Wrap yourself up well – 'tis a cold night, old man." Willie told his father as he banged the front door shut and walked out into the biting rain.

India Jennings positioned the duvet around Nathan's chest, handed him his mug of tea and some Vegemite sandwiches and put the box of man-size tissues within easy reach. Nathan had come down with some sort of virus, even running a temperature, and was shivering on the couch as his red-rimmed eyes tried to focus on TV.

"It's this bloody country, it's so cold and wet, I don't know how you guys don't all get pneumonia," Nathan sniffled.

"I guess we're kind of used to it," India sighed, "but I've heard it can take a person months to acclimatise to a new country and you've landed in a completely different hemisphere too, Big Boy, so I suppose you can't help but catch a few bugs."

"My throat is like a cut wound," Nathan complained, wincing as the tea scalded his delicate insides.

"You shut up then, baby, and I'll do the talking," India soothed, making a pretence of dabbing his beaded forehead with a man-size tissue. "Did I tell you I ran into that committee woman, Maura Simmons, the other day? She wants to organise a Bealtaine or May Day festival for Cloonsheeda – there's a meeting being organised."

"Ace – what kind of things will you be doing?" Nathan asked, still gazing mindlessly at the TV and huddling further under the duvet.

"Well, the thing is, I don't know if I can take on another festival, not with everything else I'm doing, but

I suppose I'll give her some ideas. May Day, Bealtaine or what the Scots call Beltane go back to the pagan era – it's kind of like Halloween – you know, another one of those times when there's meant to be a gateway between this world and the Otherworld of the fairies. In olden days there would have been bonfires lit on hills and dancing so I'll probably pick up on the fire theme with fire-eaters or fire-jugglers and dancing drummers – something like that – course then there's all the kids' stuff too – puppetry, drama, that kind of thing . . ."

"Yeah?"

Nathan's apathetic response to her ideas was disappointing. True, it wasn't his fault he'd developed chills and a fever but she'd been working so hard the last two days so she could spend a quality evening with him, followed she hoped by a night of quiet seduction.

"I might as well head to bed then," India said finally, realising that physical activity of any description would more than likely put Nathan on a life-support machine.

"Good idea, I might just lay my head here for the night. I don't want to give you any of my nasties," Nathan answered, still looking directly at the TV.

After scrubbing her teeth and cleansing her face India hopped into bed and stared at the ceiling. Tense from her day's work she kicked the duvet with her heels and tried to get comfortable but her jaw ached and her back was rigid from driving. Right now, more than anything, India Jennings needed to be stroked, devoured and pleasured. Right now more than anything she needed a fully-functioning man in her bed. But it wasn't Nate's fault he was sick, her grown-up self reasoned. Timing, everything comes down to timing, her mother used to say. Pity timing was always rotten, India's spoilt inner child sulked.

It was after eleven and Liesel was excited and agitated all at once.

"Don't worry if the doors are shut – we'll just do 'the knock' to get in," Mark placated her as he drove her to Keogh's, and Liesel, not at all used to the ways of Irish rule-breaking and late-night drinking seemed genuinely mystified at this explanation, but then her face went sulky and Mark sighed. Late home from work he'd only offered to drive her to Keogh's to break up the palpable tension between the young au pair and his wife.

At the pub, with Liesel at his side, he did the special coded rap on the door and it was opened by the publican himself, Jasper Keogh.

"Hey, Liesel, get the lads to order you a taxi when you want to come home – I'll pay," Mark told the girl as she slipped through. "Foreign she is – from Germany – Rebecca got her to look after the boys," Mark explained as she disappeared and Jasper gave him 'the nod', the guarantee that she'd come to no harm, at least not in his establishment for the night.

Downstairs the TV was flashing out blue light from the darkened sitting room when Mark got home and, not finding Rebecca in any of the downstairs rooms; he took the carpeted grand stairs two at a time. Quietly he opened the boys' bedroom and, seeing that they were sleeping soundly, shut the door carefully. Rebecca wasn't in the main bedroom and instinctively he walked into one of their guest rooms and saw her silently swirling around her silver dance-pole in her underwear, throwing herself upside down, hooking onto the metal with the back of her knee, twirling, letting her flame hair unravel towards the floor. For a minute he watched her sneakily and then he saw her right herself, then swear softly as she began to slip steadily down the pole. Silently he embraced her from behind, untangled her from the metal and held her in his arms.

"You're home," she laughed, putting her arms around his neck. "Somehow I thought you'd meet up with one of your cronies and stay out for the night," she teased. He was taken with her naturalness at that moment and her warmth. Mark loved such rare moments as these where she was caught off guard and feeling mellow, instead of her brain racing a hundred miles a minute and her body tight with tension.

"Why are you laughing?" she quizzed him.

"It's just I like it when you dance – you like it when you dance," he said, shrugging his shoulders.

"Well, what was the point in doing my pole-dance course if I wasn't going to dance at least now and again?"

"And then you got pregnant," Mark smiled mischievously.

"No, then *you* got me pregnant, Mr Gleeson, and all plans I had to teach pole-dancing went out the window," she narrowed her eyes, then broke out into more laughter and shook her gorgeous hair. Yes, he truly loved these unpredictable moments when Rebecca softened, when she switched off all her career and life plans. Nestled now into his chest, she sighed, and he tilted her head up by the chin and gazed into her eyes.

"What's up?" he asked.

"Just I feel so overwhelmed sometimes with all the things I want to do," she admitted.

"The problem is you want to do so much so fast, Mrs Gleeson."

"And you don't?"

"Well, the new au pair should help you manage your time a little better," he soothed her.

"Do you think she's working out okay?"

"I'm not thinking of our new au pair right now but I do have such exciting plans for your lips, Mrs Gleeson, if you'd only keep them still!"

Slowly Mark ran the pad of his thumb along her lower lip until he coaxed her warm, soft, mouth apart, then sliding his fingers deep into her hair he pulled her face up close so he could brush her lips with his own.

"Rebecca," he whispered urgently.

Lifting her off her feet, he staggered to the bed, kissing her everywhere at once from her throat to her collarbone and back to the soft hollows behind her ears. Dropping her on the mattress, he continued to play his lips on her skin, pausing momentarily as his eager hands splayed her breasts, delighting in the possession of such a great prize.

Her eyes were lit from within with desire and Mark smiled to himself – yes, on the few occasions when his wife was in the mood she was such an intensely physical woman – sex tonight was going to be nothing short of mind-blowing.

"Mark?" she said urgently.

"Yes?" he panted.

"I've just remembered I have to email off a proposal

to Professor Winterbottom. I'm really sorry but we'll have to stop. Maybe you should just go back to our own room and get some sleep – I'm going to be a while on the computer."

"For you, Fraulein, your first of many a pint of Guinness I hope, and as we say here in Ireland there's both eating and drinking in it! No, no, put away your money, this one's on the house," Jasper Keogh insisted.

Enthusiastically Liesel accepted the creamy sustenance; after all, anything with eating in it would be readily welcomed by her growling stomach, for apart from a miserable cup of powdered Miso soup and some slimming crackers that tasted of sawdust, poor Liesel had had nothing to eat at all since her miserly lunch of dried-up salad.

The pub was gorgeous, just as she imagined, snug with the glow of a turf fire and quaintly dingy in its overall decoration with painted, yellowing wallpaper stuck to the ceiling and used as a lining to roughly hewn shelves behind the bar. In the corner musicians were playing traditional songs and tapping their feet wildly, a portly red-faced man with a ginger moustache hammered away on the bodhrán and a young lad of about seventeen played the guitar and sang sweetly. Both were accompanied by a pale-skinned woman of about thirty whose fair hair fell about her face as she made sweet music from the folds of her heavy accordion.

After two minutes of soaking up the atmosphere, Liesel had already knocked back half a pint and felt the pleasure in her belly and a warm excited feeling in her head. Suddenly there was a lull as a tall, dark-haired young man walked into the pub with an instrument underneath his arm and the girl with the squeezebox laid her instrument aside and hugged the visitor tightly.

"Willie, great to see you and the pipes with you and all!" she enthused, planting a tender kiss on the young man's cheek.

Then Jasper Keogh came up from the bar and clapped the young hunk on the shoulder. "Young Cleary, good to see you, lad – I have your pint already on," Jasper assured him, squeezing the young man's two hands tightly in his.

"Sure you might as well just send it straight over to Skeehan – where is he tonight anyway?"

"Gone off with that sophisticated, leggy Swedish one from the village. I think she's married but herself and the husband are 'open' about it if you know what I mean. He said something about he had a feeling you might be in later yourself to clean your own pipes," Jasper teased and Willie just rolled his eyes and shook his head.

For the next hour or two Liesel swayed to the music and she never had to put her hand in her pocket once. People kept buying her drink and at one point she was even lucky enough to be bought a packet of dry-roasted peanuts. All night, even as her vision blurred, she couldn't keep her eyes off the strangely familiar young man who played what looked like bagpipes with his elbow, making beautiful, mournful music escape from the long black stems of wood, music that spoke to her soul. This was what she had come to Ireland for; this truly was the Irish experience she craved. This was worth all the nonsense she'd put up with from her Irish Hausfrau, this was living in the moment, this was truly heaven.

Rebecca awoke from her dream with a start and snuggled closer to her husband. In his sleep, with the bedside lamp glowing softly, Mark was an older version of her beautiful boys. Touching his cheek with her palm she smiled to herself – the sex she'd given into had been out of this world. Closing her eyes, she replayed the best parts of her romp with Mark and then quite unconsciously thoughts about the hot Aussie at the leisure club with the sun-bronzed skin began just as images of the mysterious Henry Winterbottom, who intrigued her with his academic knowledge and his self-confidence, began jostling for premier position in her brain. Suddenly Rebecca felt uneasy.

It was only a few short years since she'd walked out on her marriage and had almost had a full-blown affair with a toy boy several years her junior and here she was letting her thoughts and desires run away with her once more. The idea hit her like a truck. Maybe she was a sex addict, someone always in need of excitement and maybe this constant lust that drove her would one day blow her marriage apart. It could be she needed proper help to get an insight into herself and her bothersome sexual desires. Shutting her eyes she breathed deeply, then allowed herself a little smile. Oh who was she kidding? She was just a busy woman whose sex drive sometimes went askew; there was nothing wrong with that, she concluded, as she sighed contentedly and spooned into her husband for the night. Her archaeology proposal could wait; she'd get up at the crack of dawn and email it straight to Professor Winterbottom . . . Professor Winterbottom . . . even in her sleep her mouth began to water.

A dull thud shook Mark from his sleep. As the protector of his family he was always on alert like the butcher's dog waiting for the first sounds of trouble. Quietly he got up from the bed and went in search of the hurley stick that he had stowed away for protection. Probably it was nothing, but still he was cautious as he crept down the stairs, the hurley over his head ready to swing. Hearing scuffling in the sitting room, he hit the lights full force and braced himself for attack.

It was then Liesel screamed.

"Don't scream – you might wake the boys," he whispered in her ear as he instinctively cupped a hand over her mouth.

Silently she nodded and, as he removed his hand, Liesel began to giggle and sway and then she lost her footing completely and fell onto the couch.

"Are you okay?" Mark asked, feeling awkward but unable to stifle a smile. It was obvious she was completely sozzled.

"Yes, I am fine but I think I had too much of the 'eating and drinking' Guinness," she giggled again. Her long blonde hair was falling over her eyes and he noticed her cheeks were flushed pink and her eyes sparkling. Fighting hard not to laugh himself, Mark watched her adjust herself on the couch and handed her some cushions for her head.

"Mr Gleeson?"

"Mark," he corrected gently.

"Yes, Mr Mark, I think I might be in love," she announced breathlessly.

"Really?" Mark felt his gut tighten with her unexpected announcement.

"Incredibly in love, with a beautiful, dark-haired Irishman."

Instantly Mark felt his jaw clench and his mind race. God, it wasn't him, was it?

"He plays those pipes with the elbow, I can't remember their name . . . at Jasper's pub. I never heard his name, but he will never love me back," Liesel continued mournfully.

"Uilleann pipes, they're called uilleann pipes," Mark said, feeling both relieved and disappointed. "Why don't you think he'll ever love you then, this beautiful Irishman?" Liesel's heavy breasts heaved gloriously in her low-cut purple-satin top and Mark couldn't help running his eyes over them as he watched them rise and fall.

"I am not stupid, Mr Mark. I know I am plain, and fat like a milk cow with a big backside and wide hips, and he is *so, so* beautiful!" she sighed, then began to giggle uncontrollably.

Instinctively Mark wanted to tell her that she was beautiful, that men never wanted a stick insect anyway, that her hips, thighs, belly, bum and breasts were like soft hills where any man would be proud to lay a hand or rest his head – but he just about managed to contain himself and pulled off her shoes instead – she was never going to make it from the couch tonight.

"Mr . . . Mark, I think I might be too drunk to look after the children tomorrow," Liesel yawned as Mark covered her with a blanket from the back of the couch.

"That's okay – you've been working very hard since you got here. Rebecca can handle being a mother for just one morning."

"Oh and this, this is for you," she said as she removed a crumpled-up piece of paper from her hand with an IOU written in biro for six euro accompanied by a taxi receipt. "For the taxi," she announced to no one in particular as she snuggled into her cushions.

"Hey, Liesel, I don't expect to be paid for the taxi," Mark insisted as Liesel yawned again.

Why was the kid operating on an IOU basis anyway? Rebecca. It had to be because of something orchestrated by Rebecca. What was his wife playing at?

"Goodnight, Liesel," Mark said as he turned out the lights.

"Goodnight, Mr Mark," she murmured in reply and Mr Mark smiled as he took one last look at her soft sleeping form, shut the door tight and allowed himself to dream.

10

"Well, what do you think of herself getting drunk as a skunk – not very responsible, is it?" Rebecca fumed the next morning.

It was nine o'clock and Liesel was still snoozing on the sofa and the boys, out of bed since the crack of dawn, were being placated by watching telly in the grown-ups' sitting room.

Mark completely ignored his wife's interrogation and knocked back his morning tea, a no-nonsense look carved on his face.

"Rebecca, what's going on with these IOU's Liesel was talking about last night?"

Immediately Rebecca's body language stiffened and it was enough to signal to Mark that she didn't want to talk about such matters.

"It's just I was on some of the internet boards where people said you gotta be a little bit mean with money to keep these au pairs on their toes," she said as she stirred some artificial sugar into her strong black coffee, "otherwise they start getting above themselves and before you know it they're the ones giving you the orders."

"Well I'm telling you to stop being even a 'little bit mean' to her. She's a nice kid – okay, she's a little bit sozzled this morning but so what? Give her the day off and maybe you could give yourself a day off from world domination as well and just be a mother. If it stops raining, why don't you do something hands-on in the garden with the kids, give them a few memories? 'Digging' I think they call it – it's not a world away from archaeology. Why don't you do a bit of hands-on archaeology with your boys instead today?"

"Ha bloody ha," Rebecca scowled as she cradled her coffee.

Tipping her chin with his forefinger, he looked earnestly into her eyes. "I *mean* it, Rebecca, give that kid a break and spend some quality time with your sons. Believe me, they'll grow up fast." Quickly he branded her with his kiss before heading for the door, leaving a very bored and restless Rebecca in his wake.

All morning Liesel snoozed and snored, all morning the boys ran riot, and worst of all, all morning it bloody rained. Suffering from intense cabin fever, Rebecca eventually went completely stir crazy at midday. Booted and wet-suited, she gathered her young sons up and let them splash in puddles around the house with her splashing alongside and, despite having an essay waiting to be written for her next evening class with Professor Winterbottom, Rebecca laughed just like a little kid.

"I love Mammy," Sam said suddenly, grabbing her at the knees and nearly toppling her over.

"I love rain!" Jack said, splashing in a mucky puddle and drowning his brother in the process.

"I love you both!" Rebecca squealed back and at that moment she never spoke a truer word.

At the local coffee shop, bookshop and health-food shop owned by Maura Simmons and run by bush-jumper mother Sylvia and Tilda, the long-legged Swede, India handed over the information posters and leaflets she'd designed for Cloonsheeda's first village festival.

"There's some more details there about government grant bodies you'll need to contact for funding and legal requirements along with some other stuff like who designs good brochures."

"Wow, this is fabulous, India, and I see you even have ideas for turning our Bealtaine Festival into a family event," Maura congratulated her.

"I'm glad you like what I've come up with . . . just to emphasise again, Maura, while I'm willing to help out and maybe source acts and do a few other bits and pieces on an ad hoc basis, I really can't commit to anything formally," India asserted in between sipping unappetising chicory-infused coffee. "I just have too many events of my own to organise and now that it's already February I'm gearing myself up for all the summer madness again."

"Uhm . . . oh, of course, India, I completely understand . . . I just wonder what we should call the festival – we really need to think of a good name, don't you think?" Maura chewed her biro, her mental energy somewhere else entirely.

"Well, that really will be for the community to

decide," India said, slightly agitated as she shuffled her papers together and shoved her phone into her bag. "I'm sure you can do a bit of brainstorming at your first meeting whenever you organise it." She really was anxious to head off and get back to her own life problems.

"So, Maura, what do you have in the way of tackling bugs and viruses? I've got a boyfriend at home with chills and a sore throat and, being an Aussie and a health nut to boot, he likes his health supplements strong and by the kilo."

"Oh poor guy! I'll just ask Sylvia if we got in that stock of super-strength Manuka honey we were expecting. I think Tilda said the order came in and she put it out the back. Being an Aussie, we'd better get him some tea-tree oil too – great for gargling."

Maura excused herself and, left alone with her chicory coffee, India studied the room properly and to her embarrassment realised it had been taken over by a gaggle of breastfeeding mums – one homely woman in particular who seemed to be leading a discussion on correct nipple attachment techniques and winding methods for colicky infants.

"Ah, I see you've discovered our breastfeeding support group, set up by Tilda and our local midwife – it meets here every week," Maura said as she reappeared with half a ton of bug-nuking new-age supplements concealed in a tree-friendly, no frills, heavy-duty, brown-paper bag. India could hardly conceal the horror on her face.

"Of course I missed out on all that but you still have it all ahead of you," Maura said, making light conversation.

123

India sincerely hoped that she did not, as she paid her money for Nathan's health kicks and left in horrified haste.

At lunchtime a dishevelled Liesel appeared in the kitchen, looking green about the gills.

"I'm *so* sorry, Rebecca! Last night, everyone kept buying me the pints and I'm not used to them, you see. Still, I don't think I drank more than four altogether, maybe five?"

Rebecca silently seethed at being addressed by her first name. Maybe she should have stuck with the Hausfrau thing – it would have kept things on a much more professional footing.

"Oh never mind, Liesel – a nice long hot shower and some strong black coffee will fix you. Do you fancy porridge again?"

Liesel visibly winced at the offer.

"How about some mini chocolate muffins then? A little bit of sugar rush never did any harm?" Rebecca cajoled.

Mark had bought the goodies at the late-night petrol station on the way home the night before. They were already a source of temptation to a dieting Rebecca and there was a limit to the amount of muffins she could shove into the boys without turning them into hyperactive monsters. Thankfully, in two minutes a hung-over Liesel managed to inhale four or five effortlessly with some coffee.

"So, what do you have planned for the afternoon?" Rebecca asked brusquely. Already she could tell her au pair wasn't going to be much use for the rest of the day so she might as well take the boys to the pool. Besides, she wouldn't mind that hunky lifeguard seeing her in a sexy high-cut swimsuit with her two handsome little boys in tow.

"Perhaps I should just stay here?" a tired Liesel asked hopefully.

"On your day off? Nonsense! I have a far better idea. Now, I probably forgot to tell you when you arrived, but there's a community market on today till half three at the eco-village – very Boho – and, well, I think a bit of fresh air would do you the world of good. I have a big surprise for you as well. Come and I'll show you!"

Reluctantly Liesel followed her employer to the enormous garage where Rebecca pointed out a very basic man's bike concealed under some torn grey tarpaulin.

"You see, Liesel, with Mark being directly involved in the eco-development at Cloonsheeda, we're not too eager to get you a car just yet – it wouldn't look too good for our green image, you see, and I'm not sure if I can put you on my insurance that easily. So, since we're halfway between Cloonsheeda and Carrigmore town anyway, I thought on your days off you could cycle around a bit. Fabulous exercise, cycling!"

Rebecca beamed and Liesel found it very hard to suppress a scowl as she wondered if she was some kind of slimming project for her Irish Hausfrau – between the lack of calories and now the presentation of a bike as her official mode of transport she'd soon be burning enough calories to run a small country.

"I have heard that Irish roads are very bad – do you think I would be safe on this bicycle, especially with the amount of rain that falls?" Liesel quizzed somewhat defiantly.

"Our roads? Ah no, sure we've redone loads of them over the years and, look, the rain has eased off now too. Did I tell you that the market at Cloonsheeda today is not just clothes, plants, books and the like, but there's a proper food market too and they're always giving away lots of free nibbles?"

At the mention of food Liesel was smitten.

"How far is it to the village by bike?"

"Oh fifteen minutes, twenty max, depending on how fast you cycle," Rebecca announced over-optimistically. "Do you have a raincoat?"

"No – I thought I would buy one here as soon as I got some money."

"No problem – I have an old rain jacket somewhere just in case it does rain. Hang on till I find it."

Ten minutes later Rebecca waved her off enthusiastically. Hopefully the fresh air would revitalise the au pair enough so that Rebecca wouldn't have to look after the boys in the evening. But in the meantime the pool beckoned.

Aussie Sex God, here I come!

The loneliness of life ahead was boring into Anna Gavin's middle-aged bones as she swept a strand of hair from her forehead, accidentally smearing a streak of black paint on her right cheek and nose. Both her boys were now ignoring her texts and calls. How was it that she'd reached the age of forty-five and had no one to help her through one of the blackest journeys in her life? And to think she was once a vibrant, attractive, financially-sound woman in her own right!

Still in her teens she followed her dancing dreams to

London, first training as a ballet teacher, then winning small parts on the West End – not having any money but hanging out with pop stars, celebrities and Flash Harrys from the city and partying as much as her body could stand. Then she had a blast working the cruise ships, bluffing her way into dancing flamenco or the cancan or whatever was required on any given night. Then, still in her twenties, she'd the sense to come home, setting up her first ballet school in a cold school hall and having more cash in hand than she knew what to do with. Soon there were more dance schools around the country, each with her name on them, and without even trying she was a successful businesswoman overnight, with poise and beauty and an independent streak that attracted the eye of Paddy Gavin, then a young County Councillor about to stand for election as a member of parliament in his late father's constituency.

"You're my Jackie," he told her. "I need your grace, beauty and brains to help me on the campaign trail," and after months of rejecting his advances, she succumbed to his flattery, enjoying having her picture in the paper, got the rock of a ring for her engagement, had a ton of people she didn't know at her wedding, had the boys young and tried to keep her ballet schools going until she accepted that being a political wife to a man who had his eye on a ministry was always going to be an all-consuming affair.

It was only now that Anna realised that she'd spoiled her sons as much as Paddy, tucking them in at night when Paddy was at a function, driving them to matches when Paddy was at the opening of a supermarket, making their lunches, lacing their shoes . . . but they didn't respect her servant's work and lived instead for the snatched moments when their father might see them play a match or speak a part at a school play.

Now, stupidly, Anna had thought that every fortnight one or other of her sons might grace her with a visit and when they came to visit they could decide how they wanted the spare bedroom decorated, but she sensed now it was never going to happen. All morning she'd driven around looking for a bed to replace her deflated blow-up mattress but her equally deflated heart wasn't into buying anything as symbolic as a bed, so she bought paint instead and in a frenzy she painted the walls of the spare room, where her sons would never stay, the colour of her soul, the colour of her pain – the colour of the nothingness ahead: all-encompassing mind-numbing black.

Liesel's whole head looked like it had just recently emerged from the spin cycle of a washing machine as great puddles of water ran down the back of her neck and pooled on her shoulders. The journey to the eco-village on Rebecca's rickety bike took nearly forty minutes and by the time she made it to Cloonsheeda and negotiated the huge, Irish water-logged puddles, she had a puncture as well. Her black leggings and long grey knitted sweater were stuck to her skin, thanks to Rebecca's borrowed coat which had turned out to be anything but waterproof. Frozen and drenched, she wheeled her broken bike to the bike shop, but it was locked with a '*Back in 15 minutes*' sign on the door. Deciding to leave her bike leaning against the front door of the shop, a tired Liesel wandered towards some cream canvas tents in the centre of village, which turned out to be the focal point of the market.

Big black ugly rainclouds still dominated the sky and it was as much for shelter as for anything else that Liesel made for the huge tarpaulin protecting the market stalls. Inside she beheld an array of cheeses, pickles, relishes, chocolate, sausages and meat pies, home-made pastry and breads, clotted fudge and an array of vegetables with clods of mud still stuck to their skins. Everywhere she looked, Liesel saw luxurious, tempting food and now that she'd breathed in fresh air she was hungry, ravenously hungry for any sort of delicacy or sustenance and she successfully ate her way around the stalls, trying sample after sample – loath to spend cash on any actual purchases.

"Would you like to try this goat's cheese? We make it from the milk of our own community herd," Sylvia, who was wearing a yellow jumper dyed with natural dye, cajoled Liesel who helped herself to several small wedges – plain, with garlic and with herbs.

"Miss, some creamy Irish fudge laced with chocolate and rum for you," a middle-aged man cajoled her, handing Liesel a slice of creamy, soft fudge off a large flat knife. He smiled as he watched his confectionary melt on Liesel's tongue. Willingly she parted with two euros for a thick mint-laced fudge wedge, packaged in an eco-friendly green paper bag.

It was the same story of little food gifts at the bun, soup and food counter, run by Rita Skeehan and two other farmers' wives, where the sellers, now eager to finish up and return home, were giving two-for-one offers and reduced-price deals to last-minute shoppers.

Wrapping her hands around some gorgeous minestrone soup, Liesel drank deeply and inhaled, then bit into a large chunk of farmhouse bread which she dipped in the thick tomato and spelt-pasta meal. Smiling, she almost felt human again; she'd have to eat here more often, making sure to arrive late of course to avail of any deals. Delighting in her new well-fed self, Liesel didn't realise she was in the presence of the beautiful man from the pub until he was right up beside her, receiving cash discreetly from the man behind the vegetable stall, even though bizarrely the beautiful man had made no actual purchases.

"What's that, my dear? Are my fruit and veg organic?" the vegetable man, as orange as a carrot from his head to his fuzzy chest and arm-hair joked, as a shopper looked over his stock. "Well, not exactly organic but next door to organic if you know what I mean?" He put a tattooed forefinger to his mouth in mock secrecy and Liesel noticed his little finger was stumpy, severed completely at the second joint.

And as the beautiful man turned to move away, for one split second he looked directly Liesel's way and held her gaze for just a few moments.

Realisation hit Liesel piecemeal – this guy looked remarkably like that Irish personality – the papers were always full of how he'd grown up in a family of artists and writers and how one of his brothers had once penned the winning entry for the Eurovision. What was his name? God, it was on the tip of her fudge-coated tongue!

"Hello again, Fraulein, did you enjoy yourself last night?" Willie smiled as he nodded curtly to the nearby artisan cheese-maker and accepted a cracker and cheese.

All Liesel could do was open and shut her mouth several times, then blush deeply as she watched the mystery man's teeth crush the dainty cracker to pieces and, when he licked the stray crumbs from his lips with an exploratory tongue, her heart pounded like a trapped animal in her ribcage.

"I'm sorry, am I speaking too fast for you to understand or maybe it's my accent?" Willie said curiously, enunciating every word as if Liesel had a learning disability.

"I understand you perfectly well," Liesel stammered. "And yes, thank you, I had a lovely time last night." Then out of nowhere his name hit her like a missile, her mouth opened and shut like a fish again, and she remembered now it was the actor David Ron Dwyer, yes, that was it, David Ron Dwyer – and here he was standing talking to her! "Can I just say I really *love* your work?" she gushed.

"My work?" Willie answered somewhat shiftily, thinking perhaps she was making some sarcastic comment about the wad of notes in his wallet, profit from his exchange with the market-vegetable man who was sometimes tempted by the cheap 'next-to-organic' overflow from the big city's bins.

"Yes, especially your last film with Lauren Hopkins – it was a very challenging role and all the magazines said the director was crazy, yes?"

It was Willie's turn for his mouth to open and shut like a goldfish. "Ehm . . ."

"See you next week, Willie?" the vegetable man said softly, with a cute-hoor squinty wink and a crooked smile showing crooked teeth, and he began to take down his stall as the heavy clouds overhead burst with determination.

"Why does he call you 'Willie', David?" Liesel asked in a whisper, huddling close under the tarpaulin, her eyes big wells of puzzlement.

Looking at her, it suddenly dawned on Willie that this young girl really believed he was David Ron Dwyer in the flesh. Her big cow's eyes searched his face repeatedly and he watched the blush start on her beautiful peaches-and-cream cheeks and throat.

Seeing a look of unease cross Willie's face at her questions, Liesel began to stammer and tried to hide her blushes behind her mane of soft, luscious hair.

"I'm sorry, I am being rude – you perhaps are trying to keep a low profile," Liesel apologised.

"No, don't worry about it. Do you want to come with me – my place is just down the road?" Willie said, grabbing Liesel by the elbow and steering her away from the market as they sprinted to avoid the stinging rain and headed for Willie's rundown cottage.

The rain couldn't mar the sunshine in Freeda's heart as she ran back to her bike shop with her takeout scone and bean-sprout salad sandwich along with a ton of aromatherapy oils, vitamins and herbal teas from Maura's health-food shop. The purchases were part of her 'homework' from Demelza, part of the process of honouring her inner goddess and being tender with herself as she got over the grieving process of having loved and lost. Puzzled, she saw the unfamiliar bike outside her shop but then, seeing one wheel was deflated, took it inside the door to doctor, trusting the man who owned it would show up eventually. Trust – Demelza recommended trust as the medicine for the bruised and broken heart.

"Is this where you live?" Liesel asked, amazed, as Willie fumbled for his keys in his pocket outside the dirty, rundown little dwelling off the main street.

Pushing her inside the opened door, Willie tried to answer Liesel's questions as cleverly as he could, intrigued by his own brazen ingenuity.

"Yes, for the moment. I'm trying to lie low from the paparazzi but I'm sure you're aware that I'm also a method actor and for my next film I'm playing an Irish layabout who lives in a crap house and I like to remain in character right through till the last take. In fact, if you don't mind, I'd actually prefer if you called me 'Willie', Liesel just to keep my focus – Willie's the layabout character in my next film, you see."

"How exciting! Of course, David, I mean Willie, I will do exactly as you ask!" The young German flushed pink right down to the tops of her bosom which was now centre stage as her wet top clung to her ripe curves of girlish flesh.

Mesmerised, Willie found he couldn't stop looking at her tits, imagining how good it would feel to trace the edge of his tongue along the soft pink mounds of her nipples.

"Fancy something to eat, Liesel? There's a ton of food in the kitchen, we had the crew round earlier on," he lied as he rightly sensed food was Liesel's Achilles' heel.

An hour later, after he had annihilated his German Fraulein's resolve with a selection of vacuum-packed mussels, olives, bread, cheese and Italian sausage, he pulled her through the door of his room and backed her onto the bed, all the time kissing her wildly and ripping off their still damp clothes. Mid-tussle, the doorbell began a fiercely incessant ring.

"Jesus Christ, is there never a moment's fucking peace in this house?" Willie raved, annoyed that his attempts at sexual conquest were being so rudely interrupted, probably by some man with a tortured sheep.

"Who is it, Willie?" Liesel asked nervously as each ring made her flinch like a startled deer.

"Goddamn paparazzi probably!" Willie feigned annoyance as he put on a slight American accent and tried his best to ignore the bell buzzing, but three minutes later, just as he'd Liesel stripped right down to her knickers, the ringing stopped but a hammering on the door began instead.

Cursing loudly, Willie strode to the front door in his boxers.

He was faced with a man with a whimpering greyhound.

"My dog's hind quarters are fierce bad . . ."

"Fuck off and don't come back!" Willie roared at the unwanted visitor and banging the door hard went back to Liesel, who was feeding off all the drama of being in the company of David Ron Dwyer.

Willie was living off the excitement too. Very, very briefly the thought did enter his head that it might be a mean trick taking advantage of a girl who thought he was a movie star, but what was the point in being the spit of David Ron Dwyer if he didn't occasionally get a lucky break? Besides, he hadn't had a ride in ages and this plump German milkmaid was a surefire thing as she sat cross-legged on the bed and waited for him adoringly.

"David, David!" Liesel moaned as he fell back into her arms and explored under the elastic of her large cotton granny-knickers with a feathery touch then traced his hand along the edges of her pubic mound, causing two plump warm thighs to part slightly in anticipation.

"Willie," Willie corrected as he worked her clitoris slowly with the edge of one tobacco-stained thumb.

"Oh yes, Villie!" Liesel gasped, momentarily lapsing into the German pronunciation of this chancer's name as she was driven wild with excitement. Collapsing backwards onto the pillow, her nose began to twitch in surprise.

"Villie, it is quite a smelly room, is it not?"

"Yes, but then my Irish layabout is quite a smelly character," Willie explained bluntly as he travelled the length of Liesel's lovely soft body from her creamy white throat to her navel and beyond with his hands and tongue, working her to a hot molten mass of longing until she could stand it no more and bit him on his shoulder like a feral animal, snared but genuinely loving every moment of her captivity with a real live Irish movie star who only had eyes for everything Liesel.

11

Willie sat propped up in bed, his head against a hard and lumpy pillow, sighed and took a long drag of his roll-up cigarette. After nearly two hours rolling around the smelly sheets of his double bed, Willie had groped, licked, touched and worked Liesel into a frenzy but he still hadn't actually been inside her and when his second condom unravelled from exhaustion Liesel began to sob.

"I'm sorry, Willie, I'm so sorry. It's just my body doesn't know what to do. I didn't want you to find out but I am still a virgin, you see," she cried, her breath raspy and her eyes swollen.

The news was quite enough to put the longing off Willie straight away. Deflowering virgins was never one of his biggest turn-ons. Liesel was snuggling in close to his chest and, not sure what to do, he started to stroke her arm in a play of reassurance.

"Willie, thank you for being so kind and patient . . . but I think . . . I think I am willing to try again," Liesel sniffled, lifting her blotchy face up to gaze adoringly into his eyes and Willie cringed inwardly although he effortlessly faked a caring smile.

"Back in a sec, Liesel, just got to check on something in the kitchen," he lied, jumping out of bed and racing for the door.

In the grimy kitchen, Willie considered what he should do as he smoked his roll-up to his fingertips. A virgin, who the hell was a virgin at nineteen any more? The pressure! What was a guy to do? What would David Ron Dwyer do in a situation like this?

Then knowing the answer, he determinedly stubbed out his cigarette into a sloppy chipped china saucer. David Ron Dwyer would get the job done, that's what he'd do, he'd find a way to penetrate the impenetrable, he wouldn't let a female fan go away disappointed from the biggest thing that had probably happened to her in her entire boring, innocent little life.

Promptly Willie strode across the room to the fridge and opened it wide, looking for a little special *je ne sais quoi*. Somewhere near the back shelf he found just the culinary little wonder he was looking for and grabbing a bottle of cheap red plonk from the worktop and two supermarket wineglasses headed back into the room.

"Are you mad with me?" Liesel sniffled as she sat up, pulling the duvet around her shoulders.

"You? No, never you! You are fantastic, beautiful and completely special!" Willie realised he was now beginning to think and speak like some kind of luvvie actor without even trying.

"But my virgin news, it is okay with you?" Liesel pursued, pushing a strand of hair behind one ear, brushing a tear away with the back of her hand in the process.

"I admit I was a little taken aback . . . but I'm flattered, honoured even, that you've chosen me," Willie reassured her as he placed the bottle of cheap plonk and a plate of black goo on the bedside locker.

"What's that you have?" Liesel asked quickly, her mouth already watering at seeing the large slab of what was most definitely some kind of dessert.

"That, my sweet, is something almost, but not quite as sweet as you . . . Black Forest Gateau," he said, handing her a glass of wine.

"Oh, my grandmother used to make Black Forest Gateau when I was a child!" Liesel squealed, her eyes filling again with tears as she took in large gulps of the wine. "We used to have just this cake on weekends when we went to visit her . . . when she was still alive . . ." she trailed off, the floodgates beginning to open properly now.

"There now, don't cry, it's alright . . . relax and enjoy as I spoon-feed every last piece into your delectably kissable mouth," Willie promised.

The wet kitten eyes filled with longing.

Slowly, Willie placed a forkful of cake in Liesel's mouth then deftly slipped his tongue through her opened lips, running the edge of his tongue along her pointy white teeth then deepening his kisses until she was drowning in emotion, the sugar hit of black cherry chocolate sauce and the fumes of cheap Cabernet Sauvignon.

"Willie, don't stop, Willie, I want you, I want you!" she insisted after she'd devoured her cake completely crumb by crumb.

Fifteen minutes later, Willie's mouth was curled in a

smile as he wiped a trickle of sauce away from the corner of his lips with his tongue and swallowed a swollen black cherry whole. Snuggling flush with his body, Liesel began to murmur nonsense in his ear as she ran her hand along the curls of his pubic hair in post-coital bliss.

What had she said?

"More, I said I wanted more!" Liesel insisted loudly, her voice guttural, her body wanton.

It was just as well his father had taken off for his annual weeklong devotion to the Holy Shrine of Knock with the widow woman from Carrigmore Town, thought Willie, as he ran his hand the length of Liesel's generous hips and cupped her delectably large buttocks as firm and delicate as any warm ripe peach on a lazy summer's day.

"Be nice to her, treat her well, he says! See what happens when you start treating these girls well, Mark? They start believing *they're* the ones who run the show, just as *I* said!" Rebecca laid on the sarcasm thick as she tried Liesel's mobile one more time and found it just kept ringing out. She'd been irritated when she found the sexy Aussie lifeguard was off sick from work after she'd taken her boys for a splash in the pool but, now that her hired help had done a runner, she was fit to kill and anyone would do.

"Give it a rest, would you?" Mark snapped, trying to wrestle the boys into their Batman pyjamas. "How was I to know she was going to disappear for hours on end? We'll track her down once we have the boys in bed. She doesn't strike me as the type that's going to run away and join the circus!"

"It's the bloody cheek of it though," Rebecca fumed. "She had last night off already. Does she really think she can disappear tonight as well when I have so much work to do before I go on the archaeology dig this weekend?"

Rolling his eyes to the ceiling, Mark groaned as he remembered that he would be in for a weekend alone with the twins.

"Don't tell me you forgot? Really, Mark, it's my first *ever* archaeological expedition away and I need your *full* support!" Rebecca seethed.

"Okay, okay, I admit I forgot but it's nothing I can't deal with. Although since you won't let me dump the kids on my mother it's a good thing Liesel will be here to lend a hand."

"Just be careful where she puts those hands she'll be lending," Rebecca warned, her eyes narrowing as she deliberately avoided any conversation about Mark's mother.

"God, you really think I have a thing for foreign birds, don't you!" Mark retaliated, knowing full well that he was baiting her and deliberately reminding her of the time she thought he was having an affair with their beautiful, blonde Polish cleaner Mariola. Rebecca's jealousy had been the catalyst for her walking out on their marriage. Mariola had since left the country with her husband and in her place Rebecca had hired a big-boned middle-aged Irish country mammy with arms like tree trunks and a head on her like a good-sized boiled ham. Not the stuff of any red-blooded man's dreams.

"Why are you trying to wind me up with your 'foreign bird' remarks?" Rebecca asked huffily as she stood hand on hip.

Mark threw his head back and laughed good-naturedly. "Jesus Christ, you were the one who hand-picked our new German au pair yourself for her plainness if I remember rightly. Are you having second thoughts now about your judgement?"

"You know I'd never do anything to lose you?" Rebecca said suddenly and, as soon as she said it, she wondered if it was really the truth or was it just one of those casual phrases that married people threw around from time to time – just because.

Washing the blackened paintbrushes in her kitchen sink and seeing the darkened swirls disappearing down the plughole, Anna wondered for a minute if she was going slowly insane. Painting a whole room black while experiencing rage was not normal behaviour but then, since Paddy had told her of his affair (two hours before some cheap tabloid paper threatened to expose his infidelities to the nation), life had suddenly stopped being normal in any way and everything she had thought was certain was suddenly thrown into disarray.

The separation itself had taken forever, any goodwill she might have offered dissipated on legal advice from her solicitor who warned her not to cut the charmingly manipulative Paddy any slack. Still, there were occasional little moments during the warring when Paddy was nice to her and it seemed as if maybe his little indiscretions could be forgotten and they could get on with their lives again, get on with the business of being normal, being respectable. But in the end it ended and she'd never really felt ready for all that freedom.

Bereft of a husband, with no one to visit and no ballet

schools to run and no chance of any sons visiting despite that silly Wii thing she had purchased for them to play games on TV, Anna recognised the anxious feeling that clung to her flesh and buzzed through her nerves as boredom, coupled with paralysing fear about the future. With her forefinger she mindlessly caught a trickle of black paint that ran from the brush and doodled a dancer on points on the white ceramic surface of the sink and her back began to stiffen as she remembered that grace, poise and strength were something ingrained in every dancer. Like lightning the idea came to her.

Washing her hands and putting on some lipstick, she hurried to the mini-supermarket for some blank sheets of printer paper and a child's box of happy-coloured markers.

Mossy came in from an hour or so or cleaning down smelly cattle stalls and was met at the door by Jangle. It was hard to believe the animal was ever sprightly; he moved so slowly now, his whole body far removed from the loose collection of puppy-dog muscle, bone and sinew. Now diagnosed with arthritis, Jangle didn't have much time left on this earth and was allowed to rest in the back porch of the kitchen most nights. Looking at him, Mossy felt he and the dog were at the same stage in life – waiting.

"What's for dinner?" Mossy asked Rita, who was painting in one corner, wearing one of Mossy's cast-off shirts, her brush poised to put the finishing blue touches to the ears of a Friesian.

"Well, whatever it was, it's long since burnt," Rita said somewhat snappily, not that she ever expected him to keep regular mealtimes. If she'd learnt anything over the years it was not to expect much from a farmer – not to expect him to have the cash for a new pair of curtains if she wanted them or a new set of table and chairs and not to ever see him early for dinner, especially one she'd gone to any trouble over.

Lifting the lid on the casserole, Mossy saw that his meal for the night was beef stew, and although it was a little bit dried up, by his low standards it certainly wasn't inedible.

"Bit dried up, still edible," he muttered to himself. Stopping to get himself a plate, he sat at the table and blessed himself before shaking salt on his dinner and digging in. Momentarily, he paused aware of Rita watching him with cold eyes.

"What?" he asked mid-forkful.

"It's just something that has entered my head a few times lately – that here you are waiting to die while I want nothing more than to live," Rita said plainly.

"Jesus, woman, what a thing to say! Are you trying to put me off my food?" Mossy wiped a used knife clean with his finger so he could butter some soda bread.

"Why then have you been spending so much time at the tree stump lately, praying to something that isn't even real?" Rita snorted, not caring one bit if she put Mossy off every forkful.

"Had things on my mind that I thought Herself might help me figure out, that's all. Now, would you ever give my head some peace?" Mossy glowered as he ripped into his dinner like a feral animal.

"Well for some, having such time to waste," Rita huffed as she started to flick through her digital camera, studying different cow shots until she found the one she wanted to paint. "I never had the luxury of time with children to rear and I still managed to bring my baking and garden flowers to market to earn an extra few pence! Took my canvases to market this week for the first time, if you're interested . . . sold two and got a commission for another."

"What kind of a commission?" Mossy asked suspiciously.

"The Daly calf – you remember it nearly died when it was born and the children took it for a pet and reared it – the family wants me to paint a picture of it for the hall. I took some photos of her today!" Rita announced triumphantly.

"More money than sense, that Daly lot!" Mossy snorted.

"And I've booked the library in Carrigmore. They don't have a spot till next year but I'm going to have an exhibition of my work – there'll be wine and cheese and fancy little finger things," Rita continued, putting her camera down and squinting at her canvas with one eye, trying to fix something indefinable.

"For Jesus' sake, woman, you've lost your mind with all this cow nonsense!" Mossy thundered, wiping his mouth with the back of his hand and jutting out his chin.

"Have I? Well, what do you expect me to do? The children are grown and you're no company – still farming, not wanting to give the land over to one of the girls, even though all of them have the love of it and Sinéad having the agri business qualification too."

"We've been over this a million times. It's no life for a woman, farming." Mossy shook his head definitively.

"And who are you to judge?"

"No matter – there'll be no handing over of *this* farm while there's life in me yet," Mossy blazed, his appetite completely ruined.

"It's stubbornness, that's what it is. You can't bear to stop farming because it'll be the end of your name and you can't bear one of the girls taking up where you've left off because they'd have the name of their husband on your land."

"I'm going to take my tea inside to the TV and then I'm going to bed!" Mossy shouted and the ears of old Jangle pricked up at the sharpness of his master's voice, then he shuffled over from his lying place in front of the tumble dryer and put his weary head in Rita's lap and let her stroke his silky ears and dry snout.

"You're like two old bachelors, the pair of you, and there's no teaching either of you new tricks," Rita sniped as she pushed the dog away and started on her first ever painting commission.

Sinéad Winterbottom was busy washing clothes for Henry's weekend away on his university archaeological dig. He'd need plenty of T-shirts to keep him going as well as two casual easy-iron shirts and one pair of chinos. The casuals were for when he and his distance-learning and post-grad students stopped work for a beer and a meal. Well for some, she thought. Other essentials included two pairs of cotton boxers and two warm winter fleeces. He would pack the lot himself; Henry hadn't ever thought much of Sinéad's packing ability.

"Don't forget to wash my long johns – weather like this and I'll freeze without good thermals," Henry instructed matter-of-factly as he poked his head into the laundry room where Sinéad was sorting the washing into their different laundry baskets: whites, reds, darks and light coloureds.

"I'm on it," Sinéad grunted, not even lifting her head as he disappeared back upstairs to his office – they hadn't spoken much since the night she'd rejected his baby-making advances. Henry had written '**Have baby sex with Sinéad**' into his computer to remind him of his responsibilities to the species and had been miffed when he couldn't write '**goal completed**'. Looking at a heap of red-and-pink clothes belonging to herself and her daughter, Sinéad loaded up the washing machine and deliberately stuck Henry's white thermals in with them. Accidentally on purpose she forgot to put in the sheet of colour-catcher for catching the pink dye that would without question escape from a never-before-washed generic red 'mummy' top bought cheaply from the big supermarket chain in Carrigmore town.

India Jennings thought for one moment that she was actually going to die. Lying motionless in her bed she was panting furiously, her hair matted and slick with sweat and her nightdress stuck to her clammy breasts. Desperately she wanted to pee but she didn't have the energy to put one foot outside the bed. Beside her Nathan was also lying motionless, his mouth dry, his glazed red-rimmed eyes glued to the TV screen, watching nothing and everything simultaneously. Every now and then he'd take a sip of water or erupt into a man-size sneezing-fit worthy of the man-size tissues that rested on his lap.

"Nate, I think I'm dying," India finally croaked.

"Me too, told you this bug was a bastard," he answered, every word an effort.

"It just came from nowhere and cut the legs from under me," she panted in disbelief.

"Yep, me too." He started to flick the channels then abruptly turned the TV off and just stared at the wall.

"Will you make me a cup of tea?" India pleaded in her best damsel-in-distress whispery voice.

"Nope, I got up last to make Vitamin C drinks, remember?"

"You're *such* a gentleman," India seethed, pulling herself up in bed to a sitting position. Every muscle was cramped, every sinew and nerve on edge and every bone was like stone as she hauled herself out of bed, went for a pee and then endured the boiling of the kettle even though the noise of screeching steam ripped through her ears and tore strips off her brain. Pouring the milk into the mug, she took a sip and winced. It tasted vile – she should have stayed in bed.

Sitting on her barstool in her kitchen, Anna surveyed her handwritten posters and smiled. There it was in black and white with lots of happy colours in between, the notice that she would be setting up a new dance school for children. Thank God she'd done that UK course in general dance – she could teach musical theatre, freestyle and tap as well as ballet. This was it, the start of her new life; she would just sit back and let the eager mammies ring her for lessons. First thing tomorrow she would even go out and buy a new bed – a dance teacher couldn't afford to compromise her posture. After all, good posture was one of the few things in life that Anna Maguire had left.

12

It was late, very late for just lounging in bed since the afternoon, almost nine o'clock at night, and Liesel's soft, feminine petals had not only been deflowered but, on her specific request, almost torn asunder by the obliging if ever so slightly shattered Willie Cleary.

Post-coital, lying in his strong arms, inhaling his male musky scent, she'd forgotten about the real world entirely until shortly before nine when she awoke with a start and remembered that she was meant to be in charge of very small children.

"Willie, wake up! Willie, I have to be home!" she told him in a state as she shook him vigorously and switched on the light, jumping around the bedroom trying to retrieve her granny knickers, bra and outer clothing.

Squinting under the bright lights, Willie was like a rabbit caught in the headlights.

"Have you a car? Can you drive me home?" Liesel wailed as she snapped her plain utility-style bra shut and pulled her jumper over her head.

"No, sorry, what's the rush?" Willie questioned, shielding his dazzled eyes with one hand.

"The children – Rebecca will kill me!" Liesel blurted out as she continued to dress quickly, pulling on her socks and shoes in a jumbled dance of hopping and cursing.

Children, Willie was puzzled. What children? Hadn't she just told him she was a virgin? It suddenly entered Willie's head that he hadn't the slightest clue about the personal responsibilities or habits of this new lover and that a few more questions mightn't have gone astray.

"I know we didn't talk much . . . but I'm an au pair, didn't I mention it?"

Willie chewed his lip as he considered the question, then slowly as he pondered the data of his brain he shook his head, got out of bed and started to get dressed too.

"So, who's Rebecca?" he asked as he jumped into his denims and ran a hand through his bed-head hair.

"My Hausfrau and she's not exactly friendly – I don't know what I'll tell her about being here all day!" Liesel wailed.

"Tell her a lie, the best lies are those mixed with truth. I don't know, tell her you got a puncture and got drenched in the rain and your phone went dead, although it didn't matter much anyway as you can tell them you had no credit in your phone to ring or text back."

"That's almost the truth – she still owes me money from my expenses," Liesel fumed.

"Well, make sure you add that bit in too – make her out to be the inconsiderate bitch and you the innocent little foreign girl. Let your Hausfrau know that you tried ringing from the pub but couldn't because it's shut till the evening, which it is this time of year. What's the man of the house like if this Rebecca one is a cow?"

"Nice, friendly I suppose."

"Then tell the whole thing to him instead. Trust me, if he thinks his wife has been taking advantage of you and his good name, and feels sorry for you, it will start a row between them and they'll probably forget all about you once they start fighting."

"That's brilliant, how did you think all that up?" Liesel gushed.

"Hey, baby, when you've read as many film scripts as me, thinking up plots is never a problem," Willie continued, the fake American accent back in full swing.

Suddenly she bear-hugged him tight and kissed him heartily.

"Thank you for everything, Dav – I mean Willie," Liesel blushed.

"No worries, kid. I'm afraid I can't walk you to the pub to make your phone call though, don't take this personally or anything but I can't risk being seen with you – my ex-girlfriend, well, she doesn't accept the break-up and I can't risk everything being splashed across the papers."

"I have seen men about with cameras, and reporters too, but I did not know why they were here until now."

"Blood-sucking parasites, the lot of them, they follow me everywhere, what I wouldn't give for some anonymity!" Willie moaned tragically.

"Don't worry, Willie, your secret is safe with me – I will not tell anyone that we are lovers," Liesel assured him matter-of-factly as she turned on her heel and said goodbye. Walking towards Jasper Keogh's she wallowed in her new ex-virgin, nymphomaniac status – it was hard to think of anything else as the muscles at the tops of her legs were tender from the weight of Willie's hard body on top of hers. Momentarily Liesel winced as the soft skin of her inner thighs, already chafed from Willie's scratchy stubble chin, rubbed together. With each bow-legged step towards Jasper's Liesel smiled a little more as she remembered being handled deftly by international movie superstar and all-round hunk, David Ron Dwyer.

It wasn't in Liesel Hoffman's nature to play games or tell lies and that's probably why she got away with it when Mark gently but firmly questioned her in the kitchen about her unauthorised disappearance from the family. Somehow Liesel knew he had decided to speak to her instead of Rebecca who was probably a human tornado of rage at the other end of the house.

"So, that's what happened, the bicycle was old and the road was bad and I got so wet and couldn't ring you, here's the IOU from the taxi home . . . I will pay you back soon." Liesel held out another handwritten note to Mark which he looked at in embarrassment.

"Jesus, Liesel – I expect to pay for your taxi home if the bike fell apart on the road and I don't want any IOU's – didn't Rebecca talk to you already about this stuff?" Mark said, exasperated.

Liesel's eyes filled up with tears and she sniffled miserably and shook her head just as Rebecca's enraged energy force appeared at the door.

"Well, if Liesel doesn't mind *too* much now that she's

back maybe she'd like to clean up the kitchen a bit and load the dishwasher since she wasn't around to help out with the children today!" Rebecca blazed, one hand on her hip, her eyes flashing with anger.

"She's not doing *anything*," Mark bristled as he lanced his wife with a knife-like stare.

"*What?* I think –"

"The kids are in bed for the night and there's nothing that needs to be done."

Mark's black eyes narrowed and, furious at being rebuked in front of the hired help, Rebecca's jaw jutted out defiantly.

"That's not how I see it!"

"Rebecca, I think we should talk about a few things upstairs." Mark took his wife firmly by the arm and began to steer her out of the kitchen.

"I think I will just watch some TV for a while," Liesel said, smiling sweetly at Mark, knowing with whom to side in future.

"Sure – just put your feet up and relax," Mark offered, before pushing Rebecca out the door.

Liesel spent a respectable fifteen minutes channel-hopping before overhearing some muffled shouts upstairs. Curiosity got the better of her and she sneaked up the grand staircase and passed by the upstairs office and main bathroom. She could hear raised voices from the main bedroom.

"And if you didn't see her off on that crock of a bike today she wouldn't have got lost! As it is she might have got killed or caught bloody pneumonia!" she heard Mark lash out.

Smugly, Liesel smiled to herself. It was just as Willie

had said: the Gleesons were having a row and the man of the house was siding with her and rebuking his wife.

Willie was chain-smoking one minute and smiling the next as he thought about the incredible day of seduction and sex – a right little goer that German one was. He was still lost in his own world when Tom pulled up in his heap-of-junk car and rapped on the door.

"Willie, I'm picking up Spud and Hackett out the road, man – they're back from Manchester for the weekend and we're all heading out to my Uncle Mossy's for some lamping. Do you want to come?"

Invisible fingers chased a shiver down Willie's spine at Tom's suggestion. He would rather rip his eyelashes out one by one than be squeezed into a banjaxed motor with Murphy and Hackett from primary school. Not known for their brains or the quality of their conversation, the two lads had spent the last few months in the UK picking up casual labour, and the thought of spending a night dazzling bunnies with headlights and blowing their little furry heads off didn't appeal on any level.

Sensing a moment's hesitancy, Tom went in for some mental arm-twisting to try and get his friend to succumb. "A farm can get overrun with the long-eared big-toothed feckers, so it's not a crime to take a few of them out. It's the way of the country, Willie, killing stuff when they over-breed, why I remember I shot my first rabbit when I was in the –"

"Primary," Willie finished for him and Tom scowled at his friend's flippancy.

"Yeah, well, we'll be hanging tomorrow – if you fancy a game of pitch and toss let me know, otherwise we'll be down the kids' playground having a few before we go to Keogh's."

Willie shook his head. "I'll skip the playground, thanks, skip the pub too."

"What, no pub? But sure you have to go out on the beer with us! Spud and Hackett are home from *England*, it's your patriotic duty to come out and help them drown their sorrows!"

"Sorry, Tom, I've decided, I'm going on the dry for the next while."

Stunned, Tom's face went blank for twenty seconds before his eyes creased and he broke into a huge grin. "Yeah right – sure how would you cope without booze? Going on the dry, don't talk soft!"

"Doesn't say a lot about my character if drink is the only way I can exist, now does it?"

"You're talking shite, man. Look, I'll let you off tonight because I know being a bunny-murderer would have you up half the night with your conscience, but tomorrow we're going on a bender, right? You, me and the returned emigrants!" Tom punched Willie in the shoulder to emphasis the point and a flash of annoyance passed over Willie's face.

"Skeehan, meant to tell you for some time now."

"Yeah?"

"Stop punching me in the fucking shoulder, man!"

Having watched his annoyed friend start his motor, the exhaust coughing like an old man, Willie shut the door and wondered what he was at announcing he was off the drink. Taking a break from the pub was social suicide, although with Liesel around that might be no harm. If he kept hanging out in Keogh's she'd be sure to work out his identity eventually but staying away from the pub would make perfect sense if he told her he was deliberately trying to keep a low profile.

Although going stone-cold sober was about more than keeping Liesel as a plaything and about more than saving some much-needed cash. In her innocence Liesel thought he *was* somebody, somebody important, and having her around believing that for the last few hours had had a strange effect on the way he thought, the way he even spoke. Out of his pocket Willie pulled a crumpled piece of newspaper ripped from one of the recent red-tops where David Ron Dwyer's sneaky face was caught coming out of that top model's apartment in London.

"Just you wait and see, one day I'm going to be screwing models too," Willie announced loudly as he speared the photo of his doppelganger with a thumbtack and stuck it on his bedroom wall.

Anna just couldn't believe it. All day the phone hadn't rung once asking her about children's dance classes. In the past, in the heyday of her ballet schools, she only had to announce that she was setting up and the phone would hop. Today Anna had put six hand-drawn posters up around the village and not one phone-call had followed. Surely it wasn't because of the recent bad publicity with Eddie Ferris at the welcoming reception for her new home? Damn that comfort whiskey for making her look like a lush and damn that little wagon from the national media, Isobel something or other, who had turned the presentation into an embarrassing national comedy event.

The doorbell rang. Anna answered almost absent-mindedly.

"Hello, I'm sorry – I hope I didn't disturb you."

Outside, Eddie Ferris, wearing a red-spotted bowtie, yellow tank-top and faded blue denims, held a large bouquet of green leeks in one hand and one or two things wrapped in purple tissue paper in the other. It was like horrible déjà vu. Almost unconsciously Anna started looking for cameras and big-voiced reporters behind the halo of Eddie's perfect red-brown curls.

"It's just I was passing through, doing some ground-work for a new TV series, and I just couldn't get that day of your formal welcoming to the green village out of my mind. It was so obvious you hadn't a clue what was going on and, well . . . well, like I said, it's been on my mind ever since. So these are for you, to sort of make amends." Without any fuss Eddie shoved the leeks under Anna's nose. "Oh and two bottles of this too – organic red wine. I buy it for a friend of mine sometimes – she usually gets terrible bad headaches from red but not from this little beauty, no horrible sulphites, you see," Eddie continued.

"Funny presents," Anna said indifferently, not caring in the least if she came across as rude or ungrateful.

"Sorry?" Eddie coughed nervously.

Anna still hadn't taken his gifts despite his outstretched arms and his trademark big cheery smile.

"Presumptuous presents too," she said. "The leeks, for example, presume I can cook, when I am actually the worst cook on the planet. And the wine . . . well, how do you know I'm not an alcoholic? That day you first met me I was as pickled as a corpse if you remember."

Immediately Eddie turned puce from his ears to his throat. "Oh God yes, now that you mention it; it is stupid to bring wine. You're right, of course, for all I know you could be in AA and my present could push you over the edge or off the wagon, whatever the expression is. How terribly inconsiderate of me and, yes, presumptuous of me to put you in this position . . . and, dear me, the leeks . . . I wasn't presupposing that you were some kind of domestic goddess by bringing them here – you're more than entitled to be a non-cooking kind of feminist or some kind of activist or –"

"Would you like to come in?" Anna asked wearily, not wanting to hear any more of his ramblings and not really wanting his company either, but some company and some conversation from another human being was better than none.

"Oh, yes, that would be lovely. Maura's in Dublin for work and I'm in the mood for a chat," Eddie answered breezily, cranking up the trademark smile to full wattage now.

"I warn you, the place is pretty sparse on furniture – I don't even have so much as a couch." Anna gestured to the floor space behind her which was still all boxes and tattered rugs, assorted bits and pieces and two large shapeless beanbags.

"No worries, sure sitting on the floor is very good for the spine," Eddie announced magnanimously, slithering yoga-like to the floor and adopting a natural bendy Buddha pose.

"Is that so?" Anna went rooting in the kitchen for a corkscrew that she knew she'd tidied way in a big cardboard box marked 'kitchen utensils'.

"Sure."

"I'm not an alcoholic by the way but if you've got the time I'd very much like to get just a little bit tipsy," she then announced in a manner that suggested she expected complete compliance.

Not that Eddie would have done a runner anyway. He was too much of an old-school gentleman with a built-in radar for ladies in distress to refuse her this very little indulgence . . . and Anna Maguire was very much a lady in distress in need of plenty of indulgence, he thought, as he poured a large amount of wine into her glass, cocked his head to one side in friendly subservience and adopted the kind and sensitive expression that always, *always* made the ladies want to tell him absolutely *everything* that was wrong in their lives.

13

India Jennings' body had transformed into a river of sweat. Like an over-exercised stallion, steam was actually rising from Nathan's naked six-pack. Both of them were wiped out by whatever bug was percolating in their systems but, having been bed-ridden for a day, boredom was setting in and India's fingers started wandering as her brain schemed about having her wicked way with her currently immobilised boyfriend. With monumental effort, a sex-starved India managed to straddle a whimpering Nate to begin a brief exploration of her boyfriend's nipples but moments later she slithered slug-like off his torso into total flu surrender.

Listless of body but restless of mind, she reached out her hand and grabbed her mobile phone beside her bed which had been shut down the last 24 hours and began checking her messages. Immediately she was bombarded. The first message was from Maura Simmons, 'Just wondering could you put in an appearance for our first meeting on the festival scheduled for next week?' Angrily India stuffed the phone under her pillow. Hadn't she made it clear to this woman that her services were strictly limited?

"Nate, will you get me some fizzy orange – we've none left beside the bed," she pleaded, determined that *someone* should do something for her for a change.

Turning his back, Nathan pretended not to hear.

So much for Australian blokes being big and bold and strong and wanting nothing better than to protect their Sheilas, India thought, as she peeled the sheets from her skin and went on a hands-and-knees hunt for some dyed and sugared water.

Henry Winterbottom hadn't stopped ranting since he'd found his pink long johns in the airing cupboard.

"Impossible, it's impossible that this should happen," he raved as he brought the long johns within an inch of his nose for better viewing. "I even bought some of those colour-catcher things to put in the washing machine, Sinéad. Why on earth didn't you use one and why were you washing my underwear in a red wash anyway?" he fumed as he held his unsexy underwear up to his nose once more and shook his head in disbelief.

Feigning ignorance of colour-catchers and washing in general and citing weaning problems and on-going sleep deprivation, Sinéad brushed aside her husband's piffling distress.

"I swear, Mummy Winterbottom, you wouldn't have lasted two minutes in boarding school!" Henry lashed out in a final attack.

Sinéad just smiled a crooked smile. Boarding school was where Henry had been sent from the age of eight to learn basic survival skills in being a man. Naturally, being Henry, he lapped it all up – the sports, the spartan communal living, never shedding a tear for Mummy and not caring that food was always scarce and poor quality despite the exorbitant fees his parents were paying. Discipline and training, the pillars of self-belief, were ingrained in Henry's nature ever since and became an essential part of his faultless personality.

Folding his newly girlified underwear into his well-packed suitcase, Henry managed to regain self-control.

"See you Sunday," he said ten minutes later, kissing Sinéad briskly before leaving the house and getting into his sparkling 4x4, where all traces of children had been forensically removed. He was heading off before lunch to get things sorted for the dig.

Not even bothering to wave him off, Sinéad turned on the radio and began the daily grind of dishes, laundry, and tidying up toys. The cleaning journey continued upstairs where she got the bright idea of combining her housework with Demelza's 'homework' as her next appointment was looming. Rooting through her drawers, Sinéad fished out some saucy scarlet French knickers and a matching satin camisole. To complete the harlot look, she tried on some seldom-used and very high, black-patent heels. This was the only way to do the vacuuming, she thought, as she jiggled her bum to Dusty Springfield's 'You Don't Own Me', practised switching on her Hara point (according to Demelza, the source of sexual energy two inches below her navel) and went on a hungry hunt for dust.

Mark was at home trying to get last-minute instruction on how to run the household for the weekend from his somewhat sour-pussed trainee-archaeologist wife. Dressed only in knickers, fleecy socks, a long grey T-shirt and a sports bra that hugged her boobs tight, Rebecca was in the ensuite rubbing moisturiser into her face when Mark, wearing only his boxers and a fleecy dressing gown, came from behind and squeezed her right buttock hard. Immediately she winced – he'd gifted her the previous night with a nice big love bite on her flank as a kind of teenage going-away memento and it was already turning seven colours of the rainbow underneath her knickers.

"Hey, beautiful!" Mark started pulling Rebecca's exotic red hair out of the way as he began the process of tickling the back of her neck with his mischievous tongue.

"Don't, I'm cross with you," she snapped, pulling away from his embrace and applying chocolate lip gloss to her natural pout.

"What about?" He couldn't resist pulling her backwards against his chest so he could play with her copper love-curls under the waistband of her pants.

"As if you didn't know! My bitten ass for starters – I only hope there aren't communal showers at the hostel – I don't fancy people knowing I'm married to Dracula!" she snapped, not pulling his hand away but not showing any obvious enjoyment in his fondling either.

"Is that all?" His busy hands were expertly unsnapping her bra and darting to her breasts now, twisting the hard little nubs of her nipples.

"Get lost, Mark," she growled as she made a show of stopping his hands from cupping his favourite playthings.

"Oh come on, Rebecca, you're going away for the whole weekend! Let's not fight," he pleaded, ploughing both hands into the pockets of his robe in an act of good-natured diplomacy.

Turning to face him, Rebecca flashed him a practised snotty-nosed look of contempt.

"And just for the record, I had sex with you last night *only* because sex is a fabulous way to burn up calories and I'm watching my figure!" she sparked, hauling on her denims and an expensive woollen sweater.

"God, I love watching your figure too," Mark teased but, still playing the part of indignant wife, Rebecca stormed down the stairs and kissed the boys goodbye without even one perfunctory look at poor Liesel who was standing behind the boys awaiting some sort of instruction or at best some sort of encouragement from her Hausfrau. Pointedly, Rebecca turned away from her and addressed Mark who'd sauntered down the stairs behind her in his dressing-gown and socks. "After two years of being a parent I expect you will know something about looking after our children until I get back. I'm not expecting much. Just try and keep them alive." She arched an eyebrow as she hauled on a gorgeous red-leather jacket.

Liesel hurriedly took the boys inside to watch a DVD.

"So much maternal instinct – when did that kick in?" Mark asked Rebecca boldly, then seeing her bristle changed the subject. "Aren't you going to kiss your husband goodbye before you leave?" He couldn't really understand why she was so prickly when they'd had such a fab time in bed the night before.

"No, I am not," Rebecca hissed. "You embarrassed

me in front of Liesel last night by undermining my authority and, while we might have had great sex, don't think that I'm not still awaiting your apology this morning!"

"*Great* sex . . . surely *mind-blowing* sex is more accurate?"

"If you won't apologise then I guess we're at a stalemate," Rebecca shrugged, eyes flashing as she pulled on a scarf and tucked it inside the collar of her jacket.

"What is this – the United Nations? You know; if you don't kiss me goodbye, Rebecca, you might regret it. You might have a terrible accident and be killed on the way to your dig and you'd regret then that your last words to your husband were fighting ones," Mark insisted, his dark eyes burning as he hauled her towards him by her winter scarf, still angling for his parting kiss.

"Regret? I doubt it. Don't you know the dead are just dead, Mark, they don't regret anything," Rebecca snorted as she prevented him from garrotting her with her woolly neckwear. "Besides, do you think I would be so careless as to accidentally kill myself on the road knowing that you might end up in the comforting arms of our new au pair?"

Her words of venom still in the air, Rebecca disappeared with a bang of the door and a flounce of her flame locks.

"Bloody childish woman!" Mark swore under his breath as he opened the kitchen door and saw Liesel propped up on a stool at the breakfast bar, dreamily looking out the window towards the mountains and fields in the background. He stood and watched her popping open her plump pink lips to lick her forefinger slowly and hungrily, then sliding the finger back into a newly bought jar of peanut butter for another swab of food before sliding her finger mindlessly back into her mouth for another bout of hard sucking.

Making an introductory cough, Mark padded across the floor, threw open the fridge and realised that, bar the peanut butter he'd bought the night before for the kids, there was genuinely nothing to eat in his home.

"Think I might have to take you out in the car later on – do a bit of shopping," he rattled off to Liesel as he shut the fridge door and frowned.

"Hhmmm?" she said dreamily, her peanut-covered finger paused mid-air, her vacant eyes searching his face.

It was at that moment that Mark realised Liesel was wearing a particularly low-cut top that exposed the roundness of her breasts to perfection.

"Talk to you later, Liesel, I'm just going to go and have a shower," he excused himself as he pulled his dressing-gown belt tight and bolted for his ensuite.

It was late morning and Anna and Eddie had spent an innocent night together as Eddie listened to Anna's tales of marital and maternal woe while they both downed the too-drinkable organic wine.

"So now you know it all," Anna sighed as the day's rays filtered through the blinds. "Big Paddy Gavin was, correction, *is* a total bastard and my boys have abandoned me to old age and senility."

"Still, who would have known that the Wii you got the boys would have been so much fun once we set it up."

"Drunken sports in your living room – best thing ever, virtual tennis imagining every ball I was hitting was Paddy's face! I didn't even know what that blasted Wii thing did until you showed me, Eddie!" Anna laughed as she moved in her beanbag, a mother duck on her nest. "I'd offer you breakfast, but I know for a fact I've nothing to tempt you."

Eddie smiled a wonderfully genuine smile that lit up his lovely brown face. "I hope you didn't think I planned to be here for breakfast, Anna. It was such a spontaneous night! But you having nothing here to eat is very fortunate – I get to take you out for breakfast instead."

Anna was struck by the fact that it was not only power and sex appeal that could light up a room but kindness and gentleness too.

"Surely you have so many more interesting people to meet than me?" Anna stammered.

"Nonsense, you'd be doing me a favour. Don't run yourself down, Anna, just say 'Yes please, Eddie!'."

"Yes, please, Eddie – I guess I accept your breakfast proposal then," she said, smiling.

"Excellent. One thing puzzles me though, Anna – why do you not have a proper bed – surely beds are the one essential requirement for comfortable living in a new home?"

"Oh God Eddie, if I never saw another bed again, it would be probably too soon! My marriage bed was custom-made, a fabulous indulgence at the time, but Paddy would only have the best and, even though he wasn't always in it, even though he probably betrayed me in it, it was still a symbol of our marriage vows, the

166

marriage vows that *I* never broke. I slept in my marriage bed till the night I left Galway and sold the house with all its contents, and somehow I just can't bring myself to buy something as personal as a bed again – ridiculous and all as that sounds."

"A bed is a practical thing, Anna – the emotions you feel about something as lifeless as a bed are entirely in your head, are entirely of your own making," Eddie insisted.

"Well, perhaps you're right and I suppose if I don't get one soon my posture will be ruined and any chance I have of doing something with dance will go with it," she mused.

"So, it is agreed then, straight after our wonderful breakfast we will go on a hunt for a new bed?"

"Well . . ."

"Just say 'Yes, please, Eddie'."

"Yes, please, Eddie," she answered, almost feeling assertive.

And Eddie smiled again that radiant smile that could light up any room.

Demelza watched and listened to her new client carefully. The woman in her counselling room was roughly the same age as herself, dressed in a blouse of pale blue which brought out beautifully the violet in her troubled eyes, and a scarf of green, gold and pink that brought colour to the face, which was losing some of the pigment of youth. In contrast, her denim jeans were scruffy and frayed round the ends and her boots were splashed with flecks of dried mud around the toes and heels. Beside her on the table the woman gently placed a camera which seemed to be as important to her as any lady's handbag.

"Thank you for agreeing to see me at such short notice," the woman said, brushing a stray blonde-grey lock away from her ear with a hand that hadn't been pampered but had known real work all its life. As she did so a delicate blue and silver earring bounced playfully and Demelza smiled as she noticed a streak of dark-blue paint behind one lobe.

"I be only too willing to help if you tell me your trouble," Demelza said gently, smoothing her pearl-pink satin dress over her knees.

"Well, it's stupid really, but it's just my husband really upset me the other night when I told him about my first real art commission. He wasn't supportive and it got me thinking about all sorts of things . . . to tell you the truth, I'm not really sure I should be here at all . . . I've been through the menopause, you see, and perhaps . . . well, perhaps I'm just expecting too much of life at my age."

"So, Rita, what do you think the alternative be then – to lower your expectations? Do you mind if I call you Rita or would you prefer Mrs Skeehan?"

Her client squirmed in her seat at the suggestion of formality. "Rita is fine by me, far less stuffy – and being stuffy, being stuck to the past is part of the problem. Well, if I'm to be honest, I think the problem is actually with my husband Mossy. He's only a few years older than me but I just can't relate to him any more. He seems to be focused on who'll get the farm when he's dead – we've all daughters you see, no sons, and it's like everything is over for him, there's nothing worthwhile ahead. And while I see the children leaving the nest as an opportunity for us to grow again, experience new things, he . . . well, he even dresses so old even though he's only sixty-two. You see Hollywood actors his age all the time who still have the spark of life in them, still care about their appearance – it's not that I want anything special and I know he's a farmer, not a film star, but occasionally just occasionally I'd like him to make an effort and –"

"So the sex be not the best then?" Demelza interrupted.

Rita laughter was like little bells on the church altar. "Oh my word, what a question! Sure I don't bother with any of that any more – I have my photos and my painting to keep me happy."

"So why come here?" Demelza asked, propping her chin up with one hand as she watched the woman's flustered body language scream for help.

"Well it's not just sex therapy you do – it's general relationship stuff too, isn't it? And I don't know why I'm here exactly but it has definitely something to do with my relationship. Maybe I'm just wondering should I bother still being with him, or whether I should give him one last chance to do something more with his life and to take the journey with me."

"And have sex?"

Again there was a small, tinkley little laugh. "Do people my age still actually do it then?"

"But from your date of birth I see you're only fifty-seven, Rita, and people still have vibrant sex lives in their seventies and even older. Naturally, there might be some hurdles to get over, nothing insurmountable if there be understanding – arousal for lovemaking begins primarily in the brain, you see, and communication is key. Now, tell me, Rita, when did you last have sex with your husband?"

Rita's hands and feet fidgeted as she did some mental arithmetic. "If I remember right it was the night of Roisin's Confirmation."

"And how old is Roisin now?"

"Twenty-two and just out of college, enjoying herself in London."

"Ah, there be some serious work to be doing then," Demelza said, nodding, as she noted the clock, steadied her pen and paper on her knee and settled down and just listened for the next hour and a bit.

"So, Liesel, would you like to go shopping with me in the afternoon?"

Liesel stared at a fully dressed Mark as if he'd just spoken a language from another planet.

"For food . . . remember I mentioned it earlier on?"

"Uhm . . ."

The question was irrelevant really – it didn't matter where Liesel was or what her body was doing, from now on she'd be opening unknown doors into all the rooms of her head, living a dream life with David Ron Dwyer by her side.

"The shopping centre in Carrigmore is our best bet. Maybe there's some German style food you would like – we could have a look?" Mark continued, hoping for just a little show of enthusiasm. What the hell was wrong with her? It was like some alien life force had taken over her brain.

"Now?"

"No, I said this afternoon. I have to go to work for a

170

few hours, but in the afternoon we can go shopping and talk about car insurance as well. Rebecca really should have sorted out something about a car before now – I'm sorry about the delay."

"Rebecca thinks cycling is better for the environment and having a smaller carbon footprint is important for your image. Funny, even though I got wet and lost and the bike got a puncture, I really enjoyed cycling – in fact, I wouldn't mind getting a bike instead of having a car since spring is coming anyway."

"Are you *serious*?"

"Absolutely." And she was. Liesel had quickly realised that if she had a car she'd rapidly become a stressed-out nanny, ferrying the boys everywhere and running shopping errands for Rebecca instead of having any down time. Besides, she didn't care about stocking up on food any more – Willie had a ton of it and the butterflies in her stomach batted away the rest of the hunger. Cycling would also help expend the constant nervous energy that was circling around her core and bursting out into little ticklish bubbles of longing and desire from her head down to her toes.

"Okay, but we'll have to get you a decent bike. There's a very good bike shop in the eco-village, maybe we could look there later on," Mark agreed tentatively. For the life of him he couldn't understand why she would voluntarily cycle the wet roads of Ireland instead of being warm and dry in a car, but then she was a woman and if years of marriage had taught him anything at all it was that women were nothing if not unpredictable.

"*Danke*," Liesel nodded, unconsciously slipping back

into German as she snuggled up to the lovely hunky David-Willie memories in her head and Mark slipped off to work half-worried that when he came home his children might not be alive.

14

"I can't Eddie, I just can't do it!" Anna wailed, nearly having a panic attack in the large furniture shop in Carrigmore as bed-frame after bed-frame was shaken for sturdiness, as mattress after mattress was tried out by two new friends whose fully clothed bodies made the plastic bed-wrappers crunch noisily in virginal fright.

"It's hard, Anna, I know it's hard but you can't go on making a bed of beanbags and duvets every night – your back will be destroyed," Eddie cajoled.

"The Japanese do it – sleep on the floor – never seems to do them any harm," Anna sighed miserably as they lay back on a super-king-sized bed with frilly everything as standard: cushions, pillows, matching throws and duvets.

"Has Madam seen anything she likes?" the salesperson enquired, a big professional, smile on his face, not noticing Anna's eyes were fit to flood with tears and only backing away when Eddie made some obvious eyebrow-raising and frowning gestures.

"Why can't you buy a bed?" Eddie persisted as he followed Anna round the shop as she looked aimlessly at towels, home-ware trinkets, anything and everything with glazed-over eyes.

"Because . . . because if I buy a bed, well, what will I do then? It will be a big taunt to me forever more, screaming 'Ha, ha, ha, Anna Maguire, you've got yourself a nice big bed but you should have saved yourself the trouble because your days of passion are over!'"

"Oh, Anna!" From out of nowhere Eddie produced a giant, clean and pressed cotton handkerchief for her to blow her nose as her eyes began to stream and her nose swelled to bulbous proportions.

"I'm sorry, but I did warn you last night and again over breakfast this morning that I was a basket case," Anna sniffed.

"So, when you agreed to hire a tandem from the bike shop to get here you weren't being spontaneous then, you were just being mad, were you?" Eddie teased.

"Wait, that's it!" A definite mad look flashed across Anna's face as a momentous thought crashed into her brain. "It's a slightly mad idea but I could live with it – a compromise of sorts."

"What is it?"

"I think . . . yes, I think I just might be able to buy a bed-settee . . . that way the bastard won't be able to taunt me with its 'bedness' because most of the time it will actually be a couch, and I need a couch as much a bed – beanbags are a tad too studenty, don't you think?"

"Well, perhaps a bit studenty, not that I would ever judge," Eddie said diplomatically.

"A bed-settee it is so and this one here is perfect, the fabric so soft and the colours so easy on the eye."

Instantly Eddie's face took on a troubled expression as he pondered the bed settee. "Anna, the frame seems to be made of hardwood – that's not at all environmentally friendly, you know – and the lacquer on the wood, I would worry about the exact chemical content there as well and the fabric is definitely not of natural materials either."

"Eddie, it's either this or I'm going back to my beanbags," Anna bristled.

The salesperson was again hovering hawk-like. This time he was the one shooting non-verbal signals in Eddie's direction, signals that reeked of, 'Give the lady what she wants, mate, trust me, you'll be better off in the end.'

"Would you be able to deliver today?" Eddie asked quietly as he approached the till to seal the deal.

Mark put in a very brief appearance at work before he knocked off early to take Liesel shopping for groceries. Funny, he'd always assumed she'd like her food but now they were in the supermarket she didn't seem to be paying any attention to any of the wonderful culinary delights on offer. Ice cream, chocolate biscuits, cakes and expensive microwaveable dinners promising dubious French cuisine in showy cardboard boxes – nothing caught her eye. In fact, if anything Liesel was cruising down the aisles like a Stepford Wife, not seeing anything at all and not even noticing that the twins seemed to be killing each other in their double trolley.

"Liesel, I said would you like steak tonight?" Steak was the only thing Mark could cook but he could cook it well, but then he remembered she was a vegetarian.

"Sorry, what did you say?"

Not getting anywhere with his conversation, Mark pushed the boys around the supermarket himself, feeding them bananas, bread rolls and cartons of juice while loading up on essentials and all his favourite things that had mysteriously disappeared recently from the kitchen shelves and fridge.

"Wanna go and take a look at a bike in Cloonsheeda now – see what happened to the bike you left there after the rain?" Mark asked after they'd unloaded the boot and packed everything away in cupboards.

Liesel gave him another couldn't-care-less expression that made her employer wonder why he wasn't booking her on the next flight home instead.

The bike shop was quiet and Freeda was skimming over the festival notice for the May Bealtaine Festival. Something about the whole idea of a May Day festival seemed so novel but old-fashioned and she barely heard the shop bell tinkle before a broad-shouldered dark-haired man, accompanied by two manic little boys and a woman with long hair came through the door.

"Hi, my bike was left here a few days ago outside your shop," Mark began as Liesel bent down and tried to prise Sam and Jack away from a pink girlie trike.

"Ah, *you* left it! Don't worry, I fixed it," Freeda beamed.

"No, it wasn't me – actually Liesel was riding it. Thanks for repairing it but we've come here today to get something more suitable. Liesel, come over and see if anything catches your eye."

At that moment Liesel pulled herself up from her crouched position and as she did so her lovely light hair fell back from her face and Freeda heard the rush of blood avalanching to her ears.

"A ladies' bike is what I'd like, maybe even with a basket, do you have such a thing?" Liesel asked brightly and Freeda had to force her eyes away from the rose-cheeked beauty and force the cogs of her brain to turn.

"Yes . . . yes . . . of course, I'll show you what we have in stock, although we can always order something you might like from the catalogue." She led Liesel through rows and rows of shiny metal bells, spokes and bars.

"I like this one . . . this one is nice, not too heavy and not too light."

Freeda hardly knew what the young girl was saying. She hadn't fallen so head over heels in love since she first saw her Irish lover, Maeve O'Meara, throw her head back and laugh out loud in a sushi bar in downtown San Francisco and until this moment she wasn't quite sure if her heart still even functioned as an instrument of love – until this extraordinarily unexpected moment of a young girl with honeyed hair buying a bike in her very own bike shop.

As promised, the bed-settee had arrived just in time to be toasted by an evening glass of red organic wine. Eddie had already started on some fancy thyme and oregano meatballs which he was cooking up in a fancy basil and sweet tomato sauce. While Eddie cooked and sang bad light opera in the kitchen, Anna ripped the plastic sheeting off the couch and laughed softly at the racket Eddie was making.

"Well, here's to your new bed!" Eddie toasted as they ate their rustic Italian meal at the breakfast bar and knocked back another fantastic red bought at the exclusive wine shop in Carrigmore.

Anna couldn't help but feel happy as she clinked her glass and ran a hunk of garlic bread around her thick tomato and basil sauce.

"My new bed-*settee*, you mean," she corrected.

"Oh yes of course, we can't have it taunting you with its 'bedness'," Eddie smiled.

"And you don't mind too much that it's not environmentally friendly?"

"Well, it wouldn't be my first choice but then it wouldn't be right for me to interfere, Anna, especially since I've only known you for a day."

"Although it feels like I've known you for longer," Anna said sincerely.

"Yes, I know what you mean, no awkward silences – just like old friends – remarkable, isn't it?" Eddie added, circling the rim of his glass with his forefinger.

"And today . . . today when you took me for breakfast, I'd almost forgotten how beautiful an experience eating can be when you're tasting quality ingredients . . . handmade herb sausages and bread, that gorgeous spicy tomato relish and the organic chocolate and coffee to follow!"

"I'm glad you liked it, you needed spoiling," Eddie said, patting her hand.

"But I think it was the tandem ride I liked the most . . ."

"Well, when you said you didn't know how to ride a bike, it seemed the most logical thing to hire from the bike shop."

"But the thing is, you didn't give up on me . . . you

found a way to still give me the experience of a first bike ride, of feeling the sun on my face and the wind in my hair." Without knowing why, Anna began to cry.

"Hey, there now, don't cry," Eddie consoled her as he squeezed her hand in sympathy.

"It's just I've felt so dead inside for so long, Eddie . . . and, well, I know this is kind of stupid but I've been wondering what to do with myself since I got here and the thought came to set up a dance school again and usually, well, I know it's been a long time, but in the past whenever I put up the notice the phone would be hopping immediately, but *nothing* has happened, *nobody* has phoned and I just don't know what to do!"

For a moment Eddie was silent and he swirled the glass of red in his hand in time perhaps with the thoughts that were swirling in his mind.

"Too boring perhaps!"

"What's too boring?"

"Ballet . . . what you have to remember, Anna, is that you've deliberately moved somewhere a bit more Bohemian, somewhere where people might want to try new things. For example, I have a sister now and she's a divil for anything new – only last week she was doing this biodanza stuff in Cork and she's done every kind of belly-dancing you can think of – Egyptian, Moroccan, Bollywood – you name it!"

"But ballet, what I do best, is at the core of all dancing – ballet is where all the discipline is and belly-dancing is just fluff compared to it!" Anna snorted.

"Well, if ballet is the core of all dance, you shouldn't have any problem branching out then. Look, after dinner I'd like you and me to try something a bit different to open up our perspective on life a bit, okay?"

"God, it's not tantric sex or anything, is it?" she laughed a little nervously.

Kindness seeped from Eddie's face as he patted her hand and smiled his perpetual smile and reassured her of his noble intentions.

Pity, part of her would have really enjoyed tantric sex, she thought, as she drained her glass of lovely wine.

The boys were worn out from the day's shopping, busting up the bike shop and an hour in the playground and were already in bed after a fairly healthy dinner of pasta and meatballs, which Liesel had made from scratch. Mark couldn't deny her culinary skills were impressive once she had access to decent ingredients and she was even a good sport, making a meal with meat. When Mark complimented her though she just shrugged her shoulders and sighed.

"Eldest child – my mother expected a lot – I grew up fast," she said matter of factly, all joy drained from her face.

"So how is your mother? Have you called her to tell her how you're settling in?" Mark asked as he sat down to his own steak. Funny, he thought a big girl like Liesel would need feeding but she was picking at her vegetables and sighing at the effort of cutting through the nut cutlet on her plate.

"We don't get on too well – she thinks my being here is madness, wants me to come home to Germany and be a teacher or something boring – not that she has ever asked me what *I* want."

"Oh, and what do you want then?"

Liesel shrugged her shoulders. "Something more exciting than just teaching. My mother was a great beauty, a singer and actress before she had children. She would say to me, 'It's a pity you're not pretty, Liesel, but you have a good enough brain, I suppose.' Now she wants me to use my brain to be a nice quiet girl with some sort of nice quiet job, living near enough for her to interfere in my life every day!" Liesel was ranting now, the venom just past simmer and threatening to boil over at any minute.

"Oh right – I see, not the best situation so." Mark was beginning to feel uncomfortable. The conversation was getting far too emotional and the effort of making small talk was sapping his energy and, although he'd entertained notions of getting out for the night and leaving Liesel in charge of the children, he'd enough parental responsibility to see that at this moment she was in a strange mood.

"Liesel, do you want me to call you a cab and have you dropped off at Keogh's?" he asked, itching for the silence of his own company.

Immediately, Liesel's face lit up at the suggestion.

"The only thing is you're not tell Rebecca I let you off and I need you back tonight sober enough to help me with the kids tomorrow, okay?" Mark smiled.

"I'll just go and get ready and thank you, thank you, Mr – Mark," Liesel beamed as she ran off to get ready, leaving most of her meal on her plate. Being in love was doing wondrous things for her figure.

The phone beeped out a message and Willie Cleary

scowled. The German au pair was sex-mad and he couldn't deny it was a turn-on her thinking he was some Hollywood big-shot but tonight he wanted some respite from his newly found 'fame'. Deliberately he ignored Liesel's **'can we meet later?'** texts and started to ponder Tom's words that it would be his patriotic duty to go out drinking with the two lads home from England for the weekend.

"Skeehan, where the fuck are you?" Willie queried as he heard Tom answer the phone.

"In a feckin' skip ten miles out the road – there's some chairs I'm rescuing – what you want?" Tom snapped back in his trademark grouchy tone.

"Meet you and the lads for a pint when you get back?"

"Ah good man, I knew you wouldn't let us down with all this going-on-the-dry shite," Tom said, his tone softening immediately. "I'll just throw these few bits into the boot – see you there in about forty." The phone went dead.

Anna and Eddie were sitting cross-legged on Anna's beanbags while Eddie tried to explain the finer points of Buddhist mysticism.

"People often wonder how I stay calm, even in the face of adversity," Eddie said softly.

"Gosh, yes, I mean I've seen you on TV where people are expecting to design an eco-house and things go really wrong and they go nuts and I've wondered how you don't ever collapse into a heap of quivering jelly," Anna spluttered.

"It's because I practise the Buddhist principles of

stillness and nothingness where there is no form or feeling, no suffering, no fear, no touch, taste, sound or form," Eddie explained and Anna nodded, thinking that was an awful lot of nothingness alright.

"So we're going to leave the stresses behind, the worry about the ballet, the worry about your marriage breakdown and your children, everything will be as nothing as we journey beyond thought into nothingness. Shut your eyes."

For two minutes Anna did as she was told but, try as she might, she just couldn't switch her thoughts off. Why did nobody want to send their children to ballet, old hat indeed . . . were the boys okay and eating anything half-nourishing in college or living off drink . . . was Paddy in good health – she hoped with all her heart he wasn't . . . maybe she should go back to retrain in dance, she should investigate that a bit more next week . . . what the hell was biodanza anyway?

"*Anna*, I can actually *hear* your mind whirring!" Eddie snapped, temporarily losing a little bit of his Zen as his eyes rolled open like steel shutters.

"What? I'm so sorry, Eddie. Maybe I'm just more of a keyed-up personality than you – in fact, would you mind if I switched on the news? I haven't heard a bit all day."

Without waiting Anna switched on the national airwaves and couldn't believe her ears or eyes.

"*Good evening . . . more again on that somewhat unexpected story about TD Paddy Gavin being given a new ministry in the government reshuffle. We're switching live now to Government Buildings to discuss the matter with our chief political correspondent, Sam*

Quinn. Sam, some surprise in government buildings tonight?"

Anna just couldn't believe this, she *really* couldn't. After all the years she'd put in being the good wife, now that she was separated everything was coming to Paddy on a plate and that floozy Paddy had taken up with would be getting all the benefits of being a de facto minster's wife without the years of blood, sweat or tears.

"Anna, are you okay?"

"If you'd just excuse me for one minute, Eddie – nothing to do with your lovely wine or anything but I think I'm going to throw up."

It was after one and the lads were in the kitchen, making inroads into the father's whiskey, having a laugh, singing a few songs, smoking themselves hoarse and bemoaning the fact that they were soon to be on the boat back to England.

Willie thought he'd never get rid of his school buddies, then Spud and Hackett finally decided to stagger home, muttering something about playing a football match in the morning – as if. Only Tom was for staying and Willie let him stretch out on the couch before going into his own room, whipping off all his clothes and collapsing into the bed. Immediately he found warm hands around him and a devilish tongue working its way from his mouth down past his navel.

"Hello, Willie, you left the back door open so I came in and waited for you!" The voice was clipped but husky.

"Liesel!"

Willie had drunk too much alcohol and was far too

turned on to berate her for her excellent entering and breaking, not to mention stalking skills, but an hour and a half later, after a marathon sex session, a thought entered his head that even he, Willie Cleary, Sex God and all that he was, wasn't seventeen any more.

15

Henry Winterbottom drew his tall frame up to its full height and surveyed the dig which was rapidly turning into a mudslide as the rain continued its relentless assault on the land. All around him a dozen students, three quarters of them female, were on their knees, trowelling through the soil and beginning the painstaking excavation of the ancient Christian site.

It was Henry's idea to take the college students away in winter to be buffeted by the elements on the southwest fringes of the Irish coast. Up until now the college had mollycoddled the archaeology wannabees, never taking them away until after Easter to digs, but Henry's argument that the students needed to face the realities of archaeological excavations early on to see if they were cut out for the physical and mental demands of the job had won through. In real life rain, hail, sleet and biting cold were ignored by archaeologists who were often up against deadlines in commercial digs, with little protection against the elements except for a good waterproof raincoat and some decent pull-ups.

From a distance he watched the leggy redhead with the good looks of a catwalk model shift position to guard against leg cramp and rub her stiffening thighs. The night before at the 'breaking the ice' dinner she'd been somewhat standoffish – he bet she would be the first one throwing a hissy fit before they even broke for lunch.

"Right, what have we got here then?" Robert, a friendly PhD research student who was acting as supervisor, asked Rebecca as she took off the top layer of grass and began to trowel just under the surface.

"I don't actually know," she answered honestly. Her limbs were aching; she had known the dig would be hard physical work but she hadn't counted on how badly the muscles on her arms and shoulders would burn or how her legs and kneecaps would seize up from endless sitting.

"Okay, remember we talked this morning about how changes in the colour of the soil are an important sign of something going on?"

The information seemed vaguely familiar although after a late night out and a half-eight start on the dig, Rebecca was somewhat spaced and it was only half ten now.

"Okay, well, what you've got here are postholes left from where wood from the site rotted away." The supervisor pointed with his finger.

Peering past his finger, Rebecca nodded. She had spots in front of her eyes even though she had ditched the diet for the weekend – you couldn't be an intrepid explorer of the earth without some serious fuel combusting in your system.

"So what you need to do now is stop for a moment and draw this feature," Robert prompted gently.

"Yeah? Oh yeah, right, of course." Rebecca, who had lost the ability to form words, just nodded.

Drawing would at least be a break from trowelling and she'd be able to switch position a bit to restore some blood flow to her legs, although every bit of her was pinched from the elements despite being a walking clotheshorse of long thermal underwear, tracksuit bottoms, pull-ups, hiking boots, rain jacket and as many layers of tops as she could swaddle on her body and still be able to move.

Slowly, her cramped fingers began to draw the postholes. For some reason she felt she was being watched and looking up she saw Professor Winter-bottom gazing at her critically then look away. There was something about Henry Winterbottom that excited her and made her shy at the same time. Maybe it was the knowledge that underneath all that wet gear he would have a magnificent body from his years of field work and also had that brain that knew so much about the past.

"You did a good job," Robert said, praising her sketch.

"Back to trowelling now?" Rebecca asked, weapon poised.

"'Fraid so, soldier," Robert patted her shoulder.

An hour later and all she'd found was a tiny piece of bone which she bagged under Robert's instruction as competently as any forensic expert on one of those sexy TV crime programmes. Professor Winterbottom looked her way again and gave her a curt nod. It was no wonder she couldn't speak to him last night at dinner; he was that elusive mixture of brains and brawn that all women fantasise about and never think they'll encounter for real but here it was, all packaged in the form of the enigmatic Henry Winterbottom.

In bed, with the German nympho finally asleep, her head resting on his chest, Willie congratulated himself on having the stamina of a mountain goat as the light streamed through the crack in the frayed curtains, showing up the dust in the room hovering in mid-air.

He was having a few pleasant drags of a joint when the door burst open and Tom roared out a greeting, his throat raspy from lack of sleep and too much drink.

"Cleary, get up, you lazy bastard! You don't want to miss the five-a-side. Did you see what Spud and Hackett did to my hair? Came back while I was asleep and cut off loads of it, the bastards! Jaysus . . . who's the fine mare you've got with you in the bed?"

In fright a startled Liesel woke up and sat straight as a broom, her hand drawing Willie's dirty sheets self-consciously to her bosom, and Willie would have hauled a shoe at his ignorant oaf of a friend except that Liesel broke the silence with an astonished gasp and an instant prattling of both German and English words.

"*Mein Gott*, are you, are you who I think you are – Conan Mallon?" she gasped.

It took Willie, whose tongue was glued to his mouth and whose brain was ossified from drink and the few puffs of cannabis, a few seconds to realise that Liesel believed his layabout friend was famous Irish actor Conan Mallon. For with the pony-tail chopped off and the morning stubble shadowing his chin there was a definite resemblance Willie had never really seen before. Besides, Liesel had smoked a joint earlier and could still be a bit stoned. God knows what she saw through her innocent German eyes.

Tom's face remained a puzzled blank.

"*Gott im Himmel*, you're Conan Mallon! I can't believe it! How lucky am I? First, David Ron Dwyer and now Conan Mallon?"

Years of near-brotherly telepathy told Willie that Tom was close to blowing his cover, so with a scrunching of his eyes and a tiny shake of his head he warned Tom to keep quiet, and out of nowhere the 'luvvie' actor voice and persona took over.

"Yes, Liesel, this is Conan – he was here with some of the crew last night who were . . . ehm . . . talking a bit *too* loud, in the kitchen. Myself and Conan are making a new film with director Nic Gerard. It's very much a pet project of Gerard's, very small budget – in fact, we're not actually getting paid for this film – we've agreed to take a percentage of the profits instead, isn't that right, Tom?"

Tom's jaw was nearly on the floor with this startling piece of information, as he watched Willie nod furiously from behind Liesel's head.

"You called him Tom?" Liesel's face broke into a huge grin. "Ah . . . Tom . . . so you are a method actor too?"

Finally the twin-like telepathy from years of 'the Primary' kicked in as Tom looked to Willie for a cue and decided to play along with whatever was unfolding.

"Got it in one, babes," he drawled in a cheesy American accent.

"I *knew* it," Liesel chirped excitedly, clapping her hands like a child as the sheet around her chest began to slip downwards and Tom got his first glimpse of big, excitable German puppies. What happened next wasn't planned – it just sort of evolved in the madness of the moment. After all, Willie had known Tom since 'the Primary' and Liesel was a girl with such a big appetite for love that even Willie realised one man alone would struggle to satisfy her completely.

"*Ich liebe dich,*" Liesel cooed into Tom's ear. Didn't he just know it?

It was Rita's second therapy session. The silence, except for the constant whirring of Rita's brain, was beginning to get to Demelza.

"Well . . . anything at all, any of the sexy memories of your past coming back to you?"

Rita eyebrows were knitted. She was trying, Demelza could tell she was definitely trying. Finally, Rita smiled and her eyes lit up with absolute pleasure.

"London . . . our honeymoon, we did it in a chair in the hotel – it was very much like in that film, you know, with Richard Gere . . . *An Officer and a Gentleman.*"

"Okay . . . good, but it be still only one memory . . . think some more, remembering the Mossy of the past as sexy in the past will help increase desire, you see."

A deep frown threatened to crack open the front of Rita's forehead as she wrapped a strand of hair around her finger and dug deep into her memory chest for possible hidden 'sexy' treasures.

"See, what you have to understand is that farming isn't exactly sexy, Demelza. Mossy would never be one for dressing himself up in good clothes – there'd be no point. He did have a pair of jeans once, I bought them for him but he never kept them good, never saw them as anything special. Farming is hard, physically hard, and often he'd be too tired to even think about sex especially when we had the dairy herd and the children were young and to tell you the truth I was so busy and tired myself I was sort of grateful to be left alone, if you know what I mean."

"Right, well, the memory of doing it in a chair and of Mossy in jeans be a good start anyway," Demelza nodded, keen to wind up the session and give out the homework.

"Why? Why is it a good start? It doesn't make me fancy him any more, not now. Do you know what he said to me the other day? He said: 'Woman, at our time of life all we have to look forward to is OAP specials.'"

Demelza cringed, but she hid it well under her professional veneer.

"Well, like I said, we be a long way from the end but today be definitely a good start – trust me on this, maid. Now, Rita, have you ever tried meditation? I'd be keen to pick a nurturing goddess for you, someone strong who can be in your mind as you make your journey the next while."

"Oh, just tell me who she is and what I need to do – I'll try anything once," Rita insisted, half-excited, half-worn out from her session.

"Excellent, your attitude be excellent, Rita, having a good attitude be a very good start."

The northern-hemisphere bugs were still making inroads into India's southern-hemisphere Boy God but India was recovering slightly faster than poor Nate who was still either shivering or sweating buckets. In a perpetual feverish sleep he was making short bursts of snoring that were driving into India's brain like a pneumatic drill.

Not able to stand it any longer and notwithstanding her still weak legs, India decided to make a quick stagger to the spare bedroom. 'Ooh, in all the years your father and I were married, through babies, sickness and snoring, we never slept in separate beds, not if we were under the same roof and your father wasn't even a Sex God!' she heard her mother chastise. 'Oh shut up, Mum, there's always my vibrator!' she yelled to herself as she collapsed into bed and fell into a sickly, solitary sleep.

Liesel walked up to the big gates of her host family's house, her head and feet in the clouds, just in time for a very late lunch, and hesitated for a minute as the last few hours washed over her again and again. Unbelievable, it was unbelievable how her life had changed since she'd arrived in Ireland. First she'd lost her virginity to one of the most famous men on the planet and now she'd shared herself with his friend, equally gorgeous actor Conan Mallon. Naturally she'd agreed to their insistent demands that the liaison be kept secret, especially from the press, but who would have thought that plain little old Liesel Hoffman who'd never done anything exciting in her life would start having such amazing adventures?

The front gates buzzed open and she made her way to the door and almost fell through it, it was opened so fast by her employer.

"Nice to see you finally make an appearance for work, Liesel, but I'm sorry to tell you it's the last appearance you'll be making for work in my home," Mark told her frostily. "It's clear your commitment to this job is lacking. This arrangement just isn't working out, so you can start packing your bags – you're going back to Germany."

"No!"

The single word ran through the hall like the shrill notes of a whistle and Mark was momentarily struck by her very definite and very defiant non-compliance, not at all what he'd expected from a meek milkmaid type.

"I'm sorry, Liesel, but it's not up to you to decide. You were meant to be here this morning to look after the children and you were not. I overlooked it once when you came home drunk and unable to work but not this time. You're unreliable, you've proved it – you'll have to go."

"No, please, Mr Mark, I'm not ready to go home! It won't happen again, I promise. Please, I'll do anything if you let me stay!" she implored, her big breasts heaving with dramatic passion, a look of yearning, fear and heartbreak written all over her face.

For the very first time Mark's brain felt light with indecision. As a businessman he wouldn't hesitate firing someone if they weren't up to the job and had been given all the necessary legal warnings, but faced with an adolescent on the brink of tears and with his wife away from home, he wasn't at all sure what to do.

Then the boys suddenly made the decision for him.

"Liesel! Liesel!" the boys lisped as they ran into the hall from the kids' TV playroom and each grabbed a leg and hugged tightly with obvious toddler affection.

"Okay, you can stay, but there are *definitely* no more

chances," Mark said abruptly as he brushed past her to go upstairs and heard a cry of 'Thank you, thank you, Mr Mark!' in his ears and felt surprisingly turned on by her gratitude. There was something strangely glowing about Liesel the last few days, something he couldn't quite put his finger on, and for some reason he felt an overwhelming desire to have sex with Rebecca, but what was the point in having a wife at all if she insisted on playing some kind of silly mud detective games miles away from home?

"Anna, are you okay?"

Watching Anna watching TV and poring over the daily papers, Eddie was quite concerned about the ex-wife of Paddy Gavin. The coverage of him being sought out for a ministerial post was non-stop and the write-ups in the newspaper indulgently salacious. At every opportunity journalists and columnists got in a mention of his 'hot' new make-up-artist mistress and Anna's recent 'break-down' at the eco-village opening.

The tandem bike ride, breakfast out and the new bed-settee of yesterday were all forgotten as Anna tortured herself with any available news feeds from radio, TV or print.

"Anna?"

"Hmm?"

Finally Anna turned to acknowledge him but he might as well have been a ghost. Her eyes were eaten up with nervous worry and Eddie knew he might as well make polite excuses and leave.

"The train to Dublin – I was going to head back tomorrow but I think I'll head back today instead. I get the feeling you'd rather be alone," he probed.

A slight unconcerned shaking of the head and Anna was back in obsessive mode poring over a broadsheet.

"Goodbye then, Anna."

"Yes, goodbye," Anna said, in her own world completely.

Placing his white panama hat on his red-brown curls, Eddie breathed a sigh of resignation and shut the front door behind him gently. Anna was traumatised, he could tell – she had the same agonised face as she'd worn the first time he'd met her at Cloonsheeda.

Eddie was hardly out the door when Anna grabbed her coat and left the house. She walked out of the eco-village to the little cottage on the main street which was warm and brightly painted, with smoke lazily meandering to a cotton-wool sky.

"I need your help," she said urgently to the woman who opened the door in the late afternoon sunshine wearing funky pyjamas and furry slippers and with her wet hair swaddled in a white towel with a bejewelled hatpin holding it all together in the centre.

"Come on in, maid," Demelza beckoned as Bast wrapped herself around her naked ankles and tried to trip her up. "Truth be told I be expecting you for quite some time."

In Willie's messy bedroom on Willie's filthy sheets, two childhood friends in their boxer shorts shared their second post-coital cigarette of the afternoon and reminisced about their wild sex romp with a little German girl fresh off the plane who had spectacularly turned the corner of girlhood innocence.

"Fair amazing that was but weird all the same, and I

just want to make it plain now, Cleary, I don't fancy you or anything, okay?" Tom said, trying to sum up his feelings on the three-in-the-bed session with Liesel as he blew a smoke ring at the ceiling, got up from the bed and handed Willie the cigarette while he pulled on his clothes.

"Still don't quite know how it happened," Willie said as he propped himself up on his elbows and sent another smoke ring chasing.

"Sure haven't we shared everything since the Primary . . . but still . . . I'm not messing, keep your eyes off *my* ass – not everything is for sharing, you know," Tom said with more earnestness than sarcasm in his tone.

"Trust me, your ugly hairy ass does nothing for me, Skeehan, especially when I've acres of that savage bird's flesh to bury myself in instead," Willie sighed.

"Yeah, there was plenty of her to go around alright, but I have to admit, Willie, I think she was a bit dense to fall for it, us being two film stars and all – "

"Method actors . . . we're method actors, remember?"

"Method actors . . . film stars . . . the thing is, she's not going to fall for that crap forever. I mean, fair enough, there was always a look of David Ron Dwyer about you, but me looking like Mallon was just a trick of the light. And she's probably going to be here for a year at least, minding them kids. Sooner or later she's going to suss that you and me are just regular Joes and then she'll be right pissed off."

"Maybe . . . maybe we should take off for a while, leave her guessing."

"Dublin?"

"Jesus, Tom, would you ever think a bit bigger just

for once in your life . . . Manchester . . . head over with the lads. Manchester has the same population as the whole of bloody Ireland – there has to be a few models over there worth riding for practice – maybe we could even con some of them into thinking we're big time film stars while we're at it."

"What would you tell Liesel? That we're going to some film première or doing research for a film or something? Shouldn't be too hard to convince her – you only have to open that mouth when she's around and shite falls out of it."

"Leaving Liesel out of it, what do you say? Will you go?"

"Haven't been in England since we took the boat two years ago for the Good Friday drinking."

"Exactly, it's time you had a bit of craic. Got any money saved?"

"A bit, but could do with a bit more."

"A bit's enough . . . let's get the hell out of this one-horse town!"

16

Mark was on the way home from the removal of a deceased local businessman, where he'd said a few prayers through gritted teeth, when he was overcome with an urge to pull over his car and check out the blasted Blessed Tree Stump.

There was no one praying at the moment but the hacked wooden body was covered in rosary beads, small, cheap plastic Virgin Marys and jam-jars full of dying flowers. Damn – what he wouldn't give for the shrine to get another belt of the digger but, even though daily devotions had died down and the media were off the case, vandalism wasn't an option – yet. Sabotage now would only make the whole thing blow up once more. Annoyed, Mark noticed that the tree trunk was even spouting little buds round the bark. He felt edgy enough for one drink, partly because deaths reminded everyone of their own mortality, but partly because something about Liesel was getting to him these days. No doubt about it, the little German au pair was getting too big of late for her scruffy black Doc Marten boots.

How he'd like to pull them off and explore up those curvy legs, so different from his wife's, to the tops of her thighs and her soft, swollen secrets beyond.

"A *ministerial* post, when your husband gets a *ministerial* post it's party time, time to go wild, time to buy a new wardrobe of clothes, time to get yourself a housekeeper and get ready for VIP everything after all the long, hard, lonely years of rearing children on your own and shaking hands with every gobshite!" Anna raged as she tore up a giant paper hanky in her hands then fished in the box to release another smooth white sheet and destroy it by blowing her nose loudly. "A ministerial post is the full royal treatment on planes, top hotels all the way, international banquets – and he's gone straight in as the Minister for Transport, so you can imagine all the travel that would involve. And I've *missed* it, after all the years of hard work I've missed it and some young trollop is going to get all the fun instead!"

"You be angry, justifiably angry, let it all out," Demelza soothed as Anna unbolted the locks to her inner pain and a waterfall gushed from her eyes.

"And, when *I* was his wife and he was just a boring TD, *I* only got to go on two junkets away *ever*, but it was nice, it was lavish and maybe it sounds selfish to say it but it reminded me of the years in London when I was having a ball, living for the moment. Jesus Christ, I *deserve* to be recognised for all I did to get him to the top! Did you know for *years* I hand-washed his famous blue shirts? He was always too worried for them to be machine-washed in case the colour faded, and I spent *hours* ironing out every little crease and, God forbid, if there was anything big on like the Races I was always the one who had to buy the new ties and colour-coordinate them with his shirts and now this young bitch –"

"Be doing all the mothering for him now. After all, from what you say your husband be too much of a control freak to send out his shirts to the laundry. Now that he be a minister won't he be even worse for the tidiness?" Demelza queried.

Suddenly Anna smiled an insane smile from ear to ear. "You're right, Jesus, you're right – he's *her* little boy now to have clean shirts for, not mine – and, you know, he's fiercely ambitious – Paddy fucking Gavin has his eye on the top post in the land, always had . . . nothing will satisfy him until he, as heir to the great Gavin dynasty, finally nails the Taoiseach's job itself!"

Thinking it time to calm her down a little, Demelza interrupted. "Tell me, Anna, you mentioned how you liked the odd junket away because it reminded you of your past life of fun. Before Paddy, what be your dreams . . . what did you do, do you remember?"

Anna laughed out loud and then collapsed like a deflated paddling pool into the chair, feeling somewhat better but exhausted now her wild rant about her ministerial loss had been vented and bemoaned.

"What did I do? God, I was so young. I danced, I had fun, I snogged minor pop stars who wore make-up and frilly shirts . . . it was the New Romantic era, you understand, they weren't gay or anything . . . and I flirted with soap stars and gave West End stars the eye and when I came home to Ireland after a wild stint at sea doing the cancan one day and flamenco the next, I set up

201

some bloody good ballet schools around the country and made a packet."

"Dancing be important to you then?"

"God yes, dancing used to be my *life*, something I was always sure of but dancing is useless now, I'm too old and I can't earn any money. Do you know I put up a poster advertising that I was starting ballet for children and not one inquiry did I get, not one? I used to be the kind of businesswoman who always had her finger on the pulse, knew instinctively what people wanted, but that savviness seems to have left me along with my useless husband."

"You've moved into a more experimental community – maybe they want something more of the moment, something novel, something interesting and cutting edge?"

Anna snorted derisively. "That's what Eddie Ferris said. What people don't realise is that ballet is at the core of all these technically fluffy dances that are, as you say, 'of the moment'!"

"Then you should have no problem being a success. After all, you moved here so something about Cloonsheeda must appeal to your spirit. The 'you' of buzzing London from long ago?"

A curious smile appeared on Anna's gnawed lips. "You know, I think you've given me an idea and I think I might just have to run with it," she said gratefully as she grabbed her bag and made to leave for home.

The interior of the pub-restaurant was cosy and the lighting intimate as the archaeology students piled into the eatery famed for its fresh Atlantic seafood and

Guinness heavy and frothy as whipped cream. Every bit of Rebecca's body ached from the day's exertion, her upper body from trowelling, and the hours spent carrying heavy buckets of wet earth had wracked her arms better than the Spanish Inquisition. As she studied the menu she occasionally paused to rub her poor knees and calves which still felt half frozen and cramped from kneeling in one position but right now it was her lower back that was most troublesome. It was a map of tension that even a long hot shower in the hostel couldn't melt into soft submission.

"So what are you having?" Robert asked as he seated himself beside Rebecca.

She smiled, grateful that he'd sought out her company. Robert was an encouraging and sympathetic mentor on this dig. Best of all, he never judged her harshly as she was sure Professor Winterbottom would.

"It's so hard to make a decision, isn't it? I'm starving! My body says eat the whole menu . . . mussels, Atlantic salmon and a nice juicy steak with pepper sauce too!"

"A woman with a healthy appetite," Robert laughed. "I see you've already eaten half your pint. Sure maybe you should go for the whole menu if you feel like it? After all, you never stopped for a moment today – you were really focused, really determined. You'd never be the one angling to get under the tent for a break even in torrential rain, would you, Rebecca?"

Rebecca was just about to make a jokey answer when Professor Winterbottom pushed past the two and, leaning towards Rebecca, asked if the seat next to her was free.

"Rebecca, isn't it?" he said as he sat down beside her,

with the air of a man who has supreme confidence in his own importance and ability, and reached to pour himself a glass of water.

"I suspect you already know the answer, Professor Winterbottom and, by the way, it's Mrs Gleeson to you," Rebecca answered playfully in her usual brash-flirty fashion, not believing herself that she was being so bold with the man who in recent days had caused her mouth to clamp shut with fear – maybe she was already just a little bit drunk.

"Is that right, Mrs Gleeson? Oh and I should tell you now before we go any further, I must insist it's Henry to you," he said, offering his hand.

She shook it firmly, a hearty laugh escaping as she met his eyes and saw some unexpected badness peering straight back at her.

"Cow calving on the Nugent farm is in a bit of trouble – breech more than likely – said I'd take a look," Mossy announced, one hand still on the cordless phone and one arm already in the sleeve of his jacket – ready to go, like the SWAT team.

Rita hardly looked up from her painting of the Daly calf and just gave a slight nod. Breeched cows were Mossy's speciality in the parish. Whenever a cow was in trouble in calving season Mossy would be called for, better than the vet some would say, although it was his big stature that was to his advantage – the Giant was famous for his long arms that could pull and push where others couldn't ever get a grip of a newborn.

"So don't wait up," he said as he moulded his hat to his head.

Rita wondered at his words. Sure why would she wait up? All day she'd been trying to work with Demelza's suggestions that she revive her sexy memory with Mossy but try as she might she couldn't get any value out of her London *Officer and a Gentleman* encounter of nearly thirty years ago. It was hopeless, she thought, as she fiddled with the picture of the Daly cow on her canvas and cursed as she couldn't get the shading to capture what her eye could see in the photography. Sighing, she began to clean her brushes and put away her paints. Anger and frustration had killed all her creativity in an instant – painting was such an emotional business, much more than anyone would suspect.

As he walked to his car Mossy's head was racing. At this time of the year, he couldn't help but remember his father and all he learned from him about creatures big and small; they'd kept sheep in those days too and his father was always on the go once lambing began. More than anything, though, Mossy remembered the pride: the pride of being hoisted on his father's shoulders, and men and women beaming at him for carrying on the farm's name and, although he hated himself for it, he couldn't help but envy his younger brother, God rest him, for having three boys even if all of them were eejits. The phone in his pocket beeped a message and Mossy urgently began to root it out – maybe things had taken a turn for the worse with the Nugent calf.

Uncle Mossy am going to England for a few days could you lend us a few bob?

The message from his nephew, Tom, irked him as he switched off his phone. More than once he'd wondered if he'd leave the farm to Tom as his nearest male blood relative but he was like all this generation of young men: useless and only good for an occasional bit of lamping. Mossy cast his mind back to early winter when himself and Rita had a bad flu and couldn't get anyone in to tend the cattle and he'd got Tom to do a bit of work – the waster had forgotten to feed the beasts for two mornings in a row. Still, the Giant didn't have to retire from the land yet, but who to leave the farm to was a constant worry.

On the way to the Nugent farm he stopped off for a while at the Blessed Tree Stump. "*Blessed art thou amongst women*," he mumbled in prayer, an expression that was always on his lips, an expression that always rang in his ears from the birth of his first girl and all the girls that followed. "Sure aren't you blessed amongst women?" his neighbours would say jocularly after the birth of each daughter, and although he was blessed he still worried. He worried more than a man his age should have to worry about his lot.

17

On Monday morning the little church hall in Cloonsheeda held a healthy crowd of people willing to help in some way to get the first Bealtaine Festival off the ground.

"I'm *so* happy to see so many of you here and I'd just like to thank India Jennings, especially as she's come away from her sick bed to be here this morning!" Maura Simmons gestured towards a very off-colour India.

India made a small little cough into her fist – she didn't want them to think she was hanging around forever, although she had consented to helping out a bit more than she wanted.

As Maura spoke, Rebecca sneaked in and sat at the back to see what kind of dance entertainment might make the festival bill.

"Now just a few ideas. Apparently Bealtaine is associated with bonfires – not sure if we'll be able to get that past the Council or not – they might see that as a fire hazard. Basket-weaving is another thing that's traditional and India has told me there's an artist who weaves basket sculpture that we could get as kind of an art-in-progress project for the village green. Flowers obviously are something else traditional and of course the May Pole . . ."

Rebecca tried to concentrate . . . poles . . . yes, she really had to try and get her pole-dancing business off the ground . . . when she wasn't so busy, when she was in better shape . . . something to distract her from thinking about Professor Winterbottom. Who would have guessed that her new archaeology professor lived only fifteen minutes from her home? 'I wish my wife was more like you . . . since she's had children she's become such a mouse, whereas you . . . you may be a mother but you're so vibrant, so full of energy.' Again and again she replayed Professor's Winterbottom's tribute from Saturday night when his reserve had slipped as wine loosened his tongue. It was as well his wife wasn't there; if she had been, even a normally hard-headed Rebecca might have blushed at her presence.

"Now, as you know, we're trying to advertise Cloonsheeda's straw bale passive hostel and capitalise on tourist potential. A lovely man rang me today, thinking of completely booking out the hostel for the time of the festival. There was also a coven of witches interested after the tree-stump fairy article in ahm . . . one of the national newspapers . . . but naturally I declined *that* booking." Quickly Maura's eyes darted over to Demelza.

Demelza hid any hint of irritation but seized the moment to speak up: "Fertility – I'd just like to remind you that Bealtaine is the fertility festival in the Celtic year, so shouldn't we be representing that in some way?"

"What?"

"Traditionally it be the day when the God Sun married the Goddess Earth, it be the day when sun and earth united at the height of their beauty and power and fertility," Demelza explained.

"Really? Gosh, that's eh . . . interesting . . ." Maura said, her brow furrowing slightly at this unexpected information. "Perhaps, India, you'd look into the marriages-of-the-gods thing a bit more . . . see if we can organise anything relevant around that?"

India smiled tightly, made a short note and then blew her nose loudly, signalling her near-departure from the meeting on health grounds. Fertility festival, what exactly did Maura want her to organise around that? Fertility wasn't something likely to cross her path any time soon – her still sick Australian Sex God was turning into a domestic cat these days.

"I was hoping we could have a little bicycle parade – encourage people to think about their carbon footprint – maybe make it fancy dress," Freeda suggested.

"Yes, yes, definitely like the sound of that, make for good photos too," Maura nodded as she made a scribbled note of Freeda's idea.

"Would there be a chance for people in the community to sell some art at the festival? I specialise in painting cows," Rita gushed excitedly. "Not sure exactly how I could pick up the fertility theme Demelza was talking about, though . . . could paint a few calves of course . . . yes, maybe I could even have an artificial-insemination man in the background?"

"Uhm . . . well . . ." Maura began.

India had to escape; the conversation was becoming far too nutty even for a person like herself, well used to dealing with off-the-wall characters. With great effort she un-welded her sick body from the uncomfortable seat and staggered back home to find Nate curled up on the couch watching TV.

"How'd it go?" he asked, not taking his eyes off some stupid American medical soap.

"Same as always really, little power struggles already emerging, everyone wanting a slice of the pie, crazy ideas everywhere. Someone suggested that because Bealtaine was originally a Celtic fertility festival that that theme should be reflected in the celebrations."

"Free vibrators for the Sheilas, that kind of thing?" Nathan joked.

India silently seethed. If only he knew. Joking about self-stimulation was no longer a laughing matter.

"Nate, I'm popping out for a while."

"Bring back Vitamin C, we've run out!" he shouted after her.

Frustrated, India banged the door shut. Vitamin C – they needed more than Vitamin C to survive this relationship.

"I didn't know if you'd be here or not," India smiled nervously as Demelza opened the door.

"Left straight after I told them about the fertility festival – think I took some folk by surprise with that little bit of knowledge," Demelza smiled back.

"Yes, well, happens in every festival – people have different ideas," India ventured, feeling unsure.

"No point talking on the street. Come in, m'bird, come in!" Demelza gestured with a hand, talons painted purple with sparkly jewels attached. "I was just about to start on the book but that can be put aside if you be needing me?" Of course she already knew the answer as she showed India into the cosy therapy room.

"You're going to think this is crazy, I mean I'm only in my twenties, I'm healthy, have no kids to distract me and –"

"And you not be having any sex," Demelza finished with certainty.

"How did you know?" India gasped as she collapsed into her chair.

"It be actually much more common than you think. Busy professionals out earning money, maybe spending time socialising separately and finding there be no time for lovemaking, but there be always a way even when you be too tired to care."

"But it's not *me* that's the problem, it's my boyfriend. When I met him in Australia he was a Sex God and couldn't keep his hands off me, but now he's been too busy with work, too sick . . . we're not lovers any more, we're just, oh God, we're just roommates."

"Ah, it could be the southern-hemisphere thing then. Could be you be out of sync as a couple."

"What?"

"See, in the northern-hemisphere women like you and me, pet, be friskiest and men at their most fertile around September – nature's way of ensuring most pregnancies result in spring and early summer births . . . survival, you see . . . but in the southern-hemisphere, things be literally upside down and men are most fertile around March. End of March, at the latest. See if he be more interested then."

"Are you telling me my boyfriend's sperm is in the wrong time zone and that is why I'm not having any sex?"

"In a manner of speaking – maybe."

"And what if nothing happens in March, what if he doesn't come out of southern-hemisphere hibernation and ravage me?" India asked, almost squirming in her seat. She couldn't go without sex for that length of time, no red-blooded woman could.

"Not to upset you or anything but be there any chance this Australian Sex God of yours be a tiny bit bi-sexual?" Demelza asked, leaning in close to squeeze India's hand in case she slithered from the chair to the floor in shock.

Liesel was puzzled by the text message on her phone from Willie, but more than a little excited.

Gone to UK 4 a while with 'Tom' 4 voice coach lessns, wil contact U when get bak. UR my muse baby, I think Ur going to inspire me to do my best work yet. Tom says it too! LOL Willie.

"Liesel, poo-poo!" both boys screamed from the bathroom at the same time.

"In a minute," she yelled back. Voice-coach lessons, there'd probably be VIP parties too, press interviews, models and actresses and unusual-tasting cocktails at every turn, but *she* was David Ron Dwyer's muse and Conan Mallon also said she was inspiring. Wow, she was one lucky girl! What the hell was she doing in the middle of Ireland wiping the bums of children that didn't even belong to her?

"Busy, it was busy."

That was the sole sentence Sinéad had managed to extract from her husband about his weekend archaeology dig, before he dropped his clothes to be washed and headed off to his new office in the village development of Cloonsheeda. Busy, what the hell did he know about busy? She was the one who'd had the busy weekend, the crazy weekend in fact. While he no doubt had been dining out on gorgeous food and drinking pints, she'd eaten boring kiddy-dinners, broken up rows and fallen into bed exhausted every night having cleaned the kitchen, loaded the dishwasher, folded clothes, ironed and completed a load of other tasks that her tired body and bored brain had begged to forget. To top it all, two of her virtual fish had died from neglect, a fact which even now was bringing tears to her sleep-deprived, red and scratchy eyes.

What the hell did these archaeologists do on these digs, she thought, looking at her husband's clothes? Whoever said never marry a sportsman because you'll be scraping mud off their clothes and washing them for the rest of your life was fortunate they'd never married an archaeologist. Wet, soggy, muddy, grass-stained – Henry had wanted her to try out eco-ion-exchange washing balls for ages but, looking at the state of his clothes, she reckoned she'd need bleach and a power-hose to get them even vaguely wearable again. In the laundry basket, beside Henry's sniffy pink long johns and mud-clogged trousers, was her lingerie from the vacuuming and she smiled as she remembered cleaning in her high heels with painted nails. Trouble was that the nail polish was now chipped, her hair greasy, and circles were taking up residence like inky rock pools around the delicate skin of her eyes. The battle to find the goddess of her youth, her 'lost maiden', as Demelza instructed her to was hard but not as hard as keeping yourself in tip-top goddess condition. She must remember to remind Demelza of that when they next met for a session to discuss the on-going difficulties with her 'homework'.

When Anna was a politician's wife there had never been time to browse the Internet. Politics was always much more about reality than virtual reality – well, that wasn't exactly true either, bluffing was always a big part of the game. She remembered the time Paddy had bumped into a party of New Zealanders on one of their trips away and they'd begged him to say a few words in Gaelic about the state of the world and Paddy gave them a solemn rendition of the National Anthem in Irish – the only large chunk of Gaelic he could rattle off quickly and fluently without faltering.

When Anna was Mrs Paddy Gavin there was never any means of retreating into a private world. Now, being a boring separated person who didn't have to live in the shadow of her famous husband, the world seemed sometimes scary but there was a certain kind of relief in the fear too.

"Belly-dancing, belly-dancing, let's see what's so bloody good about it then," Anna sneered as she scoured YouTube looking for anything on the art. Snake arms, the goddess walk, hip rotations – she could do this – it was a piece of cake. She could teach this, but is this what she had studied classical dance for? Somewhat frustrated, she pulled away from her belly-dancing videos and began to check out the on-line news and there it was in full colour with a picture and all included.

Controversial New Motorway Goes Ahead.

New Minister Gavin announces funding for motorway close to flagship eco-village Cloonsheeda. Minister Gavin denies the new road will disrupt locals' lives and impact negatively on the landscape.

Anna couldn't help smiling to herself. So Paddy had a new ministerial post but obviously he had to become the fall guy for this decision, likely to be unpopular with the wider public as well as with locals. Smugly satisfied, she saw that Paddy looked tired and had circles under his eyes, despite some concealer make-up, but most satisfying of all to her well-trained eye – his tie clashed terribly with a badly-ironed blue shirt.

18

Eddie Ferris was all excited at the prospect of the new motorway which would clip the Cloonsheeda eco-village on one side. Protests must be organised against its concrete path, covered extensively by the media of course. After all, Eddie was a recognisable personality in his own right and his anti-motorway stance would show all the world, especially his serious environmental activist mates from college, that at heart Eddie Ferris was still an anarchist, a bonafide anti-establishment figure with fire in his belly who just happened to appear on TV once a week, open a few restaurants or trade fairs now and then for a personal fee and who just happened to be the 'mature male' face of an organic, vegetable-based hair-colouring company as well.

As he waited for the new make-up girl, who looked vaguely familiar, to get him ready for camera, he wondered what his old college acquaintance Ailish Calhoun, a Scottish eco-warrior best known for chaining herself in subterranean tunnels and spending months in a tree-house, was doing now that her last UK motorway protest was past the point of redemption.

"Eddie, I think we'll go with a bit of powder today around your forehead, get rid of some of that sheen," the make-up girl announced as she began to attack his face with brushes, fingers and sponge. "Hair's looking great today, Eddie."

"Not bad for an old guy, is it?" he said, fluffing his locks in the mirror.

In the background the radio began to blare out a report criticising the government's stance on deciding to route a motorway so near to a flagship eco-development and Eddie realised the make-up girl was listening intently and biting her lip in agitation.

"Upsetting, isn't it, about the motorway?" Eddie sighed as she worked over his face briskly.

"Like you wouldn't believe. I know Paddy is my boyfriend and all but, believe me, he's really been the scapegoat for this one," she answered in hushed tones.

Of course – that's why she looked familiar – she was Paddy Gavin's new squeeze, Lana Phillips. Eddie had seen her photo in the Sunday papers a while back.

"There you are now, all done," she said, blending a bit of make-up under his chin and looking admiringly at her work.

Eddie couldn't help but be pleased; she'd really taken five years off him in a couple of well-placed brushstrokes. But he mustn't lose sight of the important things in life and this Cloonsheeda business would be an opportunity to let the world know that when it really, really mattered, Eddie Ferris was still a free tree-hugging spirit who cared more for his eco-warrior roots than the colour of his hair.

Since her film-star lovers had taken off to England for

voice-coach lessons Liesel had been strangely moody and agitated, a fact which her Hausfrau had picked up on as she shooed her out of the house for some mandatory bike exercise.

"Liesel, after the weekend you had cooped up with the boys, you should get out and get some fresh air, have some time to yourself," Rebecca insisted as she foisted the bike on the German teenager.

With no friends and no knowledge yet of any other au pairs in the locality, Liesel naturally gravitated towards Cloonsheeda and was excited to see a camera crew and photographers in the village green. Perhaps news of her boys' small Irish film project had broken loose. She hoped they wouldn't think she was the one who'd blown their cover.

As she locked her bike to one of the railings in the green she overheard three women, all of them she recognised from the health food and coffee shop, talk excitedly to reporters.

"This is *not* good for Cloonsheeda, not good at all. It will put off more people from moving here and if we don't have more people in Cloonsheeda we can't move ahead with big community projects like a new primary school," Tilda said furiously, her arms crossed in protest, to reporter Isobel White. "My daughter came home from primary school just the other day to ask me about the meaning of sin!"

Maura gave Tilda a sharp look. There was no way she wanted people reading in the paper anything that wasn't 100% progressive, anything that might deter them from moving to her pet project.

"Yes, it is a bit of a set-back but we will fight this motorway and send a strong message to the government and to the world, that here in Cloonsheeda we are not people to just lie down and take whatever is dished out," Maura said, enunciating every word, happy to see that every word was being taken down or recorded by eager hacks.

"What will you do then?" Isobel White asked plainly.

"Well, as it happens, at the moment we are planning a first eco-community festival for Cloonsheeda for Bealtaine at the end of April," Maura said, congratulating herself in getting the festival a plug. "And I think it may turn out to be a much more political festival than we'd intended. This new Minister had better watch out – he's not dealing with amateurs here. Now if you would all excuse me, I have a very important phone call to make."

She needed to ring Eddie and see what his viewpoint was on the whole bloody disaster. She dug in her handbag for her phone. Smiling, she realised her eco-partner was already on the case and had left a rallying text message promising as ever his full and loyal support.

Having heard enough to realise the press-scrum had nothing to do with her famous new lovers, code-names 'Willie' and 'Tom', Liesel's eyes wandered to the front door of Willie's on-street hovel and saw a scruffy-looking old man in a brown knitted cardigan with holes in it standing there, chatting to a middle-aged farmer who was holding a goat on a rope. After a bit of talk a brief examination of the beast took place, the man seeming to press his hands against it and hold them there. How strange! She must ask Willie all about the unusual man when he came back from his voice lessons in the UK.

In his new office space in the Cloonsheeda development Henry Winterbottom mused over the new motorway announcement; then allowed his brain to go into sharp analytical analysis. Motorways were big business for archaeologists; there was so much to be recorded and documented and there was a guaranteed, extremely well-paid source of income for the duration of the build. Henry's independent company had worked on the first phase of this motorway before he'd moved the family over from the UK and started the process of building his own eco-home. For the life of him he couldn't understand the current fuss over this motorway. Progress had to be made and there wasn't much at stake except a few useless trees. He picked up the phone and began to dial. If there was any more work to be done on this project, he wanted to be the man to do it for a nice fat fee.

After forty minutes on her own with the boys Rebecca was busting for a sugar hit of some kind to accompany her freshly brewed coffee. Instead she tipped a drop of organic vanilla in her brew and inhaled the powerfully sweet aroma. The weekend may have been spent eating what she wanted because she deserved it after the non-stop physical workout of filling buckets with heavy earth, but now she was back on her eating nothing but vegetables and Miso soup coupled with the odd insanely intensive workout at the gym. Losing weight, especially after the age of thirty and having children, was bloody hard work but not she noticed for Liesel who was becoming more svelte and toned by the day. It must be the bike. Then again she seemed to have forgotten to complain about not having enough to eat – maybe she was copying her employer's no-eating existence in search of the perfect figure. No, it was something more than that, that faraway look in Liesel's eyes, that mixture of excitement and desperation. Suddenly Rebecca sat bolt upright on her barstool. Love, of course, or at the very least lust. Bloody hell, did something happen between Liesel and Mark at the weekend? Immediately she picked up the phone.

Sitting in his office Mark ignored his wife's incoming phone call, finished his second cup of coffee and tapped his biro against his front teeth in a kind of nervous tic. The motorway announcement reported in all the papers was a bit of a setback. Although he'd always known the whole motorway issue was a sleeping volcano, he'd hoped it wouldn't erupt until he'd shifted a few more units at Cloonsheeda. Bad publicity was the last thing he needed but bad was the only thing that was coming his way these days. Somehow the words that strange English woman spoke about the blasted oaks and fairies were haunting him. Mark shrugged his shoulders as if to rouse himself from such daft thoughts – he was a businessman for God's sake, not some half-mad individual who was in any way suspicious of the power of make-believe fairies.

With nothing to do but mooch, Liesel found herself wander into the local bike shop and Freeda's heart thumped in her chest as all the memories of a young Maeve O'Meara, fresh from the Irish countryside, came flooding back in an instant.

"Hi there, everything okay with the new bike I sold you?" Freeda gushed.

The girl seemed surprised that Freeda remembered her. Distractedly she swept a strand of honey-blonde hair back from her lovely young face and smiled an unsure smile.

"Thank you, everything is fine with my bicycle, but I wanted to tell my Hausfrau about the trailers you sell for bicycles. I look after two small boys, you see, and have no way of getting the children out of the house – I have no car. These trailers you sell, they are suitable for children?"

"Trailers?" The resemblance to Maeve was quite striking really. Freeda remembered how soft Maeve's body had been and how creamy white before her Irish maiden had got sucked up in the West Coast's obsession with scrawny and brown. Maeve's hair had been the exact same colour as this German girl's, long, flowing past her waist.

"Yes, trailers, I first noticed them when I came into the shop with my employer, Mr Mark, and his two boys. Do you remember?"

"Yes, yes, the trailers. I have one or two made up in store and there's more you can choose from in the catalogue. If you come this way . . ." Freeda gestured and watched as Liesel walked, her generous hips swaying.

"These trailers are okay even for Irish weather?" Liesel asked as she pointed to one.

Freeda hardly heard the question as she watched

Liesel scoop up her hair in her hands, exposing the lovely nape of her neck, then watched as she allowed it to fall loosely again to her shoulders like she was a model in a shampoo ad.

"The trailers, they are suitable?" Liesel tried again.

Freeda worked hard to concentrate on an answer that wouldn't have her gushing 'I love you' or something else completely and utterly desirable but entirely inappropriate.

"I will take a brochure and come back when I show my employer," Liesel sighed wearily.

When she was gone Freeda's legs began to shake so that she had to shut the shop for fifteen minutes while she contemplated brewing some herbal tea shot through with vodka.

Home early and determined to let her phone and computer self-combust with urgent messages if need be, India was preparing a very special meal for Nathan. Today he'd gone back to work, still a bit washed out after his combat with northern-hemisphere bugs, but she was hopeful that since the thing that turned men on most was food, she'd woo him with a nice lamb shank stew with lots of root vegetables and herbs, then get him sozzled with a bottle of wine and randy with some chocolate and jump him on the couch. It was all part of Demelza's tips for setting the scene for seduction and exploring well-known tried and tested courtship rituals. Tasting a spoonful of the soupy stew, India noticed an unfamiliar car pull up outside the house and then realised it belonged to one of the guys Nathan worked with at the hotel. Peeking from behind the blinds she saw the other lifeguard go round to Nathan's door of the car and help her boyfriend out. She saw Nathan stagger as his mate helped him towards the door of their home.

"What's wrong – are you hurt?" India asked in alarm as she met them at the door.

"Oh he's not so bad, just don't expect too much action out of him for a while," his mate sniggered, helping Nathan in.

"Thanks for the lift, matey, you can bugger off now!" Nathan thumped his co-worker in the arm and stifled a scream as the movement caused a shock of pain to course through his body. He collapsed onto the couch and India sat beside him.

"What on earth is wrong with you?" India asked when they were alone.

"I've been butchered, that's what!" Nathan squirmed as he tried to wriggle free of his track pants and spasmed a little more.

"How do you mean 'butchered'? Was there some kind of accident at work?" India asked.

"Well, it's been a bit warmer lately and I found I was getting a bit sticky in work in the big-boy department so I asked the beauticians in the spa if they do back, sack and crack . . . it's not that unusual in Oz with the hot weather and all . . . well, this kooky beautician says they don't normally work on men but she'd take a punter on it . . . I mean, I thought there's not much difference between guys and girls, right? Well, it was okay when she was just waxing my back but waxing down there . . . my balls have swollen up to the size of an elephant's and I don't think I'll be right in the trouser-snake area for at least a week, babes."

India couldn't hear him, didn't want to hear him. Next week the calendar would say March and if her Australian lamb didn't start roaring like a lion by the end of it; then she'd be looking for a new boyfriend whose sperm was preferably from the northern hemisphere and who'd be ready, willing and able to give her body a new lease of life.

19

"So tell me how you be getting on with things?" Demelza began as she smiled at the bike lady with the sad face. Not that Demelza really needed to know the answer, she could tell by Freeda's body language that she not be getting on very well at all.

"Say, let's see now, I've sold a good number of bikes with the weather picking up and then the government has introduced a bike grant for anyone taking up pedal power, a green policy I think they call it. Should be doing a good trade in lawnmowers too soon and I'm going to get in roller blades and skateboards for summer –"

"Not with the shop, maid, although I be glad things are going well, but with yourself. If you don't mind me saying, you seem a bit distracted today."

Freeda sighed. She didn't want to talk about it, she did want to talk about it, it wouldn't go away. "Okay, I *am* distracted, terribly distracted. I think I've fallen in love, love at first sight and what's worse she's definitely not gay, but still I can't help thinking about her. It's awful, it's wonderful but it's *definitely* absolutely that life-threatening disease called love."

"And that be very useful right now."

"Useful? What do you mean useful?"

"Funny, the moment I ask you to spend time with yourself, to pamper yourself, to know yourself, be the moment you decide you need to fall in love. Some people need to be in a relationship to feel whole, to feel needed, but until you start looking at your relationships deeply they will always end in hurt."

Freeda shrugged. Her therapist was obviously on a roll and who was she to stop such insights?

"But be that as it may, tell me about this love," Demelza coaxed.

Thanks to an icepack the swelling had reduced on Nathan's private parts but he had nevertheless developed a strange gait in order to make the occasional hobble from couch or bed to kitchen or bathroom. Although pain was never far from his face, and despite being on the painkillers India sometimes knocked back for bad period pain, Nathan definitely wasn't fit for work at the gym for the next few days at least.

"You really shouldn't be drinking if you're on painkillers," India warned when they pulled up outside Keogh's in her jeep.

Despite his discomfort, Nathan fancied a bevy now spring was manifest and Keogh's was open days as well as evenings.

"It won't make a blind bit of difference if I pour some grog down my throat or not – I've got the constitution of a horse!" he joked as she frowned in motherly disapproval.

"Nathan," India said urgently, catching him by the arm as he went to put the novelty walking stick she'd brought back once from Vegas into good hobbling practice.

"Yeah?" He had a look of controlled agitation on his face as India's grip was hampering him from his drinking ambitions.

"Oh . . . nothing," she said softly as she saw his need to escape.

"Sure?"

"Well, it's just . . . well, you do still think it was worth leaving Australia for me, don't you, Nate? You don't have any regrets? There's nothing wrong, is there . . . you do still fancy me?" she whispered urgently.

"Course I do, babe!" he laughed, disarming her with an ear-to-ear grin that just sparkled sunshine.

"It's just, well, we haven't, you know . . ."

"Haven't what?"

Haven't had sex in yonks, you thicko, isn't it obvious!

"Nothing, it's nothing, just me being stupid, go off and enjoy yourself." Abruptly she waved her hand dismissively, kissed him goodbye and jumped back in her jeep. Well, at least he confirmed that he still loved her and it wasn't the end of March yet – the end of March – the point of the spring equinox when everything was meant to shake off the sleep of winter: trees, birds, and hopefully men whose sperm was dazed and confused in the marathon swim from southern to northern hemisphere.

Liesel was standing in the changing room of a nationwide shopping chain in Carrigmore, admiring herself in a mirror. It must be the bike riding, combined with pining for sex and having no real interest in food any more. The mirror and the clothes didn't lie – she'd dropped a dress-size since coming to Ireland and was now a voluptuous but shapely size fourteen to sixteen instead of her more usual sixteen to eighteen. With money in her back pocket – Mark had ensured that her cash was now paid regularly – she'd enough money to have a cheapo mini-splurge, buying two pairs of trousers and a few tops to show off her cleavage which was now jaw-stoppingly curvy in her newly fitted garments. After spending a pleasurable hour trying on and whipping off clothes, she paid and was just about to exit the store when she stopped at the magazine shelves and newspaper rack near the door and had a quick thumb through some of the glossies. There was no mention of her lover boys being in the UK at all; whatever kind of voice coaching they were doing must be really top secret. How she wanted them both back, especially Willie. Despite her misery she was so glad she hadn't heeded her mother's advice and stayed in Germany to pursue a boring university education – the 'university of life' was turning out to be far more interesting. Visualising her future life at film premières, posing on red carpets and 'at home' magazine specials she hopped on her new bike and headed back to Rebecca and her two-year-old charges.

Rebecca was stressed; Mark had ignored all her phone calls. Where else could he be only in the office? Business was slow at the moment – he was hardly being run into the ground trying to sell houses. Her body wanted to move, to hit, to kick, to bite, to sway, to do anything to ease her tension.

"Rebecca, boys, I'm home!" Liesel trilled as she stepped into the hall looking happy and pretty and loaded down with shopping.

The role reversal wasn't lost on the resident Hausfrau.

"So, you found things to buy then?" Rebecca asked, a touch sarcastically.

"I think I went a little crazy but I am so hot from the bike ride I must take a shower – then I will show you!"

Liesel stormed up the stairs. Fifteen minutes later she returned wearing fitted jeans, a fitted top, high-heeled ankle boots and the tiniest amount of lipstick on her flawless mouth.

Rebecca felt the jealousy boil. She also felt fearful. Women never changed the way they looked, bought clothes and watched their figure unless they'd just broken up or else had a new man on the scene.

"Is something wrong?" Liesel asked, seeing the thunder in Rebecca's face after she did a twirl in her new clothes.

"You were gone longer than we agreed, Liesel," Rebecca said, deliberately not paying any compliments about Liesel's new attire. "The boys have watched TV long enough. Some games would be good, jigsaws perhaps, maybe Mr Potato Head? I'm going upstairs to do some study." And she charged up the stairs.

Liesel heard the bedroom door lock, music being put on and then the thump of feet. From these signs she rightly concluded that her Hausfrau wasn't working on her archaeology essays but was sashaying around her metal dance-pole.

Sitting in Demelza's comfy chair, Sinéad was restless as she bounced one knee incessantly. Sighing deeply, she stopped for one moment, uncrossed and recrossed her legs, and then the jostling of limbs started once more.

"Problems?" Demelza asked as Sinéad gnawed her lip.

"Baby teething, children whinging, one virtual fish dead in the night and husband . . . husband still alive . . . unfortunately . . ." Sinéad grimaced as she remembered the last-minute row they'd had when she told him this morning she had a 'pressing appointment' and he was the chosen baby-sitter. Furious at being dragged from his work, Henry demanded to know what urgent business his wife had that required him to quit his Cloonsheeda office and play stay-at-home parent. Women's business, she had hissed back and that was enough to silence him to a grumble. Anyway it was the truth – her mind and its problems were women's business, the most important women's business of all perhaps.

"Ah," Demelza nodded, "a lot of mothering, but you must find time to mother yourself to reacquaint yourself with your inner maiden. After all, the goal here is for you to become a born-again virgin."

After staring at Demelza for a split second and realising she was serious, Sinéad contained a lunatic laugh. "I've had three children. What are you suggesting? That I get my mummy bits repaired? Mind you, I read in a magazine once that it was possible – hymen repair it's called, isn't it? Can't see the point myself of taking that much trouble to become a born-again virgin!" She cackled a bit manically. The erratic foot shaking was now replaced by the drumming of her fingers on the arm of the chair.

"I meant to become a virgin in the ancient sense of the world. In the ancient world a virgin be a woman who belonged to herself and herself alone, she be no man's property. It means independence in every sense of the word, it be nothing to do with sex."

A woman who belongs to herself and herself alone, a woman who belongs to herself and herself alone. Over and over Sinéad repeated the mantra in her head. Was it really possible to belong to herself and herself alone, now she was a mother, a drudge, her husband's secretary, childminder, cleaner and cook?

"Now I'm going to say a word and I want you to say the first thing that comes to mind," Demelza said. "Don't worry about it sounding silly."

"Okay."

Demelza paused and then said: "Bubbles."

"Fun," Sinéad pounced immediately without a trace of hesitation.

"My sentiments exactly, maid." Demelza got to her feet. "Your homework for the week," she said, smiling as she handed over a small wrapped package and saw her client to the door.

Outside Sinéad pulled the paper apart and laughed out loud. Demelza's gift was a little bottle of child's bubbles and a packet of pink bubblegum. Without hesitation she popped in the gum, blew a huge bubble which burst on her chin, ripped it off her face, wrapped it around her finger and stuck the stretchy gum back on her tongue. Then she stuck her plastic wand into her bubbles and let the wind stretch the liquid and the sun find a trail of oily rainbows to mirage. For a moment Sinéad warmed herself with the memory of being a child of six or seven at her birthday party when her mother, an artist even then, had drawn full-size cartoon characters and stuck them on the walls.

Bubbles – fun, bubbles – fun, bubbles – fun. From now on bubbles would always be fun and, even if she had to fight for it, somehow she would shed her identity of mother and wife and become a born-again virgin, an independent woman who belonged to herself and herself alone.

As she walked down the main street of Cloonsheeda she absentmindedly blew another huge bubble which exploded on her nose and chin and saw the wondrous look of a curly-haired pre-schooler who turned her blonde head for a moment to look at her strangely.

"Bubbles are fun," Sinéad whispered to her as she passed and saw the child huddle to her mother and hold her hand tight.

But she was unaware that her own mother Rita was watching her with a sense of longing remembering too that in their day bubbles had been cheap, childhood fun.

Anna was startled and a little bemused when she opened the door and found Eddie Ferris standing there with some kind of giant houseplant in his grasp.

"Better than flowers you throw away in two days. So wasteful, cut flowers, don't you think?"

"The purpose of flowers, Eddie, is that they *do* die and when they do men are supposed to replace them," she huffed dramatically, one hand on her hip where she had tied a colourful scarf to help in the belly-dance shimmies and hip-thrusts she was learning off the internet.

"Oh gosh, I'm sorry, I've done it again, haven't I – I've brought the wrong gift?"

Despite a slight hint of genuine annoyance – Anna hated houseplants, she always managed to kill them –

she smiled. Eddie was a sweet man, not malicious in any way, and Anna could do with a little bit of honest friendship in her life right now, especially a friend whose partner sometimes stayed in Dublin a few times a week.

"Don't worry, Eddie, nothing is required when you're the gift – come in, won't you?" she said as she stepped back from the door and gestured into the kitchen.

"You haven't done anything more since I was last here and you got the bed-settee?" he commented as she set to brew some coffee.

"All I need is floor space to do my belly-dance shimmies, hip-drops and snake-arms, oh and of course the goddess walk. Here, I'll give you a demo," she laughed as she walked towards him in a straight line, hips-thrusting provocatively, hands alternating between being stretched out full in front or being cupped behind one ear.

Eddie's face flushed a deep pink and then turned a scary shade of purple.

"Very . . . competent," he spluttered as he went to pour some coffee.

"I'm actually quite enjoying it, this daft style of dancing – ballet is so disciplined, perhaps a bit rigid, but this belly stuff is a bit of a laugh. I mean, I wouldn't exactly call it dance even, but I suppose I've got to think of what people want these days. Paddy was always thinking about what people wanted – what do the voters want, what do the mob want? – he never shut up about it." She untied her knotted scarf from her hip and put it aside on the worktop.

"Actually it's about your husband –"

"*Ex*-husband. We're not divorced but he's still an ex

234

to me," Anna interrupted as she poured milk into her own brew.

"Right, yes, of course, your ex-husband is part of the reason I'm here, Anna. You see, since the motorway controversy started, Maura and I have been discussing ways to protest against this whole environmental travesty. The residents of Cloonsheeda and the eco-community in general are not going to take this lying down, Anna. There could be some serious mud hurled around and I just wanted to let you know so that . . . well, so you'll know how it might be."

"For Paddy? I don't care about Paddy, Eddie – if there's going to be a mud bath or even a blood bath, Paddy can take it – he's a seasoned politician, after all," Anna snorted.

"Not for Paddy – for you, Anna."

"Don't worry about me, Eddie, and definitely don't worry about Paddy. Really, I don't give a monkey's," Anna said decisively as she bit a fig-roll in two.

"What about your boys? I know they grew up with politics but –"

"I really don't know what the boys think, Eddie, especially as I haven't heard from either of them in a while . . . but that reminds me . . . can't see the boys eating it now so we might as well indulge."

Abruptly Anna walked to her fridge freezer and hauled out a carton of ice-cream and pulled two spoons from her cutlery drawer.

"Much more fun to share, don't you think?" she said as she handed Eddie a spoon. "Now I know I'm not much of a techno girl but I believe you can buy coin belts on e-bay for belly-dancing and I was wondering could you show me how to go about that, now that you're here."

Smiling, Eddie keyed in the words to introduce his new friend to a world of exotic silks and shimmery coins.

"Oh, that one! Stop there – oh, I do like that red one! Oh and, look, they do shimmery bras as well. Red, gold or green, Eddie, what do you think?"

Eddie jammed his spoon into the tub of solid ice-cream to distract himself from the exotic clothes he was viewing and managed to bend it completely backwards.

"Hey, Uri Geller, go easy on my spoons, would you! I'm a poor separated woman of small means," said Anna as she ran a finger round the edge of the tub where the ice-cream was melting slightly then sucked the white liquid off and laughed out loud.

Trying to cool himself down, Eddie made faster and faster inroads into the luxury organic cow's milk ice cream.

In a seedy lap-dance bar in rainy Manchester, Tom and Willie had the undivided attention of a Russian redhead and a local black girl whose shiny skin gleamed in the dimly anonymous light.

"So are you or aren't you then?" the lanky black girl asked for a second time as she shook her artificially inflated boobs under Willie's nose.

"Like I said, I'm Santa Claus and this is my friend the Tooth Fairy," Willie said for the second time as a smile curled about his lovely lips.

"We're gonna be skint after this for sure, Santa," the Tooth Fairy said under his breath as his redheaded Russian shook her ass in his lap.

"I know – time to head home, skint but happy," Willie whispered back. "Hey, gorgeous, do you mind turning round?" he told the super-pumped boobs of his African lovely. "I'm more of an ass-man myself," he winked as he waved some extra notes.

Grudgingly she obliged him with a fake smile, then at his request gave him a pay per view special of her bony rear end.

20

"Peter, don't do that to your sister – sit up and eat your dinner," Sinéad snapped as she prised her son off Jane and plonked him down on a separate chair. For a second she turned her back to fix a bib on the baby and heard a scream from Jane.

"Mummmmy! Peter pulled my hair!"

"Did not!"

"Did too!"

"Did not!"

Words were then abandoned in favour of tongues sticking out and, as the battle of siblings escalated, Jane reached over to thump Peter and in her fury knocked a plate of meatballs and spaghetti on to the floor. Two pairs of wary little eyes stared at their mother who was on the brink of anger so blinding that if unleashed it could descend into a very un-politically-correct smacking frenzy followed by a torrent of tears for everyone – and at that moment Henry chose to walk into the drama, his industrial ear-muffs already glued to his head, ready for feeding.

"Ready when you are, Mummy Winterbottom," Henry told the charged air as he placed an archaeology textbook on the table and sat down to be served, not once looking at the food. Henry was always like that about food, he never much cared what it was so long as it was filling and hot – years of boarding school, he'd told Sinéad, you learned to eat what you got.

"And *where* exactly would you like it, Daddy Winterbottom?" Sinéad blazed as she ripped the earphones off Henry's head and stared straight into his face with her psychotic mad-mammy eyes.

"Well, on the plate obviously, Sinéad. What on earth is the problem?"

"*Oh you're so bloody logical!*" Sinéad screamed as she slammed the plastic ladle she was using for meatballs onto the table and got under the table to clean the children's dinner off the floor, all the time seething, mumbling then raging about her awful life and useless husband.

"Would you care for me to help at all?" Henry asked as he bowed his head between his knees so he could carry on a conversation with his wife.

"No thanks, Daddy Winterbottom. I may be a complete idiot and a total drudge but I have it all under control as per fucking usual!" Sinéad reappeared with handfuls of spoiled dinner and placed the mess on a clean plate on the table.

"Sinéad, I'm concerned. What has brought on this spectacular outburst?" Henry asked, genuinely puzzled as his wife's eyes began to dart in her head. "What *is* this about?"

"What is this about, Daddy Winterbottom? This is

about 'I am woman hear me fucking roar!'" she growled as she ran her hands under a running tap. "Feed your children yourself, would you, preferably sans earmuffs? Tonight I feel an *enormous* headache coming on."

She flew to her bedroom. *A woman who is not the property of any man, a woman who belongs to herself, and herself alone*, she said over and over as she slipped off her wedding band and popped it into her jewellery box and did some deep breathing under the duvet.

A booming laugh started India from her sleep and rubbing her eyes she went in search of the sound. It was Nathan, his Australian accent loud and strong as he ended an animated conversation in front of the computer.

"Sorry, Indy, just having a chat with Big Sis Rosie, did I wake you?" he asked as he finished Skyping and swivelled on his computer chair.

"S'alright, I couldn't have been in too deep a sleep anyway," she yawned, her mouth opening wide under the splayed fingers of her hand.

"Well, you can't expect to sleep well if you've only been in bed an hour," Nathan spoke bluntly then he whimpered painfully as India decided to plonk herself on his lap.

"Sorry, babes, still a bit raw down there," he apologised as he pushed her off, oblivious to her happy, hopeful face loosening in disappointment.

"How's your sis then?" India asked pithily, not really caring about the answer as she pulled one of Nathan's fleeces over her pink and grey cotton camisole top to hide her now scowling face.

"Ace. She's coming over next month . . . hen party of some Irish Sheila she knows."

"Nice. She can take the time to have a bit of fun and get away from work. It's nothing but festival mania for me from here on in," India groaned as she lost her hands in Nathan's too-long cuffs.

"Well, Rosie's got no worries on that score – she's still a bloody layabout doing her PhD in marine biology. Don't know why she needs a posh education when all she wants to do is swim with sharks – won't be long before she'll get bloody eaten by one and I doubt he'll give a crap about any of her topnotch uni qualifications when he's gnawing her leg off!"

India laughed. She'd forgotten how much Nathan could make her lighten up and enjoy things, when there was no TV going or anything else to distract them.

"Any idea when you'll be better?" she asked, her eyes hungrily staring at his groin.

"Couple of days yet but after that it will be all action!" He smiled widely and India's eyes lit up greedily.

"Is that right?"

"Too right."

"What kind of action?" she asked smuttily as she batted her eyelids.

"Well, that's a story. Didn't get to tell you, you were home so late, but in the boozer today when I was talking to old man Keogh about this fertility festival – what's it called again?"

"Bealtaine."

"Say again?"

"Be-ahl-ten-ah," she drew out the pronunciation lazily.

"Yeah, that's it – well, he's hoping the Be-ahl-thingy will bring in a few paying tourists. Reckons he could be on a roll if he got something novel going. So I told him about the time I did some dirt-snorkelling back in Oz and how it's modelled on bog-snorkelling which is big in Wales and in one or two places in Ireland. So he's gung-ho for it now."

"Sorry, I've lost you. Gung-ho for what exactly?"

"Bog-snorkelling – you know, when you dig a trench in some boggy land and make a lane for swimming in with a snorkel and mask! It's mostly for fun although some people take it deadly serious. So when I'm feeling up to it, me and that big Polish bloke Jerome are going to dig a trench and after that I'll be in training."

"I'm sorry. I must have fallen asleep on my legs because this is too weird. I just *gotta* be dreaming."

"Exciting, isn't it? Your lifeguard boyfriend is going into training to win Cloonsheeda's first ever Bog-snorkelling Championship at the May Day Festival!"

"For Christ's sake, Nathan, you're probably the best swimmer for a hundred miles in any direction. What do you need to go into training for?"

"Babes, this May Day festival will attract swimmers from all over the British Isles, maybe from all around the world – competition won't just be local, you daft cow!"

"But it's only a few weeks away – even if people were interested how does Keogh think he'll get it all promoted in time?"

"WWW."

"WWW what?"

"World Wide Web, darling!" Impulsively Nathan kissed her on the nose. "That's what I love about you,

India, you think you're some big-shot executive career girl but really you're so innocent." He smiled as he kissed her nose lightly again, hobbled back to bed and crawled under the covers.

India joined him and as she stretched to get comfortable she inadvertently touched her knee against his aching dangly boy-bits. Nathan made a strangled little whimper that sounded strangely feline. Sportsmen – why did they have to be so bloody obsessed with sport, India thought as she rolled away and hugged her pillow tight.

It was only when her eyes started to go fuzzy that Rita realised that painting into the early hours might be good for the bank balance, but not necessarily for her vision. All of her being wanted to capitalise on the Bealtaine Festival next month and she was busy getting ready as much work as possible. Surrounded by canvases, she'd spent the evening and night adding detail and shading to several pictures, then loaded up a big flat brush to start on a large picture of a cow and two calves suckling. The portrait of the Daly calf had had to wait as she worked on bringing her painting to a wider audience at the festival, a paying audience! All she could think of was the money the festival might generate and how much she might charge for her talents.

Would anybody from outside the locality take a shine to her cow painting? Rita barely dared hope. In her most fantastical dreams she saw herself as a successful artist, living alone, with no children, husband or animals to distract her, of spending her days working when she wanted, eating when and what she wanted, sleeping when she needed, in a little cottage somewhere near water, perhaps in the shadow of a wood or a friendly giant of a mountain, a self-sustainable life where she would support herself through her own talents, hobnob with film-makers, actors, painters, any and all of those with a theatrical or artistic bent.

Wiping her brushes on an old rag she ran them under water, careful to tease out the paint from the bristles and stand them upright in a jar on her windowsill. Yawning, she climbed the stairs and slipped into her nightdress which was waiting on a chair outside her bedroom door. Like a cat she slunk under the covers and heard her husband mumble his most important thoughts from the day out loud.

"Decided – getting some sheep to go with the cattle," Mossy murmured, then satisfied he rolled away and whistled softly through his teeth as his head moulded into the pillow. Beside him Rita's heart went cold in her chest as Mossy's annoying breathy little snorts turned to snores. So he dreamed of livestock – he not only lived livestock, he dreamed of livestock too. At a time when she wanted to cut her connections to everything unnecessary, her husband wanted to burden them in their later years with even more responsibility and his desires confirmed what she'd probably known for some time: they weren't on the same wavelength any more – he would never stop being a farmer. Maybe it was just that two people outgrew each other, maybe it was that over decades two people could shed their personalities and mutate into something entirely different and unexpected. What she knew for certain was that the man who lay beside her, heavy of limb and reeking of sweat, who once had sex with her Richard Gere style in a hotel room – that man had disappeared or maybe had never existed at all. As much as she tried, there was no magic silk that could be woven between herself and Mossy any more. Like the Gordian Knot, it would be quicker and better for them to just sever their connection.

Save for the red digital display of her alarm-clock radio, when Freeda awoke heart thumping, her breath shallow and her mind racing as fast as her pulse, she was surrounded by blackness. Three in the morning, she noted as she snapped upright from her dreams, took a frightened deep breath and eased herself slowly back onto her pillows. What dreams! She hadn't dreamt such dreams in a very long time – erotic dreams of the beautiful young German girl, her tantalising hair falling about her sweet face, interspersed with dreams of Maeve on the beach, the Pacific Ocean crashing all around her ankles, confusing dreams, disturbing dreams, stupid dreams and all of them pointless.

Maeve was no more and it wasn't as if she was going to make a move on the German au pair – she wasn't the kind of lesbian who would make a move on a straight woman just to see if they were for turning, even for one night. All of a sudden she realised what was wrong and the knowledge made her feel vulnerable, needy and incredibly angry. I'm lonely, she acknowledged. I'm lonely, I'm angry, angry that I'll never know love again – angry, lonely and wary.

Kicking the bedclothes, Freeda tried to make herself comfortable, to will sleep to come and claim her troubled mind, but after half an hour of tossing she lit four fat white candles and placed them at intervals around the white porcelain of her bath, ran a steady stream of warm water and perfumed it with heady geranium oil, then allowed her body to give in to the soft caress. Strength, give me strength, please give me strength, she said over and over in her mind as she called up her inner goddess and meditated on the past, the present and most hopefully of all, the future, her muscles relaxing, her eyelids surrendering to the warmth of the present, her mind sinking into acceptance and something else – something close to peace.

21

"Well, Tooth Fairy, my man, it's back to the homestead for us two chancers," Willie said gloomily to Tom as the provincial bus stopped at Cloonsheeda, its engine vibrating like an asthmatic having an impromptu attack. They got out and it waddled down the windy road with its last remaining passengers.

"Yep, glad to be back," Tom said as he hoisted his bag firmly onto his back, then pulled his collar closer to his chin.

"You're shitting me?" Willie asked incredulously as Tom made to light a fag, cupping his hands in close against the breeze.

"Nope, it was great to get away alright, broaden the horizons and all that but, believe you me, I *am* glad to be back."

"To this shithole? Christ, Tom, we've just been in a major city in a country of millions and you're *glad* to be back in this pissy little village?"

"Well, all I want is to get a nice pint into me at Keogh's," Tom announced brightly, delighting as nicotine coursed through his veins after the long drug-free bus ride.

"Jesus, man, you disappoint me, really you do." Willie shook his head slowly as he shuffled his own bag into the most comfortable position on his back and took long strides towards home.

"Well, what about doing a bit of a hit and run for some food later on at the dumpsters before we hit the pub? You can bet supplies are at an all-time low at home and I'm the man of the house." Tom followed behind at a half-run, his cigarette lying idle between his fingers.

"For Christ's sake, can't I live the big dream of bright lights and easy women for just a little while longer?" Willie asked, stopping suddenly and facing his friend.

"Come on, man, we had a good time but now the life of bullshit is over. Fancy a bowl of soup and a pint in Keogh's?"

Briskly, Willie shook his head. He was feeling agitated at being back in Cloonsheeda and had half a notion to keep on walking back towards civilisation: anywhere else on the planet.

"Well, I'm going to have a lovely kip in the afternoon before heading out for Keogh's again tonight," Tom announced.

"Don't count me in – this is the night the father goes for a drink with his lady friend and usually stays over."

"And, let me guess, this is the night you'll be contacting your *lady* friend hoping to get the leg over."

Immediately Willie's face clammed up; he could see the front door of the cottage and wanted to be off inside.

"I wonder did she miss you . . . wonder did she miss *me*?" Tom asked mischievously, raising one dark eyebrow, then taking a kiss of his cigarette, knowing well that he was getting under his best friend's skin.

"That time was a once-off, never to be repeated," Willie scowled.

"Serious? Ah well, nice little memory . . . hey, what say I pick you up around seven for a lovely spot of rubbish-rummaging. Don't look so sour, Cleary – have you forgotten – it's my turn to smell the bin-juice." He thumped Willie a little too hard near his collar bone, then rubbing his hands together felt the magnetic pull of Keogh's draw him near.

"You be radiant, maid," Demelza smiled as Anna sat in front of her, her hair teased into little curls, courtesy of the new curling tongs she had bought on a whim in Carrigmore, her nails painted a vibrant purple, her mouth glossed seductively and her eyelids shimmery in heavy Egyptian blue-and-green glitter.

"I *feel* radiant," Anna laughed as she kicked a shoe at the end of her foot, then kicked both shoes off completely and curled her legs under her like a smugly satisfied cat.

"So what brings this pleasure? It wouldn't be that your ex-husband be in a spot of trouble over this new motorway – might make a wife feel smugly satisfied that?" Demelza teased and Anna laughed easily.

"Paddy? Let him stew, but no, it's not my ex-husband and his problems that has me feeling good but the old reliable – sex, fabulous, spontaneous, unexpected sex – I think it may even have been some of that tantric stuff too it was so good."

"A new lover then – when did that start?"

Anna coloured slightly and then frowned as if she was trying to compose the right answer. "Oh, well, it started off with us having a few chats about this and that, life, that kind of thing . . . we were having a laugh, having some wine, he was helping me buy some belly-dance items over the computer and . . . oh God, now that I think about it, maybe it wasn't such a good idea after all, especially as he's technically in a relationship and I did all the drunken seducing . . ." Anna trailed off as she bit her underlip and looked out the window at clouds that clung like great misshapen mushrooms in the sky.

"Well, life rarely be about plans and sometimes even that be for the best," Demelza sympathised as she kicked off her own shoes and curled them under her ample rear end.

"It's just, it's just, well, ever since the split with Paddy, foolish though it may sound, I don't really know what I like any more. Some days I'm optimistic, I think 'Anna girl, you're doing okay' but every day it's like I'm trying to figure out stuff so I can file it away, so I can say, 'Oh, you don't like that, do you, Anna?' or 'That turned out marvellous in the end, who would have thought, Anna?' and it's ridiculous, it's ridiculous that I should be doing this 'Who am I?' searching at my age."

"The wheel of life be always turning and we have to keep turning with it or be crushed, but you be right to caution yourself. Until we know ourselves we often repeat our mistakes."

"It's just . . . I'm lonely. There, I admit it," Anna blurted out. "After all these years being married I still miss it . . . that connection with another human being . . . even though Paddy was married more to the political life than to me, even though he was at best a complete egomaniac and a constant gobshite, and even though I wish I had the strength to be my own woman, to not care if I have a man about the place – the truth is I *do* mind, the truth is I don't know if I could ever be like you, Demelza, happy in yourself, happy in your own company."

"Yes, I be happy in my own company," Demelza acknowledged as Bast stuck a determined paw around the door and, pushing it ajar with her nose, padded slowly over to her mistress and sprang cheekily onto her lap.

"A cat, maybe I should get a cat," Anna mused as the animal nuzzled into Demelza's waist, demanding to be noticed and spoiled.

"You could do worse," Demelza said lightly as she responded to Bast's affection with the lightest of rubs then sent her on her way.

"So what is it that I do next? What do I do with this – relationship I've started?" Anna asked, feeling suddenly panicky.

"Well, there be choices, there always be choices," Demelza nodded sagely.

Anna looked at Demelza askance, her agitation etched onto her features.

"Fancy a nice brew – I think we be needing a longer session?" Demelza asked, buying some time.

"How goes it, young Skeehan?" Keogh saluted Tom as he walked through the door and sat down at the bar next to the golden-haired Aussie and the strapping big Pole.

"A pint for the returning emigrant, if you please, landlord," Tom plamásed as he met Jasper Keogh's bemused eye.

"Oh yes, and where are you back from then?" the publican asked with a wink to Nathan as he handed the young Australian his change for his pint of light ale.

"Where am I back from? What class of landlord do you call yourself not knowing the business of your regulars? England, man! No work of course for a young fella of my talents, but sure myself and Cleary had a blast of a week all the same," Tom breezed as he fished for some change in his pocket.

"I'll be sure to tell your uncle that when I see him so," Keogh teased lightly and Tom's joyful expression fled; Uncle Mossy's few bob had helped keep the pints flowing and paid for a lap-dance, but Tom was at a loss as to know how he'd pay his uncle back his loan in the near or even distant future.

"Not much work anywhere," the meaty-armed Jerome said as he sucked his pint of beer slowly out of the glass, cradling it protectively, from time to time turning it in his hand to gaze sadly at its frothy disappearance down the glass.

"Well, none of us these days can afford to fall asleep on the job when it comes to making money and, like I've said already, I'm grateful to you lads for that idea about the bog-snorkelling for the festival next month," Keogh said with a curt nod to Nathan as he cleaned up a spill of drink on the counter with a large dirty-looking grey cloth.

"As am I grateful to you for the offer of work digging your bog-snorkelling hole," Jerome said back, raising his glass.

"What's all this about bog-snorkelling? What the fuck have I missed while I was away?" Tom asked jocularly as he inhaled his first bit of froth and was suckered with pleasure.

"I am digging a hole for Mr Boss tomorrow, four or five feet deep," the Pole said immediately, staking ownership of the job, which was alright with Tom – digging a trench four or five feet deep sounded too much like prison work for a youth of his lazy disposition.

"Then when the work is done I'm gonna swim in it," Nathan announced.

Tom gave him a look of total disbelief. "I know I was only reared here and all but what fucking bog are ye all talking about?"

"The scrap of waste bog-land at the side of the pub – there's a drain running along one side which is at right angles to the small river, so we're just tidying the drain up, taking out stones and silt and making it a bit deeper and the backflow from the river will fill it, shouldn't be more than a day's work or two – our Polish friend here is doing the job for us," Jasper Keogh explained as he shone up a pint glass with a raggedy tea towel.

Seeing Tom's jaw loose with disbelief Nathan launched in with further explanation.

"See, old man Keogh here is hoping to turn the bog-snorkelling into a national event as part of the festival with a bit of a barbie and a few beers for the spectators," Nathan announced cheerfully. "Course I'll be staying away from all that temptation when I'm in training because I'm in it to win! This here is me last pint for a month, mate, and then it's forty lengths and more a day – in the pool, that is, until I can get into the bog itself!"

"You're all fucking mad, do you know that?" Tom laughed. "Wait till I tell Willie, though – he thinks nothing happens in our pissy little village, but this shit is priceless!"

"Will he come in tonight with the pipes, do you think?" Keogh asked. "Have a céilí on in the backroom – the TV crowd are coming in to film it."

"Ah, it's not those pipes he's interested in at the moment. Could tell you a few stories there, Keogh my man, but you'd never fecking believe it!" Tom laughed, his eyes full of mischief.

At dinner Rebecca caught Mark taking a sneaky look at Liesel's chest in one of her new low-cut, tight-fitting supermarket tops and found herself seething ever so slightly like a pot on simmer, never betraying the fact that at any minute it might rage upwards and boil over in a scalding fury. Out of emotions suspiciously close to burning anger and spiteful jealousy, Rebecca hatched a plan to banish the object of her frustration out of her sight for the night.

"There's a céilí in the village tonight in Keogh's pub . . . read about it in the local paper," Rebecca said in a breathless rush of well-concealed hostility as Liesel began to stack the dishwasher for the night. "It's a one-off session . . . an Irish language programme is coming out to Cloonsheeda to make a documentary and it seems Keogh's are putting on a bit of a show."

Liesel looked back vacantly; it was the same far away expression that was beginning to get on Rebecca's nerves the last while.

"You said it was one of the things you wanted to do,

remember? The *real* Irish experience, set dancing, céilí dancing? I'll give you an advance on your wages and even drop you in if you like," Rebecca continued matter-of-factly as she hastened to stack the cutlery drawer with extra knives.

"But I won't know anyone there," Liesel protested as her phone beeped out a message. Scrolling down the text she saw it was from Willie asking her plans for later on and her face flushed with pleasure as she realised he was back and still interested in seeing her. She obviously had something special, something that celebs and models couldn't give him, but then again she was his muse. "But no matter, people there are friendly, I remember from before, I'd *love* to go, not too early though. Things only liven up in Irish pubs later on, yes?"

Rebecca looked at her au pair askance for a moment but said nothing – she was just glad Liesel would be out of her house for the next few hours at least so she could roar at her husband for having a roving eye without the hired help overhearing her every angry word.

As Rebecca drove off from Cloonsheeda, Liesel waved an overly obvious goodbye then entered the wooden doors of the pub and searched for her phone in her bag, desperate to access her latest text from Willie and find out his plans.

"Babes, come see me at the cottage after ten, 3 short nocks and 2 lng, make sure UR not folowd," came the precise instructions.

It was *so* exciting, *he* was so exciting; she thought as she walked as fast as her new red high heels would take her and after the last long rap on the door found him waiting just inside desperate to kiss her and maul her on an armchair inside his old-fashioned kitchen. So mad he was to be with her that they never even made it to Willie's smelly bedroom.

"You missed me when you were in London?" she simpered as she began to undo the three small buttons at the corner of the top she'd been wearing before he ripped it off in a frenzy.

"Of course," he said covering his lie lightly, as he tugged on her innocent heart with a thin cord of a smile. "Cake? I have some of the same kind you liked before, chocolate and with cherries?"

"Let me get it," she said, moving to the fridge, and as before she was amazed at how many packages were stuffed inside: meats, cheeses, bags of salad, desserts and lots of glass bottles, one of Greek green olives stuffed with feta cheese. Strangely, the labels were torn off most of the produce inside, a fact which bothered her as she held some items up and asked Willie to explain their ravaged state.

Since he'd invited her Willie had ripped the labels off the packages himself in case she thought his out-of-date food suspicious. Now he blurted out an elaborate explanation, amazed at the nonsensical lies that fell out of his mouth whenever Liesel was around. "Pork, some of it is pork, you'd be surprised the amount of foods that contain pork, even foods you would never think of – yoghurt for example, full of it. Some of the crew is Jewish, not all of them practising, but still when we're having lunch they don't always want to be reminded that they may be eating pork."

"Oh!" Liesel shut the fridge, accepting his explanation, then a look of puzzlement crossed her face and a vertical frown appeared between her brows. "That reminds me, there was something else I meant to ask . . . I came here on my bicycle one day when you were away, and saw a strange old man at your house talking to another man with an animal, and the first man put his hands on the animal somehow – I think it was a goat."

"Ah . . . that would have been the animal handler most likely. I have a few animal scenes in this film – the animal handler checks them all out beforehand, makes sure all of them are in good health and none of them are vicious."

"A vicious goat?"

"You'd be surprised at how vicious goats can be. I've worked with a few of them and an injury to my face could set back filming by months as I'm sure you can imagine. Why don't we stop talking about goats though? Let's head to the bedroom, take a few slices of cake with us, although you're the only dessert I need, Liesel!" Willie smiled, laying the compliments on as thick as the Black Forest Gateau he liked to feed her by the forkful.

In bed, having thrashed around with the lights on for the next two hours, Willie was enjoying a post-coital cigarette, blowing the smoke out indulgently like some carefree millionaire rock star when Liesel, who was nestled into his chest, scared the life out of him with nothing more than the English language.

"I love you," she whispered as her fingers played with his left nipple.

"What? Ow, stop doing that, would you – it hurts!"

"Did you not hear what I said? I love you, David," Liesel said authoritatively, sitting fully upright and grabbing the sheet round her chest.

"*Willie!* Remember I need to stay in character!" he corrected as he began to cough hard.

"No, David, you are David Ron Dwyer and I don't want to play games any more," Liesel said, suddenly petulant.

"Ehm – would you like some cake – there's loads left?" Willie said nervously, trying to distract her thoughts as he raised a forkful of the chocolate gateau to her lips but her eyes shone defiantly as she clamped her mouth shut into an angry, sulky line and pushed his hand away.

"It is not your cake I need but your words of love. We have something special here, David, don't we?" Liesel trembled as she pulled his cigarette roughly from his mouth and stubbed it out in the cake.

"Liesel . . . the thing is . . ."

The door opened sharply and in the wooden frame, with a fake look of surprise softened with alcohol on his face, stood Tom.

"Came in the back door, saw the light on, thought you might be up with some of the – eh – crew playing cards, David."

"*Willie!* Who the hell do you think you are, storming into my room?" his friend hurtled back, his face hidden behind Liesel's hair, his mouth clearly forming and re-forming the words 'fuck off.'

"Couldn't we get out of character for just one evening? I'm sure Liesel would like to meet the *real* David and Conan for a while, wouldn't you, Liesel?"

"We *never* break character, it's not our style, you know that," Willie scowled.

"Well, I'd like to. It's silly all of us knowing each

other's real names and never using them," Liesel said, her hands folded in front of her chest.

"My feelings exactly, Liesel. So, did David tell you all about the voice-coaching in London?"

Sulkily, Liesel shook her head.

"*David*, shame on you, you're neglecting your little Edelweiss . . . I'll fill you in, Liesel . . . Jesus, what the hell happened to this cake?"

"There's more in the fridge," Liesel sighed loudly and lay back on the bed.

"I'll get some more then – anyone for tea?" Tom asked with the over-friendliness of someone not quite sober and at that moment his and Willie's eyes locked hard.

"Maybe not tea, maybe it's more a night for whiskey so," Tom smirked as he disappeared out the door with Willie's laser eyes boring into his back.

22

Sunlight sneaked into Willie's bedroom through his cheap dusty curtains which gaped badly on the window. He'd been awake for an hour at least watching the light probe his room, watching the dust levitate, and when he wasn't watching the dust he watched Liesel and the smile of contentment on her face. Well, at least she hadn't had to suffer Tom and his antics. Willie had thrown him out after two o'clock when he'd tried to light up a spliff and get Liesel stoned.

Stirring slightly, Willie heard Liesel almost purr as she followed his heat across the sheets and snuggled in, limpet-like.

"Hey, Liesel, wake up! Don't you need to get back to your kids in the big mansion?" He shrugged as he tried to loosen himself from her dead weight.

"Hhmm?" she mumbled sleepily. "What? Oh let them fire me! They'll never get anyone as good as me anyway." She yawned, then wrapped her arms and legs round his torso like a slyly tenacious octopus.

"No, come on, get dressed, you don't really want to

get fired," he insisted as he pulled off the bedclothes and tried to lever her over the side of the mattress.

"Stop, David," she began crossly as his persistent shaking woke her to her senses. "There is no need for you to worry, we did not come to any arrangement so Rebecca is in charge." Then she smiled cattily as she played with her latest toy – his brown flat nipple. When she finally succeeded in pinching him with her sharp nails he felt wildly irritated.

"Stop, okay?" he snapped as he forcefully unglued her hand from his skin.

"What's the matter, don't you like me touching you, David?" she asked in a hurt voice and Willie shifted uncomfortably in the bed at the use of his forbidden celebrity name and the tone of ownership in her voice.

Swinging his legs out of the bed, he sprang to his feet and pulled on a T-shirt and jeans, hoping she'd follow suit.

"Let's go for an early morning walk," he said briskly.

"How romantic, David!" she beamed, sure he'd smile back and surprised when he didn't. To his relief she began to pull on her clothes.

As they left the house she linked her fingers through his and failed to notice the slight resistance in his grip. Willie was preoccupied, mulling over the best spot for walking before finally deciding on the road near the stream with the little weir. It was remote but not too far from the village, the perfect place to break up with a clinging girlfriend. Liesel could scream her head off, get it all out of her system and nobody would ever hear – yes, indeed the perfect spot, he thought, as he looked at Liesel and she smiled like a child on the way to her first day at school, unprepared for the harshness of her first real lesson in love.

"So when will this government grant scheme for buying bicycles run out?" the dad with red-rimmed, sleep-deprived eyes was asking Freeda as he perused some light-frame racing bikes with an obvious yearning, running his hands down their frames like they were the long lean legs of a supermodel while trying to balance a baby on his back and keeping a firm hold of his toddler son's reins.

"No timeline, I understand," Freeda answered breezily but somewhat indifferently; the door had opened suddenly and she saw a flash of pretty blonde hair and a turned back as a girl started looking at things on shelves in an absentminded way.

"What kind of trailers do you have for a family? We might do some touring in the summer. Is there a lot to do eco-tourism wise? We're thinking of moving here?" the man continued to rattle on as the baby on his back started to pull his hair in tight little fistfuls.

Freeda directed the hassled, hopeful dad to some tourism brochures, all the while watching the girl who had the dreamy, slow-moving body language of a professional shoplifter, but something in the movement jolted her memory – it was the lovely little German au pair.

"Liesel, isn't it?" Freeda asked the back of Liesel's head – she was mulling over lawnmowers and letting her hands trail from the handle of one to the next. When she turned Freeda could see her face was blotchy and red and her eyes puffy from crying – lovely, lovely Liesel of corn-blue eyes and skin as soft as honeyed-milk.

"I'm sorry, I just had to get away and your shop was open," Liesel snorted and Freeda handed her a clean paper hanky from a pack in her jacket pocket to blow her reddened nose, then another to stem the trail of tears that kept flowing down the full and pretty cheeks. "I met you before," the girl said, trying to recover herself as the daddy with the two young kids, sensing serious female tears threatening, made good his escape.

"Yes, of course, Liesel – I haven't forgotten," Freeda told the girl whose very name had been invading her dreams since they first met.

Temporarily unable to answer, Liesel just nodded and blew her nose again, so hard it sounded like an elephant's trumpet.

"Are you okay?"

"Not really," Liesel sniffled.

"Oh . . . look, I haven't had breakfast yet, but I bought a large fruit muffin and a date slice from the health-food shop that I can share – that is, if you need a chat?"

"You are very kind but I couldn't possibly," Liesel spluttered, rooted to the spot all the same.

"I'm perking coffee as well. It's something we both like – us Germans and Americans, isn't it – decent coffee, freshly ground from the bean?"

A moment's indecisiveness crossed Liesel's face as she considered the tempting coffee offer.

"Nothing like coffee to put a kick in your step and it's no trouble. At this hour the only customers I see are zombie parents who are too tired to buy and too nervous to buy what they really want anyway."

"Okay, I accept . . . you are so kind . . . you don't

even know me and here I am crying all over your shop and you are so *very* kind," Liesel said, catching Freeda's hand and squeezing it, unconsciously sending a spark of heart-stopping electricity straight up her arm.

"Man trouble, is it?" Freeda probed as she gently loosened Liesel's grip and tried to ignore the peculiar buzz of energy that was enveloping her torso and swirling around her head.

"Is there any other kind?"

Was there ever! Female trouble was just as troubling but Freeda chose not to burden the kid unnecessarily – she already looked like she'd been through enough this morning.

"Want to talk about it?" she asked as she brought Liesel a chair.

"I . . . I don't know . . ." Liesel sniffed again before Freeda disappeared to her kitchenette at the back of her shop.

After a couple of minutes Freeda stuck her head out from the kitchenette to shout out her progress. "Two minutes to coffee and then if you want we can have a nice girlie chat!" Then she took a few deep breaths and rubbed off some brown stains from her white coffee-cups with a worn, half-bald, tattered tea towel.

"So that's where we're currently at, I'm afraid," Eddie said as he sat opposite Maura in the wholefood café and took the first bite of his late-morning breakfast – a massive wholegrain sultana scone which was smeared with un-salted organic butter and home-made apple sauce.

Nearby sat Sinéad Winterbottom, who having successfully duped her husband into minding the children so she could have an early-morning session with Demelza, was shamelessly hanging on Eddie and Maura's every word.

"You're kidding? You can't get anyone to organise a concentrated protest for the week leading up to the festival?" Maura asked as she rattled her silver spoon around her dandelion coffee one more time and savaged her breakfast muffin with extra goji berries.

"Well, if Cloonsheeda was near a world heritage site or there was a decent national monument at stake it might be another story – the protest would attract strong personalities, personalities who if they're going to build tree-houses or chain themselves into a subterranean tunnel want there to be something really worthwhile at stake. Now I do know a pretty hard-line activist – currently she's involved in building houses in Africa but I've heard she's fighting with everyone involved on that project so if she quits we could get her here at Cloonsheeda – but it's very much an outside chance at this point."

"Would be good though, wouldn't it, having a woman heading the protest, symbolic of what this bloody motorway will do – you know, the rape of the landscape by misogynistic materialism," Maura mused and Eddie nodded but said nothing as he wiped some crumbs from his mouth.

"Excuse me," Sinéad leaned backwards in her chair to interrupt the conversation, "I couldn't help but overhear what you were saying about needing a woman to protest against the motorway. How long would it be for exactly, this protest?"

"Oh, Mrs Winterbottom?" Maura answered, a little

stunned at the interruption but her natural PR politeness came to the fore. "Just the week in the run-up to the festival – it's a symbolic protest more than anything – but having someone there 24-7 is definitely the way to go."

"And would the person concerned, this woman you're after, have to have any previous experience in eco-warrior, tree-protesting stuff?"

A quick glance and a few shrugs were exchanged between Eddie and Maura before it was concluded that eco-warrior experience wouldn't be an absolute requirement.

"Great . . . I'll do it then," Sinéad gushed.

"Really? Wow, that would be amazing!" Maura said. "You'd be someone ordinary people could readily identify with: an ordinary, middle-class mum and not just some yurt or tipi-living New Ager – not that there's anything wrong with people who live in tents and who have such a devout eco-awareness of course," Maura hastily added. "But definitely your ordinariness is your greatest asset. Are you sure?" Maura was getting quite excited at how media-friendly Sinéad would be.

"Perfectly sure. My husband is self-employed so I can't see why *he* shouldn't be able to work something out and being an archaeologist he should be the first in line to back the cause. I might need a bit of back-up with my children though for childminding – they're young."

"Don't you worry about that – if you agree to the motorway protest we'll organise a rota for baby-sitting and I'll feed you and your family for the week from the restaurant," Maura enthused.

"You will?" Sinéad asked, genuinely surprised.

"Of course, it's the least we could do for such a singularly determined young woman like yourself. 'Eco Mum Takes on Government over Motorway'! I can see it now," Maura said breathlessly. "You'll be famous!"

"Famous, do you really think?" Sinéad was lost in dreamland as she played with the naked finger where her wedding ring had once been. *A woman not beholden to man, a woman loyal to herself and herself alone,* Demelza's mantra resonated in her brain. Henry would kill her, but she'd hold firm, her born-again-virgin pride demanded that she access her warrior spirit and do something wild and free. Besides, Henry still hadn't noticed that she'd removed her wedding ring. If she was that invisible she might as well just up and disappear for real, even if it was only for the week.

Liesel was sitting on the floor in the playroom, handing pieces of Mr Potato Head to one of the twins and some wooden-block jigsaw pieces to the other, when Rebecca stuck her head in the door, just to check Liesel was interacting with the boys and not slacking – she'd become so damn listless lately.

"Rebecca, I have a question to ask," Liesel said authoritatively and Rebecca felt irked that she ever asked the German to call her by her first name.

"Can it wait, Liesel? I'm just running out to meet with my archaeology professor."

"It is just a little question. As I am entitled to holidays I wish to take some soon."

Momentarily Rebecca was caught off guard – Liesel was becoming a little too assertive these days and now she wanted holidays too!

"I want to take a few days, probably just a weekend, next weekend actually."

"I'll have to talk to Mark about it. Where are you going anyway?"

"Just a little biking holiday – it's all thanks to you really encouraging me to try cycling – it has really improved my fitness and I like the freedom," Liesel said, stretching out her legs.

Rebecca noted with irritation that her thighs definitely looked more toned.

"Like I said, I'll have to talk to Mark," Rebecca said sharply before she grabbed her keys and drove in the direction of the Village.

"Do come in," Henry gestured as he juggled the baby on his hip and welcomed Rebecca into his home.

"You're sure I'm not imposing?" Rebecca felt a thrill of excitement just seeing him again, so close and in his natural habitat too.

"If it were an imposition I would have cancelled. I had to rearrange our meeting point as my wife had an appointment this morning which she'd forgotten about, and now she's just called to say she's taking the rest of the morning off too. Suffice it to say her plans have interfered hugely with mine but I suppose one has to cope. Come in, please, and I will run through some of your assignment on Celtic culture."

"Beautiful house," she said as she passed through the hall.

"Messy house," the professor bounced back. "And it's not as if my wife actually works, can't understand what on earth she does all day."

"Daddy, we've finished tidying up. Can we watch TV now?" a little girl politely asked as her father strode through the house.

"Yes, Jane, you can watch your DVD – just leave the door open so Daddy can listen out – but Daddy has a friend over so no unnecessary interruptions in my office, please," Henry said in a level voice.

He exuded such quiet authority that Rebecca was simply melting at his feet.

"Seems like you've got it all sorted out on the home front," Rebecca praised him in wonderment.

"Discipline is important, best learned young – without self-discipline all our good intentions fall apart. My wife too would find it so much easier to cope if she'd just stick to a few rules with the children." Henry sighed wearily as he placed the baby on the office floor with some bricks and Rebecca watched fascinated as the tot gave building the Empire State his best shot.

"Enough about family stuff though . . . as you'll see from your work, I've marked in red bits which I feel are superfluous to your argument."

A thrill chased through Rebecca – she just loved the way this man spoke – his calm and certain words were more of a turn-on than even his hands chasing up and down her spine would be. One look at her work though and she was mortified. Her sheets of white were mutilated by slash after slash of angry red biro.

"Gosh, I'm sorry, I didn't think my work was *that* bad, I never went to college, you see . . . my sister was the one with the brains, while I was the one –" Rebecca stopped short and blushed. "I think I have it in me though, I think with time I could make a really good argument – it's just getting it out on paper that's the hard bit." God damn, but this man made her feel strangely shy.

"You misunderstand, I never said your work was bad – a bit naïve in parts, I grant, but not bad per se," he explained brusquely. "You need to firm up your main argument and refer to alternative opinions a bit more to have a more reasoned, well-rounded essay." Then, perhaps sensing that she was somewhat crestfallen, Henry ended with a kindness Rebecca hadn't heard before. "Archaeology isn't all about what's on paper, it's a multi-faceted thing, a hands-on profession as well as an intellectual one, and you really impressed me by the way you handled the college dig – you were tenacious, didn't whine about the weather and you listened to criticism and learned. For someone with a young family, you have drive and determination . . ."

Rebecca bit her lip, remembering the night in the restaurant when they had flirted and she had got the slightest hint of dissatisfaction in the marriage stakes.

"Henry! Henry!" an excited voice bounced through the house.

Henry didn't answer and Rebecca could hear doors open and shut as the voice went on a search.

Eventually Sinéad appeared. "Oh, there you are!" Her eyes were sparkling as she crossed the room and planted a kiss on her husband's cheek.

Henry virtually squirmed at such obvious affection and Rebecca, seeing her wear an outrageously colourful woolly scarf, gaudy fingerless gloves and a giant silk flower in her hair, instantly categorised her as a very silly, flaky type of person.

"Sinéad, what on *earth* are you wearing?" Henry asked, appalled. "And why are you home so early? I thought you'd be gone for a while yet!"

"Well, I thought I would be too but I met some new people, new friends actually. They put me in such a *fabulous* frame of mind that I just had to buy a few new bits and bobs to match my mood. Oh Henry, I have such *fabulous* news!"

"Excuse me for a moment, would you?" Henry said as he lifted the baby onto his hip, steered his wife out the door and shut it quietly behind him.

Rebecca walked to the door and listened. She could clearly hear the woman says the words 'tree-house' and 'eco-feminism' and Henry raising his voice and saying what sounded like 'over my dead body'. Then there was a sound of running feet and a door slamming.

A few moments later Henry returned, looking agitated.

"I think I'd better be going," Rebecca excused herself.

"Oh, well, I hope I've helped give you some ideas for the submission of your essay for Easter," Henry said somewhat sadly.

Rebecca felt nothing but sympathy. Clearly his wife was a basket-case who merely added to his problems.

"I'm very grateful for your intelligent suggestions and for so generously giving your time," Rebecca said honestly as she stood on the doorstep.

And for a moment their eyes met and they saw past all pretences into each other until Henry nodded his head curtly and firmly shut the door.

There was nothing Eddie Ferris wanted more than to see Anna again but he wasn't sure how she had felt about having a tussle on her bed-settee for the first time. And then there was Maura – they'd had a relationship for a very long time, too long probably, and had been attracted to each other originally by their commonality of purpose: they wanted to change the world, they wanted to make it a better place to live. But they were more like sister and brother than fiery lovers and now he'd experienced mind-blowing attraction again he couldn't eat, he couldn't sleep.

Like a thief he knocked on Anna's back door, hating himself for joining the ranks of slimy love rats everywhere.

"I didn't risk bringing a gift this time," he joked as she opened the door and Anna, although hesitant at first, flashed a small smile.

"I'm afraid I can't ask you to stay," she said as he stepped inside. "I've to meet Maura in half an hour about my plan of putting on a belly-dance display for the May Day Festival."

At the mention of his partner's name Eddie did his best to freeze his face into a happy mask. "If you're running off . . . well, maybe we can meet later on in the week instead, when Maura's away . . . maybe for a chicory coffee or even the real thing?"

"I don't know, Eddie. Don't get me wrong, what happened happened and it was great and I felt such a glow afterwards but it would be so easy to fill the emptiness in my life with someone new and I'm not so sure that would be good for me. Besides, you deserve better than what I can offer you right now. And then, what about Maura?"

"Can I call you then . . . maybe in a few days . . . just

for a chat . . . no pressure?" Eddie pleaded, not even hearing the question about Maura that Anna had tagged on.

"It's too complicated. No – I think no."

"I know I shouldn't be feeling this and I know I'm not exactly free but I feel like I'm losing a friend here, Anna, a friend I've just met but felt I've known all my life and all because we had stupid, reckless sex!"

"Fabulous sex," Anna said, laying a hand gently on Eddie's own. "And if it wasn't for you I mightn't have got my hands on something wonderfully ridiculous. Here, what do you think of this?" She took something soft, red and jangly from a brown padded envelope, shook it out fully, then tied it round her waist in a knot. "Arrived today from e-bay, my first coin belly-dance scarf," she said triumphantly as she did a hip-drop, followed by a shimmy in front of Eddie's bug-wide, mad-with-lust eyes.

"Very nice, all the best so," Eddie said as he ran out of the house and headed to Keogh's for a nice cold drink.

23

"I've decided to end it. Thank you for trying to help me but I'm going to go see a solicitor and sort out my entitlements and legal rights," Rita said matter of factly as she sat opposite Demelza who, mid-morning, was already shimmering in a tunic of gold and yellow sequins.

"Well – if you be certain. Will you let Mossy know about our sessions?" Demelza asked as she smoothed some lint off the calves of her blood-red stockings.

The farmer's wife pressed the heel of her hand to her forehead, allowing her hair to fall in front of her face like a waterfall and laughed, a deep hearty laugh, tinged with just a little sorrow.

"He'd go off his head if he knew I was even here – he thinks you're some kind of living witch but that hardly matters now we're going our separate ways. He wants sheep, you see, told me one night in his sleep and again the next morning, sheep to go with the cattle, and that's when I realised he'll never retire, that he can see no further down the line than the farm and that's no longer the life for me. I want to have a busy life, I want to meet people, I want to, as my daughter Sinéad used to say, 'rip the arse out of life' a bit more, before I'm a granny with a Zimmer frame . . . before I'm dead. Sinéad . . . there's something else that needs fixing and I have to be the one to fix it. She's seeing you too, isn't she? I saw her one day on the street blowing bubbles."

"When will you tell Mossy – that you plan to leave?" Demelza asked, not giving away from her body language that she knew Sinéad at all.

"After the festival, between now and then, I have something to focus on. I'm painting like a woman possessed every spare moment. My work, you see, who knows who might come to see this Bealtaine Festival? If I'm to branch out on my own I'll need to be seen, to be recognised. Please God I might even get a few commissions to set me up for the months ahead – if I'm lucky."

"Whether you stay or go be your own affair, but if you be willing I have a suggestion, something you might try on the night of Bealtaine itself. It be your choice, of course, but you might find it therapeutic and if not it be at least a novel way to say goodbye."

"What is it?" Rita asked, her curiosity piqued.

"Well, you'll need to be open-minded – that be the first thing," Demelza cautioned, sitting forward in her seat, her own enthusiasm evident.

"Don't hold back – I'm an artist, I can deal with strange and alternative ideas. I paint cows for God's sake and some of them abstract! Tell me your plan."

At lunchtime Mark came home from work and Rebecca could feel some confrontational static in the air, but she tried to avoid it as she busied herself in her coursework while the children played downstairs. When he rapped with his knuckles on the door and asked to come in her suspicions intensified – it wasn't like Mark to be polite, especially not in his own home.

"Rebecca, I have to head back to work so I won't beat about the bush. When the cleaner comes tonight I want you to give her notice."

"What?" Rebecca swivelled on her computer chair.

"I'm saying the twice-a-week cleaner is no more. Look, to be blunt, business is pretty crap and the units at Cloonsheeda aren't shifting at all. Maura thinks this festival will give things a boost but I know people and I know this motorway business is going to make them even more nervous. Right now Cloonsheeda is tainted and we need to make cuts – even in our own home."

"No, not a chance, I absolutely *refuse* to give up my cleaner," Rebecca sulked.

"Sorry, but unless you've got the cash to pay for her, it's not for you to say – you're lucky I'm letting you keep the au pair," Mark sighed.

"You'll get rid of Liesel over my dead body. I couldn't cope without her!" Rebecca blazed.

"Liesel stays – for the moment anyway, but you are a stay-at-home mum so what the hell do *you* have to do all day? Tell the cleaner, don't forget," Mark warned as he left.

A stay-at-home mum, what do you have to do all day? Where had she heard that phrase just recently? Not being able to remember bugged her terribly as she scrambled into her gym gear so she could burn up some angry energy before having some sort of miserable dinner only fit for a rabbit.

There was a voicemail on her phone from one of her boys. Anna must have missed it when she'd been belly-dancing in the kitchen, honing her skills so she could exhibit at the festival. For the second time Anna listened to the message which began with a '*Hi, Mom,*' a sigh and a sharp breath inwards and a final '*Talk to you soon*'. Her mother's instincts were aroused. He sounded worried, this eldest boy of hers and all he'd done was leave a short sentence of four words. Worried, Anna tried to phone Liam back and when his phone went to voicemail she felt troubled enough to want to jump in her car and drive the distance to the university, but she resisted the urge – they were both young men now, her sons, they'd bring their troubles to her if and when they were ready and until then all she could do was keep a bed ready and her fridge stocked. It was already groaning under the weight of tub upon tub of organic, luxury ice-cream.

"G'day, Mrs G – looking good," Nathan beamed when Rebecca stormed through the door, looking decidedly flustered.

"You got to be kidding!" Rebecca snorted.

"Meant every word, cross my heart – so how's the training coming along?"

Rebecca could feel a big sniffle building up inside, making her shoulders heave and before she knew it she was crying, right there at the front desk, in front of the sexy Ozzie hunk.

"You alright, Mrs G?" Nathan asked, looking genuinely concerned.

"Yes, of course, so sorry, stupid really, it's just my husband told me today that we've got to get rid of our cleaner and maybe our au pair too and, well, if I have to clean my own house and look after my kids all the time I'll get nothing done, no time for my studies, no more time to work out and lose weight –"

"Bet you've lost loads already. Look, it's dead here this morning – want to pop into the weighing room and check your measurements?"

"Well . . . I can't take too long . . . I want to do some weights and I told the au pair I'd be back in an hour."

"Busy lady, know exactly how it is. We won't bother with the cardio and flexibility tests so – all it'll take is ten minutes tops!"

Rebecca smiled. Really, he was such a friendly, open, deliciously sexy guy.

"Okay then, you're probably right – I've probably lost much more than I think," she said optimistically as she sniffled away the tears and followed him trustingly into the weighing room.

"I'm doing it, bloody hell I'm really doing it," Sinéad told her hall mirror, psyching herself up to defy Henry and become an eco-warrior up a tree or in a tunnel, anything at all to save Cloonsheeda from the blight of a motorway and give herself something exciting to do with her life. Of course, she'd probably need media training to help her deal with the press, say all the right things, Maura would help out there of course, with all her PR background. God, she hoped that no one found out that she didn't use eco-nappies on the baby or that the kids got washed with non-organic supermarket brand soap – it was way cheaper and having three kids was expensive and their super-duper eco-everything house had cost them a fortune so that cutting costs in any way was a big consideration in the Winterbottom household. Although, maybe she should buy a few eco bits and pieces that she could put on display in her house when the press came to do the 'at home with eco-mum' special. Yes, definitely a pack or two of bio-degradable nappies, some eco washing-up liquid and maybe some soap – she'd put it aside and ban the kids from using it until the photographers arrived.

Of course she'd probably have to undergo special survival training for the week-long event, do a bit of Rambo training so she could live off the fat of the land, skin bunny-rabbits or protect herself against those big-business motorway shots who'd probably try to sneak up on her in the night and evict her from her perch. Maybe she should take up something physical, something definitely not 'mumsy' – boxing or kick-boxing maybe to get her though her week.

"Fly like a butterfly, sting like a bee!" she told the mirror, fists held high like a boxer. "Just you wait, Henry – I'm a born-again virgin and there ain't no stopping me!"

"Mummy – the baby stinks!" Jane announced, coming down the hall, holding her nose.

God damn it but a week up a tree away from her kids and her husband would almost be as good as a trip to a spa.

Freeda adjusted the stabilisers on the bike for the customer buying a birthday present for his little girl and waved him off with a nice discount. Sighing, she hung two bikes off the ceiling and pushed her hands downwards against the wheels to check they'd stay firm. Telling Liesel she'd take her for a tour of the local countryside was pure stupidity – there was no way she could justify shutting the shop and besides her emotions were gone haywire. No, she'd have to put an end to this before it even started – if only she had the power to forget about that bewitching honey-blonde hair.

On her bike in Carrigmore town, Liesel savoured her freedom away from her annoying Hausfrau. Not having a car and not being on the Gleeson's insurance was actually paying dividends in the end – it meant she could sometimes escape for 'necessary items' and Rebecca couldn't object. She liked visiting Carrigmore nearly as much as Cloonsheeda. It was a decent-sized country town and had a two-storey bookshop that sometimes sold German newspapers.

She wanted to buy some new make-up at the big pharmacy, maybe a lipstick, or a funky necklace – she was sure if she had something more fashionable she could win David back, although she worried how she'd ever be able to compete on a daily basis with Hollywood starlets and pop stars who would always be competing for his love. On the way to the pharmacy she stopped at a newsagent's and was hardly in the door before her face turned white. There in gauzy print was a blurry but distinct enough photo of David and Conan with their heads up against scantily clad bums and underneath was a screaming headline 'My Lap-Dance Orgy in Manchester with Hollywood Heart-throbs.'

Voice lessons indeed! The bastards, the sneaky, rotten bastards! Liesel could feel the colour rising to her cheeks. They'd pay, they'd pay – she just had to work out how.

Rebecca was a snarling mass of discontented energy threatening to explode at any moment when Liesel walked in eating a Mars bar, a look of demonic possession on her face. Damn, but the girl was looking good – curvy yes, but toned – she was definitely losing weight. Not like Rebecca, the gym scales told the truth that she, Rebecca Gleeson, one-time gorgeous knockout had actually put on three pounds! After she'd cried buckets at the gym Nathan had told her that she'd probably created a famine-brain situation, putting her body under pressure to exercise at the same time as she'd reduced her food supply to basically different forms of grass with an occasional bit of protein. The solution, the muscular lifeguard consoled her, was actually to eat more food. Watching Liesel, all Rebecca could think of was ice cream – the craving was so strong it was nearly worse than being pregnant. Boy, she needed ice cream, besides she had to fire the cleaner in less than an hour so she *deserved* ice cream.

"Liesel, I'll be back in ten minutes just need to get something essential in town."

Not that Liesel heard, not that it mattered really. Her boys were back watching mindless telly – hopefully they'd give Tarrantino a run for his money some day in the very distant future.

Over the bath Nathan's black-and-silver wet suit was drip-drying slowly. Totally naked, he padded from the bathroom into the bedroom, roughly drying his hair as he walked.

Pulling on a clean pair of boxers he got into bed beside India who was reading and making notes by the light of a bedside lamp, wearing a cotton cami and matching boxers, night gear which was deliberately pretty but not overly sexy and, therefore, she hoped – not overly desperate.

"Don't you think you're taking this bog-snorkelling a bit too seriously?" she asked crossly, never raising her nose once from her work.

"You're joking? You should see the interest over the net – some serious contenders are travelling to Cloonsheeda for the competition – triathlon junkies for starters – but they needn't bother – this is *my* title and I'm taking it for Australia!"

India rolled her eyes. His enthusiasm for this daft competition was ridiculous – in fact it was infantile – swimming in the morning at work followed by further lengths in the pool at lunch-time, then snorkelling in the bog for all the hours of daylight. And to think that this was now March! The spring equinox had been and gone and everything that should have awoken from the sleep of winter and become frisky had done so – except for her boyfriend's stubbornly sleepy southern-hemisphere sperm.

"Indy?"

His tone of voice was upbeat, had the familiar whine about it that men used when they wanted to cajole women into sex and suddenly India was rather hopeful.

"Yes," she answered, feeling excitement tingle through her limbs and core.

"Would you turn off the light, babes – I have a really early start."

Leslie Anderson, UK spin doctor to the stars, picked up

his phone and dialled the LA number of David Ron Dwyer and waited for him to pick up.

"Hey, man – how are you?" David drawled.

Leslie smiled – they all became Americanised in the end, all the Brits, all the Irish who made it big. In the background a baby tested out a marvellous set of lungs.

"David, you weren't in a UK lap-dance bar recently with Conan Mallon by any chance?"

"You shitting me? I'm in enough trouble with my ma since I was photographed leaving that model's apartment in London when she wants me to get back with Kari Ann. Besides, I've been baby-sitting – Kari Ann's on a shoot – lucky bitch!"

"I have a newspaper photo here – it's a bit blurry but it does look awfully like you two, I have to admit," Leslie said, looking at the on-line photo.

"Mallon? That's a piss-take – you know I can't stand that bastard. We never hang out – not since the awards ceremony last year when he made a move on my girlfriend."

"Oh yes, I remember, what was her name again?"

"Jenna . . . Gemma . . . me and Kari Ann had only just split. Women, more trouble than they're worth! So tell me, what's the latest? Do I need to worry about anything here or not?"

"You never need to worry, David. That's why you pay me – this will all blow over," his media mogul answered smoothly.

"Sweet. Gotta go – the kid's chewing up my Italian leather sofa. Damn, I might as well own a bloody Rottweiler!" The phone went dead.

24

"So what do you think of the view – beautiful, isn't it?" Freeda asked as she watched Liesel hug her knees and saw the wind whip her long hair into her sad, thoughtful eyes. They were both sitting on the grassy knoll of a Norman motte, enjoying the view, feeling the heat of the April sunshine, picnicking on a day out cycling, just as Freeda knew they would.

"The air here is so fresh – German air is never like this not even in the countryside," Liesel said dreamily, ignoring the delicate sandwiches of cheese, lettuce and cucumber that Freeda had so lovingly made. "It is so good of you to spend this day with me. I have no other friends here in Ireland to share my troubles with." She smiled up at Freeda whose heart raced at the implication that she was now a valued 'friend'.

"I don't have that many friends here either – we're both in the same boat," Freeda answered, aware that if it weren't for her suntanned skin she'd definitely be blushing.

"Because we are from foreign countries living here or because you have heartache too?"

"I . . . I loved someone Irish too . . . it was a while ago," Freeda answered coyly.

"They will break your heart these Irish feckers, no?" Liesel said, her mouth halfway between a smile and a scowl. "I didn't tell you, Freeda, but my man . . . he was someone famous." Liesel suddenly felt ravenous and reached for a sandwich.

"Really – how famous – would I know him?" Freeda asked lightly.

"Very famous and I am so, so angry," Liesel announced as she almost swallowed a sandwich whole.

"Maybe you need to talk about it then, get it all out – works for us Americans!"

"Freeda, can you keep a secret?" Liesel asked breathlessly.

"Of course I can," Freeda assured her, squeezing her new friend's hand tight, cherishing every minute.

"You're very quiet today, Lana." Eddie smiled at the make-up girl as she blended his foundation into smoothness.

"Sorry, got some other stuff on my mind, that's all."

"Anything I can help you with?" Eddie asked easily as she tidied up her brushes and put them aside.

"Well, what's bothering me is not something I could tell my girlfriends about – they'd have a freak attack – or my family – my father, Jesus, it doesn't bear thinking about . . . I mean, I like Paddy, really like him and all . . . maybe it's just the age difference . . . maybe older men like yourselves expect things to be, I don't know . . . different?" Lana smiled a tortured smile.

"I see. You need some older-man advice to help you

with your older-man problems?" Eddie smiled his usual friendly guy smile and saw Lana's resolve weaken.

"Oh God, Paddy'd kill me . . . I mean, I don't even know myself if I want to hear it out loud – my older-man problems, that is," she said in a hushed whisper, looking around warily. The other girls were busy, up against deadlines, laying on the Polyfilla to get everyone looking good.

"Sure himself and myself are in the same business really – in the public eye. I can be a soul of discretion, you know," Eddie teased.

Lana laughed. "Did anyone ever tell you, Eddie Ferris, that you have the face of a priest?"

"All the time, my child . . . so tell me, little one, what have you to confess?" her priestly companion began and, despite herself, Lana began to talk.

It was Willie's fifteen minutes of fame, *his* face in the English newspapers and everyone who saw it just assuming his face must be David Ron Dwyer's for sure, not that anyone read more than the parish newspaper in Cloonsheeda. Willie spread the paper in front of him on the table and read about his lap-dance night in Manchester – most of it fabricated. It was proof though, proof that he could be more, could live a better, grander, more exciting life. It was as well to dump Liesel – she'd never fit into this grander, bigger life Willie Cleary deserved.

The doorbell rang and the farmer he'd met before with the anxious face was back, leading a sheep again.

"Same one as before?" Willie asked, nodding at the bleating heap of wool.

"It is, faith – how could you tell?" the worried little man asked, surprised.

"Not that difficult really – sure it's plain her face is still contorted with the pain," Willie answered drily, ushering the man into the back room where his father was drinking his tea.

Christ Almighty, he really had to get out of this 'one sheep' town soon and go and see a bit of the world before he became nothing more than the local bonesetter with the famous hands tending to all manner of God's wounded creatures and drinking gallons of tea.

"What . . . oh no . . . nothing like that?" Maura Simmons laughed down the phone at the man with the cultured voice who asked her would there be any witches or fairy worshippers coming to celebrate the Bealtaine Festival at Cloonsheeda.

"I suppose you read that bit in the paper a while back where a local witc . . . I mean sex therap . . . where a local *woman* said Cloonsheeda meant 'fairy meadow'. I can definitely tell you now that this festival we're organising is an intelligent, sophisticated event . . . we're not a superstitious bunch down here . . . in fact, we're a very progressive community here in Cloonsheeda . . . yes . . . yes . . . well, like I said, thank you again for booking the community hostel for the festival. I guarantee a brilliant time!"

Maura put down the phone as Tilda charged in the door scowling.

"They're back, just as before!"

"Who's back?" Maura asked, feeling happy and light

now that some proper paying tourists were booked in for the festival.

"The religious at the Blessed Tree Stump!" Tilda snapped as she went looking for her work apron. "They want to get it all *nice* for the festival – they want to build a grotto round it. That big Pole said he could do it for them but others are saying they'd like a wicker one made by that basket-weaving artist who was mentioned at one of the festival meetings."

Maura scowled, she really didn't want Cloonsheeda to get any more of that kind of publicity in the national media.

"May is the month of the Blessed Virgin Mary – the religious in Cloonsheeda think it should be all flowers and hymns starting at May Eve itself," Tilda sighed as she slipped the apron ribbons round her back and tied them quickly; ready to serve goji-berry scones and semi-medicinal blueberry smoothies to whatever customers came through the door that day.

Maura gnawed her lip as she chewed over Tilda's news. This Tree Stump Revival was a bit of a worry. How was she ever going to turn Cloonsheeda into a place where rock stars, film stars and minor celebrities might helicopter into for an overpriced chicory coffee and a scrumptious home-baked gluten-free bun?

"Hi, Mum!"

Anna was just about to run through a belly-dancing routine on her bare floors, the dance she thought she might do as a display piece at the festival, when her eldest son Liam turned up on her doorstep and crushed her to his chest tightly, making her belly-dance coin-belt jangle a startled tune of welcome.

"Can I come in?" he asked tentatively, perhaps thinking of all the times he'd ignored his mother on the phone.

"To what do I owe this unexpected visit and it's not even my birthday? Skipping lectures are we now? Shouldn't you be cramming for Easter exams?" Anna scolded jokingly.

"Relax, would you, Mum. I got the exams sorted!" Liam cheerily announced. "Found out from the start who the brainy girls were, the girls who go to all the lectures and take the best notes . . . threw in the odd a bit of charm and now I have the notes all photocopied and up to date. It's not what you know, Mum, it's who you know!"

Scoundrel behaviour! Anna knew who he'd learnt all his lazy tricks from over the years.

"So can I crash for a few days, Mum? *Please* tell me you have a bed?" Liam asked easily, not in the slightest bit guilty that he'd been giving Anna the run-around since the start of his course.

"As it happens I have a bed for both my wayward sons, ordered them just the other week. Follow me, let me show you to your newly painted room," Anna announced somewhat cattily as she opened the door of the black hell-hole and saw her son's jaw drop in amazement.

"Jesus, Mum, it's very . . ."

"With-it? Atmospheric? Rock-starish?" Anna challenged. "I'm trying to be very with-it these days." She flounced, hand on hip, causing her belt to jangle once more until her outfit caught her son's attention. "It's a belly-dance belt," she said, answering his question before the words left his mouth.

"Don't think Dad would like that rig-out much – it wouldn't be good for his image," Liam blustered, saying the first thing that came to mind.

"Well, what your father thinks doesn't really matter much any more, does it?" Anna said brusquely as she unknotted her belt and laid it aside on a chair.

"No, I suppose not," Liam said, sitting on his bed, taking in the scary black walls.

"Jesus, Mum, you're lucky I'm not depressed. These walls could send me over the edge and I can already tell you're pissed off with me," he said half jokingly.

Anna remembered his funny phone call from a few days back and parked any anger she felt at his lack of contact and became all mumsy instead as she sat beside her first-born and gave him a brief hug. "I'm sorry if I've been a bit short with you – I know you don't have time for your old mum when you're running around college having an exciting time but I've missed you all the same . . ." She was trying to be friendly but casual. "You sounded a bit down, love, when you left a message on my machine . . . problems with the love life?"

Liam sighed as he lay back on the bed, his hands cupped on his stomach, his eyes glued to the ceiling. "I tried to tell Dad but he said to stay the fuck away from him, that's what he actually said!"

"Why? What is it, Liam? What have you done?"

"It's not what I've *done*, Mum. It's what I *am* . . . there's no easy way to say this . . . Mum, I'm gay!"

And Anna breathed a sigh of relief that that was the extent of her eldest son's worries.

"Mummy, when is dinner?" Jane asked her mother who

was sweating in front of the TV doing a boot-camp fitness special with some weather-babe who'd managed to shed all her post-baby weight and now looked like she could train the marines.

"Not now, Jane, Mummy is busy," Sinéad blustered, hardly able to breathe as she followed the celeb to the floor for some goddamn awful press-ups.

"Mummy, I'm hungry!" Jane whinged again.

"Cereal – you and your brother can have cereal tonight – it's fortified with vitamins and minerals. Cereal is fine."

"But, Mummy, cereal isn't dinner," Jane gasped, shocked.

"Tonight it is," Sinéad grunted as she did some legwork with weights. Jesus, this one on the telly never seemed to stay still for half a minute.

"Besides, Jane, Mummy might be going away for a while – all kinds of people might be feeding you."

"Going where, Mummy?" Jane's face blanched.

"Up a tree, darling."

"Like a birdie?"

"Mummy, can we go swimming?" Peter came running into the room, banging a tennis racket off his head.

"No, we can't," Sinéad huffed and blowed. "After this I'm watching telly – a grown-up film, *Saving Private Ryan* – no children allowed!"

"We're having cereal tonight and Mummy is going up a tree to hatch birdie eggs," Jane whispered, eager to pass on the shocking news of motherly neglect and Peter looked shocked.

Without a care, Sinéad shooed them both out the door.

After her exercise DVD, Sinéad collapsed on the couch to watch her war movie. En route to the kitchen to drink a gallon of water she'd switched on her computer and received the news that all her virtual fish had died on-line from neglect and she didn't even feel a slight sadness – her fish were just the unfortunate casualties of war in the need for Sinéad Winterbottom to finally, finally kick some ass.

Golf umbrella in hand, India stood by the bank of the bog-hole, watching her boyfriend snorkel the muddy brown lane, turn and do another powerful length. For five minutes she watched him until she could stand it no more, then folded up her umbrella, and while he was still in the water prodded him in his backside to get his immediate attention.

"What's up?" he asked as he slithered from the waters like a giant earthworm and stood beside her, water pooling round his ankles.

India took a very deep breath. Nathan covered in mud was doing things to her, womanly things to her as she thought about mud-wrestling in her bikini and holding him as tight as slippery mud would allow.

"Nate, we've got to talk," she whimpered as they stood a breath away from each other under her umbrella.

"What about, babes?"

"Us," she nearly cried.

"What about us?" he asked as he ran his hands through his sloppy hair and squeezed out some muddy water like he was squeezing out some old dish rag.

"Okay, me then, to put it frankly I have *needs*,

Nathan, *womanly* needs, and it just seems lately like we can never get it together. God, Nathan, isn't it obvious I *need* you?" she cried as she pulled him to her, mud and all, and kissed him passionately and wonder of wonders he responded, pulling her to him by the waist, matching every movement of her mouth and hungry tongue.

Then abruptly he pulled away.

"Sorry, I can't."

"You can't! What is it?" she asked angrily, hungry for his touch all over.

"I can't."

"Why the hell not?"

"It's just – Jerome went to such trouble digging this trench for me I feel obliged to swim in it every moment I can for the training."

"You like that big Polish bloke with all his muscles, don't you? I've seen you having a laugh with him. He's fairly ripped too, isn't he? Nathan, tell me the truth," India took a deep breath. "Are you gay . . . bisexual at the very least? Tell me, please tell me, I have to know!"

"Gay? I'm not gay, why do you think I'm gay?" Nathan smiled in amusement.

"Because we never have bloody sex any more and just there when I was kissing you, you pulled away. If you're not gay then there's something wrong with me. What's wrong with me, Nathan? Please, please tell me. I have to know!"

"There's nothing wrong with you, India! I'm just in training, that's all, and I'm taking this championship very seriously – I never have sex when I'm in training – I've got to stay focused."

"This is just about bog-snorkelling? You can't be

bloody serious about having no sex while training for bog-snorkelling!" India snapped.

"I am serious. I'm in this thing to win, Indy. There's big interest in this and one of my old mates is coming over from London and there's no way I'm going to let *that* bastard win. Don't you understand – my honour is at stake here, babes. I have to be in this bog whenever I can between now and the festival. I have to win!"

India's face clouded over as dark as the boggy water.

"There's no way I suppose you'd start cooking me a steak to eat when I get home, is there?" Nathan asked warily. "Need all the protein I can get to keep me going."

"You can cook your own steak!" India barked as she flounced off, shaking with anger, her umbrella picking up on her mood, dancing a manic waltz in the wind, before wildly dancing inside out, snapping a metal spoke.

"Nice calf – be worth a bit in the marts maybe when the time's right," Mossy said, looking at one of his wife's paintings as she worked busily in the corner of the kitchen.

Rita said nothing but her husband kept hovering.

"Have you had word from the girls? Are any of them coming for Easter?" Mossy said, scratching his head for no particular reason.

"They're busy, got their own lives, very capable women my daughters, especially Sinéad, the daughter down the road to whom you never speak."

"Don't start all that again about women and farming and, as for Sinéad, I have my principles. What would you think of young Tom taking over the farm? He

helped us out a bit last year when we were both sick –
shows a bit of interest?"

"That useless nephew of yours?" Rita blazed,
suddenly getting up from her seat and shouting at her
husband, scaring Jangle in the process.

"Disinherit my daughters, would you? Just so you
could leave the farm to someone with the same name as
yourself!"

"All I'm saying is –"

"Listen here, Maurice Skeehan, the day you do
anything to disinherit my daughters is the day I leave!"

"Haven't you left me already, a long time ago, Rita?"

Stunned into silence, Rita said nothing and then
began to clean a brush.

"You think I don't notice, don't care, but I do, you
know."

"What are you talking about, Mossy?" Rita laughed,
feeling nervous.

"We're not man and wife any more, just partners,
business partners who can barely do business any more
it seems."

"Mossy . . ."

"I'm going out," he announced determinedly,
searching for his work coat.

"Where?" Rita demanded, feeling Mossy had opened
a can of worms and was now content to leave them
crawling all over her, tormenting her for the evening
while he disappeared.

"To the Blessed Tree Stump."

"Lord's sake, man, would you ever have some sense!
It's spitting rain! Why go out on a night like this to see
her? Why is she so special, you old fool!"

"Fool or not, she's the only woman who understands me and my troubles!" Mossy said quietly as he took his keys and headed out the door.

"Rebecca, come to bed, would you?" Mark snapped as he turned over and over on the mattress trying to get comfortable.

"In a minute! I just want to proofread my essay on the Celts – it has to be submitted pronto or I'll lose marks!" Rebecca snapped back across the room just as crossly, as she tapped on her laptop.

"Jesus, woman, can't you do that stuff during the day when I'm at work?"

"No, I bloody well can't!" Rebecca blazed, tears threatening through her temper. "Now that I'm down a cleaner I'm sort of short on spare time and I can't handle everything at the same time. I'm even three pounds heavier since I went back to the bloody gym. And since I got the news from my gym instructor I can't stop eating ice cream so I'm probably five pounds heavier now and now you're nagging me too!"

Mark looked at her for a moment and said nothing.

"Okay, but would you switch the light off when you come to bed?" he said as he pulled the duvet over his head and sighed a deep sigh of frustration and regret.

25

"I didn't tell you *all* my story yesterday, Freeda," Liesel said as she pulled a hunk of brown bread apart and dipped it into her lunchtime pub-grub soup.

They'd been cycling all morning, ever since they'd left the B&B in fact.

Freeda's heart had taken off like a racehorse just being in the same room as Liesel the night before, just hearing her brush her teeth and watching her brush her long, gorgeous hair.

"No?" Freeda couldn't help watching from her leather padded seat in the snug as Liesel's fingers reached from her bowl to her mouth.

"No, not everything . . . one night there was a mad moment when David was talking to his friend, his co-star on their new Irish production, Conan Mallon, and . . . well, I did it with the two of them. I felt so beautiful, but now I feel so used, so dirty, since I know what they both did in Manchester . . . and even so fat again, so ugly." She sighed regretfully. "I should have stayed in Germany – I should have listened to my mother!"

"You *are* beautiful, Liesel," Freeda said, gripping her hand and squeezing it. "And if you never came to Ireland . . . well, we wouldn't be here today, would we?"

"I'm still not so sure being here in Ireland will be good for me . . . but you, Freeda . . . I spoke so much yesterday I never listened to you," Liesel said as she shook some salt on her soup and stirred.

"My lover . . . I suppose she was like you . . . innocent, unsure . . . she came from a small town in Ireland, a place where she couldn't be herself or so she said . . . I understood that. I didn't always live in San Francisco, you know. I grew up in Africa, my family were missionaries. San Francisco was so open, such a place to be free if you were young and wanted to be anonymous."

"I am angry, angry with what he did to me, what they did to me," Liesel mused, not really listening to Freeda's story, not taking in Freeda's pain.

Freeda didn't mind. That had always been her role, to be overlooked, to be the unselfish one.

"So, so angry and, you know, I think I know how to make them both pay!" Liesel laughed, a savage look in her eye as she blew on her soup. For a moment her spoon paused mid-air and she wrinkled her nose, then abruptly put her spoon to her dish with a clink. "Perhaps I misunderstood the grammar . . . did you say 'she'? Your lover . . . 'she' came from a small town in Ireland?"

"Yes, her name was Maeve, Maeve O'Meara."

"So you're . . .?"

Freeda nodded. "I'm sorry. I should have told you before. Have I upset you?" she asked gently.

"No, it's just I never had a gay friend before," Liesel

mused. "*Mein Gott*, if Mutti could see me now, she wouldn't believe how different I am!"

Liesel smiled and Freeda laughed as they clinked water glasses and asked for the bill.

"You've lost your mind!" Henry fumed as Sinéad slung a bag over her back and went looking for her walking boots to complement her wet gear.

"Henry, a horrible, unnecessary motorway which will destroy the environment is going ahead and you expect me to remain indifferent – besides, my new outdoors home is ready for occupation. Maura gave me the news herself last night."

"For God's sake, Sinéad, sometimes progress is necessary and not everything from the past is sacred. And protesters are nut-jobs – they come from all over the world for this kind of protest nonsense – do you know how many of them I have had to fence off in the past on sites for health and safety reasons alone?"

"Well, like I said, it's only for the week – I'll be back in time for the festival," Sinéad said authoritatively as she pulled her hair back in a rubber band. God, being in control of her own destiny for the next seven days or so made her feel so powerful.

"And just how am I supposed to manage to work while you're off playing eco-soldiers?" Henry thundered, totally frustrated.

"Don't stress, Henry – it's all arranged. Maura Simmons has a rota of people to help cook meals and look after the children. But naturally you'll have to take some time off work. I can't think it will be such a problem – after all, work is hardly overwhelming at the moment."

Furious, Henry pulled her by the arm and glared in her face. "That's exactly why you can't get involved in this motorway protest. Motorways mean business for architects like me, and if this motorway is turning out to be a sensitive issue I could get monitoring work on site or be considered for future projects! But if you go ahead with this stupidity, Sinéad, it will mean death for my career. As it is, my lecturing position is only part-time and you *know* this house cost a fortune to build with all the extra eco-features we put in!"

"All of it your vanity, because you needed to have the most show-off eco-house in the locality! I would have been content with something less environmentally flashy!"

"You can't do this, this is just not *you*, Sinéad!" Henry insisted, feeling panicky now.

"This *was* me, Henry, this was me before you got your claws into me and started to suck the life-force out of me – but I've remembered, you see, I've remembered what it means to be beholden to no man, to be independent, to be free!"

"What on earth are you talking about, Sinéad? Have you gone completely insane?"

"No, not insane – just more confident. I'm a born-again virgin, Henry – it's something you're going to have to get used to. Have you ever heard of the warrior goddess Scáthach?"

"The Scottish mythological warrior, yes, of course, hardly a goddess though. What has she got to do with anything?"

"Scáthach, who was very much a warrior goddess, was so skilful that men came to *her* to be trained for battle . . . she was also called the Shadowy One and someone chose her as my role model for my life right now."

"Who chose her, what are you talking about, Sinéad?"

"Basically, Henry, I've realised it's okay for a woman to live in the shadows, to not know exactly who she is, it doesn't frighten me any more. But it frightens you and you'd better watch out because I warn you, Henry, just like Scáthach this wife of yours kicks ass!" With that, Sinéad stomped her walking boots out the door for a practice run around the neighbourhood in full combat gear.

"So tell me again what your father said, I want to make sure I've got it completely straight in my head before I kill him," Anna seethed, handing her son a strong cup of breakfast coffee.

"I met him for a pint – he did all the talking . . . said he was up to his neck in it over this new motorway and questions were being asked about the amount of money he spent on make-up services from his new girlfriend Lana Phillips . . ." Liam paused for a minute and read his mother's annoyed face at the mention of his father's mistress. "Anyhow, he wasn't in a good mood and I didn't think it was a good time to tell him but I didn't know when I'd see him again so I just got it out there, told him about me being gay, and he went all quiet and then he just told me to keep my mouth shut and stay away from him because he just couldn't take any more heat at the moment . . . and then he asked me did I think Niall might be 'batting for the other team too' because it would be better he had that information now for damage-limitation purposes."

"So he didn't ask you *anything* about you, how you were feeling about all this?" Anna asked in amazement.

Liam shook his head sadly and cradled the warm cup while his mother couldn't help eyeing up the coffee pot, couldn't help wondering what it would be like to dump the entire contents into Paddy's crotch for maximum harm potential. Of course, she'd always known Paddy was a self-centred SOB – his supreme arrogance was the reason she'd been attracted to him at first – but still she'd always thought that, if only for egotistical reasons alone, he'd had some sort of genuine affection for his sons.

"I suppose he is under a lot of pressure. That new motorway and the protestors are all over the news."

"Now listen here, no matter what your father has on his mind, you're his son and what's happening in your life matters – so don't you dare make any excuses for him and don't you feel sorry for him either – he has the skin of a crocodile. Why don't you go off, Liam, and take a walk around the village for a while. I want some time alone to think about this."

Liam shrugged on a jacket and gave his mum a quick squeeze before he headed out the door.

A dozen times Anna picked up the handset to dial her husband but she couldn't do it; she was shaking too badly to attempt any kind of ex-wife/husband rationality over the phone.

Lana was distraught; her eyes were darting around shiftily as she met Eddie in a dingy coffee shop in Dublin on her day off from work.

"It's just me meeting you could be splashed all over the papers and him in his moment of crisis over this bloody motorway," she said, looking over her shoulders and all around as Eddie took a seat. "Look, Eddie, I wanted to meet you again because yesterday I said too much. I shouldn't have said anything at all but I just couldn't help myself – the words just came pouring out."

"I won't say anything to anybody, I promise," Eddie said, not wanting to tell anybody what Lana had told him the previous day anyway.

"You must think I'm a right sap going out with a man like that, a man who . . ." Lana covered her eyes for a moment and groaned.

"Wants you to walk over his chest in stilettos – and wants to wear nappies and get you to give him a bottle of baby formula," Eddie whispered, as he uncovered her face and patted her hand.

"God, when you say it like that it sounds so awful . . . but, you've got to understand, when Paddy first suggested it I thought it was just his idea of role play, you know, like me dressing up in a schoolgirl uniform or him wanting to be a fireman or something."

"I've heard it's not uncommon for men with high-powered jobs to seek some kind of release, to want someone else to be in control," Eddie said, patting her hand some more, trying to convey a normality about the situation that he didn't feel.

"At first it was just once or twice but now . . . now he wants it that way all the time . . . this week he even bought a baby's dummy for Christ's sake and he asked me could I make him up to look like he'd a flawless baby complexion, all pink skin and rosy cheeks!"

Eddie smiled his reassuring 'priest-like' smile that unfortunately always got women to reveal their darkest torments, but underneath he was dying – this was more than any normal red-blooded man should have to hear. God, he hoped Anna hadn't had to endure this for years.

"So what do I do, Eddie? I've thought of leaving him but he's under so much pressure I'd be afraid he'd crack . . . I mean, he already loses the plot if he thinks his blue shirts have lost a trace of colour, has me hand-washing them all and they can't be hung outside in case the sun fades them . . . and, oh God, you wouldn't believe how particular he is about his ties!" Lana moaned. "God Almighty, you don't want to get me started about his ties!"

"Hello," Rebecca greeted as Henry opened the door of his home and said nothing, his blank face not even registering her presence. "I tried you at the office but you weren't in . . . I've made those corrections you recommended for my assignment . . . I'm sorry, is now a bad time?"

Before her eyes he began to thaw just a little.

"No, come in, the children and the baby are away – being minded by some woman with a funny jumper – it's a trial thing before my wife embarks on a crazy motorway protest. Sinéad's out at the moment – running."

"Some woman? You don't know who she is?" Rebecca asked, a bit puzzled.

"My wife does . . . she'll be away tomorrow for a week . . . won't you come in?"

Henry watched her as she came in and stood on his hall mat. She really was a lovely-looking woman, a proper yummy mummy, well kept, stylish, lovely figure, had time to put on her make-up, not wearing any strange hand-knitted hats or anything else too 'grungy' and her perfume was sensual and floral, not too heavy but divinely sexy all the same.

He placed a hand behind her to shut the door and invaded her personal space – just slightly. Rebecca smiled and without really thinking he leaned in and snatched a kiss.

"Oh no, I'm so sorry," he said apologetically as he released her and stood looking at his shoes, then ran a hand through his hair and smiled in embarrassment.

Rebecca drank in some air deeply and felt her head buzz. Now would be a good time to tell him off but instead she stepped forward, stood on her toes and kissed him back, enjoying the argument and pursuit between their lips, enjoying the sheer luxury of this kiss which she deepened further by cradling the back of his head but then, unexpectedly, guilt brought her to her senses in a moment of old-fashioned sense and reason.

"My assignment – I think it's good," she said and, not sure what to do next, she handed him her work. "I didn't do that . . . I mean, I didn't kiss you just to get a good grade," she continued stupidly.

"It's my fault, I really am sorry," he said.

"I'd better go," she said finally and bolted for the door, her head completely addled. She started up her car and drove away.

Then, as she was driving up the village street, her head was turned by the Goddess sign of the woman Mark called a witch.

Stopping the car, she walked towards the cottage.

Breathlessly she rang the bell and was astounded when the witch answered looking completely normal in a T-shirt and faded blue jeans.

"Do you need an appointment?" the witch asked quite politely.

For a moment Rebecca was unsure but then she nodded her head vigorously.

"Well, I be busy at the minute but come in and we'll check the book, see when we might fit you in." Demelza ushered her in with a smile.

"Thanks."

"So what be your problem?" Demelza asked as she flicked through the pages of her appointments book in the hall.

"Sex addict – I think I might be a sex addict," Rebecca blurted out and Demelza nodded kindly as if it were all run-of-the-mill in her line of work.

26

At the coffee shop Maura, kitted out in over-sized shades, bundled Sinéad into an anonymous van, driven by Eddie Ferris, and headed for the secret location somewhere along the route of the proposed new motorway. It was so exciting Sinéad couldn't help laughing out loud at the drama of her new situation.

"Sorry, it's just so unlike what I do every day, I can't help myself," Sinéad apologised to Maura, who was giving her strange sideways looks.

Despite some last-minute reservations that Sinéad might turn out to be a bit of a flake, Maura laid on the professional charm. "What you're doing here is *so* important – it will really help in the publicity," Maura said calmly. "I mean, sometimes when there is a situation like this, professional protestors can come from all over the world and locals can find it hard to relate to them, but you're a homegrown ordinary mum. That's such a *huge* bonus."

Sinéad glowed.

"Okay, we're here," Eddie announced, pulling up as close as he could to the spot.

"Trees!" laughed Sinéad.

"Yes, we couldn't decide whether to chain you into a tunnel or go for a tree-house," Eddie said, "but in the end we went for a tree-house. Trees are such an emotive issue – excellent for publicity."

"And they look good in photos, especially now it's April and they're in full foliage. We've already contacted the press – there'll be someone out later today to see you settle in," Maura added, drawing on her PR savvy.

As they got out a group of protestors appeared from between the trees to greet them.

"Okay, Sinéad, I'd like you to meet Steve and all the rest of the guys." Eddie seemed proud to know the names of all these genuine eco-buffs who looked like they never washed their hair, even with organic shampoo.

One guy stepped forward, smiling, his hair in dread-locked, dirty-blond ropes.

"Steve," he said and shook her hand.

She noticed the bulging tattooed biceps at the top of his T-shirt but when he added "Nice to meet you" in a North of England accent dripping with musicality a shudder passed through her body as she remembered the whirlwind romance with the devastating Geordie man of her youth.

"Now the first thing we need to find out is – can you abseil?" he asked.

Without a moment's hesitation Sinéad shook her head – abseiling was definitely not part of her daily routine as a housewife.

"We'll have to teach you so. The thing about trees is no stairs, you see," he said, pointing at the green canopy over their heads.

"Of course, no stairs," Sinéad said, stating what was the eco-obvious. Inside she was bursting with excitement. She, Sinéad Winterbottom, mother to three young children (four if Henry got his way) was going to learn to abseil. All in a day's work for an eco-mum like her.

"Well, what be on your mind?" Demelza asked Rebecca as she led her into her therapy room. From the outside it didn't look like there was too much wrong with the woman – designer clothes, hair made up, make-up blended to perfection.

"You help people with their relationships, right?"

"Help people to help themselves, yes," Demelza said as she lowered herself onto her favourite chair.

"Well, it's me you'll have to help so – there's obviously something wrong with me. See, I'm married to this good-looking guy. He's funny – well, he used to be but we haven't done much laughing lately. He's smart – in his own wheeling-dealing way. But even though I know he's a good thing I can't stop looking at other men, flirting with them, harmless stuff mostly, but yesterday . . ." Rebecca started to pluck the fabric on the arm of Demelza's chair as she tried to work out her feelings.

"Yes?"

"Yesterday a man kissed me and I kissed him back . . . passionately, in fact!"

Demelza gestured with her hand for Rebecca to continue.

"The thing is I didn't want this . . . not really . . . I thought I'd got all that out of my system . . . see, I separated from my husband a few years ago just for a few months . . . before we had children. He's a bit older than me and we met when I was young and maybe I wasn't so sure about us . . . even he thought maybe I needed a break to have, you know, some experiences before committing to our future."

"So if you be committed, why the flirting?" Demelza asked easily.

"I don't know . . . my way of seeing if I still have it maybe . . . since I had my babies, I . . . I don't feel right, don't feel my body is as tight as it used to be. I'm heavier and I can't lose any weight – it upsets me, I guess."

"Many women would be envious of the body you have," Demelza challenged.

"But it doesn't feel like *my* body, it feels like my body has gone away, deserted me and me being happy in my body is important to my identity," Rebecca sighed.

"So flirting be about your self-esteem, to see if you can still attract with the body you do have, this body that doesn't feel like yours any more?"

"I never thought about it that way before," Rebecca said as she stopped plucking at the chair and furrowed her brow for a moment.

"And these men that you flirt with, be they free or attached?"

"Well, there's this lifeguard I like, well, flirt with at any rate sometimes – he's young and fit – I know he has a girlfriend, she lives in the Village. And the man who kissed me . . . he has a wife, a wife who's away at the moment."

"So they be safe for flirting with then. You don't really expect them to respond except one of them did . . . and now you feel you not be the one calling the shots any more and it be scary?"

"Yes, no, oh I don't know! When this man kissed me, the man with the wife, it was *exciting* . . . it was only afterwards I felt guilty . . . oh God, I'm probably some kind of sex addict or something, aren't I?"

Demelza smiled but said nothing for a moment. "Tell me about the life you had before you married."

Rebecca's whole face lit up with animation. "Well, I used to be an air stewardess . . . did that until the passengers started to drive me crazy . . . then I trained and worked as a beautician . . . did that until the clients started driving me even more crazy . . . and then I played rugby, just for a short while – God I *loved* rugby! And I sometimes pole-dance . . . well, I did, but not so much any more, now I've got assignments to do and study . . ."

"You mostly be a physical person then?"

"Well, I'm smart too, you know! It's not all about the way I look or the way I move or putting on make-up!" Rebecca tapped her head with a finger. "People don't realise that, you know – that I've got it all upstairs too!"

"I think I be able to help you, certain of it in fact. Do you know about goddess therapy?"

Rebecca shook her head, a small, bemused smile on her face.

"It's a passion of mine, putting women in touch with the goddess that might help them feel whole, Celtic goddesses being my favourite. Sometimes we all need to realign, find the goddess that has much to teach us at one time in our lives. With you I feel there is much you can learn from Danu."

"Who?"

"She was the goddess of plenty, the mother to the Irish fairy gods. Some people in today's culture see the mother figure as being weak but she was strong, respected and loved. Her tribe was the mythical Tuatha Dé Danann who were said to walk this land of Ireland long ago."

"Tell me more quickly – I have to head back to let the au pair out for a while and, believe me, she's turning out to be more trouble than a trade union activist!" Rebecca said briskly and Demelza filled her in on her goddess homework.

Isobel White hated drab and boring agricultural towns. Dublin, where she was based, was exciting. She liked the bustle of the city centre where she worked – grabbing a latte and a cupcake or Panini before heading back into the newspaper office for her editor to yell at her – and she was itching to get back to urban life pronto. But it was an easy day's work in some ways, coming to Cloonsheeda to interview that young dimwit housewife who was learning to abseil from trees in protest against the new Minister's decision to proceed with a motorway. And someone had mentioned the Minister's ex-wife Anna Gavin was going to belly-dance at this festival lark these eco-fanatics were planning in a week – there might be a story in that too – not to mention the tree stump, that blessed heap of wood.

In fact, Isobel was at the Blessed Tree Stump at this very moment, in her trendy 'Musical Festival' wellies, talking to some of the devoted about their plans to hold vigils during the whole month of May, when she was met by a curvy, blonde-haired girl wheeling a bike.

"You write stories?" the girl asked very precisely in a slight foreign accent as Isobel flicked through a notebook.

The young reporter gritted her teeth at the banal

question. Wasn't it obvious to anyone with a brain that she didn't clean toilets for a living?

"Yes, I write stories," she sighed.

"Would you be interested in mine? I've been away for a while and had time to think and I've decided I want it to be written."

"Why, what story do you have worth telling?" Isobel said, feeling impatient. If she hurried up she could whizz back to Dublin, write up a thousand words or so, and meet some fellow journos for a bitching session later that night.

"I lost my virginity to movie star David Ron Dwyer, had a threesome with him and actor Conan Mallon where we all smoked some pot – but then David dumped me after he and Conan went to England – he told me he was working but the English papers showed pictures of them both in a bar in Manchester with lap-dancers. Now I hate him, hate them both!"

Isobel White could feel the excitement chasing through her limbs like forked lightning. For a one-horse town this little patch of boring Ireland sure had a lot of juicy secrets.

"I have some photos?" Liesel added to sweeten the deal.

"What's your name?" Isobel asked, her face sweet and inviting as a Venus flytrap.

"Liesel."

"Liesel, let's go and talk in private!" The young reporter smiled broadly, putting an arm around her catch possessively as she steered the young au pair towards her car.

"Well, some reporters from the national media came to

do initial coverage on our protest. I have to say, I think it's very clever how we're getting coverage for the festival out of it as well," Maura gushed as she sat with India in the coffee-cum-health-food shop, finalising some details for the Bealtaine Festival.

India smiled politely but really couldn't care less as she started on her festival list in a perfunctory manner. She was eager to get away and work on some paying festival work of her own.

"The council have okayed us for stalls on the village green, the art exhibition on the railings and temporary camping areas," India rattled off briskly. She couldn't wait until all this nonsense died down – Nathan had turned into a physical robot since the thing with the bog-snorkelling had started.

"And thankfully, the lighting of a community bonfire on May Eve has turned out not to be contentious," Maura added as she checked off her list. "Are you sure it's okay to do the wrapping of the May Pole on May Eve and not May Day?"

"It varies a bit across cultures but we could always leave it up and let people have an impromptu dance on May 1st too – it'll be a more relaxed day anyway with picnics on the green and the family bike day – nothing too hectic after all the fun of the day before. The bog-snorkelling is turning out to be the real star of the show – it's great we're running such an unusual event, isn't it? We can be proud of ourselves."

"Yes, fabulous idea that was, should get lots of coverage," Maura enthused. "The hostel is booked out and it's great that locals are opening their houses and doing a bit of spontaneous B&B as well. Jasper Keogh says he's got a few guys from London staying with him over the pub and there's mad jostling going on to get into the bog for snorkelling practice. Amazing how much some people want to take home the title of Cloonsheeda's first ever Bog Snorkelling Champion!"

"Uhm," India said distractedly as she totted up some artists' fees and expenses on her calculator.

"And your boyfriend – I met him on the way to work earlier on, such a laugh – he says he can't *believe* how addicted he is to the snorkelling now and to think he's planning to enter a few more competitions in the UK or maybe go home to Oz for a bit of dirt-snorkelling!" Maura laughed, shaking her head at the nonsensical dreams of the young.

"What?" India spluttered, suddenly animated.

"Your boyfriend and his international bog-snorkelling plans . . . didn't you know?"

"About his training for the Bog Snorkelling Olympics? No, I did not!" India huffed.

"Oh, sorry, didn't mean to cause any trouble. Still, it must be nice to be going out with such a *fit* young man all the same!" Maura said with a twinkle in her eye, that twinkle that India knew meant 'You're so lucky, I bet he *never* lets you out of bed!'.

"Actually there are times when I'd settle for him being a typical Irish bloke, a few pounds overweight, in love with his pint and fast food," India said with a flash of sarcasm in her voice and Maura put her head back and laughed heartily, not believing a word.

"Eddie!" said Anna as she opened the door.

"I was in the area, helping get things ready with the

motorway protest and Maura had to go to Dublin for a meeting."

He stepped in but halted then as she hovered anxiously in the hall.

"It's just a tiny bit awkward at the moment," she said. "My son is staying with me and he needs a bit of mothering," Anna explained, her brows knitting together as she tried to convey the seriousness of her mothering requirements.

The 'mothering' word made Eddie cringe slightly as he thought of Anna's ex-husband and wondered what kind of 'mothering' Anna had to endure during the years, in addition to Paddy's shirt-washing and obsessive-compulsive behaviour over his ties.

Seeing his face caved in from disappointment, Anna capitulated and patted his hand.

"Later, come back later. I know Liam's going to the pub for a pint in the evening – there's a real buzz down there, now that Jasper has a few foreigners staying with him."

"I'll cook for you," Eddie announced, his face brightening.

"The bane of a woman's life, a mother's life, cooking – that would be lovely," Anna smiled.

"It's important not to mother *too much* in this life," Eddie announced seriously and Anna gave him a peculiar look.

"Later then, Eddie, and bring some of your lovely wine," she said as she ushered him out and shut the door.

He'd been walking the fields. Rita could hear him taking off his boots downstairs and she steadied herself and pulled the belt of her silky dressing gown tight. She really didn't want to do this bit of her homework but Demelza had coaxed her to give it a go.

"Up here, Mossy, in the bedroom!" she called and heard his step on the stairs, heard him shuffle around in the bathroom before opening the bedroom door.

"Take your clothes off," she said matter-of-factly as Mossy froze in the doorframe.

"What?"

"Just do it, would you, Mossy? And here, this sack is for you."

She handed Mossy a black plastic refuge sack which seemed to contain nothing but air, then with one motion she let her slinky dressing-gown fall to the floor.

"Rita, it's been so long," Mossy said awkwardly, the nervousness apparent in his voice.

"Don't worry, it'll be longer yet," Rita said wearily as she picked up a black refuse sack of her own.

"I don't understand . . . if we're not going to . . ."

"Just take your clothes off, Mossy. I've been going to counselling lately and this is part of my assignment."

"Counselling for what?" Mossy asked accusingly but he was nevertheless carrying out his wife's instructions and was down to his vest, pants and socks.

"Later, I'll tell you later," Rita said as she reached inside and found a ping-pong ball for her fist.

"Apparently we throw them at each other, one by one, taking turns, and if we want we can unleash any angry thoughts. That way we get any negative thoughts out but we can't hurt each other. Perfect, isn't it?"

Mossy laughed. "Jesus, Rita, you've lost your head!"

"Right, I'll get things started by throwing the first

one," Rita sniped, throwing the light ball as hard as she could at Mossy's chest. It fell like a raindrop and made a light pop-pop sound as it dropped on the floor.

"That's . . . that's just for everything!" she said, feeling suddenly furious.

"Well, I'll just aim one at your tits then, seeing as you haven't let me near them in years?" Mossy said in a ridiculous voice, taking aim across the bed with two balls. "One for each of them!"

"You stopped caring about the way you looked from the day we got married, you dress for me the same as you dress for the animals!" Rita said in a fury, not sure where her spiteful words were coming from, only aware that they were being unleashed with surprising ease. A ping-pong ball bounced off Mossy's nose.

"Stupidity, daftness and more stupidity! What did you want me to wear, a tuxedo every night?" Mossy fired a ball at the curve of Rita's belly and it slipped quietly to the floor like a whisper.

In a craze Rita rummaged in her bag and fired two handfuls of balls at her husband with huge force. Still the damn things made no impact.

"That's for being a misogynistic bastard, not content that we never had a son, not seeing our daughters as being good enough to run a farm!"

Mossy fired a ball at Rita's head, curious to see what would happen if the ball found a harder surface – the results were unspectacular.

"You know I care about them greatly – I just would prefer they didn't have such a hard life – I've seen the toll the life has had on you. I wouldn't wish it for a daughter. Can I stop throwing balls now, Rita? This is ridiculous!"

318

"I'm not finished yet!" Rita roared as she threw a few more balls as fast as she could, emptying all the balls from her bag in a frenzy.

"They're all, they're all just – just *because*, you worthless bastard!" she said breathlessly.

Mossy started to laugh, a trickle of noise first that built to a roar.

"Why are you laughing?" she asked. "I've used all my balls up – let me see inside your bag!" Rita grabbed Mossy's bag and poured his ping-pong balls over his head, letting them plip-plop to the floor like a light shower of rain.

Spontaneously, Mossy pulled her to him and smiled – he was aroused, very aroused and began to stroke his wife's face – but when he bent to kiss her she pulled away.

"No."

"What?"

"My counsellor said I'm not allowed to rush my homework. Tonight was just about anger and a few harmless balls." Rita pulled on her nightdress and hopped into bed.

Mossy stifled a moan. He had no idea what he'd just partaken in but, as he switched off the light, for the first time in a long time his body was flushed with heat and his dormant man-bits had the vaguest memory of something pleasurable – it was almost strange the way they were heavy and ached.

27

"Nothing happened, of course, but I still want to take care of her somehow – she hasn't been treated well since she arrived in Ireland," Freeda sighed as Bast walked around the room, her tail stroking the air with fiery determination as she sought out a soft chair in which to snooze.

"Shoo!" Demelza scolded, picking her up and putting her out of the room, much to the animal's annoyance.

Freeda waited anxiously until her therapist settled herself again.

"Ah, yes, distraction in the shape of the little Fraulein – distraction be easier than doing the hard work on yourself," Demelza said. "I told you that before."

"You think I'm looking for a project to get over my troubles then and Liesel is it?"

Demelza said nothing, knowing silence would encourage Freeda to keep talking.

"It's stupid, I know, but she reminds me of Maeve . . . every time I see her I see Maeve . . . all that long, beautiful, hair, all that innocence and wildness mixed together," Freeda sighed.

"This Maeve, when she first came to America, why she be so special to you then?" Demelza queried, her pen poised to make notes.

"Oh, Maeve when she first arrived . . . she stood out for being so natural . . . she was only finding out about herself, about what it was to be gay and San Francisco was freedom to her coming from rural Ireland, but maybe a little overwhelming. I guess you could say I took her under my wing, protected her because I thought I came from a similar way of life . . . I grew up in Africa, my parents were missionaries, life was basic, there was no TV, cars had to last forever, things like that . . . Maeve and I . . . well, over time she changed, got sucked into the whole West Coast thing, whitened her teeth, lightened her hair, had Botox, wanted to morph into an All American Barbie Doll and had lovers, men as well as women . . . she became cruel."

"Your parents, what did they think of you being gay?"

Feeling cramped by the question as much as by her chair, Freeda squirmed.

"They don't know . . . they still don't know. I went to San Francisco to disappear and never told them."

"And found someone to fuss over so you be not needing to deal with your own problems. It doesn't make for very equal relationships, nor healthy relationships, does it?" Demelza challenged.

"Stop, please stop, just tell me what my homework is for the next day so I can go!" Freeda said, clearly frazzled.

"Same as before, spend time with yourself, learn to love yourself, to treat yourself as the most special person in the world – and stop being a doormat," Demelza said sternly.

Freeda scowled, not at all liking the 'love thyself' mantra that Demelza insisted she learn.

"The finest!" the vegetable man winked as Willie handed over a supply of 'dumpster' carrots and got a folded handshake of notes for his trouble.

Passing by the corner shop Willie stopped dead. A newspaper headline screamed at him: **Sex Rat David Ron Dwyer Steals My Virginity**. Underneath was a picture of himself and Liesel doing a cheesy kiss for the camera. He rushed inside and picked up a newspaper. Hands shaking, he opened the pages and saw a two-page special complete with a moany interview from Liesel about relationship woes. There was an inset of the lap-dancers again from Manchester taken from a mobile phone and juicy bits were done in bold text. **Au pair Liesel Hoffman speaks of betrayal, bizarre method-acting in rundown Irish cottage** . . .

"Tom, have you seen today's papers?" Willie hissed down the phone.

"What?"

"We best disappear for a few days! Do you think your heap-of-shite car is up to a long journey?"

"Dublin?" Tom asked incredulously and Willie snapped.

"No, not Dublin, not far enough, nor remote enough neither . . . get your gear packed, Skeehan – I'll explain it all on the way!"

"Sis, this is the finest publican in the northern hemisphere, Jasper Keogh . . . Jasper, this is me Big Sis Rosie, the finest sister a man could ever wish for!" Nathan said grandly in the bar.

"Don't make such a fuss about it," Rosie said, giving her brother a friendly dig.

"You're over for a wedding, I believe," Jasper said as he pulled a pint.

"A girl I know is getting married," Rosie smiled.

"Who's the lucky chap?" Jasper asked jocularly.

"Me – I'm Maeve, Maeve O'Meara, and I'm the lucky 'chap'!" a tall, tanned, toned, bleach-haired woman introduced herself, enjoying the blush of embarrassment on Jasper's face. "I'm here having my hen weekend before I get hitched in a civil ceremony. Didn't know there was a festival on soon – think we'll have to pop down for a bit of bog-snorkelling, what you think, ladies?"

A cheer went up from her group of friends.

"Don't think you're gonna just walk away with that snorkelling title, little bruv!" Rosie warned, giving Nathan a steely stare.

"That right?" he joked back.

"It's women and men all together on the big day, isn't it? Not girls and blokes racing separately?"

"That's right but the competition would be better staying at home, this is a title I'm taking for Australia," Nathan boasted.

"You bet, but we'll have to see which Australian takes it!" Rosie smirked, raising her pint in a friendly toast.

All morning Liesel's phone had been hopping and she'd been having whispered conversations in the hall. Rebecca couldn't read the girl's body language: one minute her whole being seemed to bristle with excitement, the next she seemed to go rigid with fear.

"Liesel, please turn your phone off!" she eventually snapped. "The boys need you and I am going out."

"Yes, Rebecca."

Rebecca pulled her trainers on hastily.

"Rebecca, do you think I am pretty?" Liesel asked suddenly, and Rebecca froze to the spot at the question.

"Pretty . . . well, of course, Liesel . . ." She wanted to deny it, play it down somehow but the fact of the matter was that Liesel was pretty. Still very curvy, but since she'd lost a few pounds through moping and not eating much, she was pretty – very pretty, now that she thought about it.

"Do you think I could be a model? One of those plus-size models?" Liesel asked meekly.

Rebecca was flummoxed.

"Well . . ."

"No matter," Liesel added abruptly and gave Rebecca a knowing small cat-like little smile.

The smile bothered Rebecca greatly. Who was this saucy madam? Where was the meek and mild Liesel she'd first employed?

"Don't forget to give them scrambled eggs for lunch – just as a break from the sausages," Rebecca said tetchily.

"Eggs, yes, I know how to scramble them just as the children like," Liesel said smoothly.

Rebecca flinched. There was something different about Liesel, something she couldn't put her finger on, but something different and bloody annoying all the same.

"Actually, I've changed my mind. I'm going upstairs Liesel."

Liesel shrugged her indifference and Rebecca bristled even more.

"Damn au pair," Rebecca seethed as she swung out of her dance-pole but after five minutes of twirling she started to feel unexpectedly happy. Dancing, there was nothing like it in the whole world for putting her in a good mood.

"Was I in Ireland banging some German teenager and with Conan Mallon? Are you for real?" David Ron Dwyer laughed down the phone, a little bit of stress plainly evident in his tone.

"David, there are pictures of you with the girl concerned. Have to admit it does look like you – *really* like you."

"Hey, I'm in LA minding my kid, remember? And I'm chewing my nails right now – Kari Ann's making me give up the fags because of the baby."

"You sure you weren't over? It would be better to come clean right now. They say you were doing method-acting in a rundown hovel in Ireland."

"The only method-acting I'm doing now is stressed-out dad! And I'm not too gone on these film parts that I'm getting to read lately – not as macho as they used to be. Look, this German teenager stuff – you *can* sort this out, right?"

"Leave it with me. I'll get to the bottom of this thing – that's a promise."

Eddie and Anna sat on the bed-settee staring straight ahead, neither of them speaking after their unexpected wine-fuelled tussle on the cushions. Eddie had lipstick on his cheek and Anna didn't know whether to brush it away or leave it there; she did her best to ignore its guilty imprint. Maura wasn't even away this time – this was definitely reckless behaviour.

"Eddie . . ." Anna started, feeling awkward.

"I understand," Eddie said, waving his hand to discourage her from talking more.

"It's just my mind is on other things," Anna told him cautiously. "To be honest, all I can think of is that bastard Paddy. Liam met him a few days ago for a chat and after what my son has just told me I'm shocked and really, really angry about Paddy's attitude to sex and sexuality – appalled, to be brutally honest with you – you have no idea what kind of monster I was married to for twenty years, Eddie!"

"Actually, I think I do, but I wondered did you . . . what that man did to you over the years . . . liking to wear nappies and suck soothers and his wanting to be walked over in high heels and tied up, and sometimes locked in a box . . ."

Anna's jaw nearly hit the floor in disbelief and Eddie heard her gasp.

"This is what we're talking about isn't it, your husband's unusual fetishes?"

"What the hell, Eddie? My eldest son is gay, just gave me the news, and he tried to tell his father a few days ago but Paddy's response was so old-fashioned and selfish poor Liam ended up walking off upset! Nappies, tied up in a box, who in God's name told you all this?"

"Oh God, damn wine!" Eddie moaned.

"Forget the wine – what are you talking about and who told you about Paddy and all this weird stuff?" Anna demanded.

"I wasn't supposed to say . . . Jesus, I can't believe I

let it out after all that I promised! Anna, can you keep a secret?"

"Eddie, I was married to a politician for twenty years – 'secrets' is my middle name," Anna said firmly as she made known with her body language that she was settling down for a long and frank disclosure about everything to do with the new Minister for Transport.

Henry stood in a cleared area of the woods with Jane and Peter at his side, but he couldn't see Sinéad anywhere on this pathetic protest lark.

"I'm looking for my wife, Sinéad Winterbottom," he finally had to ask a man in combat trousers and thick leather boots. Henry saw the man's thick biceps were covered with Celtic and Polynesian tattoos and he wondered how long it had been since he'd washed his dirty-blond dreadlocks or any other part of himself for that matter.

The man with the hair like rope held out his hand to be shook and introduced himself as Steve.

"Look, Mummy is in the trees!" Peter pointed excitedly and Henry watched horrified as Sinéad effortlessly abseiled down to the woodlands floor right in front of his nose.

"Sinéad," Henry said firmly, trying to keep his anger under wraps, "your baby is at home being minded by the village midwife and before that by that woman who wears jumpers of dyed sheep's wool and who could give birth herself any minute."

"How lovely, just like in a genuine tribal system – we really live in a *fabulous* community here at Cloonsheeda, don't we, Henry?" Sinéad said happily in a sing-song voice that made Henry want to do something vaguely violent and satisfying but not at all logical, like cracking every single one of his knuckles on both his hands or giving his wife a good shake.

"Sinéad, I will be blunt – if you do not come home with me now I will not be held accountable for what might happen," Henry said in a tight voice full of suppressed anger.

"For heaven's sake, Henry, what could possibly happen?" Sinéad said lightly, picking a leaf out of her long, tangled ponytail. "The children are being minded by loving earth-mother figures, my protest is only till the start of the festival a few days away and I really don't think I'd be up to battling council workers and the cops if we're moved on . . . but then again, being out here in the forest makes me feel strangely invincible."

Henry noticed her face was smeared with dirt; he longed to wipe it clean, wipe all of Sinéad clean in fact; maybe even dip her in disinfectant and check her for lice or other creepy crawlies.

"Sinéad, I will ask you one more time, are you coming home? You're still my Mummy Winterbottom and I *need* you," Henry persisted.

"Did you see my coverage in the newspapers – there's a lot more press coming later on?" Sinéad inquired, deliberately ignoring her husband's question.

"Yes, yes, I saw every word and I wouldn't be so proud if I were you. Your publicity is terrible for my business, I'll never be asked as a consultant archaeologist on a big-build government project again. Sinéad, as your husband I absolutely *demand* you come home right now!" Henry said, fit to bust.

"I've thought about it – the answer's no," she said calmly.

"Well, I hope you realise that this is a turning-point in our relationship," Henry warned, his eyes narrowing.

"Yes, Henry, I know," his wife said, looking him steadily in the eye.

"Sinéad, we're going to have a drumming session to pass the time and provide a focus for the cameras – are you joining?" Steve asked in his sexy North of England accent as he appeared at her elbow.

"Gotta go, darlings, Mummy just loves the beat of the African drums – be good for Daddy now," Sinéad said, kissing her two eldest children goodbye.

"Mummy, you hanging out of trees is cool, just like Spiderman!" Peter said proudly as she released him from a hug.

"Thank you, darling," Sinéad responded and, as she kissed the top of Peter's head and deliberately withheld all affection from Henry, much to her satisfaction she saw her husband scowl.

"Some of your daughters might be dropping home for the festival," Rita said bluntly to Mossy as he walked into the room where she was painting.

The frisson between them was uncomfortably electric; it was a mixture of anger and something else – something dangerous but sad.

"You do know that cow is blue?" Mossy pointed out as he surveyed Rita's latest work.

"I'm going through my Van Gogh phase. I've no idea what these people at the festival will want and I want to give them a good selection of cows to take home," she said, feeling annoyed, but something else too as she felt his energy encroach on her personal space.

"Rita . . . last night . . ." he began slowly as he came up behind her and put one hand on her shoulder.

His touch thawed out something frozen inside her ever so slightly and she winced from the unexpected burning pain.

"I told you . . . just homework." She shrugged off his hand.

"Who are you seeing that gives you such strange homework and why?"

"You have Your Lady up in the field that you speak to when things get too much and I have mine, although mine is real and isn't made of wood," she said, wanting to cry.

"Will there be any more homework then?" Mossy asked, looking small and strangely hopeful.

Rita shrugged. In a few days' time she'd know if she was any good as a painter, if anyone at the festival would buy her work. In a few days she might see if she could fund a lifestyle where she might live alone. In a few days she'd tell him it was all over. But she'd keep her bargain to Demelza to wait until May Eve itself before saying goodbye to her husband of many years.

28

Anna couldn't quite get over the shock of it. Calling Paddy now was impossible. She didn't know who he was any more, this grown man who liked to dress and behave as an infant in his spare time, and she almost felt sorry for the woman who'd landed herself the country's Minister for Transport. Who would have guessed that the great and arrogant Paddy Gavin liked a mixture of pain, humiliation and some mollycoddling in nappies? Eddie had even told her the new mistress had been asked to don spiky high heels and walk across his chest. Jesus Christ, who the hell had she been living with for all those years?

"Mum, is it okay if I have a friend over?" Liam asked, breaking her reverie for a moment as he came into the kitchen, showered with just a towel around his waist, his hair damp and sticking up like the fluffy feathers of a baby duck.

"I suppose . . . whatever you like," Anna said distractedly, biting her lip.

"Great, he's just texted, actually he's outside the door," Liam said happily and exited the room.

A moment later he returned with a beautiful young man, his muscles sleek and hard, his eyes dark and deep, his features noble and beautiful and totally arresting, his skin a gorgeous shiny black.

"My name is King," the handsome young man said in a warm African accent.

"We're going back to college together," Liam gushed.

"Are you over seventeen, King?" Anna asked wearily as she took in this latest information.

"Of course," King answered in his mellifluous tones again.

Anna gave a mother's blessing and went for a walk. What the hell did she know about anything any more?

"Jesus, Willie, how much are you paying to rent this hole?" Tom Skeehan asked as he chucked his rucksack into the corner of his bedroom in the damp cottage they'd rented in the wilds of Mayo. The decor was all 1970's, the room a time-warp of purple, orange and brown.

"How much are *we* paying?" Willie corrected, throwing his own bag into the corner and lying on the bed. The mattress was like lumpy porridge, the padded velvet headboard smelt musty and was the colour of dried blood.

"Them curtains are like what you'd chuck up after a night out," Tom said, shaking his head mournfully as he sat on a straight-backed chair with padded arms, the kind of flock chair found in a grubby doctor's surgery, shiny with engrained filth and smelling of body odour.

"You're right, the curtains are vile – you can have this room," Willie said meanly, eager to find out if all the beds in the rundown house were equally as lumpy.

"This is mad, Willie – us being here at all," Tom said, suddenly feeling overcome by their musty environment and the dirty plush pile carpet on the floor which once had been a vivid orange. The huge solid-wood dressing-table in the corner with the curvy mirror stained the colour of tea in parts lent an even more depressing quality to the room.

"It's the best place to be till all this stuff with Liesel blows over. No one will think of looking for us here and, besides, I brought the pipes so we can have a pint and play some music in one of the local pubs. Keep your nerve, it will be an adventure."

"A few days – that's all I'm giving it at most," Tom said frankly as he ploughed his hands into his pockets and walked out of the room.

"Mark, good news, RTÉ are committed to doing something on the motorway protest," Maura gushed down the phone.

Mark suppressed a sigh. Publicity was all very well but what he really needed was publicity to get people to buy property in Cloonsheeda, not any news that might put clients off the place completely. What he desperately needed was something to raise the Village's profile.

"What about the people arriving for the festival? It's only a few days till kick-off. Anyone at all interested in actually buying a property?" he asked hopefully.

"Oh yes, the festival – well, the nice man who booked the community hostel a while back arrived today – very respectable, very well-dressed, *definitely* the kind of person we'd want to be attracting to Cloonsheeda long-term – you know, progressive but well off and educated.

And the Tidy Towns committee are doing an amazing job planting flowers and doing window-boxes and encouraging everyone to give their premises a lick of paint for good appearances."

"Right, so nobody actually has talked to you about buying in the Village then?"

"Well no, not exactly, but isn't it great about RTÉ coming down to meet our gal in the trees?"

Considering that the last time the media had been on his doorstep the whole world had got to hear about Moving Holy Tree Stumps, Mark wasn't so sure.

"Suppose it can't hurt," Mark said, wanting to hang up and get away.

When would Cloonsheeda start to pay off? The worst-case scenario is they'd end up bulldozing units, not a very environmentally friendly scenario and, worse, not a very financially sound one either.

"Bye, Maura – let me know if any well-known actors or musicians want to buy a house for a huge mark-up price, won't you?" he said as he hung up, wishing for the hundredth time that he had never got involved in the damn Village project at all, wondering if that local witch Spargo had really turned the fairies against him for having the stupid Blessed Virgin Oak Tree felled on the meadow. No, that wasn't possible, was it?

"Hi, I'm Rosie – you rent bicycles for the day?" the tall hard-boned Australian asked Freeda as she charged right up to the desk and flashed a warm, sunny smile.

"Yes, yes, I do," Freeda said quickly, reckoning this was one of the tourists in for the festival and eager to capitalise on their arrival.

"Would you have ten bikes for hire?" Rosie asked.

"Ten . . . ten would be a big ask, but I also have two tandems if you're interested?" Freeda said, doing some rapid mental calculations on her feet.

A jangle of noise at the door alerted Freeda to the fact that more customers were entering her shop, all women, all giggling and in good form.

"Hang on till I ask one of the lucky ladies myself if she'd like to tandem with me, the chief bridesmaid!"

"Maeve . . . over here! This lady here wants to know would you be interested in a tandem?"

Still laughing, Maeve walked to the counter and hardly saw Freeda at first. Then her face blanched like a sick child's.

"Y-you!" she stammered, completely stunned. "What are *you* doing here in Ireland?"

"I . . . you were always telling me how beautiful it was in Ireland so I came to see for myself," Freeda answered in shock.

"Hey, you girls know each other?" Rosie asked happily.

Suddenly, Maeve turned on her heel and ran out of the shop like a frightened bride running from her altar on her wedding day.

"I've been pole-dancing – quite a lot actually. My big college assignment is submitted so the exams are a formality really, and I've been doing all the other course work throughout the year," Rebecca said as she got herself comfortable in Demelza's therapy room.

"Good. You be happy then with your achievements?"

"Yes, I suppose. I always dance when I'm happy and

me and my pole we're best friends when we're together but we haven't been together much since I started my course, that's the thing . . . which has got me thinking . . . why am I doing this damn course at all if it's not the thing that gives me the most pleasure?"

Demelza said nothing but Rebecca caught her eye and started to babble.

"Well, I know why I did it, applied for the course, that is. I've always liked practical work but I wanted to prove to everyone that I had a thinking brain too . . . but now I've done the first year I know what's involved and I know eventually I'll get my qualification, but it's all going to take years and even then I don't know if I'm ever likely to get a job as an archaeologist. But dancing, dancing I can do it now and it gives me so much pleasure, makes me happy right now, right this very moment!"

"Great news," Demelza said, smiling.

"No, it's not great news, that's the thing. I'm so confused. I thought I wanted a life of study but now I wonder if it's making me miserable, not leaving me enough time to do the other things I love."

"If you had six months to live which would you be wanting to follow, which be the bringer of happiness, the dancing or the archaeology?"

"See, I'm such a physical person, but that doesn't mean I don't use my brain," Rebecca said, chewing her lips, trying to think of an answer that wouldn't cause any distress. "But if I don't slog it out and keep doing archaeology people will think I'm stupid."

"Life be all about decisions and they don't always have to be perfect. We know what be in our hearts by our behaviour. Look at your behaviour and you'll see your heart's desire," Demelza said softy.

"It can't be that easy," Rebecca grimaced.

"It not be half as hard as you think," Demelza said with assurance.

Isobel White felt very pleased with herself on selling her au-pair story to a UK paper. Of course she would have loved to have seen her name in print but it was better that some other reporter got the glory and she the money – she didn't want to piss off her boss in Ireland – not really. Still, there was more to this story. The name Skeehan rang a bell – and the Bold Willie had to be related to the old farmer whom she'd interviewed at the Blessed Tree Stump. So far she'd pieced together that Willie Cleary and Tom Skeehan were real guys and not made-up aliases for famous Irish actors. That much she'd been able to tease out because people's tongues were loosened from the festival, but the chancers themselves were nowhere to be seen. The guys in the pub clammed up when she went in at lunchtime for a bowl of soup and the old man at the rundown hovel where all the action with Liesel supposedly had taken place, had shooed her from the door, saying his son was nowhere to be found and had taken off with his playing pipes.

From a distance she saw Mossy Skeehan, standing at the Blessed Tree Stump where the Pole and a basketry artist were making a wicker grotto for the honouring of Mary at the start of May.

"Mr Skeehan, Isobel White. Do you remember me from the interview you first gave about the tree stump and the sex therapist down the road?"

"Indeed and I do!" Mossy stuck out his thick hand to be shaken and smiled.

"I got a bit of flak for calling the sex therapist a witch," Isobel said, "but I said it was important to quote you correctly and *witch* was the word you used, wasn't it?"

"There wasn't a wrong word in the whole piece. I stand over everything I said," Mossy thundered, his face turning shades of purple and pink.

"A lot of hard work is going into this festival, isn't it?" Isobel said lightly, trying to take a relaxed approach to her interrogation.

"Good though, brings people together," Mossy said, nodding, his mind somewhere else.

"You got sons and daughters coming to it then?"

"Not sons, only girls – one lives nearby . . ." he trailed off. "The closest I have to sons is a nephew Tom, but between you and me he's not up to much, living the life of Reilly he is, owes me a few bob – in fact he sent me a text today from Mayo that he'll have some payment for me next week, not that I believe a word."

"Mayo?"

"There's a spot there his friend Willie favours – wild beautiful beaches, peaceful all the same."

Isobel sighed and looked into the distance as if a great burden rested on her own shoulders. "I've been meaning to take off somewhere peaceful myself, Mr Skeehan, but I can't afford to go abroad, not on what I earn." Isobel smiled sweetly from under her eyelashes.

"Well, if you had the time you could do worse than check out the place in Mayo," and Mossy rattled off the name of Willie's West of Ireland coastal haven and Isobel smiled and made her excuses to leave.

"Hello, can I speak to Liesel the au pair, please, about her recent three-in-a-bed session with David Ron Dwyer?" the male voice asked briskly.

"What – who the hell is this? No, you can't!" Rebecca snapped.

A second later the security gate buzzed, with another similar request, this time from another man.

Upstairs in her room Liesel was squashing clothes into her case and putting on some scarlet lipstick.

"Liesel, there are people ringing my house asking about you and some ridiculous affair with that womanising Irish actor!" Rebecca fumed, struck for the first time at how vampish Liesel appeared as she blended in some black eyeliner.

"You have heard then. There are too many questions – it is time for me to leave you and Mr Mark," Liesel sighed.

"Leave, what do you mean leave? You can't leave, what about the boys?" Rebecca wailed.

"I will miss them but London is my big chance." Liesel smiled in polite regret as she brushed her long hair into a shimmering, golden sheet.

"London? Don't you mean home to Germany? What are you doing going to London?" Rebecca asked in disbelief. Her gym and study plans would be shot to hell now.

"After the publicity in the papers I got a phone call from a plus-size modelling agency – I'm going to do a photo-shoot for a department store," Liesel smiled happily and picking up her luggage she left the room.

"Liesel, this is very unsatisfactory," Rebecca threatened as Liesel made it to the front door, having kissed the twins goodbye.

"For you maybe, but not for me," Liesel said with a saucy raise of an eyebrow. "Goodbye, Rebecca, my taxi is waiting."

And Liesel walked through the front door and out into an exciting new life.

"Excuse me," Jerome said, asking Rosie to move to one side. His huge tanned forearms were on display as he drove the last remaining stakes into the ground by the bog-water's edge. The waters of the bog could be black as slick oil but today they were red-brown and murky. Rosie kept the stopwatch in her hand and watched her brother move through the water like a fish.

"How am I doin' for time, sis?" Nathan asked as he surfaced and shook the dirty droplets from his mask.

"Not bad, wouldn't call it a winner's time yet though!" Rosie teased and Nathan smiled cockily, knowing for sure now that his time must be good.

"Well, regardless of your time you'll never look as good snorkelling as us!" two of the bridal party challenged. They'd got in on the festivities and had decided to enter the fun fancy-dress swim dressed as the front and back end of a zebra instead of going for the fastest time in the serious competition.

"Or me! I'm going for the real event!" another yelled. Her legs, arms and face were painted in large blue warrior-like dots and as a visiting camera crew moved close she smeared herself with mud and made victory signs in the air.

Beside Rosie, Maeve O'Meara was quiet and worried. The bicycle day and picnic for the girls had been called off, Rosie still didn't know why.

"Excuse me, I have to go and do something," Maeve said, slowly getting up from where she was sitting on the bog bank.

"You okay? Not having any last-minute nerves, are you?" Rosie asked.

"Nothing about my future life bothers me – it's the past that needs dealing with," Maeve said cryptically as she left her girlfriends behind and started to walk towards the village shops.

Despite business being brisk, with people buying snorkels, flags for bikes and other bits and pieces, Freeda was just about to close the shop. Liesel had stopped in en route to the airport to say goodbye and tell her that she was a good support after the Irish boys had treated her so badly. Saying goodbye to Liesel reminded Freeda yet again of her past but how was she to know the past would catch up with her so literally?

At the door, Freeda, still thinking of the lovely Liesel, saw Maeve and was frozen to the spot.

"Can I come in?" Maeve asked tentatively.

Freeda shook her head and gulped. No, she wasn't ready for this, she'd never be ready for this, but she opened the door anyway as if in a trance and let Maeve inside, automatically bolting the door behind them and pulling down the blind.

"Coffee, you want coffee?" It was all she could offer,

something that would do in an emergency like taking a nip of whiskey after an accident, not at all sure if it would or could do any good for the hungry, raw feeling of pain.

"I never really drank coffee till I moved to the States and met you. You couldn't get a decent cup where I was from when I left all those years ago," Maeve rambled as she followed Freeda into the backroom and waited as she got the pot out and unfolded a clean white filter, watched as her hand shook out the scoops for brewing. Both of them looked at the pot with anxiety, both of them knowing that it would take too long to have something in their hands which they could hug to their chests defensively, maybe even for comfort.

"Actually, do you know, I'd prefer some tea. If you don't have the Irish kind I'll take one of your herbals – you were always big on them, weren't you?" Maeve tried in a falsely optimistic voice but within a minute she had something warm in her hands, which was all she really wanted.

Freeda said nothing, just looked in darting glances at Maeve.

Maeve looked too, then began playing with the tea bag in her cup.

"I'm sorry, it's just I'm in shock," Freeda said abruptly, her words almost gulped to nothing.

"Me too – wasn't expecting to ever see you in my own country. I've been back a year."

"And you met someone special." Freeda tried to say the words with indifference but they came out raw and stinging all the same.

"Yes, she spent a few years in Australia but I met her

in America – she's Irish-born like me. We decided to have separate hens . . . our friends from home and a few we've picked up from our travels around the world and the Ozzie girls are on a world tour anyway . . ."

"You walked out on me, Maeve," Freeda said shortly.

"Yes," Maeve whispered, nodding her head.

"Had affairs with everyone, men, women, treated me badly."

"I needed to grow – to know who I was," Maeve said, cradling her cup tight.

"I tried to protect you against everyone who might hurt you, but you left without even a goodbye."

"It was cruel, I know, but you could have found me easy enough," Maeve defended herself.

Freeda sighed deeply and, more to have something to do than anything else, threw out her tea and filled a clean cup with coffee.

"I've come to ask you . . . will you come to my wedding? It's in the hotel in Carrigmore."

Freeda laughed, laughed so hard her shoulders shook, until Maeve came and steadied them with her hands and looked her in the face earnestly.

"I was a child and needed to grow and you did all the mothering when I needed it but I don't need that now. I'm inviting you to my wedding as an equal. Please come."

Freeda shook her head sadly. "Go, Maeve, please go," she said, tidying the cups away on the draining board of her kitchenette.

The bell jangled as Maeve unlocked the door and walked into the street.

Freeda shut the shop for an hour and cried until there was nothing left but emptiness.

29

The nice well-groomed man that Maura Simmons approved of left the community hostel with a companion and headed up towards the eco-houses of Cloonsheeda, up by the hill near the Blessed Oak at the crack of dawn on the start of May Eve.

"What do you think?" he asked his companion, a geeky man of thirty who had greasy black hair and post-adolescent spots, as he surveyed the countryside.

"It's a definite possibility – it has that certain vibe," the geek said jocularly, pushing his square spectacles back from his nose as he spoke.

"My feelings exactly – I'm blown away by it to tell you the truth. I think we're bound to have some success here with our investigations. Do you still stand by your view that there's likely to be more activity tonight?"

The geeky guy scratched his stubbly chin and pushed his jaw out a fraction as he considered. "Like I've said already, in Celtic times it would be the night closest to the new moon . . . that would be tonight."

"Tonight it is so – got a good feeling about this place,

344

a real good feeling. Let's round up the rest of the lads for breakfast and work out our plan of attack," the well-dressed man said as he took his smartphone from his shirt pocket, stabbed in a few important lines of text, then looked at the rising sun.

Demelza smiled as she rubbed the morning dew into her cold cheeks. Today was a very sacred day, a day when the Sun God greeted the Goddess Earth. Later on she would make a basket of flowers and hang some hawthorn from her doors and take a light from the community bonfire that was to be lit on the hill and use it to light a fire in her own hearth.

"Today be a day when opposites unite, when men and women draw strength in who they are. Bealtaine be a time when anything can happen," she told her computer as she wrote down some illuminating thoughts for her future goddess book.

At first light Rita jumped out of her bed and ran downstairs to the kitchen, feeling suddenly fearful. Switching on the light she surveyed her offerings for the festival ahead, fifty canvases, all of cows, to be hung on the village green, each one more than a painting, each one a possible meal ticket to a new life away from this place, away from Mossy, away from wifely duties. Immediately she made the decision to get dressed and load up her 4x4. She wanted that life immediately, she wasn't willing to wait a single second more.

Maura Simmons was feeling the pressure of being the kind of woman who could cope with everything at once.

Today would be an adrenaline rush but there was so much to do. The coffee shop would be flat out with orders and all the events had to happen on time. Most of all she was worried about the bonfire which was meant to be lit at moonrise, it was traditional for cattle to be driven through the flames and people to jump through the flames as a purifying ritual for the year ahead but she hoped nobody knew about the flame dancing – such spontaneous behaviour would have the local Council in a flap. It was just gone seven but she rang India, knowing well that the girl was a workaholic and bound to be up and doing something fruitful.

"The maypole – did you get the ribbons?" Maura asked, rattling out her top concern.

"Oh hi, Maura?" India made herself a herbal tea with one hand as she held the phone to her ear. She hadn't quite switched on her computer yet, but was almost there. "Yes, that's all covered – the ribbons are sorted."

"The pavement art contest for kids – did we order enough chalk, do you think?"

"Plenty – anything else?"

"The dancing maidens around the pole – have they all been costumed and told to braid their hair – braiding is traditional?"

"Everything's ready."

"Lord – I've got to put in an appearance at the motorway tree-top protest too this morning, then rescue our housewife maiden in time for her to dance around the maypole. I'm just so sure I'm going to forget something," Maura fretted.

"Relax, Maura, at this stage you have to go with the flow. Stuff might come up we weren't expecting but we'll deal with it. It is, after all, meant to be an enjoyable time for everyone."

"Yes, I suppose," India could hear the air whoosh out of Maura as she suddenly relaxed.

"That bog-snorkelling contest this afternoon looks like it's going to be the hit of the festival – so colourful too – UTV are doing a piece – I suppose you're betting on your boyfriend to win?" Maura teased, feeling playful now stress wasn't allowed.

India pursed her lips as she picked up a photo of herself and Nate in Australia and remembered what a hot love god he'd been in his own hemisphere. To be honest she didn't care if he won this bog-snorkelling business at all – all she cared about was getting him back in her bed after the stupid bog-training was over, raring to go and fully operational.

"I have to see if he's worth betting on, Maura," she finally answered, and she meant it in more ways than one.

This being one with nature, being outdoors under a canopy of leaves with the sun risen and the birds singing, was better than any holiday. It brought life to Sinéad's veins, made her feel like someone who could write stupid, flowery, woodland poetry about being one with nature, about being feminine and free. To think she had to go home after this, go home to the old life of drudgery with a house she hated and kids that frustrated her and a husband that quite frankly was from another century.

"Breakfast?" Steve's enquiring voice asked from the woodland floors.

At the sound of his North of England voice, Sinéad felt all tingly and bright.

"Yes, please, that would be lovely!" Sinéad yelled back through the green shade and minutes later breakfast of nuts, berries, cereal and mint tea arrived on a pulley system direct to her outside paradise.

Lovely, but then she deserved lovely, she thought as she sipped her tea.

Rebecca was sitting at the breakfast table open-mouthed like a goldfish, not saying anything, shaking her head, then sighing before repeating over and over again, "She's gone, I can't bloody believe it – she's actually – gone!"

"Well, maybe if you'd treated her nicer when she arrived she'd still be here working," Mark said bluntly, shovelling his cornflakes into his mouth – today was likely to be a busy day.

"We'll have to get another au pair – I'm going to start looking immediately, before the boys are out of bed," Rebecca announced, sitting up straight as if she'd just been electrocuted with the idea.

"Why, why exactly do we need another au pair? Why can't you just stay at home for a while and be a mother to our children and do what you really *want* to do, Rebecca, and not what you think you *should* do?" Mark ventured.

"Stay at home full-time! Are you mad? I've worked so hard putting in the hours for my archaeology course, and in a year or two I should be able to transfer to university and do a degree," Rebecca said haughtily as she blew carefully on her breakfast tea.

"Exactly, you are years away from accomplishing anything solid . . . and newsflash . . . this country doesn't need more archaeologists just now!" Mark said bluntly.

"So you want me to stay at home and just look after

our sons? That's not really a life though, is it and besides, what would your mother say?" Rebecca fumed, wanting to weigh down her toast with butter but resisting the urge.

"I can't win, can I? All I want is my wife back, the one who used to be fun, remember her?" Mark said, hurrying from the table.

"Mark, come back here, you can't make a statement like that and just leave!"

"No time – enjoy the festival, Rebecca!" Suddenly he turned on his heel. "And I mean that, Rebecca – just for today, enjoy yourself and stop worrying about the future – anything might happen in the future, but today the sun is shining. Lose it or use it, babes!" He smiled as he ran out the door.

In the kitchen, Anna was shaking. Paddy had left a message on her phone to say he was going to a race meet and function not far from Cloonsheeda and wanted to drop by to see her and talk about Liam. She'd agreed to meet him later on that night, when all the activity had died down . . . and she'd be ready for him. She had a plan. Her hands shaking, she reached for her hip-scarf with sewn coins and began to shimmy around the kitchen and tried some hip-slides. In the afternoon after dancing around the maypole she was going to give a fifteen-minute belly-dance demonstration for the public and tonight as the bonfire blazed she was going to shake her stuff on Cloonsheeda's hilltop and then . . . and then she'd meet Paddy on her own terms, on her home turf and get her satisfaction.

It was barely eight thirty but Rita was already hanging her pictures on the railings of the village green, feeling doubtful all of a sudden that she had any worthwhile talent. The blue cows in particular made her feel uneasy – she'd been mad to think she could pull off her attempt of a 'Van Gogh' cow. A trailer was setting up on the corner of the village, ready to hand out baked potatoes, coffee and chocolate bars. On the green itself the market was beginning to come alive; boxes of second-hand books were hauled out of vans, little pots of lavender and herbs were on sale, as was hand-made jewellery from glass and bits of metal, and second-hand clothes on metal hangers and old shop rails. It was going to be a busy day. She'd grab a coffee and start sketching the activity, a break from cow-drawing for a while; she had to diversify, from just painting placid bovines. She might try painting pets perhaps or children. Thinking of her grandchildren all of a sudden made her feel sad and ashamed – she had to resolve this thing with Sinéad, she couldn't allow it to just go on.

"Could you girls turn around, please? We'd like to get some shots of you in your excellent zebra costume," the photographer asked the two Aussie lasses who'd decided to enter the bog-snorkelling as a duo in the fancy-dress event.

"Wow, this is mad, isn't it? So much better than getting our nails done and having a facial," Rosie laughed giving Maeve's shoulder a friendly squeeze.

Sitting on the side of the bog lane, hugging her knees, Maeve O'Meara tried to pretend she was having a great time, but all she could think about was her past and not what should be an amazing future. Gingerly she looked towards the bike shop, knowing that Freeda was probably doing a brisk trade, kitting out whole families for the bike parade later on. She remembered one of their biking tours in Europe not long after they first met and smiled a smile that was somewhere between sweetness and sadness. In her mind she'd done her best, she'd forgiven herself for her juvenile behaviour and, if Freeda couldn't, well at least she'd tried.

"Excuse me," Maeve said, getting up from her grassy spot on the bog bank.

Maeve O'Meara hadn't prayed in a long time, didn't know what if anything she might believe any more but as she watched a small number of people place jars of fresh country flowers round the Blessed Tree Stump in preparation for the start of May she wondered if there was any wisdom to be got from women, whether living or dead, saint or goddess, blessed tree stump or budding oak; she could do with some healing energy from somewhere and anything that might fortify her for the days ahead had to be worth a look.

The morning was still dull but Rebecca could tell it was shaping up to be a beautiful start to summer. Still feeling shell-shocked and unsure without Liesel around to help with brushing hair and blowing noses, Rebecca had decided to bring the boys down to Cloonsheeda to sample a bit of the festivities. Face-painters offered to spider-web their little cheeks and Rebecca watched as they sat patiently waiting their turn while eating home-made iced buns bought from the market. Then she let them race around the bustling village green, full of sugar, and was surprised by how much love she felt for them and their boundless energy.

"Rebecca, so glad I've caught you!"

Maura Simmons was standing before her, a clipboard in hand.

Rebecca saw the worried frown on Maura's face and baulked; it was definitely the face of someone begging a favour.

"One of the maypole dancers is unable to take part and I've heard you are interested in that kind of thing," Maura said, deadpan, and Rebecca wondered was she trying to be sarcastic.

"Ehm . . ."

"The thing is you're about the right size for the costume," Maura continued, not to be deterred.

"It's just I'm here with my children today," Rebecca explained.

"Oh, the event itself will only take about half an hour. I'm sure we could arrange to have them minded," Maura pushed.

Have fun at the festival, take some time off from worrying about the future, isn't that what Mark said? And she *did* have a lot of experience dancing around poles.

"Okay, I'll do it," she said, seeing her boys charging around the green where people had set up yurts and wigwams full of interesting novelties and amusements. In one extra-large yurt you could even order every kind of mint tea known to man while listening to New Age music and perusing books on chakras, angels and alternative world religions.

"Excellent, I'll just go get your costume so," Maura enthused.

By necessity and by nature Mossy had always been an

early riser but he was unsettled when he awoke and discovered Rita gone. He didn't like the funny atmosphere between them the last few days and he'd wanted to wish her well with her painting, knowing how important it was to her at least, even if in his mind a cow should never be blue. Having crossed the town to feed his animals, he stopped off to buy a coffee and a bun at the market and as he munched it down to its paper skin he spied Rita by the railings, discussing her work with passersby. He moved closer to where she was.

"Do you want me to get you a coffee – lovely buns, very fresh," Mossy said awkwardly, stepping up to her when he spotted a lull in her conversations with the public.

Rita shook her head, annoyed that he was interrupting her day and her thoughts.

"Did you sell anything yet?" Mossy probed, aware as soon as the words popped out that the question would have been better left unasked.

"No, not yet, a few inquiries though," Rita said uncomfortably.

"Not everyone cares for blue cows, I suppose," Mossy said, sucking the froth from his coffee.

"The colour has nothing to do with it – there's just not enough people here yet!" Rita snapped, her voice deliberately turned down to simmer instead of scream.

"Rita . . . when you come home tonight . . ." Mossy began slowly.

When you come home tonight, the phrase sounded vaguely ridiculous, but Rita had promised Demelza she would wait at least until this night before telling Mossy of her unhappiness.

"Not sure when I'll finish up – you'll see me when you see me, Mossy," she said and felt a stab of unexpected pain as she watched her tall, well-built husband give her a curt nod and disappear across the green.

"I will pick you up – no worries – I am strong," Jerome the Pole assured Rebecca as she realised she was meant to place the wreath of flesh flowers on top of the wooden maypole. Already she felt ridiculous in her bare feet, long white robe with green belt and fresh flowers in her hair.

"Come, we do it now!" Jerome signalled with his hands.

"Actually, if you don't mind, I'll do it," a deep voice said from behind and Rebecca flushed as she turned around and caught Mark's amused expression.

"What are you doing here?" she said crossly but felt excited as he pulled her into his arms.

"Just came to see the fun," he said jocularly and before she knew what was happening she was hoisted on his shoulders and tentatively she looped the wreath around the wooden stick to whoops and cries from the crowd.

"Thank you, Rebecca – the Earth Goddess has now symbolically married the Sky God!" Maura announced to the crowd with a nod in Demelza's direction. "And now we'll proceed to the traditional wrapping of the maypole!"

"Wrapping a pole – you should be in your element with all this pole stuff," Mark teased as he backed away from his wife and saw her blush again as she joined a circle of dancers.

On the outside ring, amongst others were Rebecca, Anna in her belly-dance hip-belt, Sinéad Winterbottom with a dreamy smile on her face and Tilda the Swede and on the inside ring were eight local schoolgirls. The system was easy enough; every dancer took a ribbon attached to the pole, an outer ring of dancers then danced clockwise, the inner ring waiting for the outer ring to stop so they could begin an anti-clockwise dance. All the while Rebecca could feel Mark watching her and couldn't stop blushing. This was ridiculous, she'd known her husband for years, but for some reason she felt like they'd only just met. The pole-wrapping with ribbons went on for half an hour, Irish jig-like music playing, hair flying, the soles of her feet being stained with grass and the whole time her husband never moved from his place once, even when his sons crashed into him and demanded to be held aloft.

"That's the housewife from the tree protest," a cameraman muttered to a journalist alongside him as they watched the hypnotic swirl of ribbons round the wood.

"Wow, real earthy, isn't she?"

"Yeah, I know what you mean – I definitely would!" the cameraman said softly, then laughed.

Henry, who had been watching Sinéad, thinking how ridiculous she looked, how irresponsible and flaky a mother she'd been lately, was suddenly irritated.

He turned to the two men, his face beetroot with suppressed rage. "Do you mind? That's my wife you're talking about."

"Sorry, no offence . . . just saying, well, you've got a real wood nymph there, plucky woman too, sticking with that protest – you must be very proud," the cameraman said deferentially.

Sinéad plucky, a source of pride? Such thoughts had never entered Henry's head before. He watched Sinéad dance, coloured ribbons swirling around her head, a dreamy, carefree expression on her face – and watched Rebecca Gleeson dance barefoot beside her, all trace of the sophistication he liked about her gone as her hair went flying over her shoulders.

"That was fun," Sinéad said to him breezily as the dance finished, her hair in a mess around her, her cheeks pink and glowing.

"Good, maybe you can look after your children now," Henry said huffily.

"Oh no, Henry, I don't think so. I'm going into a yurt next to have an angel reading," Sinéad announced stubbornly, holding together her bright smile.

"What on earth for?" Henry hissed in annoyance.

"To see if I have an angel," Sinéad said as if the answer should be obvious.

"I can't believe you would waste the money – there is no scientific basis for this witch-doctor mumbo-jumbo stuff, Sinéad!" Henry bristled, pushing back his spectacles from his nose in complete incomprehension.

"I'm doing it for the fun of it, Henry – remember fun?"

Henry's face was blank.

"No, I don't believe you do much fun, do you?" Sinéad said, shaking her head in disbelief, skipping around like a girl on the village green, in search of angels, in search of anything at all that might give her wings.

30

The moon had risen over Cloonsheeda. On the hilltop the community bonfire was being lit and people were dancing around the crackling branches. Beside Jasper Keogh's pub the bog-snorkelling was proceeding. The 'headbanger' sections had been completed with Spud and Hackett getting cheers for being dressed as the front and the back of a Friesian cow – they were now trying to mate with the Aussie zebra girls as the true athletes were lining up on the banks to be timed by the ever-affable Eddie Ferris. Two hardcore but good-humoured snorkelling buffs from London had already swum the length of the trench with good times as men smeared in blue paint banged African drums and Maeve's bridal posse whooped like tribal women at a rain dance and blew police whistles.

"Wish me luck, sis," Nathan implored as he went to adjust his snorkel and took his first steps into the inky blackness.

"No way! Not when I'm going for the title too," Rosie snorted ungraciously.

"No worries, I'll kiss my girlfriend then instead," Nathan said as he went to clinch India to his wet and muddy sides but she managed to jump clear of his embrace like a scalded rabbit. "Okay, no love from the women then!"

Nathan touched the wooden starting pole in the lane and took off like a bullet, a line of water powering after him, the crowd cheering him to the end and back again.

"Best result of the day so far, one minute thirty-eight!" Eddie Ferris said, announcing Nathan's time to the crowd through a megaphone.

"Not bad! *Neeeeigh-thon!*" the girls who'd dressed up as a zebra teased and Nathan shook his head and swore.

"Bugger – not as good as I thought," Nathan cursed, hauling off his mask and snorkel.

"Oh Lady Luck, shine on me instead!" Rosie beseeched, rubbing her hands and looking at the rising moon as she went to take her starter position.

"You won't do better than me," Nathan said, shaking big mucky drops out of his hair.

"Wow, the arrogance of men!" Rosie sniped as she adjusted her mask and gave the signal to Eddie Ferris that she was ready to begin the challenge.

"Rosie! Rosie! Rosie!" the chants of women all along the line began as Rosie took off like a torpedo, pausing only once for breath until she reached the finish as fast as when she started.

"A new Ladies' record! One minute forty-five!" Eddie yelled in an excited flourish.

"Well done, bruv!" Rosie said magnanimously.

"Put it there, sis – you were the best woman here

today – you're up for an award," Nathan said, sticking out his hand.

"Rosie!" the bridesmaid troupe squealed as they danced around her, hugging her tight and admired her bog-snorkelling award, presented by Ferris.

"Where's Maeve?"

Nobody knew.

As the flames licked the bonfire on the hill Maeve O'Meara, having meditated for a time at the Blessed Oak, danced like a woman possessed, completely aware that hers were the actions of a lunatic woman who was supposedly getting married in two days' time.

"You're a bride to be, I hear," Mossy said out of awkwardness as he inadvertently caught the attractive young woman's eye. "If you jump the fire with someone you love there's meant to be a blessing for you – it's the old ways," he said as Maura Simmons did a jump so impressive it would nearly have qualified her for the Olympics.

"Well, she's not here, so that's that then," Maeve smiled, doubly so when she saw the farmer's confused expression.

"You can jump it for luck too," a voice said from behind and Maeve shuddered.

"F-freeda . . ." Maeve stumbled over the words.

All around the bonfire people were whipping themselves into a frenzy. Anna was shaking her hip-belt, blue-skinned mummers were belting their drums and swaying, Demelza Spargo was almost in a trance of joy.

"It's alright, Maeve," Freeda said, putting her hand on the shoulder of the younger woman. "You were right. You were young and you did what the young should always do – you explored. So shall we jump the flames for luck, for good luck for your wedding day, for good luck for both of us?"

Seizing Freeda's hand tight, Maeve took a deep breath and as the flames crackled she jumped through them, blessing the life with an old love while wishing for good tidings with the next.

On the other side of the bonfire, Sylvia gave a shriek as her stomach seemed to ripple with wave after wave of life. "The baby hasn't done that before," she gasped, looking at Jerome's face, alarmed.

"It's time," Jerome said, offering his strong arm for his wife to lean against.

From out of a small wooded area Tilda emerged, smoothing her hair, followed a minute or two later by Spud and Hackett with smiles on their faces.

"Tilda, Tilda, it's time! I am having the baby!" Sylvia gasped and she was glad to see her alternative pharmacist friend seem cool and unruffled.

"Don't worry, we have the birthing pool all set up – I'll call the midwife. How exciting! A new life for Cloonsheeda!" Tilda squeezed her friend's shoulder affectionately.

"If she is born by tomorrow I would like to call her Mary after the Blessed Tree Stump," Jerome said, looking intently in his wife's eyes.

A severe cramp temporarily took Sylvia's breath away. "We can call her whatever you want – just so long as I can get her out!" Sylvia puffed and blew and Jerome put his arm around her, taking all the weight he could from his sensible, labouring wife.

Maura Simmons was feeling a bit light-headed as if she'd

drunk just a bit too much wine. It wasn't every day of the week that she did something as 'earthy' as jumping over licking flames, but one day of maypoles and yurts and bog-snorkelling was about as much wacky alternative living as she could take. The festival was all very fine but really she wanted wealthy, respectable academic green types to move to Cloonsheeda.

With the Sacred Oak coming into view she stopped and took a short breath. There was a small gathering around the slain oak – all cross-legged, eyes closed, hands turned palms up to the moon above – and in their midst that nice well-groomed man who had booked the community hostel several weeks ago.

"Hello, everything alright?" Maura heard herself ask in a tight voice.

"Yes, thank you, we are just meditating near the roots of the oak to see if we can detect a haunted atmosphere," the nice well-dressed man told her.

"I beg your pardon?" Maura said, sure she'd heard wrong, although to date this blasted oak was attracting all the wrong attention completely for Cloonsheeda.

"A haunted atmosphere – indicative of there being fairies about. Steve in particular has possibly been blessed with the fairy sight. This place Cloonsheeda means 'fairy meadow', you know, an indication of it being a fairy haunt," the well-dressed man continued.

Steve smiled and Maura recognised him as one of the head honchos from the motorway protest. With him was that half-wit housewife Sinéad Winterbottom, looking half-spaced.

"Trees especially are sacred," Sinéad said as she stroked the protruding roots of the oak.

Maura's mouth was set firm. The trees on the motorway route were important, she didn't want any noisy motorway passing anywhere near her utopian Cloonsheeda, but this blasted magical oak tree she could do without.

"Did you say fairies?" she asked the meditative group in her most strident voice, then heard herself emit a nervous cackle.

"Yes – although some people think the fairies might really be aliens," Steve said knowingly. "Same thing really – bright, shining – there might be different races of fairies of course, just as there might be different races of aliens – we're open to possibilities but May Eve is considered to be like Halloween – it has potential for traffic between the two worlds."

"How illuminating and how exactly would *you* know all this, if you don't mind me asking?" Maura continued huffily, visualising all the PR damage to Cloonsheeda this latest clap-trap lunacy could start.

"Oh, we do this on a regular basis as part of PIG – Paranormal Investigations Group – UK and Ireland," the well-dressed man intervened.

"I do research anyway for the government – human statistics, gathering information is what I do – although I would prefer if nothing about my being here gets passed on as some of my colleagues are extremely conservative," a geeky guy interjected as he pushed his glasses back from his nose nervously and looked around as if he was certain he might be under some sort of government surveillance.

"I don't believe this! When our hostel was booked I thought you were a party of tourists – in fact, I distinctly remember being told you were tourists!" Maura snapped.

"We are sort of tourists, psychic and paranormal tourists, that is – we travel all over to check out 'the haunted atmosphere,' if in fact it exists," Steve continued.

"Hey, Steve, that light over there!" one of the party began shouting excitedly.

"It's silent and moving quite fast – quick, someone get it on camera! It might be a spacecraft!"

A massive chase began all over the hill by the PIG's after a bobbing light in the distance. Maura took a deep breath – when she got home she was going to have a nice shot of whiskey on her own. Eddie was still dancing on the hilltop, all this New Age pagan stuff was mad, it wasn't good for people's mental health such lack of order, such spontaneity . . . maybe she'd just make that whiskey a double.

Up on the hilltop, still leaping over flames, Anna twirled and laughed and shook her belly-dance belt joyously.

"You seem to have forgotten all about ballet dancing," Eddie said admiringly.

Anna didn't pick up on his praise – she was in too much of her own world.

"I'm going to take a lighted branch to light a fire in my own home," Anna said, picking up some fire and twirling it around energetically so that Eddie became a little worried.

"You want to light your wood-pellet stove in this weather and at *this* time of night?" Eddie asked, genuinely puzzled.

"You're right – I think I'll just symbolically light a fire

in my own home. After all, it's time," Anna said a look of scary determination on her shadowy face.

Her presence and her mystical determination filled Eddie with lust. If he could be with her tonight it would be especially exciting as he'd have to get up extra early to slip back into Maura's bed.

"Anna, can I come with you – please? I don't care if Maura finds out. You're intriguing, amazing, I just have to be with you!" he asked, tripping over his words like a little boy.

"Not right now, Eddie – tonight I have some work to do."

"What work?" Eddie asked, his perpetually friendly face almost sulky.

"I told you already, Eddie – tonight is a night for burning," she laughed as she took a branch of sparks and, waving it in front of her, giggling, headed for her home.

As they chased the light further and further away from the village and into the open fields, Sinéad, still dressed in her floaty maiden costume but with the addition of sandals, tripped in a ditch and she screamed like a caught rabbit as both her hands went to her ankle.

Immediately Steve, who was one step ahead of her, turned and came back and went to investigate the injury.

"Damn – I hope I haven't broken anything," she panted, trying to hold in the pain.

"Can you stand?" Steve asked gently, his big tattooed arm around her waist for support.

"I don't know – I'll try. Ow!" She hobbled a bit, then fell against his chest for support.

"Right, I'll carry you," Steve said, picking her off her feet.

"Oh, this is nice," Sinéad cooed, aware that she was flirting, feeling young again, like the young girl who flirted outrageously with men in nightclubs and didn't give a damn, the Sinéad before she was a mother and became bound by Henry's restrictive ways of doing and thinking.

In the distance, by the light of the moon, some playful bog-snorkelling was still in full swing, but suddenly they heard the disappointed PIGs scramble back over the ditch full of the woes of searchers for the paranormal.

"Pity that – a Chinese lantern, I'd say, although you never can tell for sure, must keep an open mind," the well-dressed man told the group.

"Where's Steve and Sinéad?" someone asked, sounding puzzled.

Instinctively, Steve melted into the bushes and Sinéad looked at him and smiled.

"Dunno – maybe they've headed back to the hostel," someone else said and they went off with all their paranormal and psychic equipment to look.

"You've lovely eyes," Steve said, still holding Sinéad close so she could feel his heart thudding.

"Bit cheesy that – you've a lovely accent," she offered back as she rubbed her head up against his stubble.

"That's real cheesy that," he said back, every syllable like melted chocolate.

"Shut up and just put your mouth all over me," she laughed and felt the thrill as his lips brushed her lips then traced down the line of her throat.

On the grass he laid her down and she put her arms

up to him to lace around his neck and touch his hard, ropey, dreadlocked hair.

"Don't stop kissing," she said urgently. "It distracts me from the pain."

"In your foot?" he asked, worried now that he was crushing her with his weight.

"All of it, all my all-over pain, your kissing makes it go away," Sinéad laughed and had never felt more feminine, more womanly as she enjoyed the desire she provoked in this man, this man who, unlike Henry, never once asked 'Is this good, Sinéad, do you like this, Sinéad, would you like it harder, faster, slower, Sinéad?', this man who just desired her and made her feel desirable, this man who was part of the earth and who shook her with his passion.

31

Back inside her own kitchen Rita made herself a cup of tea the old-fashioned way, one heaped teaspoon for her, one for the pot and, out of habit, one for Himself. Her paintings were still outside in the boot of her car, only two had been sold this May Eve and none of them were blue. Of course, she should have known. Her great escape was just a stupid dream. She wasn't an artist, she was just plain old Rita Skeehan – a farmer's wife and not much more.

Upstairs she ran a bath, her big toe plugging the drippy cold tap as she soaked herself in a trance, and when she eventually dragged her leaden body out of the tub she found him standing waiting for her in the bedroom.

"I've had a think about it," he said plainly but with some kindness. "If it's the sheep that's worrying you then I won't get them."

And Rita, wrapped in her bath-towel, bent in two from hilarity although to the casual onlooker she might have been suffering from acute appendicitis.

"Sheep? Good God, sheep! Is that what you think has me the way I am?" she laughed.

"Isn't that why you've been out of sorts with me the last while," he said, "because you think the sheep would be too much and that I should be slowing down in my old age?"

"No, not really, Mossy. Well partly, but to be honest I just wanted to do something with my life before I die. I want to be around people more, I want to feel young and not feel like I'm waiting to shuffle off and I want *you* to move with the times and realise that, just because our daughter hasn't her children baptised, it isn't such a big deal. You're missing out on seeing your grandchildren, Mossy, out of stubbornness and they're only up the road – and you're missing out on Sinéad, the one out of all our girls who was most interested in the land!"

"Not that she did anything with it – went to England and got herself mixed up with that big girl's blouse Winterbottom – what a name – and had all those babies!"

"Well, what encouragement did she get from you to ever use her qualifications?"

"I don't believe farming is for women, it's too hard," Mossy's face flushed purple with the intensity of his belief.

"And who are you to judge? That girl was made to farm. Was there ever a child so interested in tending animals? And she's fit too – all those athletics medals she won as a child – underneath that slim frame of hers is pure muscle. But I don't want to talk about it any more. Take your clothes off and lie down on the bed, face down! I've some homework that needs doing!"

"What? Is this your nonsense homework again?"

"Yes, yes, it is actually . . . now do what I ask or, I promise you, I'll walk out the door this very minute," Rita said, her voice wavering.

"Stuff and nonsense!" Mossy blustered as he lay down on the bed with just his shorts on.

Furiously Rita poured massage oil from a bowl on the bedside locker into her hands and slapped it onto his neck and back. He groaned – she wasn't sure whether it was from pleasure or pain. All the while she bristled at the thought of promising Demelza that she'd complete this act before saying goodbye to her marriage. Full of venom she attacked the slab of muscle around his neck, certain she had to be hurting him. "That's good," he almost purred. "Do it harder, woman. God damn, that's good!"

"Be careful what you wish for!" she told him as she straddled him at the waist and pounded him with her knuckles, grinding hard into his shoulders with all her pent-up emotion and to her surprise she could feel her hands begin to unknot the tensions in his muscles.

"Strong fingers," he grunted, a trace of pleasure discernible even in his discomfort.

"It must be all that blue-cow painting I was doing," Rita said sarkily as she slid her fingers from Mossy's shoulders down his forearms, noticing that her husband's body was still in excellent shape, hard and muscular from all the years of farming. Despite herself, she began to feel a slight tingle of desire – Richard Gere desire from long ago.

The heat was building in her hands as she moved in large sweeping strokes down his back to the tops of his muscular buttocks and she remembered the time twenty years ago when he was in pain from a trapped nerve and she'd rub cream into that spot. They'd been close then, she remembered, and a sob stuck in her throat. Down his hairy legs she stretched the muscles underneath the skin, the oil making his black hair glisten and stand up and she saw the gash on his leg which needed stitching when he bashed himself against an errant gate. Next she ran her hand over his gnarly feet and toes, squishing the big toe with the bad nail which had become a thick horn after the cow stood on his foot not long after Sinéad was born. Pulling herself away from her memories, she forced some steel into her voice.

"Turn over. I'm meant to do your face." She wanted to hurry her project along as best she could.

Starting with his forehead, she made small circular movements with her forefinger, pinched the skin around the eyebrows with her finger and thumb, and made small circular movements under his eyes. Next she moved her focus to either side of his nose, pinched his chin lightly and stroked under it as if she were giving Jangle a good old scratch. Mossy's face was peaceful and Rita discovered that for that moment at least she didn't hate him. His hairy chest soaked up oil like an old sponge and, as she did her best to make him supple and elastic, he purred deeply like a lion after a feed of gazelle.

"Jesus, Rita, such hands!"

Finally, when she was spent from the hard work, she lay back on the pillows and sighed. Instinctively he moved towards her and she could see he was fully aroused but she was having none of that business – not now.

"Keep your underpants on, mister! It's your turn to massage me, not that I really want you to but the homework lady says I must," she instructed as she went to pour more oil into the bowl. She stripped off her towel and lay on her belly. Above her she could feel him hesitate and then he went to work on her shoulders, awkwardly at first as if she was some kind of animal needing mending or shearing or some such practical activity.

"Ow, too hard, soften it up!" she yelled at him.

It didn't take him long to settle into a pleasant rhythm. Gently he travelled down her sides and spent a lot of time massaging her buttocks.

"That's enough," Rita chastised, feeling Mossy was probably caught up more in his pleasure than hers. As his big hands pulled down her thighs and shins she felt the tightness leave her body, then felt the droplets bead behind her eyes. Nosily, the tears collected on her pillow.

"Your front next," Mossy grunted.

Rita closed her eyes as she let him loosen her shoulders and slide his hands around her flaccid breasts, across the stretch-marks of her abdomen and down her wobbly thighs, feeling with each stroke all the anger she'd kept close to her for years, as her own personal property, miraculously fall away. At intervals she felt Mossy brush against her and knew he was as ready as a bull to take her, to cover her with hungry kisses. Opening her wet eyes she drank him in and felt his energy all around, not old energy but the energy of a man with a strong life-force still as strong as his physique.

His first kisses rocked her, cracked her hard shell wide open, making her like molten lava wanting to rush

372

out and find a hard, sure place to gather. Encouraged, Mossy made to move on top of her but she resisted, shaking her head.

"It's been so long, Rita, too long, I thought these days were gone," Mossy pleaded.

"I'm not allowed, the homework lady said we could touch and kiss – not that I expected that to happen – but no actual penetration," Rita said, feeling a school-girlish excitement.

"What? Why not?" Mossy protested.

"A week of touching, she said, to increase desire."

Resigned, Mossy rolled off his wife and lay panting beside her on the bed.

"I don't know what that was all about, Rita – you're a mystery to me," he said, piqued.

"A woman's prerogative, that – to be a mystery," Rita said, simpering happily.

"Can I hold your hand – is that allowed?" Mossy asked with put-on grumpiness.

"No harm in that," Rita said, then she turned on her side and felt him move in close, felt the weight of his arm around her as he clasped her hand in his own.

"So if it's not about the sheep, what did you want to tell me then?" Mossy asked, feeling weary.

"Nothing – nothing at all."

Demelza had done her part. Rita hadn't wanted to engage in this nonsense but still she was looking forward to the next five days of touching but not touching with this hard-muscled husband of hers in this big old marriage bed.

In the hot shower Nathan was whistling, happy after all

373

the bog-snorkelling and dancing round the bonfire, and India felt her desire rock from her toes, travel at breakneck speed through her body like a daredevil on a motorway and explode through her head. In her book it was always better to woo a man, to hint, to be coy, to let him know by look or body movement that she was ripe for chasing, but with Nathan all of that was useless. She still didn't like to be the aggressor when it came to sex but she had needs, raw, womanly needs and subtlety was for wimps, she thought, as she tore off all her clothes.

"Indy – whoa!" Nathan could barely see her through all the bubbles on his hair and face.

Although he tasted of soap from every pore, India couldn't help herself as she ran her tongue and mouth over her Antipodean Sex God like a woman quite literally starved.

"I've waited for you too long, way too long, and in case you've forgotten this is what we were made for!" she berated as she kissed him hard and deep, suds and all.

"It's just between the big move and the new job, me getting sick and the training –"

"Don't speak, do anything you want, but don't speak," she warned as the water from the shower-head coursed down her neck and pooled round their feet.

Their eyes locked and there was the glint of danger, that old spark from the first days they met. For five minutes India devoured him, relishing his tongue, chafing her cheek against his stubble, feeling the hardness of his torso against her chest but as much as she stretched on her toes she couldn't get in a comfortable position to have sex. Leaving the shower running, she opened the shower door and stepped out, Nathan following with kisses as if his lips were surgically attached to hers. "Let's go to bed," she panted, making for the door.

"Too long," Nathan replied throatily, sweeping all her beauty clutter off the bathroom worktop and lifting her up on to the tiles.

"Nathan!"

"Don't speak – remember!" he reminded her.

Inside, waves of pleasure built until she felt she could be floating in another stratosphere.

"Nathan . . . this weekend . . . this weekend you're mine," she finally said when she'd recovered enough from his kisses to pant a coherent sentence.

"Bonzer! I won't bother putting any clothes on then," Nathan quipped, shooting her a seriously wicked smile that announced all his bad-boy intentions and making India's pulse race.

Walking into her home, still raw from Steve's kisses and with a leaf in her hair and the scent of lust on her body, Sinéad didn't even register her husband waiting for her on the landing.

"Good, you're home – I've been having a big think about the last few days," Henry said. He took her by the hand, led her into the bedroom and sat them both on the bamboo bed.

"First things first: I'm prepared to forget about your whole involvement in the treetops protest and even though I was a bit taken aback at your dancing around on the green half-naked and barefoot . . . Sinéad, your feet are quite filthy, are you actually aware of that? Anyway, what I was thinking is maybe it's time we reconnected – we still haven't actually made our planned baby number four, so let's get in a practice run tonight, shall we?" He pulled back the soft white cotton fabric at her shoulder and started to unbutton the small white buttons at her chest.

"No." Sinéad stood up instantly and shook her head.

"What?" Henry huffed.

"I'm leaving you, Henry," Sinéad said decisively as she re-buttoned her dress.

"What? Don't be ridiculous. I'm your husband and you're still my Mummy Winterbottom!" he whined.

Sinéad visibly winced.

"Yes Henry, I'm *definitely* leaving you and I'm going to sell this house you chose and I've always hated – it's too perfect, too clinical, too soulless and too bloody expensive as well – our heating might be peanuts but with everything we've put into this house we can hardly afford to live! Besides, I like a bit of imperfection, Henry – doors that don't shut properly, cookers with half the dials worn off. Never again will you be able to tell me how *you* think *my* mind should work. Being an atheist for an example – I'm not sure I actually am one. I want to explore other things – I like the earth beneath my feet, God damn it, I like my feet being dirty, maybe I'm a Pagan, maybe I'm a Buddhist but of one thing I'm sure – I need to leave you behind, Henry. You are slowing me down in my journey to find out who exactly I am!"

"Sinéad, this is not like you at all – you're distressed – you need to calm down," Henry implored, feeling suddenly panicky.

"Unfortunately, Henry, it's too late for calming down. Tonight I had sex with another man. Actually sex is too clinical a word – it was a whole body/mind experience. We hardly said a word, we just connected, and the best part was he never once said, 'Do you like this, is this good for you?' or, worst of all, 'Did you come?' He *knew* I had an orgasm, he didn't need to ask – the tremors could be felt for miles!" Sinéad said coldly and with masterly calm.

"I can't believe you did this. It was that Steve hippy bloke, wasn't it?" Henry ranted as he ran his hand though his hair distractedly until it stood on end in an unsightly mess.

"All you need to know now, Henry, is that *I* am a born-again virgin, *I* am a woman beholden to no man and your time with me is up! Now I'm going to bed to relive all my lovely memories of the last few days, especially tonight, and you should move out – tonight would be preferable but I'll settle for tomorrow morning at a push. Turn the light off on the way to the spare room, Henry, I'm whacked from all the day's excitement."

The festival had been a bit of fun, the bog-snorkelling in particular a clever bit of PR but there were still no massive orders to move into Cloonsheeda, despite tours of the village being offered to any prospective buyers. But really what kind of buyers were interested in moving to a place where a tree stump was being worshipped and paranormal investigators wanted to explore the alien/fairy realm on this May Eve night of possibilities between worlds. Mark thought of all this as he arrived home.

Then his phone beeped.

"**Meet me in the bedroom, Mr Gleeson,**" it said and Mark shook his head and smiled.

He wondered if she was still wearing that white peasant gypsy dress with flowers in her hair – she had seemed so comely, so maidenly. At the thought of all that comeliness, he flew up the stairs.

"Hello, Mark," Rebecca said coyly as she sat on a chair, crossing her legs, making sure he got a good flash of thigh.

She was still wearing that dress and her feet were still grass-stained and dirty. There was something about those dirty feet that made Mark feel quite primal and raw.

"Hello, wood nymph – kids asleep long?" he asked as he tugged off his tie and started on his jacket and shirt, his un-gentlemanly intentions plainly obvious.

"Hours – must have been the excitement of the day and all that exercise," Rebecca purred – slowly, deliberately unbuttoning the tiny white buttons on the front of her dress. "Mark, today . . ."

"Yes?"

"When you picked me up at the maypole and I put the wreath of flowers on the top of it, do you know what that symbolised?"

"Well, Maura said it, didn't she? Something about the union of the Earth Goddess and the Sky God?"

"And what do you think that means exactly?" Rebecca said, unbuttoning until the orbs of her breasts were showing provocatively.

"Sex?" Mark said hopefully as he tugged at the waistband of his trousers.

"Yes, sex, of course, but something more."

His blank stare caused her to sigh.

"It's a symbol of fertility, a time when everything blossoms and comes alive."

"Right, sex, just like I said," Mark mumbled quickly as he threw his trousers roughly over a chair and moved in to nibble his wife's lips.

"Mark, I want a baby, right now," Rebecca said urgently, breaking away from his caress. "I know I'm fertile and I want one. I want a little girl."

"What? What about your wanting to become an archaeologist? What about your wanting to get back into your dancing, for God's sake?" he asked, shaking his head in disbelief.

Her hand was on the waistband of his shorts, playing with the dark curly hair of his stomach. "I don't want to be an archaeologist any more. I know I can do it, I've done it for a year but what you said struck home – I'll be years studying, getting wrinkles from the stress," she ran her hand along her forehead and shuddered. "And then I probably won't even get a job. And the dancing, oh today dancing I felt so free! But I can do some dancing, even when I'm as big as a horse – I want a little girl, Mark," she coaxed, her hand was down his shorts now.

"Jesus, Rebecca, there's no guarantee we'd even have a girl," he said squirming, trying to hold a serious conversation but wanting to just give in to her touch.

Irritated, Rebecca broke away and stood up, hands on hips. "Tonight if we have sex I know I'll conceive and, don't ask me how, but I know it'll be a girl!"

Quickly Mark did the calculations in his head: he'd wanted another child anyway but thought Rebecca might be too self-centred to get pregnant again. And a pregnant Rebecca was easy to live with it – she'd lost all her restless energy and had gone completely bovine with the twins – and if Rebecca had three children under the age of three she'd be more worried about getting sleep than dreaming big life dreams that always seemed to put her in a bad mood. Another plus: her boobs got bigger. Big boobs reminded him of Liesel . . . strangely, he missed her about the place . . . he wondered what she was doing now.

"Come here, gorgeous, let's make a baby," Mark said with calculated seductiveness as he kicked off his shorts and clinched his wife in tight to his strong, manly chest.

The back door was open. Willie saw his father asleep beside the fire, a blaze going despite the weather, and smiled. The old ways, his father loved the old ways, and on May Eve it was traditional for households to take fire from the bonfire and bring it to the home hearth. In his hand his father had an empty whskey glass and Willie gently loosened his fingers and placed it on the mantelpiece, thick with dust and grime.

"Well, old man," he said kindly as he placed the famous bone-setting hand on the arm-rest and went to his room.

Switching on the light, he was amazed to see a young blonde with short salon-bobbed hair sitting on his bed, wearing flowery festival wellies, over-the-knee socks and sexy denim shorts. She wasn't from these parts, for sure, but something about her was familiar – he'd seen that face before.

"Isobel White," she suddenly announced as if able to read his mind. "You're a difficult fella to track down. I've been to Mayo and back just to talk to you." She smiled catlike.

"Why's that – am I famous or something?" Willie

said as he collapsed into a chair and dangled his boots over the side.

"Not as Willie Cleary you're not, but as David Ron Dwyer naturally I and the public would be *very* interested in your every move. I know everything about you, Willie," she said urgently. "I broke the story about you and Liesel and I ran it fast, didn't have time for in-depth digging, but now that I've been around I've figured out how you and the eejit Skeehan fooled her with your Hollywood cock-and-bull pretence and I've even heard a rumour that you and Skeehan go dumpster-diving for food. I'm going to write all about it in the paper. I just wanted to know if you had anything to say first." She gazed at him haughtily as she crossed her legs and jigged a coloured welly in time to her own beat.

"Sounds like you've got it all worked out right down to my quotes," Willie said angrily as he swung his legs back to the floor and sat forward in the chair.

"Well, it's customary to ask, but if you've nothing to say . . ." Isobel shrugged, standing up to show off her long legs and tanned thighs.

Willie stood up too and faced her, a smirk on his face.

"You're not very nice, Isobel White – so naturally I'm wondering when you last had sex."

A derisory little laugh escaped her lips but, like an animal that survives on instinct, Willie could sense the slightest hint of desperation.

"Why, are you offering? Not that it's any of your business but I'm a modern woman. I have sex whenever I want with whoever I want," she said with a toss of her well-cut bob.

"That's what I'm asking – *when* did you last have it?" Willie came right up to her now.

Unsettled, Isobel White's face began to flush. It had been over two months ago with a well-scrubbed, nice-smelling, designer-clad advertising exec and, of course, she didn't have an orgasm.

"I bet you only have sex with guys that are all nice and shiny like they've been done up by their mammies for their First Communion. I didn't wash today by the way – there was no hot water in the cottage in Mayo – I reek of fags and, yes, your sources are correct – I sometimes go dumpster-diving so there might be a whiff of bin-juice about me as well." Willie's breath was hot in her ear now and Isobel White felt her legs in her festival wellies go weak.

"It's rather a smelly room, isn't it?" she said for no reason as Willie cupped one of her smallish breasts and she forgot to protest.

"Believe it or not, smelliness is one of the room's main attractions," Willie said, feeling Isobel White's flat stomach and reaching to unbutton her festival shorts.

"I'm still going to write the story," Isobel whimpered, desperate to maintain her professional credibility as Willie pushed an exploratory finger along the edge of her thong.

"And when you do, tell everyone I'm well hung, won't you?" Willie teased as he bit one of her ears . . . and Isobel White, usually the huntress of men, allowed herself to be hunted down in a smelly room in the unfashionable sticks for one long, delicious night of dirty country passion.

He looked older and more tired than the last time she'd

seen him, Anna thought as she opened the front door of her home to Paddy and hurriedly belted the black silky dressing-gown at the waist. Being a Minister was taking a toll on his appearance – it was as well he had a make-up artist mistress who could patch up the growing cracks and maybe do something to cover the growing silver hairs around his temples. With a distinct sense of pleasure, she noticed that his shirt was slightly crumpled and his tie was an appalling match.

"Nice enough place, not much in it," Paddy said bluntly, looking round Anna's spartan home.

"My life was full of clutter for years and I'm in no hurry to fill it back up again," she said frostily.

"Yes, well, here I am. You wanted to talk about Liam. I won't beat about the bush. His being gay is not exactly the kind of publicity I need at the moment."

His paunch had filled out a bit since she'd seen him last – perhaps the new lady wasn't much of a cook or he was eating too heavily at functions – she remembered when she was fool enough to make him nutritious sandwiches and pack healthy snacks for his long drives to Dublin for sessions in the Dáil.

"It's always about you, isn't it, Paddy, how everything affects *you*?"

"I just call it like I see it. Can we sit down?"

Not waiting for an answer he went and sat on the couch. Reluctantly Anna followed and sat beside him and Paddy noticed for the first time that she was wearing tights, if not stockings, and high heels. He smiled to himself. Of course she was feeling lonely and missing him – why not make her happy?

"Ah Anna, Anna, can we not be friends?" he asked, putting on his most charming smile and reaching for her hand, and for a moment his wife was disarmed as she looked into what were still very tempting, sexy brown eyes.

Seeing something in her gaze, a touch of regret perhaps, maybe even longing, Paddy sighed sadly like the great actor he was and loosened his ill-matching tie at the collar, looking at it a little distastefully, knowing that Anna would understand that look which said, 'even in the little things my mistress is no match for my wife'.

Anna knew a big speech was coming – she had known him long enough to know words of weight were on their way.

"I've left her, Anna," he said gravely. "I was stupid to get involved in the first place. I was stupid to throw away everything we had together. Good God, it's only while I'm sitting here with you now that I realise how stupid I've been!" Anna was speechless, first with wonder, then with anger, then despite herself she felt a flash of lust . . . but she didn't trust Paddy. Experience had shown her that lying and half-truths were what he did naturally and what he always did to survive.

Taking her silence as acquiescence, Paddy shuffled quickly down the couch towards her so he could dominate his wife with his vice-like arms and mouth.

"No, not here," Anna gasped, coming up for air.

She took Paddy's hand and led him to the bedroom, the spare bedroom, the physical manifestation of all her hatred and pain.

"The walls – they're very black?" Paddy said

questioningly and for a moment he was thrown, hesitating like a rat seeing the corn but suspecting a trap.

"Black but perfect for what I have in mind – come, let me show you." With a growing sense of power Anna let her gown slip from her shoulders and Paddy gasped – he had never seen his wife dressed in black leather before.

"For too long I have been your wife, Paddy – tonight I am your mistress and you will do what I tell you!"

Paddy got a rush of pure pleasure as he imagined having a wife who could not only act out his sexual fantasies but take care of his work shirts as well. Then in the corner of the room he saw a big bottle of baby formula and a giant frilly bonnet and everything inside him was marshmallow happy.

So happy that he failed to notice the camera on the windowsill waiting to incriminate. This was too easy. Anna had never been so happy in her life as she alternated between scolding and taking pictures of her entranced husband in ridiculous poses. He was so turned on and so under her 'mistress' command that he left his savvy politician persona behind and let Anna click her camera away – Anna was especially fond of one photo where Paddy was on his knees sucking his thumb.

High in the clear sky the moon shone into the living room of Anna Gavin's trendy two-bed home and saw the strange acts of new beginnings in her black bedroom, saw the crackling of twigs in the Bonesetter Cleary's grate, saw two women with dirty feet, one falling in love with her husband all over again, one leaving her husband forever, saw a new baby born to the Village and christened Mary in honour of the old ways, saw a wise woman meditate with a ring of candles and her mischievous cat. The moon shone into all the nooks and crannies, into all the living spaces of all the inhabitants of Little Cloonsheeda then hid her light behind the clouds until morning came to the earth.

32

One year later

"Mum, we've another booking from America, a party of six coming in two weeks' time. It's Dad's fairy stories about the old days and ways of Cloonsheeda, not to mention his *Taxi Driver* impressions – I'd swear that's what's bringing them in!"

Sinéad shot a congratulatory smile at her father and he smiled back. It was wonderful to have her and her three lively children in the old farmhouse, wonderful to have new life about the place. Mossy didn't condone her walking out on her marriage, but he never liked that fella Henry Winterbottom from the first when he brought Sinéad home with his grandmother's engagement ring on her finger – that had always seemed like meanness to Mossy – a woman should never have another woman's marriage ring. No, he'd never liked that fella Henry Winterbottom – arse by name, arse by nature.

"I'm off to the fields, the animals won't wait," Sinéad laughed as she went to feed her two real goldfish in the hall and touch the foot of her big fat wooden Buddha beside the old grandfather clock before she left. Jangle jumped at her ankles as she left the room – Mossy had noted even the dog had perked up with the arrival of Sinéad and her family to the old homestead.

New starts, new beliefs, new life mixed in with the old, his wife running a B&B on their farm, delighting in all sorts of visitors from all over the world, organising a painting course in that new therapy centre all the women of the village had set up since last year's Bealtaine Festival.

"I've got to go get the breakfasts on, see you in a while, love," Rita kissed Sinéad goodbye,

Sinéad took her mother by the elbow and had a discreet whisper. "By the way, Mum, could you and Dad keep it down a bit – last night I thought you were going to wake the children!" She was only half-joking.

Rita blushed. Things had been good between herself and Mossy the past year – it was like they were newly married again, they were both excited about how their lives were changing, they were both celebrating being alive with new hopes and dreams and all the old contempt Rita had felt was blocking her love for him disappeared when Sinéad came home to help run the farm.

Seeing Mossy drop his grandchildren to school and playschool in the morning, seeing him get his few sheep after all and start a small pet farm – opening it up to the neighbourhood children and the children of guests – he had a way with the young she had to admit, a way that brought nothing but gladness to her heart.

"Going to the art and dance therapy centre in the afternoon – two of the guests have booked a session – and then I have to run to get the picture I painted of the

Daly calf before my photo and painting exhibition opens at the library," Rita said, smiling at her husband.

"Don't be too late back," Mossy said softly, a look of longing in his eye.

"Sure there's oceans of time now we have Sinéad here with us," Rita gushed affectionately.

"It's like you always said – that girl's a born farmer and I've more time for us now – more time for you now that I'm not such a stubborn bastard," Mossy said as he stroked Rita's cheek lightly.

"I was just thinking it again this morning – I'm glad you let go of that stubborn obsession of yours about Sinéad not having the children baptised – I'm glad you've seen sense – they're her kids and she has to raise them her way."

"Well, they might come to a good end anyway – didn't I sprinkle their heads with Holy Water when they were in the bath and said a few words – home-style baptism you could call it – if I remember correctly it might even hold up in the eyes of the Church," Mossy mused.

"Mossy Skeehan, that's shocking! I don't know what Sinéad would say about that intrusion into her children's lives!"

"Ah don't tell her then, sure what harm can it do – it's only a bit of water and a few words," he said, leaning in for a sly kiss just as a guest rounded the corner for breakfast.

"Later," Rita said throatily, her eyes twinkling with promise.

"Later it is then," Mossy winked, feeling as much of a bounce in his step as if he too were the old Jangle getting a new lease of life.

Rita nodded, full of joy, and for every minute of it in their twilight years both of them were profoundly grateful.

It was hard work farming, but it was what made her life worthwhile, Sinéad acknowledged as she checked and fed the animals on the pet farm and went to view her beasts in the field. All this was her responsibility. She who a year ago was little more than a mouse under her husband's covert oppression was now a woman beholden to no man, a woman free.

"I'm a born-again virgin after all," she told the cows, laughing out loud at the incredulity of her situation. Leaving Henry was the best thing she'd ever done. The first thing she'd done was buy two goldfish and set them up in an aquarium in the hall, real fish, real life, she was sick of everything fake. Then they'd sold the blasted house that was new and gadgeted and perfect for a fabulous price and were able to go their own ways. Sometimes Henry rang her up and whined and told her they needed to reconcile, but she remained detached from his pleadings. It wasn't that he was a bad man, it was just that a man like Henry could only bring her down. Besides, she wasn't totally lacking in male company. Steve had been an occasional and warm presence in her life and in her bed and she'd had one or two fun go's at the local Jack the Lad Willie Cleary – when he was home from America. He was a few years younger than her too, which made their encounters doubly pleasurable. Maybe one day in the future she might just turn into a farmer who was also a predatory cougar when it came to younger men.

"Ah yes, life is good," she told her fields and every word was true.

"You've good movement there, plenty of flexibility, things should be grand." Willie returned the slim, soft, slightly injured limb to its besotted owner and smiled his winning smile.

"So you're really the son of a bonesetter?" the girl gushed, feeling her skin tingle from Willie's gentle but thorough examinary touch.

"Seventh generation – of course I rejected the healing for years, saw it as kind of embarrassing, but I've just sort of grown up in the last while, accepted my talents," Willie said sagely, knowing from recent experience that this sort of talk made women go weak at the knees. "The father always said I had the power in me – I just had to be receptive towards it."

"Excuse me, but you're sitting in my seat!" A curvy girl, beautifully dressed, with a lovely clear complexion and long honeyed hair, gave the besotted usurper a slightly withering look so that she scarpered immediately and the bigger-boned lass sat down beside Willie and shot him a most disapproving look, then laughed.

"You are so full of shit, Willie Cleary," she said, her German accent hard as her reprimand.

"Come on, Liesel, give us a break – besides, I've been full of shit since we first met!"

Liesel laughed so hard she thought she might need an oxygen mask. Willie spoke the truth, he had always been full of shit, but she couldn't find it in her to be cross with him any more and anyway things had been good, really good the past year since she'd gone public with her 'affair' with love rat David Ron Dwyer aka Willie Cleary himself. There'd been the lucrative plus-size modelling contract and then she had become the face of a major women's clothing store in the UK, then there had been the advertisements, the endorsements, the times on the *Breakfast TV* couch on the telly. At first she had hated Willie but now she had to acknowledge sleeping with him, even under false pretences, was the best thing she had done in her short life to date.

Willie stroked Liesel's hand and felt relieved at her good humour.

"You've a lovely laugh, Liesel. It's weird us ending up on the same flight, isn't it?" he said, laying on the charm, and Liesel pulled her hand away and scowled warily.

"Fuck off and don't you dare try your bonesetting charms on me, Willie," she said haughtily.

Willie marvelled at how assertive she'd become in a year, quite a change from the little innocent who first came to Cloonsheeda. But he was glad things were working out for her – he'd never meant to cause her distress – it was just when she mistook him for David Ron Dwyer it was like he'd been possessed by the man himself – which he kind of was now anyway since David Ron Dwyer's PR guy had tracked him down and hired him as a photo double after the Manchester lap-dance scandal.

Isobel never ran the story exposing his identity – why would she when there was still occasional dirty sex there for her to explore – she'd even followed him to LA for his services! In the past year Willie had got to hang out in LA and smoke cigarettes, did a bit of drinking and smooching with the ladies, all things that David Ron

Dwyer couldn't do any more, now he was a dad and in a relationship – as much as any celebrity was ever in a relationship, that is.

"Man, you're going to be my lifesaver! I need someone to carry on my bad-boy reputation," David Ron Dwyer gushed on the phone when Willie accepted his offer.

It was in LA that Willie realised that the bonesetting routine went down real well with the ladies, who adored the physical touch. When he'd finished working for David Ron Dwyer he'd go into something else, something like physical therapy maybe or massage, something that would sit well with his long line of bonesetting ancestors, something that would set him up for life – something that would ensure he'd always be a hit with the ladies. Man, he had to bring the pipes to the States and see if the ladies liked that too – anything with the hands, definitely that was definitely the way to go.

"So tell me what it is like now Tom Skeehan is your legitimate half-brother?" Liesel teased, enjoying making Willie squirm.

In the last year the Bonesetter Cleary had decided to marry again – it was a whirlwind romance but not with his religious buddy, the widow in Carrigmore town, but with Tom's widowed mother.

"It's freaky, it's fucking freaky, knowing I'll never be shot of that fecker Skeehan!"

"He looks nothing like Conan Mallon now his hair has grown back," Liesel mused.

"He never really looked like Mallon anyway, Liesel – you were half-stoned, baby! But Tom is not a man for adventure, he likes his small life in a small town and good luck to him! Hey, he's my brother!" Willie gave a crooked smile.

"Here's to us!" Liesel said as she clinked champagne glasses with Willie.

"What doesn't kill you makes you stronger," Willie said, arching an eyebrow. There was life outside of Cloonsheeda, thank God, and what a year, what a life!

"Give her here, she's hungry," Rebecca said as she wrenched her baby daughter from Mark's arms and tucked her under her chest to breastfeed. Watching her suckle their three-month-old baby never ceased to stun Mark – Rebecca, who always said she'd never breastfeed and who'd got off the hook when she had twins, was willingly nursing their third child, Alicia.

"Nothing but the best for my daughter," Rebecca laughed, catching Mark's eye and reading his mind. "Besides, I can't go to Anna's 'Shimmy and Shake' class at the centre without feeding her – I might leak all over the place!" She was using her free hand to munch through wholegrain toast – there was no starving herself now, not with a child that needed nourishment.

"You love that place, don't you? Though, weirdly enough, my mother loves it too," Mark said as he placed a cup of tea off to one side where Rebecca could reach it comfortably.

At the mention of Dee Rebecca arched an eyebrow. Mark desperately wanted his wife and mother to get on and Alicia's birth had strengthened their connection – slightly.

"How could you not love a place where you can just drop in and have a chat with other women? There's always something on, painting, jewellery making, shiatsu –"

"And dancing," Mark added, drinking from his cup, unable to keep his eyes off his beautiful wife and baby daughter.

"Yes, dancing, and you know how *that* makes me feel. When Alicia gets a bit older I'm going to start teaching my pole-fitness classes – fair play to Maura and Rita Skeehan for setting up the centre and getting bookings from people wanting to come on retreat to Cloonsheeda!"

"Yes, Maura has certainly done her bit this year in helping making Cloonsheeda viable," Mark said, nodding, thinking of all the lovely money that was rolling in now that Cloonsheeda was seen as a trendy place to live, especially since the Bealtaine celebrations when there was coverage of all the festivities, the bog-snorkelling, the crazy paranormal guys who thought fairies might really be aliens and went on a search through the countryside for extra-terrestrial life, and then during the night the blasted Holy Tree Stump was almost incinerated by a bolt of lightning which left burns that looked vaguely like eyes and a nose and the devoted had returned again. It could have all spelled disaster for Cloonsheeda commercially, but instead people with money thought it might be a quirky place to live and bookings came flooding in, especially when Hollywood heart-throb, David Ron Dwyer, in a fit of madness bought the Winterbottom's old place and erected electric gates around the property, much to the annoyance of his Zen-loving, community-orientated neighbours. But Mark didn't care – the house had turned into a tourist attraction even though David Ron Dwyer himself had failed to live in it, although there were rumoured sighting of him in Cloonsheeda from time to time.

"I was just thinking, it was this time last year almost to the day when you decided to give up the archaeology classes – still no regrets?" Mark asked, draining his cup.

"No, I don't need to prove to anyone I have a brain," Rebecca smiled as she kissed her daughter's head, Alicia the fruit of that passionate decision made on the spot in her bedroom with Mark a year ago.

No longer did Rebecca need a diploma or degree so people would think she was intelligent and people like Professor Winterbottom, whom she used to think so sexy and knowledgeable, didn't attract her any more – especially since he'd lost his wife. Remembering how she used to sort of fancy Winterbottom, she turned to her husband and smiled warmly.

"You're smart too, Mark, street-smart – selling all those houses in Cloonsheeda, looking after our investments – smart the way you're planning to start the next phase of houses in Cloonsheeda. I don't tell you this often enough, I know, but you're smart and I appreciate you, Mr Gleeson."

"Wow, I think I'm gobsmacked," Mark said with put-on humility.

From another room there was a crash as Alicia's two big brothers got stuck into some serious on-site demolition.

"And even though I love you loads, I'm still off to my dance class now. You can change her and sort out the boys." Rebecca handed over Alicia, then impulsively she kissed the fluffy hair on the top of her daughter's head.

"I love her so much, she's so tiny and delicate," she cooed.

"Well, as you said yourself the night we made her, you were destined to conceive."

"Feckin' hell, how was I to know that the Goddess Danu who Demelza chose for me is also the Celtic Fairy Goddess of Fertility!" Rebecca laughed.

"Goddamn fairies got me in the end," Mark laughed. "Go on, you don't want to be late for your class!"

As she hurried out the door for Shimmy and Shake, Rebecca noted her curves in the full-length mirror in the hall. "God damn, Rebecca Gleeson but you're one sexy woman!" She winked at herself before heading for her car.

On the wooden floor of the dance studio in the newly established art and dance therapy centre in Little Cloonsheeda, Anna set cross-legged and breathed deeply in preparation for the Shimmy and Shake class she ran twice a week. Every day new things, new opportunities came her way and she grasped on to them tightly as if she'd only six months to live and be happy, because who knows maybe that's all she would have. Life was not to be taken for granted, not any more, and no one could take her for granted either.

Smiling, Anna remembered the night when she whipped Paddy into a frenzy, tied him up – all with his submissive permission – took photos of him and then threatened to send prints to the media if he didn't do something to stop the motorway from clipping the edge of Cloonsheeda. Funny how politicians could move mountains or shelve motorways when their own political asses were on the line.

But that was the old Anna, the Anna before she had

started meditating. The new Anna wouldn't ever attempt anything so vicious on a former lover – well, not unless she was provoked.

It was just as well Maura had got the idea of setting up the centre as a tourist attraction because at the time Anna was definitely in need of some calm, relaxation and self-assurance. Somewhere along the line Maura had involved the local community too, from people like Rita Skeehan and her painting classes, to women from all sorts of backgrounds who needed the reassurance of other women and she'd seen Maura relax a little – maybe realise that the best people came from all over, not just the well-heeled, moneyed, professional classes. Maura was nothing if not practical and after last year's May Eve, Anna had returned Eddie to her without upset to either woman, although Eddie himself had been a bit upset and had tried to woo her once or twice with some more organic wine. Eddie wasn't for Anna, though – a nice man but not what she wanted at this stage of life. Anna thought she might go for something more exciting, a biker with nose-rings, a tree-hugging dread-locked He Man like that fella Steve, whom she knew well Sinéad Winterbottom had taken in the bushes on May Eve last year.

"Hi, you!" Rebecca rushed into class, her face glowing.

"You're the first here," Anna said in admiration.

"Only because Mark's on standby today and tomorrow for the May Eve Festival. There's so much going on, the amount of bog-snorkellers alone coming is incredible!" Rebecca pulled off her jacket and put on her sequined shimmy-belt.

One by one the ladies of the locality came into the class and peeled off their layers of clothing, showing bodies of different shape and age, some wearing leggings, some long flowing gypsy skirts, some hiding behind long T-shirts and others happy and young enough to show off their torsos. At the back Anna spied two new women, shy and a bit uncomfortable, and smiled – one or two Shimmy and Shake sessions and she would have them looking and feeling like the goddesses she knew they were.

"Some gentle stretching first, girls," Anna said as she began to loosen up in front of the mirror.

What a difference a year had made! Her hair was longer, her clothes were brighter, even her make-up was more casual and experimental. After ten minutes of stretching, she put on some belly-dance music and couldn't help but break into a big, happy grin.

"Okay, goddesses, for the next hour at least let's shake this earth!" Anna said with a slide of her hips and a shimmy of her coin-belt.

The evening was warm and balmy. India wrapped her arms around Nathan and smiled, for the millionth time glad that she had brought her boyfriend home for his fix of Oz. It was the place where he was the sun-kissed god of her dreams and she felt truly like his besotted goddess. Melbourne was a great city too – she loved the way it had proper seasons. It was also a city steeped in culture and the arts, a great place for someone like her to get a job if she ever decided to leave Ireland – not that Nathan was ready for that yet – for some inexplicable reason he liked the drizzly Emerald Isle.

"Well, sis, congratulations on your engagement!" Nathan said, raising a glass to his sister Rosie.

Alongside him Freeda Petersen smiled. Who would have thought that so much good would have come out of Maeve's wedding? Who could have known that for the first time ever she would find grown-up love with the lovely Rosie O'Driscoll?

"Here's to us all!" Rosie said in reply as she toasted their health in front of the South Pacific where the sun cast its spell over the trendy suburb of St Kilda's in Port Phillip Bay.

On her laptop computer Demelza wrote the last chapter, of her goddess sex therapy manual, printed it out, read it aloud and sighed like a woman who knows one phase of her life is over while another is destined to begin. Finally, she had got an agent for her innovative book. It hadn't been too difficult really after last year's festival when Cloonsheeda had got acres of coverage in the media and had gone 'trendy', especially when that Hollywood actor guy had bought a property in the Village. The London agent had called back, eager to represent her, but Demelza had known she was onto a good thing by then and hadn't stopped until she found an agent she actually liked – one who knew Demelza Spargo was not a penname but Cornish through and through. In two weeks she would be fifty-one and, looking around Mermaid Cottage, boxes stacked everywhere, she knew it was time to go, time to move on and bring her ideas and ways elsewhere. One final meditation, one more night under this roof, and she'd be handing the keys of Mermaid Cottage over to Mark Gleeson and then she would head to Scotland to try somewhere new, to bring her magic to other folk in need.

Stepping outside the door, with Bast on her heels, she unscrewed her three-foot-high wooden goddess sign and looked towards the village green where big Jerome Sawicki was once again attaching festive bunting in preparation for the Bog Snorkelling Championships tomorrow.

"To everything there is a season," she said as she took one last look, picked up Bast and stroked her ears, and returned to her spartan rooms to pack her bags and leave the 'not so sleepy' village of Cloonsheeda for good.

If you enjoyed

The Goddess Village by Nuala Woulfe

why not try

Two to Tango also published by Poolbeg?

Here's a sneak preview of Chapter One

Two to Tango

Nuala Woulfe

POOLBEG

One

Through the kitchen window Jennifer O'Malley spotted her husband Dan pottering around the greenhouse, moving pots and cleaning the winter mould from the glass with a cloth and spray, in oversized washing-up gloves. Out of badness the thirty-something mother-of-three dialled Dan's mobile and watched as he fumbled about in his pockets for his phone. He was still a handsome man, she thought, as she waited for him to answer – lithe, sallow-skinned and blond with just a touch of daddy-grey about the temples.

"What are you wearing?" she asked, trying to sound sexy but aware that her voice mostly sounded hoarse and just a little bit desperate.

"Jennifer? That you? What do you mean what am I wearing?" his Newfoundland-Canadian accent, which had a strangely Irish twang about it, broke through on the phone.

"Right now – what are you wearing?"

"A fleece – it's chilly in the greenhouse, even though it's warmer inside than out," he said, completely unaware that his wife's dark eyes were studying his every

407

movement as she wound a wayward strand of dirty-blonde hair round her index finger.

"What else?"

"I don't know – dirty socks? Where are you?"

God, this was useless. Dan didn't even have the brainpower to ask her what *she* might be wearing – not that she had anything sexy to boast about these days – not in big sizes. Perhaps it was no harm; slinky drawers might give out the message that she was frisky, which she was in a surprisingly uncomfortable sort of way. Running a spare hand down her flabby mammy bits, which she'd liberally sprayed with perfume (the only thing sexy she currently had to cover her pelt), Jennifer knew what she needed right now was earth-shattering excitement. Right now at this very moment on a January morning she wanted something momentous to happen, like a Hollywood movie star bursting through the door pursued by fast cars and helicopters, telling her that in the interests of national security he needed to have sex with her now – on the couch – with all her clothes on and with helicopter searchlights pinpointing her every move and relaying images back to live satellite TV in the interests of – well, in the interests of national security.

Feeling all hot and bothered, Jennifer's eyes glanced back through the double doors at her couch, wondering would it be up to any kind of national-security action. Chance would be a fine thing. Then her roaming eyes returned to base, alighting on the remote control which was just about to be stuffed into her eight-month-old son's mouth.

"Forget it, forget I even asked!" she sighed as she hung up, pulled her baby son onto her knees to breastfeed, switched on some international TV and tuned in to

France's loveliest weatherman, the soft-spoken, dimple-cheeked golden-haired weather babe du jour, Pierre Dubois. She listened raptly as Pierre in his native French tongued a few weathery terms which might one day come in useful at her daughter's experimental French-speaking primary school, started by Irish parents of Norman descent. Straight after the weather Sophie Lloyd, the nation's glossy-haired culinary wonder came on, and was just sticking one buffed shiny finger into a chocolate pudding, licking it and having a pretend culinary orgasm for the camera when Dan appeared and hovered nervously beside the double doors near the TV.

"Everything okay?" he asked slowly, peeling off a dirty man-sized washing-up glove just as the brunette chef let forth another strangled *miaow* of fake pleasure.

"The baby's not bawling – what more could a mother ask for?" she answered briskly, not allowing her eyes to wander from the screen.

"Sure you're okay?" he tried again very tentatively.

"I'm *fine*," she snapped as she fisted a cushion into an acceptable shape before slipping it behind her back.

"Is it because I'm going away and leaving you with the kids for two nights?" he asked, not willing to give up his investigative line of questioning just yet.

"It's not your fault, I understand work is work, your computer company owns your ass, what can you do, right?" came her sardonic response.

"Jeeze, you know I hate Intech's team-building days away – I'd gnaw my own arm off if I thought I could get out of this buddy-building nonsense," he insisted as he deliberately moved a fraction in front of the TV, directly into her line of vision.

"You want to be in Galway for lunch, right? You'd better go," she said frostily. Then full of guilt she forced herself to smile until it seemed her face might crack.

God, she was such a bitch these days. A long time ago she used to be the kind of girl who'd blow kisses at herself when she passed mirrors, who'd wiggle her hips and shake her boobs just for fun, but that was such a long time ago it might as well have been a completely different person. In fact, now that she thought about it, it *was* a completely different person, somebody young, somebody fun and somebody most definitely free.

When Jennifer O'Malley was angry, she baked, which was somewhat surprising because the results were never pleasing and only led to further irritation. It was madness, she knew, but as Abby was home from playschool today (she was on probation on account of her need to taste her fellow students with her teeth) and with time on her hands before collecting Emma from 'big school' the baking urge had come upon her and she'd decided to hit the flour – hard. Today her nerve wasn't up to the dreaded scones, but she felt she had been close to success with the muffins the last time she'd tried.

So, she and Abby mixed all the ingredients together, slopped them into paper cases, then placed their gooey achievements on trays in the oven and hoped for the best.

"Mammy, this is fun," her angelic-looking three-year-old lisped.

"Isn't it just?" Jennifer laughed as she kissed the child on her soft white blonde hair. "You just stay here a moment and watch our lovely buns while I check on

Adam in the bedroom." Jennifer left the kitchen to check that her son, who'd fallen asleep in his car seat, was still breathing. It was while tenderly stroking her sleeping baby's flushed cheek that that she heard the crash and a shrill-pitched scream that turned her into an Olympic athlete in three seconds flat. Oh hell, what had the little minx done now?

Back in the kitchen Jennifer's eyes swooped on the scene and her brain proceeded to check all the relevant boxes. Hysterically screaming child – check, blood flowing from the head – check, child in need of medical attention – further investigation needed. Zooming in on the hot spot, Jennifer took Abby's head in her hands and surveyed the damage. Shit, up close there was a half-inch slash on the child's forehead near the hairline and Jennifer knew that only stitches would solve this problem.

"Were you climbing again?" she half-scolded, half-consoled.

A little sniffle and Abby pointed at the mixing bowl that Jennifer had pushed out of the way – she'd been climbing the kitchen counter to find and lick the bowl.

As she tried to calm her hysterical tot, Jennifer fired two emergency bananas, a half-packet of biscuits, several cartons of juice, soothers, baby toys and her purse into her mammy bag-sack, placed the baby in the hall in his car seat with a blanket over him to guard against the January cold, and lastly switched off the cooker knowing that the action would cause her muffins to collapse from promising mounds into a sorry soggy mess.

Reversing her car at lunatic speed out the driveway of her small three-bed bungalow and watching her middle child in the mirror with blood trickling down her face, Jennifer rang her friend Helen and prayed she'd not be working one of her mornings at the local butcher's.

"Helen, you around? We're on our way to Bannestown Hospital . . . Abby, wouldn't you know . . . cut to the head . . . it's just with Dan away I wondered could you collect Emma from school . . . are you sure? Thanks, you're a star."

Bursting through the hospital doors Jennifer's eyes scoured A&E and her breathing improved just a bit. Thank heavens – the place wasn't totally jammers, with a bit of luck they should be seen within the hour.

Helen was outside talking to Emma when Jennifer finally pulled into the sweeping driveway of her friend's enormous terracotta-painted farmhouse bungalow.

"Acting the monkey again, was she? What was it the last time?"

"Raisins up the nose," Jennifer sighed, rolling her eyes in exasperation.

"Sweet Jesus – there's no end to that one's imagination!" joked the captain of the parish rugby team, a woman with rosy cheeks, playful eyes, a swinging raven plait down her back and a fit, toned body that was always chasing action. "So, where's the stitches?" Helen stuck her nose in the car and surveyed the three-year-old's skull.

"There's none – they glued the cut – no old-fashioned stitches necessary," Jennifer answered, feeling relief that the slit looked much less intimidating now it had been cleaned and sealed.

"Glue . . . seriously? Well, fancy that," Helen smiled as she smoothed Abby's hair back from her forehead.

"Thanks again, Helen, for taking Emma," Jennifer said with genuine gratitude.

"Oh for God's sake, will you say no more! She wasn't an ounce of trouble." Helen smiled at a blushing Emma.

Of course Emma was no trouble, Jennifer thought, not her five-going-on-fifty Emma who was always adept at seeing what needed to be done and just doing it, her blonde Emma who never complained, her Emma who was always smiling – either that or biting her nails.

"You'll come in and have a cup of tea so?" Helen coaxed as her scruffy black-and-white cat moulded itself into her shins and mewed plaintively, demanding attention.

"Believe me, I'd love to, but if it's not too ignorant I think it would be better if I just hit the road, get them fed, do the laundry . . . clean the kitchen . . . ha, ha, ha, no, maybe cleaning the kitchen is just *too* optimistic!"

"Tough call looking after kids when Dan is away travelling," Helen sympathised.

"He's not travelling this time . . . well, I suppose he sort of is but it's nowhere foreign, just Galway at a team-building love-in – basically the company try and get people who normally can't stand each other to 'bond' and all the employees do their best not to reveal any secrets. I can't see Dan enjoying it much – so I suppose it's rough on him too."

"You reckon? You're such an understanding wife, I bet it's a blast," Helen teased, then cursed the cat for making a good attempt at tripping her up from under her feet.

Cross at being shooed, the cat jumped on the bonnet and Helen ignored him as she opened the door for

Emma and helped her get into her car seat. Then her quick eyes fell on the latest *Slinky Bunnies – Sex Toys and Lingerie Special* magazine – and she began to chuckle. She scooped it up, eagerly released it from its cellophane prison and began to thumb through its saucy pages.

"Good Jesus, all these frisky young ones in sexed-up gear with not a patch of cellulite in sight! Your pal Sandra still in the *Slinky Bunnies* knicker-and-bra game then?"

"Yep – business is booming – she says sex is a cheap night in and never goes out of fashion," Jennifer quipped as she pulled Abby's awkward safety belt super-tight. It was a frustrating car seat, probably designed by a twenty-something male engineer who'd rather be concepting high-powered sexy cars instead of boring kiddie equipment.

"Well, now I've got a glimpse of all this young smooth flesh I'd better check into the beautician's myself."

"Why, what are you getting done – a facelift?" Jennifer teased.

"Ha bloody ha. No, a Brazilian actually – wasn't I in the scrum only last week when I was locked in and couldn't move and a team-mate grabbed a hold of my . . ." Helen's voice dropped to a whisper, "hair . . . and I'm not talking the plait on my head, Jenny!" Helen gestured at her crotch.

"That's gross, Helen, *please* don't tell me any more!" Jennifer pantomimed a scandalised face.

"Well, gross or not, as captain I can't leave anything to chance this year – we've a tough season ahead and if we play well Bannestown might even move up a division!" said Helen with feeling as she threw the catalogue in the boot, gave the car a friendly smack, shooed the cat from the bonnet and waved goodbye from the steps of her house with the number of her local beautician's pounding in her brain.

Jennifer drove off, realising that something about the raunchy catalogue really bothered her as she'd deliberately avoided opening it and seeing the bunch of skinny young harlots parading around in their sexy drawers. Of course *Slinky Bunnies* did plus-size lingerie too, as well as comfy pyjamas, but no one with a big arse or flabby thighs actually posed in the magazine – that would have been far too depressing.

Driving home, with the stereo turned up high, Jennifer tuned into some powerful hits from the eighties and nineties, songs that lit her up from the inside. Despite Adam's bawling and the girls' bickering, it reminded her of a time when she was full of energy with a sassy demeanour and a trail of tongue-tied guys collapsing around her feet. *That* girl didn't own a single pair of cuddly pyjamas. *That* girl only wore G-strings, if she wore anything at all. *That* girl could have posed for *Slinky Bunnies* herself with or without knickers and bra, she thought, as she pulled into her driveway and took a very deep breath.

Lunch was served late, laundry washed, ironing tackled, fights broken up, an Arctic Dinner of frozen fish and chips which Sophie Lloyd would never approve of served up, and close to nine Jennifer got them all to bed. Dimming the lights to low she placed a slim white candle on the table, poured a glass of red wine into a long-stemmed crystal glass and knocked it back in one go. Then selecting a CD from her collection, she allowed a loud and silly belly-dancing track to fill the room with exotic sounds until her body began to sway in time with the beat.

As the music swelled a mood of seduction washed over her and in a moment of hip-hitching excitement she did a little dance of the seven veils with her multi-coloured winter scarf, a beautiful mesh of soft brightly coloured felts interlaced with delicate gold thread, and laughed as she practised a seductive look with her caramel-fudge eyes, then blew a flirtatious kiss to the mirror on the wall. Drunk with anticipation and with the first glass of wine already making her head spin, Jennifer padded past the kitchen into the utility room beyond and unloaded fifteen giant bars of chocolate from her store cupboard, then spread them on the floor of her living room like a shiny new pack of playing cards.

Huge, playful giggles reminiscent of childhood built up inside her as she slid her fingers along the luxuriant paper and brought the bars to her nose one by one to smell the traces of seduction within. Each bar she handled carefully, studying the ingredients – dark, milk, white or plain, filled with fondant or raisin, biscuits or nuts. Finally, her hands settled on one bar and she spliced open its shiny covering with her nail and snapped off a huge chunk of milk chocolate with hidden fondant inside. The chocolate broke in a jagged triangle and her tongue marvelled at the initial sharpness and then the velvety texture of melted sweetness. With artificially controlled calmness, Jennifer opened two more bars, getting down on her hands and knees to smell each one, bringing each up to her nose and inhaling deeply until her brain caught the scent and registered crazed and sudden interest. Organic chocolate, fair-trade chocolate, exotic chocolate; this should have been a pleasure shared, but then again needs must.

A soft and seductive belly-dance track played on the stereo and Jennifer swirled as she munched, swirled as she sipped her wine. How daft, how ridiculous – but what did it matter? The chocolate orgy, now wildly out of control, felt good. In less than half an hour she broke chunk after chunk off each of the bars until at a conservative estimate she'd inhaled, licked and swallowed three or four giant bars in all, washed down with more wine. Hers was an experiment in gluttony but strangely she didn't feel guilt, all she felt was joy. It was like being little again, like overindulging at Christmas or Easter, when eating nothing but chocolate was the right of every small child with a full set of milk teeth and no knowledge of disapproving dentists.

As she pranced behind her scarf, the candlelight glinted off the glass on the table; then mid-tummy-jostle she sauntered to the answering machine and found several unheard messages vying for attention.

"Baby, it's me, Dan . . . Jeeze, I'm such an ass. No wonder you were so quiet . . . well, I'll make it up to you, I promise. Where are you?" The message beeped into nothing.

"Jennifer, it's Dan . . . sorry, couldn't ring for ages – it's like being a Navy Seal here – they've got us drilling every moment. We're being corralled into another meeting now. Why aren't you answering your texts?" Message two faded with the first.

"Hi again, look, what I meant to say is I'm sorry and Happy Anniversary and I love you, honey. Maybe if you get a chance you'll call me back?"

As the greetings died, Jennifer mused just a little. As husbands went, Dan was a good guy, a steady guy, but she knew that she wouldn't be ringing him back – not tonight.

"Happy Anniversary, Jenny," she whispered as she blew out the melted candle, corked the wine and trudged off to her king-size bed to an acrobatic baby who had long since forsaken the cot as his natural birthright.

Taking off all her clothes, Jennifer lay down beside her baby son who was curled up peacefully beside the wall, but her own body refused to rest. Her sinews, her muscles, her very skin were charged as she remembered her wedding night seven years ago, when she was dressed in expensive white underwear from silken toe to satin lace-trimmed bra, but tonight she'd nothing of satin or lace that fitted or flattered her figure, but that was all right because there was no man to please, there was only herself.

All night, while her husband was away Jennifer was like a taut elastic band as chocolate, wine and intense primitive desire played havoc with her brain. In her fantasises she was the most beautiful woman on the planet and the sexiest guys on the planet were driven wild by her presence.

"You're *so* gorgeous, *so* funny, *so* hot," hard-bodied Hollywood Lotharios would whisper in her ear as she'd sip exotic cocktails with harlot names and flirt outrageously from under expertly glued eyelashes.

"Could you hang on a sec, Elvis? I have Paul

Newman waiting for me in the other room!" she said to herself in a suppressed giggle. Hell, it was her fantasy and who said the bloke still had to have his vital signs intact? Part of her worried that the only sane part of her left was descending into insanity, part of her didn't care for any such diagnosis, because until dawn broke Jennifer O'Malley was lifted out of the monotony of her world and transported back to her past to watch that fabulously sexy girl who blew kisses at mirrors and wore G-strings every day – that is, if she wore anything at all!

•–•

If you enjoyed this chapter from
Two to Tango by Nuala Woulfe,
why not order the full book online
@ www.poolbeg.com

•–•

POOLBEG WISHES TO

THANK YOU

for buying a Poolbeg book.

If you enjoyed this why not
visit our website:

www.poolbeg.com

and get another book delivered straight
to your home or to a friend's home!

All books despatched within 24 hours.

POOLBEG

WHY NOT JOIN OUR MAILING LIST
@ www.poolbeg.com and get some
fantastic offers on Poolbeg books